*Leicester*
*Rocks*

# Leicester Rocks

## MIKE HATFIELD

Matador
9 Priory Business Park,
Wistow Road, Kibworth Beauchamp,
Leicestershire, LE8 0RX
Tel: 0116 279 2299
Email: books@troubador.co.uk
Web: www.troubador.co.uk/matador
Twitter: @matadorbooks

ISBN 978 1838593 032

British Library Cataloguing in Publication Data.
A catalogue record for this book is available from the British Library.

Printed and bound in the UK by TJ International, Padstow, Cornwall
Typeset in 12pt Adobe Jenson Pro by Troubador Publishing Ltd, Leicester, UK

Matador is an imprint of Troubador Publishing Ltd

*For Pam*

# One

# Walking By Myself

Stan 'The Man' Booker was going through some warm up exercises on his guitar, keeping the volume down, when there was a knock on the door.

'Hi Mr Booker. Thought you'd like to know we're just popping round to Aldi with Mum. Probably for half an hour or so. OK? Have fun. See you.'

'Thanks, Lakshmi. I will. You're a star, and a proper neighbour.'

Half an hour when he could blast it out on his Les Paul, without upsetting his neighbours was a godsend. Lazy Frank, his miserable neighbour on the other side of his small terraced house, was on his night shift. *It has to be a bit of Gary*, he said to himself, plugging his laptop into the amp. The laptop was at least third hand, a hand-me-down from his close friend Phil.

Stan had worked out how to send emails, download his CDs and play his music. He checked the guitar was in tune. The karaoke backing track was for the Jimmy Rogers song *Walking By Myself*, in the style of Gary Moore. The problem for him was getting the intro right, as the first five notes were on the guitar, before the percussion came in. He pointed the cursor at the song title, tapped and counted himself in. He was bang on time, and in control. Then into the lyrics, how much he loved the person he would be singing to. This was classic sixteen bar stuff, and he knew the whole thing off by heart. Although Stan loved singing this, the lyrics were just a means to an end. The whole point of the song for him was the guitar solo, and from the onset of the second set of sixteen bars the hairs on the back of his neck were already standing in anticipation. Then he was flying. His heart leapt, and for the next half minute his body and guitar were as one, moving up and down with the music, face contorted in various shapes. He had to quickly overcome the sense of anti-climax when the solo ended, needing to come in again on those first five notes, and repeat the lyrics.

The next track was *Still Got the Blues*, Stan's favourite song in the whole wide world, and for which his singing and playing were almost note perfect. But the playing of it usually left him emotionally drained for hours afterwards. He decided to give it a miss and placed his Gibson Les Paul Standard on its stand, alongside his three other guitars, the Fender Strat copy, the nylon string acoustic and the f-hole semi-acoustic. The Gibson was his pride and joy. He stood back to look lovingly at it and, as he had done so often over the last thirty years or more, reflected that it was all very well practising in his front room (and what was he practising for exactly?), but he would love to be playing in a band. He had just never done anything about it. Never, for instance, plucked up the courage to talk to the people in the music shop, who had the contacts.

'Fuck it,' he said quietly.

Stan took the stairs two at a time, then picked up his Stetson from the chair next to the mirror in the front bedroom. Careful not to leave any marks, he brushed off one or two specks of dust with the side of his hand and pulled the hat over his long silver locks. He used both hands to tug on the brim, just enough to ensure it stayed on in the event of a breeze blowing, but without disturbing his carefully combed hair. He was sure that the steely-eyed look from Gary Moore in his signed photo on the wall indicated his approval. Usually he would spend several minutes trying on the hat, adjusting the angle slightly each time, until it suited him. This evening, however, he was slightly nervous and he lacked the patience.

He tried to picture the scene in the bar later that evening, as he buckled his holster and secured its leg-tie just above the knee. Would Wild Phil Hiscox, his long-time friend be there? If he did show, things could get tricky, thought Stan. He was still smouldering after what had happened during the morning, and was determined to have his revenge. He checked that the chamber of his imitation Colt six-shooter was fully loaded with dummy bullets then expertly spun the pistol twice on his trigger finger before slotting it into the holster.

'You'd better be ready, you son of a gun.'

He looked at himself full-on in the mirror, bending at the knees so that he could see the whole of his long lean frame. The outfit was almost complete. Stetson, red neckerchief, waistcoat over pin-striped shirt, Levis, brown shin-high cowboy boots with spurs and his pièce de resistance, a three-quarter length 'Wyatt Earp' style coat with brown suede lapels. Stan was well over six feet tall, with an athletic build. Although fifty-five years old, he thought that he still looked mean and tough, and attractive in a certain way to a certain kind of woman.

He practised drawing his Colt a few times, to make sure that it moved easily in and out of his holster, mentally rehearsing a shoot-out in the bar. Stan hoped it would never happen, but he had to be ready.

'Capow! Capow!' He'd drawn his gun and dropped onto his knee.

He applied the finishing touch, clamping the cheroot between his teeth. He would light it later. Closing the front door behind him, Stan set off along the pavement with a swagger, the clink of his spurs echoing in the narrow street. With a 'Howdy ma'am' and a touch of the brim of his Stetson, he side-stepped to make way for Lakshmi, her sister Ayaisha, and their mother, each carrying a bag of shopping. The girls looked at each other and chuckled as they walked by.

It was a five minute walk to the Working Men's Club, and Stan knew every inch of pavement. Until the events of today had cast their shadow, he had been looking forward to the club's annual Wild West night. People of all ages, and not just club members, came from far and wide dressed as their chosen character. They spent these evenings practising their cowboy slang, showing off their latest acquisitions, joining in the line dancing, lassoing and quick-draw competitions, and asking Ted and his bar staff to 'set 'em up'.

Laughter, loud voices and the sound of the country and western band warming up filled the atmosphere in the bar, along with the cigarette smoke. Stan exchanged 'howdys' with those he knew, a couple of Billy the Kids, one of the Davy Crocketts, another Wyatt Earp and a group of Texas Rangers. He spotted Wild Phil at a corner table, along with his wife 'Calamity' Jane, and a mutual friend, Rob 'Kit' Carson, but chose for the moment to prop up the bar and watch from a distance.

'A beer and a shot, Ted, when you're ready.'

Laughter came from Wild Phil's table, and there were frequent glances in Stan's direction. After two more beers and whisky chasers, he could stand it no longer and jostled his way across to the table. He scowled down at the threesome. Jane was sitting between Phil and Kit, and Stan was sure that just for a second or two Kit's hand rested on Jane's, before he hastily withdrew it.

'This is very cosy then. Sounds like you're having a laugh at someone's expense.'

'Well you took your time,' said Kit. 'I'd just said to Phil and Jane that you looked like you'd got a chin on and perhaps we'd done something to upset you. Pull that chair up and join us, you old git.'

Stan didn't budge. 'This fat so and so has upset someone, haven't you Phil! Have you told them, or haven't you had the bottle?'

Phil was staring at the floor between his feet, hands under his thighs.

'Whatever's been going on, duck?' asked Jane. No response from Phil. 'Do you know, Kit?' Kit shrugged his shoulders.

'You haven't, have you, you wazzock? Too sodding embarrassed. Shall I tell 'em? Ay?'

Still silence from Phil. Stan had now pulled up a chair from the neighbouring table. He stared menacingly at his old friend, at this moment considered by Stan to be an ex-friend, as he continued.

'Well, at nine o'clock this morning, like, I was the proud owner of a taxi, wasn't I? You know, the one I'd spent a load of my chuffing redundancy money on. Well guess what. I am no more, at least owner of one that's worth anything. Thanks to Mister Super Mechanic here, I'm up the swanny without a friggin' paddle in a barbed wire canoe.' The veins on Stan's neck were now pronounced, his face was a deepening red and he banged his fist on the table for good measure.

Roy Rogers and Dale Evans at the adjacent table broke off from their conversation, and gave a disapproving glance across. Stan glared back.

'What?' he barked. They looked away and resumed talking quietly. Jane, aware that others in the bar were looking in their direction, said in a hushed voice:

'Calm down, Stan! I'm sure my Phil can't have been responsible. Were you, duck?'

Phil spoke at last. 'Shut up you silly woman, and stay out of it. How was I to know it were a diesel? You don't have to bring your friggin' cars to my garage. And next time you can get your petrol at a proper bloody petrol station – or diesel – and pay full whack like the other punters.'

'Don't worry, I will. And I'll tell you how you know if it's a diesel. Because it tells you on the chuffing petrol cap. Fuel cap. It starts with a duh.'

'But ....'

The others waited for Phil's reaction. Kit came to the rescue.

'Phil was only doing his mate a favour, Stan, servicing your car, like, and you returned it by giving him your custom. You're in the same boat, both lost your jobs, both starting out in something new. You need to try and stick together and help each other out. I admire you for having a go, even if the car were a bit dodgy, and weren't properly licenced as a taxi. And Phil's showed a bit of initiative. Anyway, you can drain the petrol out of a tank, and re-fill it.'

'Thank you Mr Kofi Annan, but I got there too bloody late, didn't I? By the time I did, the damage was done. Mister smart arse had tried to start the car up. And do you know what friggin' happens when you try and start a diesel engine on petrol? It chuffin' well goes bang, that's what. That's how much initiative he's got. I had a full day's booking for today and tomorrow.

'These things happen, Stan,' said Kit. 'Call them teething troubles. If you get the car insured like I suggested, you'll be able to get a replacement if you're economical with the truth, and be back in full swing in no time.'

'We'll see about that. But I ain't using his friggin' cowboy outfit again. I'll find someone who knows what they're doing.'

'This wouldn't have happened, you know, if you'd given my Phil a job as one of your drivers, or gone into it as partners with your redundancy, like I suggested.' Jane had harboured this resentment since the businesses had started.

'The trouble is, duck,' replied Stan, 'the matter of a few points on your Phil's licence. The daft bugger has probably lost count of them. There's no way he could have got insurance.'

There was a moment's pause, and Stan returned to his beer. The group sensed a slight change of atmosphere. Phil slowly pulled his six-gun from his holster, held it in his left hand and looked down the barrel. He passed it over to Kit.

'Well who's got a new toy?' he said. 'What a beauty! This must be a Smith and Wesson 'Doc Holiday' if I'm not mistaken. Very nice, Phil. Must have set you back a bob or two.'

'Only got it yesterday,' replied Phil, proudly. 'A ton, that's all, mail order. Lovely weight and balance, ain't it?' Phil was clearly relieved to have got onto safer ground.

'Certainly is. I'm jealous. What do you think, Stan?'

'I think I know where my hard-earned money has been going. Subsiding his chuffin' purchases.'

'That's where you're wrong, you duffer. I put some of my redundancy aside for this.'

'Look here, Stan,' said Kit. 'Are you going to be a mardy arse all night, or are you going to let me, Phil and Jane enjoy the rest of the evening? We've already missed one line dance listening to your woes. So either buck up or piss off!'

Stan grunted and folded his arms. The others continued to admire Phil's new gun, and then moved away to join in the line dancing. For the rest of the evening, Stan circulated amongst his acquaintances, wallowing in self-pity as he related the story about what had happened to his car, which became gradually more exaggerated with each telling. By closing time the four had consumed their fair share of alcohol. Normally, Stan would have staggered with them to the 'chip ole' or kebab shop, as thousands of others would be doing up and down the country, but not tonight. He was nowhere to be seen, as Kit accompanied Phil and Jane back to their semi off the Stephenson Drive for a night cap, singing 'Four wheels on my wagon' loudly and out of tune as they went.

By one in the morning, the threesome had exhausted their repertoire of country and western songs and acted out the last scene from 'The Man Who Shot Liberty Valance'. During this, Phil had become so excited that he'd almost knocked over the fish tank. Now they were sprawled over armchairs, struggling to stay awake as they watched 'The Good, the Bad and the Ugly', as was the tradition following the Wild West Club get together. Somehow, thought Kit, it wasn't the same without Stan, who knew the part of The Bad off by heart.

Jane went to open the door when the bell rang, and there was the man himself on the doorstep, looking slightly sheepish and holding a half-empty bottle of whisky.

'Stan! It's very late. I hope you haven't come to cause more upset.'

'No Jane, duck. I've come to apologise for being such a grumpy old sod. And I missed the old film. Any chance of a cup of coffee?'

He followed Jane in and surveyed the scene. Items of cowboy clothing were strewn about the room, and he noticed Phil's new six-shooter on the table. Kit waved vaguely in Stan's direction. Phil was snoring loudly. Jane had gone into the kitchen to put the kettle on.

When she returned, there was no sign of Stan.

'Suit yourself!' She went upstairs to bed. Clint Eastwood and Lee van Cleef were oblivious to the fact that their audience slept through the last scenes.

With nothing in particular planned for Sunday and in no rush to get out of bed, Stan was enjoying a lie-in. As he dozed, he was vaguely aware of the sound of church bells mixed with children's voices from the street outside drifting over him. At times he registered the sound of car doors being closed, and thought nothing of another one being slammed just after ten o'clock, even though it was just outside his front door and therefore louder than the others. He became aware first of the dull thud of his headache and of another bell ringing, a sound that was somehow familiar, then sat up with a jolt as he realised it was his front door bell. The dull thud became a sharp pain.

Stan swore and muttered to himself, as he slipped his jeans on. Pressed against the wall, he pulled back the curtain just enough to enable him to see a young police constable standing at his door, and who happened to look up to the bedroom window at that very same moment.

'Shit. What the chuffing hell does he want?'

In the bathroom he quickly splashed some cold water over his face and did the best he could with the comb, before slipping on his sweater and slippers. Downstairs, he had a quick look round in case there was anything lying around that might incriminate him in anything. He wasn't sure what, but he looked anyway.

He opened the front door. 'Morning officer. Sorry to keep you hanging about. What can I do for you?'

'Mr Booker? Stanley Booker?'

'I suppose so. Come in off the street. This lot round here have suspicious minds. Couldn't you park the car down the road?'

Once inside, the constable had a quick look round the room and then got straight to the point. 'We've had a complaint from a Mr Hiscox, who I believe is an acquaintance of yours. It concerns a missing replica gun, which he says was stolen from his house in the early hours of this morning. According to Mrs Hiscox, you called at the house at about one o'clock, and then quickly disappeared. She feels that you might know something of the whereabouts of the replica gun, sir. Might that be true?'

Stan tried to think through the haze of his hangover. He'd sobered up somewhat by the time he'd arrived at Phil's house, and he could remember pretty clearly what had happened. He explained to the officer that Mr Hiscox was out cold when he visited the house, and had clearly been drinking heavily. He suggested that Phil had simply forgotten where he'd put his gun, and Stan was perfectly happy to go round to the house and help him find it.

Seeming to accept the explanation, at least for the moment, the officer explained that Phil was at his garage and offered Stan a lift. For the sake of his reputation, Stan refused the offer, and after a quick breakfast of sorts he walked to the ramshackle garage two streets away. He was surprised to find Phil in the process of boarding up the small window, having already fastened a sign to the door which simply read 'Closed'.

They exchanged grunts by way of greeting, each unsure of the state of their relationship. Neither could remember a time in all the years they had known each other when they had had a major falling out. They stood opposite each other, not making eye contact. Phil opened his mouth as if to speak, then resumed his work with the screwdriver.

'I didn't nick your gun, mate. Honest.'

'No? Where is it then?'

'In the fish tank. Last time I saw it a Golden Orfe had taken a fancy to it. I thought if you'd thought you'd lost it, you'd know how I felt about the car.'

'Yeah? Well. I found it.'

'You sod. Why'd you send the chuffin' copper round then?'

'To teach you a bloody lesson. You could've ruined the gun.'

Stan contemplated the obvious retort about the car, but thought better of it.

'This is stupid. Look, soz about the gun, right. Are we still mates?'

Phil put his screwdriver away in his toolbox. 'And soz about the car. Stupid bloody mistake, that's all. Course we're still mates.' They gave each other a smile and a nod. Phil then made a pretence of looking for something in the toolbox.

'So did you recognise the copper then? Nobby Clark's lad?'

'No way!' said Stan. 'Last time I saw him he must have been, dunno, thirteen, fourteen. Always in trouble. And now he's a chuffin' copper?'

'I'd heard he were in the force, like, so I phoned Nobby to get his number.'

'You what? Oh I get it. You bastard. I'll chuffin' well get my own back.'

'I'm shittin' misself already.'

'So you should be,' said Stan. Phil stood up straight and looked at him. They burst out laughing. Stan nodded towards the note on the door.

'You're closing up then?'

'Yep. Got a new business lined up.' He looked inquisitively at Stan. 'Wondered if you'd like to join me.'

'What, as a partner? Depends. No cars involved I hope'

'I'm taking Kit's window cleaning round on. He's got a job as a postie.'

'You're joking! You can't go up a ladder without passing out at the third chuffin' rung.'

'No, but you can. And you've got longer friggin' arms than me. You'll reach the windows at the top.'

'And meanwhile you're listening to radio one.'

'I'll hold the ladder for you. And I can do the ground floor windows. You'll have to drive the van though. Are you on?'

'You've never cleaned a chuffing window in your life. Nor me since I were in the cubs for that matter. When do we start?'

'How about in the morning?'

## *Stan*

Me and Phil have known each other since before we started school. In the infants, right, we became best mates. We used to roll Plasticine worms and walk round the room with them hanging from our noses or pretending they was our penises. We was probably little sods to teach, and eventually we was put in different classes. Which were probably a good thing. With some gentle persuasion from me Mum and finger wagging from me Dad, I buckled down and was soon reading Roger Red Hat and whizzing through The Village With Three Corners. Miss Banner were giving me stickers for reading and I were in danger of becoming the teacher's pet.

Phil always seemed to be getting into trouble. I would see him standing outside the Headteacher's office at play times, and when he were allowed out onto the playground arguments would quickly flare up. At some point, or maybe it were gradual, I became his protector, and I learned ways of steering him clear of flash points. Even to the extent that sometimes the Headteacher would come and fetch me from the classroom to help calm Phil down. I would just sit next to him, like, and do whatever he were doing, giving him a bit of help if he asked for it. Put Phil in front of something that involved using his hands, like model making or working with clay, and he were fine. But anything involving a pencil or reading were an uphill battle.

New Parks was a tough part of Leicester. Still is. Kids learned to fend for themselves. When Phil was nine or ten he started going to a gym where they ran boxing classes for boys. I thought that soon he would be knocking six bells out of anyone that crossed him, but funnily enough it settled him down. Word got around and he gained some sort of respect from other kids. And because we were more or less inseparable they stopped calling me 'boffin', which is a tag you don't want in a boys' secondary modern school.

So basically we've always been good mates. Which is why I was well pissed off about the cock up with my car. Like I say, he's always been good with his hands, but bloody slapdash as well. He was always going to make a balls-up at some stage. We should probably have gone into either the garage or taxi thing together. Window cleaning? When I was ten and in the Cubs I did some window cleaning for bob-a-job week. I was quite good at it and remembered being well chuffed at first with making windows shiny, and with collecting a few quid. But after two days of having the piss taken by other kids, I packed in the window cleaning and the Cubs. Where was Phil when I needed him?

## *Phil*

D for diesel. You can see it inside the cap. So bleeding obvious. I felt dead embarrassed at letting a good mate down. Just when things were beginning to pick up. I'd done a complete engine rebuild for one customer, who said Ta with a bottle of malt whisky. Knowing him, I didn't ask where it came from. But he'd said he'd recommend me to his circle of friends and business people. Jane is sorting out the mess I was in with the paper work. But truth be told, I'm not really cut out for running a business, like. Not after thirty years of working on the shop floor with a boss looking over my shoulder. I suppose winderin' is a kind of business, but with Stan on board there's less chance of cocking it up. And he can reach the top of windows with those chuffin' long arms.

Great of Kit to let us take it on, like. He didn't have to, but mates should look after each other, and he is a good mate. He reckons a lot of punters pay cash, so we could be creative with the accounting, as he put it.

I was never a great one for climbing trees as a kid. Gave me the colly-wobbles. So does climbing ladders, for that matter.

# Two

# Come On In My Kitchen

The wind whistled round Stan's head and shoulders as he secured the top of his ladder to a bracket supporting the gutter, just below the eaves of number twenty two Mount Pleasant, a detached house in a leafy suburb of the city.

'Oi! I hope you've got a grip on this chuffing ladder,' he called down to Phil. 'It's blowing a friggin' gale up here, and the last thing I need is a fat lazy git daydreaming on the job while I risk life and limb.'

Phil nonchalantly dropped his cigarette onto the pavement and extinguished it using the heel of his boot, before gripping the ladder at shoulder height with both hands. 'Of course I've got hold of it.' He put his left foot on the bottom rung very deliberately, to emphasis the point, as Stan shook the ladder from the top to test its security. Stan then made his way down to collect the bucket and cleaning tools.

Three days into their entrepreneurial venture their modus operandi was still developing. Initially there had been the inevitable teething problems. Standing outside house number one on day one, they realised they didn't have any water. To add to their feeling of stupidity it took twenty minutes for them to work out how to call Kit on Stan's new mobile phone.

'Sorry! Should have told you,' said Kit. 'Those two plastic barrels I dropped off are for you to take your water in. Put them into the back of the van first before filling from a hose. There's a list of houses in the glove compartment where you can connect a hose if you run out. Mostly outside taps which some of the clients have let me use. By the way, the lady at twenty two Mount Pleasant is one of the punters who'll provide most of what you'll need, if you talk nicely to her. You'll see the score out of ten in the left hand margin of the accounts book. Just remind Hiscox he's a married man.'

Having managed to get started an hour or so later, they tried working together on each window, both applying soapy water with his sponge. Stan was all elbows, Phil all belly and backside, and Phil quickly became soaked working below Stan's long gangly arms. They wisely saw the advantages of taking a window each, and twenty minutes later the boys stood back to admire their handiwork on the four ground floor windows. The soapy water dried quickly in the mid-morning sunshine, leaving the windows looking very streaked. 'Mmm,' was their joint verdict.

Stan was back on the phone to Kit, examining the bits and pieces in the back of the van as they talked, whilst Phil sat in the front looking through 'The Sun'. Phil had turned the contortionist on page three upside down on his third visit to the page, when Stan appeared at the open window.

'Right! Sorted!' And from that moment Stan was in charge.

He lined up the sponges, chamois, drying cloths and the items Phil said resembled wipers on a Morris Minor, and explained their functions. Stan demonstrated the washing, wiping and drying technique on window one of house one, and smiled with pride at the end result. He was not so pleased with Phil's efforts, once they had re-cleaned all of the ground floor windows, and he set to work wiping them all again to rid them of the smears.

'We'll have to do better than this, sunshine,' which Phil took to mean *he* would have to do better. 'You hold the ladder while I do the upstairs windows.'

The pattern was becoming established. They would work in tandem on the ground floor, Stan would inspect those done by Phil, and promptly proceed to go over them again until they were to his satisfaction, before attending to those on the first floor, and occasionally second floor windows. Phil's alleged aversion to heights meant he was quite happy to play this subsidiary role.

His status was elevated somewhat when Stan agreed to let him do the ringing of door bells and collect the payment from each client. 'If it's a cheque I want to see it. We don't want any of these punters screwing us. And if it's cash it goes in here.' Stan held up his bumbag then resumed wiping a ground floor window, as his chubby workmate almost skipped down the driveway to knock on the door of the residence. However, this aspect of the job was not without its challenges for Phil. It would sometimes take him as long to extract payment from customers as it would take Stan to clean the ground floor windows, and after suffering the embarrassment of being unable to write a receipt, Stan resorted to signing and dating all the receipts they might need for a shift.

Outside twenty-two Mount Pleasant, they rehearsed what had now become part of the routine before Stan climbed gingerly back up the ladder to start cleaning.

'Is that friggin' water ready?'

'Course.' Phil produced the bucket from the back of the van.

Stan tested the temperature. 'Chuffing hell, Phil!' He recoiled, blowing on his hand to try and cool it down. 'Half and half, you plonker. Even you can get that right.' He filled a plastic cup with cold water and mixed it with the warm soapy water. Phil looked on, smiling inwardly. He was still chuckling to himself as he leant against the ladder and pulled out his copy of 'The Sun', while Stan set to work at the top, giving a fair rendition of 'When I'm cleaning windows' as he did so.

'God's in his heaven, the sun's shining, and all's well,' Phil muttered to himself.

'It's nice to hear somebody's happy in his work,' came a voice. Phil dropped his newspaper and lost his balance as he tried to stand up straight. He managed to avoid falling over by hanging on awkwardly to the ladder, almost pulling it away from the wall. The resulting wobble in turn caused Stan to drop the sponge as he fought to steady the ladder. The sponge bounced off Phil's head and onto the path in front of the cause of the commotion.

She was standing at the gate, dressed smartly in lime green open-toed shoes, a navy blue skirt which hugged her curvaceous hips and thighs, and a light blue low-cut top which did nothing to hide the fact that she was well-endowed. Over one arm hung a jacket to match the skirt, and from the other a pink leather hand bag. With a pleasant face, the minimal amount of makeup apart from red lipstick, and slightly greying hair pinned back, she was not unattractive, though clearly the wrong side of forty. Nonetheless, the boys would agree later that she was wearing well. At this particular moment it struck Phil that she was in the prime of her life.

For a few seconds the two near-sexagenarians were speechless, and stared open-mouthed.

'That's a fine welcome for a lady coming in through her own front gate.' She laughed. 'The previous bloke had much more to say for himself. He did say he'd handed the round over to someone. I'm Mrs White. Mandy. Knock on the door when you're ready for a cuppa.' And she was gone, as quickly as she'd appeared. Stan was the first to recover his senses, descending the ladder quicker than he thought possible.

'This could get interesting, Phil. I'm just nipping up to the shop for some fags, and we'll have that cuppa.'

On his return, Stan stood at the gate gaping in disbelief at the sight of Phil near the top of the ladder, now in position at the second window. He seemed at first to be frozen with terror and to be hanging on for dear life, until Stan realised that he was peering over the ledge at something through the window.

'What the chuffing hell's going on?' was all he could say. Phil came down looking a bit sheepish.

'I thought I ought to try going up the ladder to see whether I could help out a bit more. You know. I don't want you to feel I'm not pulling my weight.' He looked back up to the window. 'And I reckon it's a piece of cake, once you get the hang of it. So I'll do this one, duck, and you hold the frigging ladder.' With that, he grabbed the bucket and sponge, and climbed the ladder with a speed that belied his age and his weight.

'Here!' called Stan. 'I know your game, you randy old sod. Too many page threes, that's your trouble. Well you look fine on that ladder, so I'll get started round the back. Give me a shout if you need me.' But Phil didn't seem to hear him.

Stan's knock on the back door was answered after a few seconds.

'Hallo big man. Sorry, I was upstairs. Come in if you want a cuppa.' Stan followed her into the kitchen, where she offered him a seat at the table.

'Tea or coffee? And what about your friend?'

'Oh Phil's OK. He said to take him a cup of tea out in a few minutes. He's married.' After a pause, he added 'not that that has anything to do with anything. Coffee please, duck, milk, one sugar.' She gave him a warm smile before filling the cups from the kettle. He eyed her up and down, liking what he saw.

'Nice place you've got here Mandy,' he said, looking around. 'Your husband must be on a good earner. I'm Stan, by the way.'

'You don't waste any time do you, Stan?' She sat opposite him. 'I kicked him out last year. Playing away, I think it's called. Obviously I wasn't good enough for him.'

They looked at each other over the rims of their cups, eyes twinkling. Stan took in her high cheek bones, full lips and long graceful neck, and thought to himself, '*God, I'm in love.*' They chatted for a few minutes, until they heard Phil calling from the back garden. Stan said his goodbyes then found Phil in the driveway.

'Brought you a tea, my old mate. We'd better crack on and finish round the back here.'

'So haven't you done it then? What've you been playing at?'

'Well I couldn't stop her talking. You know how they are. Tell you what, though, she's coming to the club on Saturday. Says she knows the band.'

'You crafty old bugger.'

Stan skipped down the drive, jumped in the air and tried to kick his heels together. His timing was wrong, and he landed awkwardly, holding his right ankle.

## Stan

That Mandy seems a bit of alright. So how much of an eyeful did Phil get when he was up that chuffin' ladder? Anyway, he's stuck with going up the ladder now.

As I get older I find that the age range of the women I find attractive gets wider. A few years ago I wouldn't have been eyeing up a woman in her forties or fifties. Now I see some very attractive ones. I'll always say *Morning me duck. How are you today?* to a bit of talent. Usually I get no eye contact even, sometimes a bit of a smile, and very occasionally an *Hello* back. I do get it though. I'm a working class bloke, so to them probably a bit of rough, and there are some dodgy characters about. In their shoes I wouldn't want to give any sort of encouragement.

After just a couple of days on this job, we've seen all sorts, me and Phil. From people almost down and out, to posh gits stepping out of their Mercs, or taking the pooch for a walk, one that'll have more bleeding bling than you'll see in a jewellers. And collecting off people when you've done, like, or when you go round the jobs where people are out working, can be the worst part. Some will make you feel like beggars, the lowest of the low, and those with plenty of money will often make up excuses for not being able to pay you. Phil, especially, won't budge till they cough up. Those who can least afford it are most likely to tip, which I try and refuse. What we've decided to do to avoid all the hassle and time involved is to push an envelope through the doors of those out on the day we've cleaned. Inside it, there's a return addressed one along with an invoice. Fingers crossed.

## *Phil*

Stan has always managed to pull the birds. For a while, when we were kids there was a youth club up New Parks, until they closed it after the third time it were wrecked. The girls would give him the eye, and if there was one he fancied, he'd give me a note to pass on to her, asking if she wanted to go out with him. They usually did. 'Going out' meant having a snog behind the club house, sometimes meeting up after school so he could walk the girl home, and after a week or two walking her to Western Park in the evening, to see how far he could go. Sometimes I would make up a foursome, if his girl insisted on bringing her mate. Me and this other girl would usually follow Stan and his latest, us walking mostly without saying much, and feeling embarrassed, while Stan and his partner chatted away, occasionally stopping to kiss. Stan had a favourite wooded spot in the park where he would disappear with his girl. Once or twice I managed to get a snog and a grope, but usually I didn't fancy the one I were with and she didn't fancy me.

I felt like a right chuffin' peeping Tom up that ladder, which I suppose I was. But I could only see her shadow moving about. A very nice distraction from the job though, and you can see that Stan is star-struck. I think he needs to tread carefully. But it looks like I'll have to do my share up the ladder.

# Three

# Come Rain or Come Shine

**S**tan loved this place. Whether on a Sunday afternoon for a pint and some football on the telly, or in midweek when you could find a quiet corner and relax, but especially on a Saturday night when it was heaving, like tonight, and a live band would be playing. After a few drinks everybody would be dancing, and Stan would join in the fun, taking the micky out of the 'disco dads'. This, in Stan's mind, was a proper working men's club, and all his friends belonged to it, plus men he'd worked with at the cabinet makers and many shared his passion for rhythm and blues music, especially from the sixties and seventies.

He stood at the bar, soaking up the atmosphere. As the place gradually filled there was the usual slapping of backs, banter, handshakes, and exchange of kisses. The band was setting up on the stage, the DJ was playing the Spencer Davis Band's *Keep on running*, and a few couples were already on the dance floor. 'All is well in the world,' he thought to himself. 'God is in his heaven, *and* I have a date.' He could feel a warm glow inside. Casually glancing towards the entrance and then at his watch, he told himself it was early yet. Ten past eight. He'd told her things got going at around nine. Be nice to have a drink and a chat before it got too noisy, he'd suggested. She knew where the club was and would find her own way.

'A beer and a shot please, Ted, me duck, when you're ready. Oh and here's his lord and ladyship. The usual for them I would think.' Phil and Jane had just walked through the entrance. They waved and walked over.

'I've got them in for you,' Stan said. 'The usual, I assumed.'

'Thanks, duck,' said Jane. 'Plenty of soda and ice please, Ted. It could be a long night, aye Stan, nudge nudge.' She winked and gently elbowed him in the ribs.

Before she could go on, Stan quickly retorted, 'So, are you on a promise then, duck? Is Phil feeling like the old ram tonight? Mind you it's a bit parky out there, so any hanky panky will have to be at home. Does that mean we miss the chips and the old film tonight?'

They laughed. With slow exaggeration, she said 'Oh no, we won't miss the fish supper and film tonight, but I think you're hoping you will. So where is she then? Mandy is it?' She looked around. 'Not here yet? I assume you'll want her to meet your best friends.'

'Just so long as you're on your very best behaviour. I'll hang about here if you want to go and grab a table.'

At around a quarter to nine Stan was still stationed at the bar, by now getting just a little anxious, when he spotted her. He had to do a double take, because she wasn't at the entrance door. Wearing a white T-shirt, blue denims and pink fashion trainers, she smiled as she walked towards him from the stage and across the dance floor. *The Peter White Band* was emblazoned across the front of the T-short. He smiled back awkwardly, feeling clumsy as he stepped towards her, not quite knowing what to say or do. He was keenly aware of many sets of eyes watching her every move.

She walked up to him, stood on tiptoe, and kissed him on the cheek. 'Hello Stan. Sorry if I've kept you waiting, but my taxi was late, and we've had to set up. Great club you've got here.'

'Don't worry. The night's still young.' He paused. 'Set up? Sorry, I must be missing something.' Then things suddenly fitted into place. 'You're in the band? Don't tell me you're in the chuffin' band.' Mandy was nodding. 'Well that's amazing. I've always wanted to be in a frigging band, and here you are doing it. I guess you're not the drummer, either. Probably the singer?'

They were having to stand close together and speak loudly now to make themselves heard, and he was becoming heady with the scent of her perfume. 'I've been doing it for a couple of years now. It's Chalkie's band, The Peter White Band. I've known Chalkie since school. He lost his singer and knew I liked this stuff, so he persuaded me to have a couple of practices with him, and ....Look, I have to get back.'

'Well, will we have chance for a dance and maybe a couple of drinks?'

'I hope so, Stan.' Then she was gone. But he did enjoy watching her walk back to the stage.

A few minutes later, to enthusiastic applause, the band was introduced onto the stage by Stan's friend Kit, who was the club's usual MC. About the same height as Stan, and with similarly broad shoulders, Chalkie White dominated the stage. He wore a waistcoat over a sleeveless shirt which showed his muscularity, along with the kind of hat he had seen Van Morrison wearing. Stan warmed to him as he introduced himself and the band members, which included another guitarist, bass guitar, keyboard, drummer and Mandy, who received a big cheer. There was just room on the stage for the six. They opened with '*Don't Rock the Juke Box*', and almost immediately the dance floor filled with couples, plus others who wanted to stand and listen to the band. Stan drifted to the back of the dance floor where he could watch and enjoy the whole scene. Chalkie played lead guitar and led the singing, with Mandy harmonising. Good choice of opener, Stan thought, a real country song and great to dance to, and the band made a good sound together. As always, when watching a live band, he was envious of their ability to stand up and play to an audience. Usually he would spend time watching each band member, to try and get a sense of how good each one was, but like all of the other men and many of the women in the room he could hardly take his eyes off Mandy. He enjoyed watching her move around the stage, and listening to the smoothness and accuracy of her voice. In fact, he was mesmerised.

The next fifty minutes or so passed quickly. The band performed a mixture of rock, pop and country songs that were all great to dance to, including *Da Doo Ron Ron* and the Buddy Guy number *Some Kind of Wonderful*. Stan knew most of them, and he applauded loudly with everyone else when the first set ended. Kit reappeared to announce that the band had agreed to come back on stage to accompany anyone who wanted to take part in the open mic session, which was about to happen. Stan sometimes took part in these, but without his guitar he was going to give it a miss. In any case he was likely to feel intimidated by the presence of the musicians. This didn't stop a couple he vaguely knew doing a rendition of 'Islands in the Stream', a Dolly Parton and Kenny Rogers duet. On another occasion they would have sounded quite good, thought Stan, but the band had just about rescued them. Nonetheless, they received a good round of applause. He was beginning to feel conspicuous where he stood, so he tried to slip away towards the bar. As yet no one else had come forward to pick up the mic.

Kit's voice came over the speakers. 'Stan, are you going to sing for us tonight? Where are you, my old son?' A few people started a low chant: 'St-an, St-an, St-an.'

'You bugger,' Stan muttered. Fortunately the chanting petered out. He had almost reached the bar, when he found his way blocked by Mandy.

'Hallo,' he said, grinning sheepishly. 'You were great. Love your voice, and the band sound really good. I can't wait till the second half.'

'Well thank you Big Man. But aren't you going to give us a song. Some people obviously think you should.'

'Yeah, well, I might've done, but I forgot to bring my chuffin' guitar. Anyway, how can I follow you lot?'

'Oh come on. I can get you a guitar. I'm sure Chalkie will let you borrow his. And if you do then we could sing something together. What do you think?' By now she had dragged him half way towards the stage.

'No, no, no. These guys just want me to make a fool of myself.' Mandy was now on the stage talking with Chalkie, who handed over his guitar. Stan was getting a distinct sinking feeling in his stomach, and to make it worse Kit was now announcing that Stan had been found and was approaching the stage.

'Chuffin' Nora,' was all he could say. Then Mandy bent down to speak to him and he found himself staring into her ample cleavage. Intoxicated once again by the scent of her perfume, he found himself climbing onto the stage and then onto a stool, guitar in hand.

'Well done, Stan. You show 'em.' It was Jane, standing with Phil and a group of friends near the front of the stage. Stan was now feeling overcome with nerves.

'So over to you, Stan,' said Kit. 'What're you singing for us tonight?' He hadn't yet thought about this. He'd been bashing away at a couple of old Ray Charles songs recently, and the chords for one were relatively straightforward. Better still was John Martyn's *Bless the Weather*, which only involved D minor 7 and G minor 7. He strummed then finger-picked the chords on Chalkie's guitar, a Gibson, and the feel and tone of it eased his nerves slightly.

'Um, well, this is an arrangement of a John Martyn song I've been working on. I loved the bloke cos he reminded me of myself. Lost his way a bit.' He told them the title. There was clapping and cheering from the floor. He became aware of how quiet the audience had become, which in itself was unprecedented.

He broke into the first chord, then immediately stopped playing. There were groans from the floor.

'Hang on, hang on! I forgot that I could do with a bit of bass in this. Does your bass player know this one?'

'You play it. I'll work something out,' came the reply. 'Give us a clue though. What key's it in?'

'I dunno about keys. I'm playing D minor 7 and G minor 7. Join in when you're ready.' He relaxed somewhat after this little exchange. Stan launched into the eight bar introduction again, this time with more conviction, and happy to hear the bass come in supporting.

He sang. Four short lines, followed by the chorus, the part the weather played in bringing and then taking his loved one away.

His performance became more self-assured as the song developed, and there were cheers when he broke into the solo. There was a chord change and short pause, long enough for him to look up and see Mandy three or four metres straight in front of him, smiling.

The applause was generous and appreciative. As they clapped, Stan stood awkwardly then realised he should hand back the guitar. He thanked Chalkie and complimented him on the quality of the Gibson.

'What a great voice you've got, Stan,' said Mandy. 'Where have you been hiding it all these years? And such a great sense of timing. John Martyn would have loved it.' Stan was too modest to know how to reply. Two others had gained enough courage to have a go at singing along with the band, receiving polite applause. Then he was back on stage, this time to perform a duet with Mandy.

'I only know one,' he'd answered when she asked if he could think of anything they could sing together. 'A Ray Charles song, *Come Rain or Come Shine*. Will the band know it?'

'That's like asking me if bears poop in the woods, Stan. But you'll have to quickly remind me of the lyrics. It's years since I've heard it.' They went through the lines a couple of times, but she told Stan to be ready to prompt her if she forgot any. The audience had flocked back to the floor to watch them.

Singing along with someone else was a new experience for Stan. He felt slightly awkward and avoided eye contact with Mandy, until he realised she was gesticulating to get his attention.

'Quick. What's my first line again?' He told her, and this helped him to focus. He was going to have to lead. He played the intro, then launched in. They gained confidence from each other as they sang, helped by the backing from some of the band, just loud enough for them to hear.

'Well done,' she said as they soaked up the applause. 'I enjoyed that. We should do it again,' she kissed him lightly on the cheek.'

After an interval, during which he bought Mandy a soft drink and shared five minutes with her, the band was back on stage to play for those who wanted to dance. The second set was at least as good as the first, and included popular dance standards such as *Hi Ho Silver Lining*, and *Sweet Caroline*. Stan felt they saved the best till last, with a great rendition of *Dancing in the Street*. Mandy led the vocals, and although a hint of huskiness had crept into her voice, Stan began to think it might be the best female voice he'd heard.

Stan hung around at the bar as the room slowly emptied, hoping that Mandy would want to have a quiet drink in a corner, where they could discuss perhaps going for a meal somewhere. Phil came over and ordered beers for himself and Stan.

'Well, me old,' said Phil. 'Chuffin' great night so far, and it's still young, as they say. Is what's her name going to be able to come over and meet the gang, do you think?'

'I'd like to think so, Phil, but we haven't really had chance to discuss what's going to happen now. I never thought she'd be with the friggin' band, and although she has a great voice and that, it all feels sort of complicated.'

'Yeah , great voice. You're dead right. And the band must be one of the best we've had. And tell you what, Stan, you was inspired. What was all that about?'

'I dunno. Maybe she brought out the best in me.'

'We'll be around for ten minutes or so to finish up, and then off for a fish supper and you know what at our place. So you know where we are if you don't get a better offer.'

As Phil walked back to his table, Mandy strolled towards the bar, carrying her coat and handbag. She sipped a glass of dry white wine as they sat on stools facing each other.

'So what would you like to do now, to relax?' he asked. 'Do you fancy a bite to eat somewhere? There are some good curry places around here.'

'That's a lovely idea, Stan, and thank you for asking, but we always go out together for a meal after a gig, the band that is, and going solo is always a bit frowned upon. And I'm sorry, I should have told you I was with the band tonight. I realise you might have thought we were here together on a date.'

'Well you did take me a bit by surprise, like. But we could always make a date, like, if you want. You know, how about next week?' He could see that this was probably leading nowhere. Mandy had looked away. He could see that she was working out how to lower him gently.

'It's OK to say no,' he said, 'if there's a problem, like.'

'The problem is, Stan, that my life is a bit complicated at the moment. You might find you don't want to get too involved.'

They chatted for a few more minutes before Mandy took her leave. She reached up and kissed him lightly on the lips, leaving his head filled with her scent once again. Life's a bitch, he thought as he walked over towards his friends. They looked up at him.

'Right then.' He whistled the first few bars of '*The Good, the Bad and the Ugly*' and they joined in with the rest.

## Stan

She is such a sexy woman. I mean, I got a hard on just watching her walking back to the stage. Sometimes on these nights I manage to pull. Like I said, one of the things about getting older is that it widens the age range of the women I fancy.

One or two of the older women down at the club are a bit of alright. They've worn well and kept their figure. It's often the divorced ones and the widows are the ones that come onto me, randy as hell. But after a couple of dates, some of them start to get serious, like, talking about how they need a big man to look after them, or how they could look after me, cooking and cleaning and stuff. I've talked to Phil about this, and in his own way he's quite a philosopher, like. Second time round, he reckons, women, whether widows or whatever, for various reasons have often been left with not much in the bank, and are rattling around in a house struggling to pay the rent or mortgage. So they are looking for a bloke, usually a bit older than them, with a bit of cash, is solvent, fit and healthy, and can give the woman a bit of security, like. Blokes, on the other hand, are looking for someone younger, still up for a bit of how's-your-father, and who will be able to take care of them when they're old and knackered. I don't think that's me. Yet!

After my first time round, take it easy, don't commit is my motto. Especially when it's warm and sunny like today when I love seeing the young ones out wearing just their short skirts, or shorts and a little top.

Back to Mandy. Yeah, take it easy, see how it goes. I suspect she might have something going with one of the band. But she's so easy to be with and talk to, and has this way of making me feel good about myself. No one has told me before that I have a good voice. Maybe she was bulling, but I'll take it.

## *Phil*

I've always thought Stan was wasted working in the furniture place, but he seemed to enjoy it. 'There's no pressure, Phil, and I'm good at it,' he would say. I remember that he didn't cope with the pressure at school, when there were exams on especially. He would fall to pieces. And even when loads of his mates have told him he's good enough to perform solo, or play in a band, you could see what goes through his mind. He will sing and play at the club, because he's comfortable there. He knows us, and he's OK. But he thinks he would crack up in front of a crowd he didn't know. It's a big shame.

# Four

# It's a Jungle Out There

'Get rid of it! Stop pussyfooting.' Phil's command was aimed at the left back of *Fosse Boys*, the working men's club under twelves football team, but it was what he usually shouted at all of the players. The third weekend in August was the start of the season for the dozen or so teams playing on a still, grey afternoon on Victoria Park. Some were junior teams in which boys held hopes, shared by their dads on the touchline, of being the next Ronaldo. The haircut was as close as any of them could get, certainly as long as the Phil Hiscoxes of this world were running the teams. Most of the men playing in the other games did so for no other reason than to run off the beer of the night before or of

Sunday lunchtime, or both in some cases. On Victoria Park on Sunday afternoons the 'beautiful game' was reduced to the lowest common denominator of kick and chase.

The left back did manage to kick the ball aimlessly upfield, only to be scythed down by the opposition's winger. 'Referee!' came the shouts from the touchline. 'Book him. Send him off. That's three times now'. The referee blew his whistle, allowing Stan to run on with his bucket of cold water to apply the magic sponge to the boy's injured leg. Job done, the lad back on his feet, Stan ran back to resume his role as linesman, or 'assistant referee' as it had recently become known, blowing hard as he ran to keep up with play.

Life for Phil and Stan had begun to settle into a rhythm of sorts since they'd started the window cleaning round. Phil had some mysterious reason for not being able to work on the last few Fridays. Stan had at first used the time to catch up on the paper work so that he could wind up the taxi business. That done, he was happy enough 'winderin' by himself, and had found a few new customers locally, including some of the businesses on the Fosse Road not far from his home. Stan usually spent Saturdays with his eighty-six year old mother, who lived in managed accommodation in Birstall, a northern suburb of Leicester, taking her shopping and for a bit of a walk if she was so inclined. Sunday was his one day off, although being sponge man and linesman so that his friend's team could chase a ball about did feel to Stan like the least relaxing part of his week. Especially when he was being accosted by the opposition team's manager.

'Next time you flag for offside, when my striker is friggin' onside, I will come and stuff that flag up your jacksie. Understand?' The man's close-cropped hair and tattoos on his neck suggested an ex-squaddie look to Stan, who towered over him.

'Well if you can do the job better, you're welcome to it,' replied Stan.

'Just remember what I said.' Stan watched him walk away, marching almost, swinging his arms as if he was on the parade ground, although there did seem to be something unnatural about his movement.

Stan was able to listen in on Phil's motivational half-time talk, basically a reminder to kick the ball up to the two big strikers when attacking, and for defenders to chop the opposition down before they got into the penalty area.

'And remember what we said in training, Pricey. And Moz. If they so much as touch you in the area, you fall over for the penalty. Put in a couple of rolls for the referee.'

'My Dad says we shouldn't dive, and we should pass more,' said Moz.

'Well when your Dad is running the chuffin team you can do what you like, but I'm not having any nancy stuff. Route one is how we play.'

Ten minutes into the second half, Stan waved his flag when one of the opposition forwards was at least two metres offside. There was some barracking from parents on the touchline, and the next thing he knew, the tattooed manager had pushed him in the chest, pulled the flag from his hand and had proceeded to hit Stan around the head with it, swearing profusely. The referee came running across the pitch, with much blowing of his whistle, and managed to intervene before Stan was able to swing the right hook which would probably have knocked out his assailant, if it had found its target. The team manager was shown the red card and told to remove himself and retreat to the changing rooms. After much protesting he marched off, calling back to Stan.

'You'll keep.'

There was loud heckling and barracking of the referee by the parents of the opposition team, which clearly unnerved him. When one of Phil's team's defenders tackled the opposition striker in the penalty area, the referee awarded a penalty and sent off the defender, perhaps in an effort to placate the vociferous parents. Incandescent with rage, Phil carried his fourteen stones as fast as he could across the pitch, then swore at and pushed the referee, who lost his balance and fell over. Inevitably, Phil was also shown the red card and told to leave the pitch. From a distance, he watched as the opposition striker scored the penalty, and then a parent seemed to be reorganising the ten players left in the team. Towards the end of the match, the boys were passing the ball well and managed to score an equalising goal. Phil couldn't face having to give the post-match team talk. He walked to his car and drove home.

Back at work the following morning, barely a word was exchanged between Phil and Stan until they were sitting in the van for their mid-morning break. To an observer, it would have been difficult to decide who seemed to be sulking the most about the outcomes of the weekend. The football match apart, Stan had spent much of Sunday going over the events of Saturday evening. His disappointment only deepened as he realised he'd liked so much about Mandy. The way she walked, head held high, hips swaying ever so slightly. Her smile, and the glint in her eyes. She moved and sang so well on stage, as well as any professional, he thought. And he'd enjoyed the moments when they'd been close, the touch of her hand, the scent of her perfume.

'At least the rain's held off,' said Phil. Stan grunted in reply.

Phil continued. 'My missus, yeah? She reckoned your singing and playing on Saturday night, like, was the best she'd heard from you. We've said it before, but we reckon you could be good enough to have your own chuffin' band, like, if you worked at it, and play your own gigs.'

This was high praise from Phil, about as good as it got. For a minute or so Stan thought about how to respond.

'You know, I reckon she, Mandy that is, must have really inspired me or something. But it was a pure one-off. And as I've said before, me old, I wouldn't be good enough to sing and play with a band. Besides, I'm too old to start something like that.'

'Well in my humble friggin' opinion, you're never too old to try something different and you ought to think about giving it a try. You're a long time looking at the chuffin' lid.'

'Hark at doctor friggin' Hiscox, philosopher and thinker. Shame you can't apply that to your football coaching.' He glanced at his watch. 'We'd better get back to work before you convince me you're right.'

They were working on the third house in a leafy street in Aylestone, Phil on the ground floor windows, Stan on the first floor, when Stan noticed a man carrying a TV out to a van parked in the adjacent drive. He felt there was something familiar about him, but thought nothing of it at first. Two minutes later the man re-emerged carrying what looked like a microwave oven, which he also placed in the back of his van. Could be moving house, Stan thought to himself. Then the man briefly looked up at Stan, who recognised him as the tattooed team manager who had accosted him the previous afternoon.

'That bastard.' He called down to Phil. 'Oi, Phil. Remember that pillock who had a go at me yesterday? Got red carded.'

'What about him?'

'He's here. Well, next door I mean. I've seen him carrying stuff out to that friggin' van. Doesn't feel right to me. He doesn't strike me as the sort who could afford one of these places.'

The tattooed manager reappeared, this time pushing a sack barrow on which was loaded a washing machine. He struggled to lift it into the van.

'Aye mate, need a hand,' called Stan. The man looked up.

'No thanks pal. I'll manage. This is the last one. The lady here has asked me to fix this stuff for her.' He suddenly seemed to be in a great hurry. Having got a corner of the machine onto the back of the van, he managed to push the whole thing in, and then quickly covered it with an old sheet and shoved the sack barrow in, before getting into the driver's seat and reversing the van into the street. Stan's speed of thought and movement increased. He noted the van's registration number and slid down the ladder, as the van drove away.

'Phil, put your sponge down and get your phone out. Call 999 and tell them there's been a burglary, number 41. Where are we?'

Phil called out the name of the road.

'Right. White van, driving towards the Aylestone Road.' He called out the registration number.

Phil was punching in the numbers. He repeated the registration number. 'You sure it's a burglary?'

'Ninety five per cent. He couldn't leave quick enough. I'll check inside, and see what damage he's done.'

Stan found the back door of the house open and broken glass on the floor just inside.

'Hallo, anyone home? Hallo.' There was no reply. The back door opened directly into the kitchen. A drawer was open, and on the worktop next to it was a carving knife and a lump hammer. Just in case he was disturbed, thought Stan. He walked into the hallway, calling out again. He moved through the house, being careful not to touch anything.

Back outside, he heard Phil give his name and address to the person on the phone.

'Tell them there's no one at home,' Stan called.

'Well?' said Phil, when he'd finished the phone call. Stan described what he'd seen.

'Empty house. The sod must have known no one was at home.'

A neighbour appeared from across the road, and said she would get in touch with the house owners. Phil and Stan carried on working down the street, after half an hour seeing first a woman get out of a car and walk into the house that had been burgled, followed shortly by the arrival of a police car from which emerged a rather portly constable.

'Who's eaten all the pies then? No wonder they stuck him in a car,' remarked Stan.

They explained to the distraught house owner and the constable what had happened. Whilst they were in the process of giving a statement in the back of the police car, the constable received a message that the car had been intercepted and the driver apprehended. The boys decided it had been a long morning and they deserved a pint with their lunch.

'Why do I have a funny feeling we haven't heard the last of this?' said Stan.

They were working in the same neighbourhood the following day. Mid-morning Phil pointed out a white Ford van which he had noticed earlier driving in the opposite direction.

'Couldn't be lightening striking twice, could it?' he asked.

They had their answer a few minutes later, when the same van pulled up in front of their own van, parked a few doors down from the house where they were working. Three large men, each carrying a baseball bat, emerged from the white van and immediately set about smashing the windscreens and bodywork of Phil and Stan's van.

'What the fuck? Oi!' Phil shouted.

'Phil, stay where you are,' called Stan, who, worried Phil might try some heroics, couldn't get down the ladder quickly enough.

The three men had said nothing, hadn't even looked in their direction, and were already climbing back into the white van. It was driving away by the time Stan and Phil reached the pavement. They walked slowly up to what only two minutes previously had been a perfectly good vehicle, and was now a wreck, a write-off. They stood and stared.

'Chuffin' Nora,' said Phil.

'This is yer man from yesterday, sending us his pals with his best wishes.'

They sat on the low wall at the side of the pavement, silently reflecting.

'I didn't like the van anyway. Wrong colour,' said Stan.

They discussed the idea of calling the police, but decided against it. 'Those nob heads'll come for us next,' suggested Stan. 'Plus the police would start asking awkward questions about the business and stuff. Let's just tell the insurance people that we had a prang.' For a few minutes neither of them spoke.

'Life used to be so bleeding simple, Stan,' Phil said eventually. 'We went to work, clocked in everyday, like, bit of overtime now and then, and we got our wages every Friday afternoon. Why are things so friggin' hard now when we're just trying to make a go of it?'

'This is just bad luck, my old mate. We can still make a go of it, but maybe window cleaning isn't the right thing. It doesn't exactly use a lot of brain power.'

'I thought that was one of the advantages,' said Phil, and they laughed. 'So have you got any more bright ideas?'

'Well, not that'll bring in the chuffin' bread, like. But I was thinking about what you and your missus had said. I might try and put together my own band, like you suggested. It's something I've always fancied, like, but never known how to go about it. I thought I'd have a chat with Mandy and maybe that Chalkie, see if they could point me in the right direction. As my old man used to say, it's no good dying wondering what if.'

'Now who's the chuffin' philosopher. Anyway, you'd need some help. I could be your roadie or whatever. You know, fight the crowds back, specially the girls. Cart your gear around, fix plugs and fuses, like.'

'Sounds like you've just writ the perfect job description for yourself,' exclaimed Stan, smiling. 'Right up your chuffin' street. It's so bleedin' obvious.' There were a few moments of contemplation, Stan stroking his chin. 'Gordon Bennett, Phil. It would be a hell of a thing to try. For a start, where do I find musicians who'll play with an old git like me?' He turned to Phil with a look of determination. 'But do you know what, with a bit of help it might just work. Let's give it a whirl.'

They set about clearing the broken glass and general mess around the van, then loaded the ladders and washing equipment. Stan called his friend Jasper who owned a garage and pick-up truck, and they arranged for him to collect them and the van.

'He can drop us off at Ursula's place for a bit of nosh. Just the chuffin' pick-me-up we need.'

## *Phil*

The ref said he wouldn't report me to the league committee, so that was a relief, like. Fair dos, you shouldn't lay a finger on the ref, but he got that penno wrong. It's all very well that lad Moz going 'my Dad says do this, do that, pass the friggin' ball around', but half them kids don't know how to pass. When I played for the school team, well, the under-fourteens, the teacher always told us to belt the friggin' ball up the field for the lads up front to chase. We had two big fast kids who frightened the shit out of most teams, so it usually worked. I played right back. Stan would say right back in the pavilion is where I belonged. My tactics was straight forward. First tackle against the winger I'd go in hard and give him a bit of afters and some verbal. I might give away a free kick, but more often than not he wouldn't go anywhere near me or the ball after that. Which meant I had plenty of time, like, to get the ball up to the strikers. These kids, they're pussy-footed, if you asked me.

And that arsehole who started having a go at Stan. What's that about? Nasty piece of work, he was, and them parents not much better. It could get a bit tasty next time we play that lot. Makes me wonder why I got involved in this coaching lark in the first place. I blame Stan. We'd had an early pint and was walking across the park one Sunday a couple of years ago, between the pitches, like, when in one of the games we saw a bit of a scrap going off, on the touchline. It was the parents having a right go at each other, and the kids had stopped playing to watch it. The ref calmed things down, and then one of the blokes, who turned out to be the manager of one of the teams, stormed off, shouting *Blow this for a game of soldiers. I've had enough. Find some other mug to babysit this lot.* Or words to that effect. Stan and me recognised some of the others and eventually realised that their kids were playing for our working men's club team. After the game, we got chatting to the boys and their Dads, and somehow or other I was persuaded to take over as manager. I will never again drink on an empty stomach.

## Stan

The worst thing about those Sunday games is the parents. They shouldn't be allowed anywhere near, in my view, as they haven't got a friggin' clue. And Phil's as bad as them. Always bellowing at the poor lads, all negative stuff. There are one or two good players, but they don't stand a chance with all that shouting going on. The trouble is that's how the Dads used to play, if they played at all, and nobody has shown them any better. Apart maybe from the one bloke who seemed to take charge after Phil was sent packing by the ref.

As for that wazzock who had a go at me, there was something about him that I couldn't put my finger on. Something that suggested trouble was never far away with him around. And so it proved. Turns out the statement from me and Phil will see the bloke going to court, so he might end up in the nick. Who knows? I have no doubt our paths will cross at some point in the future. His nasty mates had the look of military men about them. Either that or they work out at the gym regularly. Or both.

God, I would just love to be in a band, like. Maybe I am good enough, as Phil says, but what does he know. The trouble is I'm fifty-five, so who is going to want to play or sing with me? Where do I find decent musicians? There must be some around Leicester, judging by the bands you see in The Brown Cow.

My hero is really Gary Moore. I was lucky enough to see a couple of his concerts. Manchester Apollo in 1990 was the first, when I went up with a couple of mates. He was playing the *Still Got the Blues* album, one of the best. I took my Gibson Les Paul with me, hoping he would sign it, because it was the same model that he played. I had to hang around for an hour or so after the show, and eventually his chuffin' minders let me in to see him. We had a good chat for probably half an hour, which was just unbelievable. He even went through a few of his rifts, to show me how they worked, like the opening to

*Moving On, and* the solo parts in *Texas Strut.* We had a quick blast on that one together. He said he was amazed that I wasn't playing in a band myself, but he might have just been saying it. I put a bit of varnish over his autograph, so you can still see it. By the time he played in Birmingham in 2009, he was a megastar. I thought I'd be able to get to see him again, like old mates meeting up, but I couldn't get nowhere near him.

## Five

## Ursula's Café

'Stanley! Philip! My friends, where have you been? Wie geht's? Come and give me a hug.' Stan gave a big smile, at the same time grimacing as Ursula wrapped her strong arms around him, before embracing Phil. Stan knew that Ursula gave all of her regular costumers the same warm welcome, but also knew that she had a particular soft spot for him. At six feet tall, she had few costumers taller than herself. With her booming voice, solid build and Germanic features, she cut an intimidating figure, which at first belied her friendly and gentle nature.

'Put us down, duck. You're squeezing the breath out of me,' complained Phil, also smiling at the ebullience of the welcome.

'Let me look at you, Stanley,' she said as she put a firm hand on each of his arms and gave him the once over. 'As always, you look undernourished and in need of a good woman to look after you. I live in hope, but you still play hard to get. Tell me what I have to do to convince you, Stanley. What is the way to your heart?'

Stan was used to this open flirting from Ursula, and he felt no need to pretend that he didn't enjoy it. What he was unsure about was her sincerity, and the extent to which she was genuinely attracted to him. He wondered if she was trying to hide her insecurity, following the divorce from her husband five years previously. Ursula had fallen in love with an Englishman she met on holiday, and as he owned a business based in Leicester she agreed to move from Germany to live with him. They married, but after a few months she realised he was having an affair with a member of his staff, so she moved into a rented apartment. In the year she had been living in Leicester she had quickly grown to like the city, and had established a network of friends who proved to be very supportive. So rather than returning to Germany, she was determined to stay put and make a go of things. She used some of her savings to open a café on the Fosse Road North, not far from the busy junction with the A50 Groby Road, and five minutes walk from Stan's. She had a natural talent for the business, and quickly sensed what suited her clientele. This included a mixture of the local white working class residents, who preferred strong cups of tea, bacon butties, and meat with potatoes and two veg, and a student population who had a more sophisticated taste for the modern coffee menu. Being more adventurous, they would try her homemade German dishes. Straddling both groups, in terms of taste, was the passing trade of white van delivery drivers and reps. She quickly put down anyone who took the micky out of her strong accent, or made reference to Germany losing the war, which Stan had done initially. This reinforced the respect in which she was held by her customers. Ursula also had a talent for attracting the local gossip, and little escaped her notice.

'Well we could start with a plate of the old liver dumplings, your best fried potato and sauerkraut,' said Stan

'OK, Leberknödel mit Sauerkraut und Bratkartoffel. And you Philip, the same?'

'Nein danke, ta duck. You know me. Bacon, fried eggs, sausage and chips will do nicely.'

'No problem. Take a seat. By the way, a little bird tells me that your singing went down well at the club the other night Stanley.'

'So your chuffin' spies are still out there then. You probably know what I had for breakfast.'

'Well I can't help it if my customers want to tell me about their weekend.' From the kitchen door she called back, 'And I believe it was Weetabix and toast. Sorry, chuffin' toast.' Phil, Stan and some of the customers chuckled, as her waving arm followed her through the door.

Stan liked to sit where he could survey the whole scene, so they chose a table against a wall. About two thirds of the tables were occupied. A waitress moved between them, serving coffee and clearing away used crockery. They both ordered tea. The aroma in the café was that of coffee with a hint of frying onion. There was a steady hum of conversation, but anyone choosing to listen to the music could just make out the voice of Phil Collins from the CD playing.

'I love this chuffin' place,' said Stan. 'You have to admire Ursula for what she's done here.'

'I think you might admire her for one or two other things. Her dumplings, for instance.' Stan smiled back at Phil. For Stan, one of the compensations of losing his regular job was the fact that he could visit the café more frequently. They turned their minds to the earlier events and discussions. Stan reflected that the idea of getting a band together was really just a pipe dream, and that perhaps they should look for a proper job. Phil asked him if he was a man or mouse, and accused him of lacking balls. They needed to keep the 'winderin' going, he said, so they would have to find the money for a replacement van. But he was sure that, in a place like Leicester, there are bound to be good musicians around. It was just a case of finding them.

Ursula brought their food to the table. 'Here we are. My best dumplings for Stanley. For you Philip, also the best. The eggs are free range, and the sausage and bacon I get from the marvellous butcher down the road. I will leave you to enjoy it.'

Stan sampled the liver dumplings. 'Wunderbar,' he said, pushing the fingers and thumb of his right hand together against his lips, and then away, with a kissing sound. As they ate they came up with a brief plan of action. They would each contribute five hundred pounds towards a replacement van, plus what they would receive from the insurance company. In the meantime they would try and borrow a van, or hire one if necessary to keep the business ticking over. Stan would try and meet up with Chalkie and Mandy for some friendly advice. Then they would perhaps advertise for musicians, or hold auditions. This part of the plan was where they were in uncharted waters, and it all felt rather vague.

The café slowly emptied after the lunchtime rush. Stan and Phil took their time over the rhubarb crumble and custard, then Stan waved to Ursula and asked her to sit with them for a few minutes.

'That was a cracking meal, as always, duck. No wonder business looks good.'

'You know Stanley, it gives me a lot of pleasure to see people enjoying my food. I just hope I can keep things going.' Phil asked her what she meant.

'Well, I have a new landlord, who recently bought the building from the previous owner. He is already talking about putting up the rent. Not just a little increase, but huge. From three thousand a year to five. If that happens I don't know if I'll be able to keep my lovely café open. Things are very tight already, and I would have to increase prices, which would mean I would lose customers.' Her eyes welled up as she looked at Stan. 'I don't know what I would do then, Stanley. I love running this place, and meeting the people that come here. It's my life.' The tears were now flowing freely. She blew her nose into a handkerchief, and tried to wipe her tears away. 'I'm sorry. I shouldn't make you listen to my problems.'

'That's alright duck, you go ahead,' said Phil. 'This is not like the Ursula we know, so it's obviously upsetting you.'

'It's not just your problem though, is it duck?' said Stan. 'It's ours and all your other customers' as well. We need to make sure you keep this place going, so tell us what we can do.'

'Well for a start we get a petition going, right,' said Phil. 'Get all your customers to tell this nob head to leave the frigging rent as it is, and that we don't want to lose this café we all love so much. And while we're at it, we should get in touch with radio Leicester and tell them about the petition, and that telly programme with Ann what's-her-name, East Midlands whatever.'

'Today,' Stan told him.

'Absolutely. Strike while the iron's hot.'

'No, you duffer, the programme. East Midlands Today. But yes, good idea, Phil. Occasionally you do get them.'

They looked at Ursula, who was wiping her eyes. 'I don't know what to say? Do you think it's important enough for the radio and television people to be interested? And will anyone take any notice of a petition?'

'It's what we do in this country, duck, in our spare time' said Stan. 'Sign petitions. Or hadn't you noticed? And people will sign if we have anything to do with it.'

Phil suggested that they needed to get in touch with influential people, such as local celebrities, like Leicester City footballers, and Leicester Tigers rugby players. Councillors, even the mayor might be interested if they thought there were votes in it. Stan asked him how long he'd been an expert on petitions, to which Phil replied that he'd signed one once, so had an idea what they looked like.

Ursula produced some paper from her office and together they drafted something which they thought looked like a petition. This received the approval of the customers still left in the café, one of whom had overheard their conversation. He claimed to work for the local paper and offered to see if he could generate some media interest. He also suggested some changes to the wording of the petition. Stan followed Ursula into her office, where she deftly typed up and printed some copies of the petition. Phil had no trouble in persuading those in the restaurant and several passers-by he accosted on the pavement to sign. In just a few minutes the first sheet was half full of signatures.

Phil and Stan were sipping a final cup of tea and contemplating phoning friends who might be able to loan them a van in the short term, when two men in their twenties, dressed in trendy casual wear, made a very ostentatious entrance, as if they were used to attracting attention, looking round to check that everyone had noticed them. They sat at a window table, from where one called out to Ursula.

'Fraulein, service bitte. Could we have the menu?'

'Cocky buggers,' Stan said quietly to Phil. 'Let's just keep an eye on this, right, before we push off.'

'You know who they are, don't you?' Phil named two professional footballers.

The two men laughed at something one had said to Ursula. The same man put his arm around her waist and tried to squeeze her bottom. She calmly removed his hand. When he tried again she moved out of his reach. She avoided eye contact with Stan and Phil as she walked to the kitchen with their order.

'Come on me old; let's go and get a couple of autographs,' said Stan. Phil followed, as Stan collected the petition from the bar and walked over to their table.

'Excuse me gents,' Stan said politely. 'I expect you guys get pestered a lot wherever you go, but I wonder if we could ask you to sign this petition for the café owner.' He explained the reason for the petition, and the two men agreed happily to sign. They also agreed to Phil's request for a photograph of them both with Stan and himself, which another customer took for them.

'I know Ursula will appreciate your support,' said Stan. Then looking towards the kitchen and then back at them, he added quietly, as if taking them into his confidence, 'She's a bit of alright, our Ursula,' said Stan, who, deciding to push his luck, pulled out a chair and sat at the table. 'Don't you think? A bit of a goer, maybe.'

The two looked sheepishly at each other, before one replied, 'Yeah, I wouldn't disagree there, mate.'

'Have you been here before? Do you know her, like?'

'No,' replied the same one, 'but I understand she might be, umm, available.'

'Oh, and what makes you say that?'

'Well, shall we say she's been quite friendly with a mate of ours, if you know what I mean?'

'And what, you're hoping she might be friendly with you as well? I mean, I wouldn't blame you.' Stan was all smiles and bonhomie.

'Well no harm in trying, is there?' said the young man as he leant back, looking confident, one arm over the back of his chair.

'Possibly. But I tell you what, me old,' said Stan. He stood up, towering over them, so that they had to look up at him. Phil came closer to add his sizeable presence. Stan leaned across the table, looked hard at the two men, and said quietly, 'If you lay one chuffin' finger on her, then we'll be coming after you, with a lot of friends. We know who you are, right, we've got your photo taken in here, and if we have to, we'll circulate this and anything we need to say on Facebook, twitter, you chuffin' well name it.'

After a suitable pause, Stan politely added, 'Thanks again for the signatures boys. Enjoy your meal.' As they walked away Phil asked Stan how long he'd been using Facebook and twitter. Stan replied that he wouldn't know where to start, but those cocky buggers didn't know that.

Ursula had the sense to send her waitress over with their food, and was making coffee at the machine.

'You're paying nothing, Stanley and Philip,' she said when Phil asked to settle their bill. 'It's on the house today, for all your kind help and support.' Stan asked Phil to stay at the bar while he and Ursula had a quick chat in private.

Back in her office, he asked her, 'Have these two been in before, duck? You know? The bum pincher and his mate.'

She hesitated, before replying. 'No, but I think a friend of theirs has been.'

'So what do you think's going on, Ursula? They come in, and start touching you up, like, and one suggested, you know.... Well, I don't know what he was suggesting, really. Maybe I'm just guessing.'

Ursula stood sideways on to him, arms folded, looking away from him.

'I'm sorry, duck, it's none of my business. I'm sure you can take care of yourself. But, any problems, you know, just give us a call. Alright? I'll leave you to it.'

But he had misread her body language. She looked back at him, eyes once again welling up.

'Oh Stanley, it's such a mess.'

'Now don't worry, duck. We're on the case, and we'll do everything we can to keep this place open.'

'I know. It's not just that.' She was fighting back the tears. 'I don't know why I should tell you. It's not your problem.'

'So what is it, pet? Is it something else? You've got to chuffin' well tell me now. Come on, sit yourself down.'

'No, it's OK. I'll stand.' She blew her nose, wiped her eyes, and after a pause of a few seconds, continued. 'You know, I'm thirty five years old. My husband left me, well I left him, and since then I've avoided any casual relationships. Then along comes this young, good looking man, who showers me with compliments, invites me out for drinks with some of his footballing friends. I felt like a young girl again. Then I had a few drinks, one thing led to another, and, well, you can imagine the rest.'

'So, when was this?'

'Four or five weeks ago.' She paused, before looking at him and adding, 'long enough for me to know I've missed my period.'

'Oh. I see. Shit.'

'And I never miss my period.'

'Do you know for sure?'

'I've bought a test kit but I haven't had the courage to use it yet, so no, not for sure. Oh Stanley, how can I be so stupid?' The tears and self-pity had been replaced with anger. 'Stupid in so many ways. If I am pregnant, then have a baby, how will I be able to keep my café going? There are no petitions for that.'

'Don't get ahead of yourself yet, duck. The first thing you need to do is have the test. Today. I'll stand here and make you do it if I have to, but I'm sure you must have female friends who you could confide in. I mean, I'm chuffed, well I think I am, that you've told me all this, but this is girl stuff really, isn't it.'

Ursula went on to say that she had friends, but felt none were close enough for her to talk to about this situation. She felt comfortable talking to Stan, without being able to explain why. She promised that she would carry out the pregnancy test soon, when she could face doing it. Stan said he would call in again during the next few days, for a coffee and chat, and if Ursula behaved herself he might even clean her windows free of charge. She laughed and reached up to kiss him on the cheek, thanking him for being 'a star'. After drying her eyes and running her hands through her hair, she led the way back out of the office.

Half an hour later, Phil and Stan were at Jasper's garage, negotiating the purchase of a replacement van with a contact of his, when Stan received a text message on his phone. 'Test negative. All good. Just late. Lesson learned. Love. U'.

## Stan

Chuffin' Nora. I mean, like, thank God there was a full stop after the 'Love' in that text message. I have a lot of time for Ursula, and I'd do anything for her, sort of thing. And I do admit to myself that I fancy her, like, but I do not need my life getting complicated. What about her confiding in me like that, like I was some sort of what-you-call-it, one of those women you write to in the papers for advice on stuff like that. Those friggin' footballers should know better, as well, thinking they can play around with someone like they were going to. If I catch the bastard that got her into bed, he deserves a good lamping. They're still kids really, with too much money in their pockets. My old Mum is right when she says they're paid too much too quickly, and don't know how to handle it. She blames Jimmy Hill.

Those liver dumplings are a bit special, like. One day I'd like to visit the butchers in Bad something or other, who make them. People travel from all over Germany to queue outside his shop on a Friday morning, when he sells them, so they must be good. A couple of years ago, right, a group of German folk dancers from this place came over to Leicester. Ursula had invited them to come and do some dancing around the centre of town. She used to dance with them apparently. They were great fun. The blokes liked a drink. They brought a load of wine over with them and had a cracking party in the café. Really nice people. A lot of them spoke good English, better than me, some of them. What surprised me was how many of them had never travelled out of Germany before. Some had been a bit worried about how we would treat them, right, because of the war. But they were bowled over by the welcome and hospitality they'd had from the locals. A couple of them asked me how I would vote if there is a referendum on leaving the EU, and how I thought it would go. I'd never thought about it, to be honest. It occurs to me that most of us don't know enough about this EU thing, and the chuffin' politicians don't help, with their lying crap. Basically, I wouldn't trust a politician a bloody inch, especially that tosser with the scruffy blond hair.

## Phil

It were great the way Stan sorted those two duffers out. It reminded me of how he used to look after me at school, if there were kids trying to give me a hard time. He would draw them in, like, getting them to think he was on their side, and then sort them out one way or another. When I learned to box, right, I could return the favour.

There you go again. Ursula. Another woman that fancies Stan and struggles to keep her hands off him. Not my type. Too big for a start, and over-confident. I'd struggle to get a word in. Jane's bad enough. I think she would have gone for Stan if he'd shown any interest, but he would never do that to a mate. She seems to be off me at the moment for some reason. It's been a while since we had any sex. Is it just what happens as we get older? Mind you, I'm still up for it. I know I could lose a bit of weight. I've put a bit on since leaving the steelyard. I used to keep reasonably fit working there. Maybe I should get back in the gym and into some sort of shape. Fewer fry-ups too. The trouble is you can't beat a good fry-up.

# Six

# Not Alone

tan was in good spirits, singing Gary's *Moving On* at the top of his voice.

'Give it a rest, Stan,' called Phil, from the garden below. 'That's the umpteenth sodding time I've heard that chuffin' song this week. And, by the way, playing air guitar at the top of the ladder is frigging well not safe.'

'Alright, keep your hat on, me old. I've heard you singing along as well. Or warbling more like.' Perhaps he had done the song to death, he admitted to himself.

Stan had become a man reborn. A man with a new lease of life, a new-found purpose, a sense of destiny. All down to the decision to try and form his own band. He certainly had a spring in his step, as did Phil to a lesser extent. With Jasper's help, they had managed to find a van in good working order. It had an

MOT certificate, road tax, and was at a price they could afford. So they had been able to resume work immediately on the day after what they had decreed to be VD day. Van Death day. Every now and then there was a nervous pause in the washing and wiping, whenever a white van drove past, and at one point Stan descended the ladder very quickly to join Phil next to their new van, when it looked as if one of the passing vans was going to be parked. There were sighs of relief when it moved on.

Stan had launched into his very mixed repertoire of rock and blues songs, developed over the years since he had made his first record purchase in 1973, Status Quo's 'Caroline'. Phil was very happy at first to hear Stan singing as they worked, and by Wednesday, having heard some three or four times he was able to la-la to the melodies, even join in some choruses. By Thursday, however, he'd had enough and told Stan that he needed to find some new material quickly. There were mixed reactions from some of the householders on their rounds. One had appeared on the pavement outside the house where they were working as Stan was singing 'Hey Jude'. She cheered and clapped.

'I did enjoy hearing that, thank you. It took me back a few years. My era, the sixties.'

'Do you do requests?' shouted a man from across the road, later that day.

Stan turned and smiled. 'Possibly, mate, if I know it.'

'How about shut the f... up?'

Stan was reminded that rock music is not everyone's cup of tea.

He launched into *Black Magic Woman*, singing the first verse.

'Remember that one Phil?'

'Not really, and to be honest mate, I'd love to have the radio on for a bit.' He turned on Radio Two.

As it was Thursday they worked through lunch, aiming to finish at four o'clock. They then adjourned to the nearest decent looking pub to celebrate the end of their working week. They knew The Peacock Inn quite well, and were drawn to it when Phil noticed a board at the car park entrance advertising a nineteen seventies rock music evening in two weeks' time.

'I gave Mandy a call yesterday and arranged to pop round and see her tomorrow,' said Stan, after they had savoured the first few sips of their pint of bitter. 'See if I can't set the ball rolling, sort of thing. Thought I'd go and see the old girl first, instead of going on Saturday, for a change. What you up to?' Although he sensed that he shouldn't pry, Stan had often wondered what Phil did on Fridays which meant he had to take the day off.

'Tomorrow? Oh, same thing as the last couple of weeks. Something I've started to do.'

'Like a hobby? How about twenty questions, see if I can work it out?'

Phil looked flustered. 'It's just something I like to do. Leave it Stan, all right?'

'Have you got a minute, Stan?' Christine, the manager of the block of sheltered accommodation called to Stan as he was about to ascend the stairs.

'Yes duck, sure.' She closed the door to her office as Stan sat on the one chair available for visitors.

'What's she been up to then?' He knew that Christine called in on Audrey, his mother every morning, as she did for all of those residents who she felt needed a close watch. Phil's wife Jane had suggested to Stan that he had a look around the place and meet Christine when it became clear a year ago that Audrey was no longer able to manage properly living on her own. The crunch came after she called him in a distressed state of mind to say that someone was trying to break in to her house through the roof. She had also called the police, and a patrol car was outside the house when he arrived. After seeing two workmen on the roof of nearby houses in recent weeks, she had got it into her head that they were burglars, and that noises she had heard during the night were caused by them trying to break into her house. One of the policewomen talked to neighbours, who confirmed that they had had their houses reroofed in the last few weeks, but there had been no burglaries. A visit to her GP followed by a scan at the hospital confirmed that Audrey was suffering from vascular dementia.

This had opened up a whole new world to Stan, who had assumed that the increasing episodes of confusion, forgetting where things were and who people were, and not being able to make simple decisions were all part of what comes with growing old. She was eighty-six, after all. But he knew people in their eighties that were living independently, were fit and healthy and enjoyed a drink at the club. While she enjoyed her regular drop of malt whisky in the evening, Audrey had gradually dropped out of her whist and bowling clubs, no longer used her car and had become increasingly isolated. What she needed, according to Jane, was to be with other people and 'to do stuff'. 'Loneliness is the enemy,' she had said.

Christine had also talked with him at length about dementia, how it affected some of the residents in the block of apartments, and what he might expect to happen to Audrey. The accommodation was basic, but gave Audrey the independence to come and go as she pleased. Stan and Jane agreed that Christine was just the person to keep an eye on her.

'She's been wandering, duck,' she was saying now to Stan. 'At least I think it's Audrey. A couple of other residents have complained about someone wandering the corridors, banging doors and calling out. All this in the early hours, in the last few nights. Also when the poor lass comes back after doing her shopping or whatever, she hasn't been able to find her way back to her flat, not without some help.'

'Oh shit. I'll have a chat with her, duck, see what we can do.'

'There's probably not a lot you can do really, Stan. I've had a chat with her and she does find the layout of this place confusing. I think the wandering at night is probably caused by her waking up in the night and being confused about where she is. Then she struggles to find her way back to her room.' She paused, while Stan registered this. 'I've seen this happen before, and what I've done in the past, which usually works, is to put a coloured square of card on her door, at eye level, and in one or two places, like the door into the corridor from the top of the stairs, to help her find her way. She thought this was a good idea when I suggested it, and she chose the colour of the card herself. Bright yellow, like this.' It was about the size of a beer mat. 'You'll spot them as you go up to her room.'

A yellow square was staring him on the face a few minutes later, as he pressed the buzzer for Audrey's flat.

'Aye up me duck,' said Stan. Audrey stood in the doorway. It was a few seconds before she replied.

'Oh, hello stranger. Long time no see.' Stan had become used to this greeting and stopped taking it personally when he realised some time ago that this was her way of stalling for time, until she could put a name to the face.

She sat down in her usual place, a chair beside the dining table from where she could look out onto the busy road. Opposite was a hand car wash business, run by a group of

Eastern Europeans, mostly Polish, where Stan had taken his taxis a couple of times.

'Those men work hard all day long, you know. Washing cars, whatever the weather. They do them all by hand, you know, as well. Such hard workers. Foreign too, going by what I can hear when the traffic goes quiet.' At some point during his visits she would make almost exactly the same comments. He could imagine her sitting and watching the action in the car wash all day, like a curtain twitcher, and wondered if the guys opposite were aware of their audience.

He observed her from the small sofa, thinking how thin she was looking. Casting his eyes around the room, it seemed empty of something. Then he realised most of her paintings and family photographs were no longer on display. On his last visit he discovered that she had thrown out most of her paper work, including letters she had kept for years, bank statements, and receipts. It was as if she was trying to eradicate signs of her existence. Or possibly, Stan thought on reflection, she is trying to save everyone else the trouble of tidying up after she's gone. He asked after her health and whether she had enjoyed the trip out with the luncheon club.

'Oh it were alright. The food was a bit bland, and it was the usual same people. But I shan't go again. They're all old and not quite with it.'

*Whereas you're a spring chicken and obviously still got all your marbles, me duck,* Stan thought to himself, smiling.

'And they fart. All the chuffin' time. You should smell that coach when we get off it. If someone lit a match it'd go off with an almighty bang. Then the police would think it was a terrorist attack, and then where would we be?' He'd heard it all before.

'You've got a good point there, Ma. But it does you good to get out of this chuffin' flat. It'd be a shame to stop going.'

'Oh I do get out. I fetch my paper every morning, and go for a stroll around the park. I get plenty of exercise.' Stan knew that this was make-believe, sadly. She concentrated on the car washers for a moment. 'I go bowling as well.' *I wish*, he thought. She pointed to her mantelpiece, where there was a twenty year old photograph of a ladies' bowls team.

'Have I ever shown you that photo? We were top of the league in those days.' She turned her attention to the car washers again, but Stan could see the tear rolling down her cheek.

'And from what everyone tells me, Ma, you've still got what it takes. But you haven't told me how you are.' There was a puzzled look on her face as she looked at him, as if to say 'who are you? Do I know you?'

'It's funny you should ask. I've been wondering what this rash is.' She rolled up the sleeve of her cardigan to reveal an angry rash on her forearm, then raised her leg to show the same rash on her calf. The psoriasis had plagued her since her teens, but this was the worst that Stan had seen it for some time. Audrey then complained about noticing a pain in one side of her neck and shoulder. He decided that they should call in at the surgery on their way back from the supermarket, to try and arrange an appointment with her GP.

'Oh, and I've had this letter. Looks official.' She waved a white envelope. 'Perhaps you should look at it.' Stan read it. It was a report of the review meeting that social services had held in her flat a few weeks ago. In the report was a recommendation that Audrey should use the services of a private care company to support her with the preparation of meals and keeping her flat clean. She was entitled to the attendance allowance, which would cover some of the costs, but she would have to pay the balance.

'What do they mean? I don't need them blooming well interfering. If you ask me, they don't know shit from clay.'

'Listen, Ma. They just want to make sure that you're doing alright. You know. None of us are getting any younger, like, and just now and again you do get confused and a bit forgetful, you have to admit. And these people would be able to help with the cooking, or doing your laundry and that.' He didn't like to add that there was the unpleasant smell of wet knickers lingering in the flat these days. Audrey had previously refused point blank to allow anyone in to her home to provide any sort of help, insisting she could look after herself. She wouldn't claim any benefits to which she was entitled, such as the attendance allowance. 'Give it to someone else. I don't need charity,' she had said. It was only after much persistence and persuasion from Stan that she agreed to grant him Power of Attorney for her health and well-being, but she was adamant that she could still manage her finances, and didn't want anybody interfering with her them. 'You'll have your hands on my money soon enough,' she told him, to which Stan took great offence.

'I'll arrange for these people to come and have a chat, and we'll see what they have to say.'

Audrey grunted, then produced her shopping list and handed it over to Stan, who knew it was a rough guide only. Most of her purchases would be impulsive. As had become the routine, once in the supermarket, which was a few minutes drive from her flat, she sent Stan in one direction with a trolley, while she went off in another carrying a basket. 'I'll meet you back here,' she said. After a suitable length of time had passed, Stan made his way over to the aisle where wine, beers and spirits could be found, along with Audrey, who, as always, was placing a bottle of Famous Grouse on top of the crisps, chocolates and cakes already overflowing in her basket.

'Well, it'll soon be chuffin' Christmas, and I need to stock up, don't I?' All Stan had ever seen at her flat were empty bottles and packets.

At the surgery, the receptionist managed to find a slot for an appointment the following week for Audrey.

They lunched at her favourite greasy spoon café nearby. She ordered gammon, egg and chips, adding, as usual, 'I haven't had that for ages.' Stan carried their mugs of tea.

'Hallo my dear. It's lovely to see you again,' she said, out of habit, to the waitresses and other customers, most of whom were total strangers. Stan steered her towards a vacant window table, so that Audrey would have something to talk about. She would never let there be a gap in conversation, and if ever one looked imminent she would be inventive. Increasingly, she would come out with something nonsensical.

'Have you got your bags all packed then?' she asked him. 'You know, for your trip.' Stan sipped his tea, looking at her over the rim of his mug.

'Depends which trip you're thinking of, Ma.'

'Your holiday. When is it you go?'

'I haven't got owt planned, Ma. Be nice to take a holiday, though.'

'I'd like to go on a trip,' said Audrey. 'Just into town would be nice. Buy a few clothes, see the sights.'

'What, like you've never seen the sights in Leicester?'

'I'll tell you what I would like to see. King what's-his-name's coffin in the cathedral, and the centre they've set up, all about him. I haven't seen that.'

Stan thought for a moment.

'Tell you what then, Ma. Sometime in the next few weeks, right, I'll take the day off. We'll do the King Richard stuff in the morning, and have a nice lunch somewhere.

'Oooh, that does sound exciting, Stanley. Especially if we can go to John Lewis as well.'

Their food arrived. Stan had become concerned about how thin Audrey had become, and watched as she picked at her meal. She ate a few chips, dunked in the egg yolk, and about half of the gammon, before putting her knife and fork down. Stan couldn't persuade her to eat any more, so he scraped the leftovers on to his plate.

'Want not, waste not, aye Ma?'

As he continued eating, Audrey started a very one-sided conversation about nothing that made much sense to Stan.

Stan drove her home, and left her to unpack the shopping. He called Phil from his mobile phone. There was no answer so he left a message

'I bleeding well need a pint and someone normal to talk to. But I called you instead. What are you up to? If you fancy a drink give me a call back.'

The traffic was moving slowly in Birstall as Stan made his way over to meet Mandy at a city centre café. He had plenty of time and wasn't too concerned when a bus pulled out in front of him and crawled along to the next stop in front of a row of shops. He waited patiently for the opportunity to pass the bus, from which all of the passengers seemed to be disembarking. His chin dropped in surprise when he saw the last person get off. There was no mistaking the familiar figure of Phil. The bus pulled away and Stan was able to slot the van into a space from which he could observe his friend. Seemingly deep in thought, head down, Phil walked past the row of shops and cafés and on into Wanlip Lane.

'Right, you old bugger, let's see what you're up to.' Stan waited a few moments until he thought it was safe to start the engine, and drove the car at crawling pace. Phil crossed the road and a few yards on turned down a side street, then took the first street on the left. As Stan drew level, he spotted his friend going up a path towards the door of one of the houses. Turning into the street, he parked as closely as he felt it was safe to do, in time to see the door opened by a woman who was obviously expecting Phil. Hallos were exchanged but no kisses, or handshakes even, and Phil entered the house.

He emerged a few minutes later, carrying a football and accompanied by a boy who Stan estimated to be fourteen or fifteen. The lad carried what looked like a large book wrapped in a plastic cover. Stan slid down as far as he could into his seat when they turned to walk in his direction. Fortunately the two were in deep conservation, and Phil didn't spot the van. Stan turned the van around as soon as they were round the corner, and parked on the main road, intending to follow on foot.

In the nearby park Phil and the youth used one of the sets of goalposts to play at penalty taking, taking it in turn to take the penalties and to be the goalkeeper. Phil was unusually expressive, cheering loudly whenever his companion scored a goal, and even more loudly when he, Phil made a save. The boy, on the other hand, seemed to be very inexpressive and lacking in emotion. He also had a slightly strange gait, thought Stan, walking and running very stiffly, clearly not very athletic. After two turns each in goal the pair set off back towards the village centre, where they walked into a shop full of brightly lit gaming machines. Stan watched from the bookmaker's opposite, where he placed a couple of bets on horses tipped by the Racing Post. It was fully half an hour before they came back onto the street, and Phil was clearly very happy about something. The lad had just the beginning of a smile on his face, but no more, as Phil patted him on the back in a manner suggesting fondness. They didn't walk far. Just a few doors down the road in fact, to the fish and chip shop where they gave their order and then sat at a table by the window. Stan wished he could hear their conversation, although it seemed to be Phil doing most of the talking. The boy became more animated when he unwrapped the book he had been carrying, and the two spent some time pouring over and talking about the contents.

At the point at which their food was served, Stan realised it was past twelve o'clock and he had arranged to be with Mandy by one. A lorry had stopped outside the fish and chip shop so he took the opportunity to slip out of the bookmakers and cross the road to beyond where they were eating. When he took a quick glance over his shoulder he wasn't sure but he felt that Phil had been looking in his direction. Head down, he made his way quickly back to the van. The smell of fish and chips had lingered in Stan's nostrils, so he stopped at the first opportunity to buy some for his lunch.

'The most important member of your band, in my opinion,' said Chalkie, 'is the singer. A good singer can carry the band to some extent, not the other way round.' Stan was surprised to find Chalkie sitting opposite Mandy when he arrived, but guessed that she had asked him along as a chaperone, as well as for his advice. Stan didn't mind one iota, as he knew he had a lot to learn, and quickly.

'And fortunately, from what I've heard Stan you've got a great voice. It sounds natural, it's strong, and you keep in tune. That may sound daft, but it's surprising how many bleeding singers wander out of tune, even if it's just half a tone, and people notice.' Stan was nodding in appreciation and agreement. Chalkie went on to advise Stan to find a singing teacher to help him develop his vocal range and strength. The key thing, he said, is the breathing, and a tutor would help him improve this.

Stan absorbed this for a few moments.

'What about musicians?' he asked. 'How do I go about finding the right musicians? Where did you find your guys?'

'Depends to a large extent on what sort of material you want to sing and play, and obviously who's around to play it.

You'll find, though, that there are loads of people around who fancy their chances as a rock or pop star, and think that by joining your band they're doing you a big favour, like, and also expect to make the big time overnight. You need to find people who are prepared to graft, and practise regularly'

Stan listed the songs that he had in mind to include in his set. Mandy chipped in at this point.

'Sounds a bit Gary Moore heavy, duck. I made the mistake at first of wanting to sing all my favourite songs, but it's what they like to hear that counts. Rock has such a wide range. So include some of the more recent stuff if you can. For most gigs people will want to dance and enjoy themselves. But slip in one or two oldies and ballads when you and they need a rest.' Stan hadn't imagined he would be in a band playing music for people to dance to, but he kept that to himself.

Chalkie offered to put the word around that Stan was putting a band together and was looking for musicians. He used a room at the back of a music shop for practices on Saturdays, but wasn't using it on the following Saturday. Stan was offered the use of it for auditioning.

'You're both amazing,' he said. 'This is like another friggin' world to me, and I really appreciate the help.'

'It won't be easy, Stan,' said Mandy. 'You really have to work at it. Practise, practise, practise. There are some places you'll play at first where the audience isn't interested, but you have to stick at it, show you're enjoying it.'

The conversation turned to Chalkie's band and what they were singing and playing at the moment, before Chalkie and Mandy left to return to their places of work. Back in his van, Stan sat alone with his thoughts for a few minutes. 'It's just possible,' he said out loud as he turned the ignition key, 'that I could at long last become part of the chuffin' music scene.'

'OK, for fuck's sake. His name's Daniel, and I see him for a couple of hours most Fridays, like, while it's still school holidays. It used to be Saturdays, until the business went tits up.' Phil and Stan were sitting on bar stools in the club, sipping beers after watching Phil's team win their match earlier. Phil had been very quiet, which led Stan to believe that he was sulking because the team had played good passing football, rather than the 'kick it long' variety. It was the first round of the county cup competition, and unusually Phil had simply said to the boys 'go out there and enjoy yourselves.'

Which they duly did.

Stan had been itching to ask Phil about the lad, after seeing the two together on Friday. Making conversation was proving difficult. Any comment about the match from Stan was met by a grunt and followed by a long silence. Stan could stand it no longer, so decided to wade in, regardless of any sensitivities Phil may have had.

'I was driving back through Birstall the other morning, after seeing Ma, like. I could've sworn I saw you walking towards the park.'

Phil glanced sideways, making brief eye contact. He didn't know whether to admit or deny he'd been in Birstall. 'I might have been to the garden centre,' he said.

'Was that before or after the park? You seemed to be playing football with a lad, looked about fourteen, fifteen.' Stan just looked straight ahead.

'Oh him,' Phil replied after a moment's thought. 'He was just a kid who was having a kick about and asked if I wanted to join in.'

Stan remarked that they must have got on well, because he could have sworn he saw them together in the chippy a bit later. Phil had taken a deep breath before opening up.

'Just a kid I know,' he continued, 'who has a few problems, like, so I try and help him out. I had a bit of a thing with his mother a year or two back, right, and I hit it off with the lad. I suppose because we both found school difficult and I could, you know, see where he was coming from. Eventually I had to stop seeing his Mum. I thought the missus was getting a bit suspicious, like, and weighing everything up, being how things are and all, I thought it best to stick with the devil you know. Trouble was, the lad had, has, his own view of things. One of the things with Daniel, right, is that he needs routine, so when I didn't turn up one week and his Mum told him why, he went ballistic. He did the same the next week so she asked me if I could manage to see him once a week. This was all around the time we lost our jobs. The kid's behaviour is all over the shop, like. He can be as nice as pie one minute and having a mega wobbly the next. Anyway, I didn't mind, right, as I think the lad and me had a bit of a bond. If it helps him, that's fine. But you really have to understand the kid and I'm learning all the time. This thing about routine, or even obsession. Come rain or shine we always have to go to the park and I'm always in goal first. He even takes the penalties in the same way each week. He kicks the first three to my left, right, then the next two to my right, and so on. I have to pretend I don't know and let him score, but only the ones he wants to score. We've had a few tantrums, like, before I twigged. And of course we always have to have the fish and chips. Once, they didn't have haddock. He didn't cope with that at all well. You'll have seen he's a bit gangly and uncoordinated, like, so most people find him…., well, strange at first, cos he doesn't really mix easily. But he isn't half good at friggin' Maths. For instance, you remember from school what stuff like four squared is. Four squared is sixteen, four times four. Well he can tell you what any number squared is. Like two hundred and fifty-four, straight the way, without thinking. I don't know what it is by the way. And another amazing thing is that he plays the drums, right. Not just crash bang, but properly. He's got the gear, a proper drum set in their spare room, which his Mum has had to get sound proofed. He has this special thing, like, a gift. He can listen to a tune once and play the drum arrangement straight away from memory. He can play rock stuff, pop, even chuffin' jazz. Incredible.'

Suddenly aware of how animated he had become, Phil stopped and went back to sipping his beer.

Stan just stared at him, not knowing what to say. Eventually he managed 'Well bugger me.' Then raising a smile, he added, 'You crafty old sod.'

'Turns out, right, she soon had another bloke in tow. I met him, and he gives me the creeps for some reason. Anyway, I was thinking. The lad, Daniel enjoys playing along with rock music as well.' His eyes were fixed on Stan.

Stan's quizzical look changed as it dawned on him what Phil was trying to suggest.

'Oh no. You can piss off. There will be no spotty youths playing in my band. You can get that idea out of your head.

## *Phil*

About the best thing that's come out of me running the lads' team is the day I met Esther. I hadn't been managing them long, like, when one match this gangly kid were standing next to me. He seemed dead interested in the game, fascinated even. I asked him if he played. He shook his head. Did he live near, I asked. Birstall, he said. Do you have mates to kick about with? No, he replied. Then this woman turns up, all apologetic, saying this is her boy. He's very shy normally, and she hoped I didn't mind him watching the football.

I liked the look of her and we had a bit of conversation, like, which doesn't necessarily come easily to me. She struck me straight away as very gentle and kind, quite ordinary to look at until she smiled. Esther has this lovely smile. Daniel seemed, how can I put it, a bit strange. He never looked at me. No eye contact. And he didn't seem to like his Mum making a fuss, like stroking his hair, or even just touching him. He wouldn't hold her hand when they walked off, like. It might be just because he's at that teenager stage, I thought, too old for that kind of stuff.

Just before the final whistle, they came over to say goodbye and thank you for letting them watch. Well, she did. The lad then asked whether the team played every week and could he come next week. I had to explain the home and away thing and lo and behold, he was at the next home match and the few after that, so I got to have a good few chats with his Mum, Esther. We seemed to hit it off, one thing led to another and we became, as they say, an item. The hardest thing was not telling anybody. I'd never had sex until I met Jane. No other woman had ever really shown an interest in me. Eventually, I slept with Esther and the next morning I just couldn't Adam and Eve it. I had to pinch myself.

## Stan

He's a dark horse, old Phil. Who'd have thought? I mean, I would have said he thought the sun shone out of Jane's arse, like. She was probably the best thing ever happened to him. Phil always found it difficult being around girls. I don't mean he was gay or owt. You could see that he just felt awkward, like. It's all to do with going to a chuffin' boys' school, if you ask me. Totally unnatural it is.

And this lad. Sounds a bit weird to me. For a kick-off, I can't see that anyone would be able to play the drums or any instrument to a song from memory, just after hearing it once. So I don't know. Was Phil pulling my plonker or what? You'd have thought there must be some decent drummers around who were looking for a band to join. That's the trouble when you're new to this lark. You don't know the people or have the contacts.

I hate to see the old girl going downhill. Breaks my heart, when you think about what she was like in her prime. Well, until the last few years really. I don't think anyone could have a better Mum than she's been. I've had my ups and downs and bits of trouble, like, but she's always been there when I've needed her. Some people found her a bit fearsome and I could see what they mean. She's always been chuffin' stubborn, never takes no for an answer. And if say you had a complaint about something you'd bought, like in John Lewis or wherever, you'd be happy to stand behind her if they were being awkward. She would always be willing to give a lesson in customer relations. 'Now young man, you're being very unhelpful. We know our rights, so are you going to deal with this, or shall I talk to your superior.' You knew she'd win.

Like you did at election time. She was a labour councillor for over thirty years, and people knew that if there was a problem to be sorted out, she would usually be able to do it. There was one MP, she gave a right old dressing down when he hadn't done something he'd promised someone he'd get done. She sorted it instead. People trusted her. She'd spend hours on the phone listening to them going on. There was more than once I had to rescue the meat from the oven. And everyone knew her. They'd stop her on the street and bend her ear. I think it's one of the things that drove the old boy away in the end.

## *Phil*

Stan once said to me that he thought his old girl might have had a thing going with my dad. He had heard her talking to him on the phone, reckoned it all sounded a bit lovey-dovey. Once or twice she would put the phone down and get her coat on, saying she was just popping out on council business. True, my old pop would never hear a bad word said against her, but I couldn't see it somehow. For a start he was too bloody lazy, sat on his arse all day at work, then in front of the telly all night. A boring old fart really.

She always kept us on the straight and narrow as kids. She would always say to me that if I needed to chat at any time, a shoulder to lean on, then to go and see her. And I did, more than once. She knew I had a short fuse, like, that I would get into bother with other kids, sometimes if they so much as looked at me. It was her idea I went to boxing lessons. Said I needed something to get the anger out of my system, like. And she were right, it chuffing well worked. Well, most of the time. She also saw that I was good with my hands. When we was little she would make us some playdough, and later would buy me Meccano and Lego kits.

A lovely woman. It's a shame to see her going downhill.

*Seven*

# Crossroads

T he practice room consisted of a table and two wooden chairs, a music stand and an amplifier with built in speaker. On the table was an hour glass, a bottle of water and three glasses. There were some out of date posters on the walls, advertising performances at the De Montfort Hall and Leicester University from three and four years ago. Stan had brought along a large portable CD player, and a CD that he had found in the shop downstairs with some backing tracks he could use during the audition.

By three o'clock they had almost lost the will to live. Four people had turned up for auditions, but had shown themselves to be novices or incompetent. As Stan turned the hour glass to relieve the boredom, there was a tentative knock at the door. Phil shouted come in.

A figure covered in a hooded coat entered, carrying a guitar case. He closed the door, turned, put the case down and removed his hood.

'What the fu…' said Phil.

'Shit,' said Stan.

'Are you two running this friggin' audition?' In the doorway stood the boys' football team tattooed manager with whom Stan had an altercation two weeks previously, the same man they had seen stealing from the house next door to where they had been working.

It was a few seconds before his face revealed that he had registered the situation, by which time Phil had picked up the guitar case and was standing at the door to bar his escape.

'Sorry mate,' he said to Phil, and reached for the case. 'I'll take that. I think I'm in the wrong room.' He turned towards Stan when he heard the scrape of the chair legs on the floor.

'Well, well, well,' said Stan as he walked slowly towards the centre of the room. 'Look what's crawled out from under the woodwork. We'd love to hear what you've got to sing, so don't run off. Don't tell me. *Been caught stealing, or Stealing in the name of the Lord.* Or maybe *Stand and Deliver.* Better still *Wreck on the Highway.*' He moved closer, so that he towered over the man.

'You give me one good reason,' he continued, 'why I shouldn't give you a good hiding.'

'You could always try.' A hint of a smile crossed the man's face.

Stan mentally took a step back. 'My guess is that you was in the military.'

'Two tours of Afghanistan, Royal Marine Commandos.'

The words *unarmed combat* crossed Stan's mind. 'That doesn't excuse the way we've seen you friggin' behave, you bastard. Stealing from people's houses, smashing up our van, threatening me in front of kids.'

A tense silence followed, broken only by the sound of the playing of a bass guitar drifting up the stairs from another practice room. The man clenched and then unclenched his fists, and shuffled slightly on his feet, looking up to the ceiling and then at Stan. He sighed heavily.

'Yeah, well, it's been difficult. I'm trying to sort myself out. I'm sorry about all that stuff. But I guess you won't want to hear me play, in the circumstances.'

Stan perched on the table, one foot on the floor. He looked towards Phil for some sort of guidance, but Phil just shrugged his shoulders.

'So what made you come here? I mean are you into rock music, like?' asked Stan.

The former soldier explained that he was, but didn't like some of the more recent stuff. He'd learned to play the guitar as a teenager and had tended to play rock and jazz. Whilst in the sixth form, then again when in college, he had played in a band, and had missed being able to play when he was in the marines. Life had been too hectic and unpredictable, but now back in Civvy Street he was able to get back to some serious practising and was keen to join a band. It didn't matter too much what music they played, as long as he could enjoy himself. As he talked he seemed to lose some of his pent-up aggression. There was a slight easing of tension in the room.

Phil held up the guitar case, as if to ask 'should we hear him play?'

'Don't raise your hopes, cos we've been listening to people all day. And remember, you owe us for our van.' Stan let this sink in before continuing. 'But show us what's in the case then.'

Taking the case from Phil, he pulled out a guitar with a red-brown finish, held it in front of him and kissed the back. 'This beauty is a 1959 Les Paul. A few modifications. Bought it with some of my lump sum when I came out. Want to hear it?'

Phil pointed out the amp and power points. 'What's your name by the way?' he asked.

'Malcolm will do for now.' He plugged in and quickly checked the volume and tuning on the guitar. 'Anything you want to hear especially, or shall I just give you a quick blast?' They agreed that a quick blast would do for the moment. Malcolm went straight into a bluesy riff, showing that he could play the full range of notes. The tone of the guitar was instantly impressive.

'OK, so you can play a bit,' said Stan. 'What we'd like to hear is some rock stuff. What we've asked others to do is to use two or three tracks from this play-along CD. We'll play each song and at the point where I give you the nod, be ready to pick up the tune with a guitar solo. Know what I mean?' Malcolm nodded. Stan gave him a choice of three: *Smoke on the Water, Johnny B Good, and Stairway to Heaven*. He went for the Chuck Berry song, and asked for the first few bars so that he could check the tuning. Malcolm played quietly along with the melody, then as Stan gave the nod he eased effortlessly into an improvised solo. Stan had to resist a smile and to stop tapping his toes. The same happened when he put on *Stairway to Heaven*.

'These are all very well,' said Malcolm, looking from Stan to Phil, 'but can I play you something not on the CD? The great J J Cale is one of my influences, and this piece is, well, just chuffin' brilliant.'

Without waiting for a reply he accompanied himself singing a ballad, *Magnolia*. Stan frowned from start to finish.

'Not really rock is it,' said Stan. 'A bit bluesy.'

'Isn't that one of the great things about rock though,' Malcolm protested. 'It's all a matter of interpretation. With a full band line up behind it that could be amazing.'

'Up to a point,' said Stan. 'Anyway, I'll be doing the singing.'

The three stood looking at each other for a few seconds.

'If it helps, I play the sax and write my own stuff as well.' Stan and Phil remained dead-pan. 'Well, is that it?' asked Malcolm.

'I think so. We'll be in touch if we need to hear more, but we've heard a few guitarists so don't raise your expectations.'

'Not what I was told downstairs,' said Malcolm, now standing at the door, 'but please yourself.' He gave them a phone number on which he could be reached then took a step away from the door. 'So, seriously, is there a chance you'll want me in the band?'

'Well, seriously, is there a chance we'll get our money back for the van?' responded Stan.

'Maybe you can take it out of my first couple of gig fees,' Malcolm said with a chuckle. Phil and Stan were unmoved.

'So what's happening then?' asked Stan. 'Presumably you're being done for the burglary, if not our friggin' car. What are the cops doing?'

Malcolm looked distinctly sheepish.

'They've dropped the case. The house belongs to my ex-wife, and she isn't pressing charges.'

'You are fucking joking. You've got away scot-free, like. Just like that.'

'Afraid so. I'll leave you to it then.'

Malcolm closed the door quietly behind him.

Stan and Phil busied themselves tidying up, in unspoken agreement that they were finished for the day. 'What do you think? He could certainly play,' said Phil

'But not in my chuffin' band,' replied Stan, angrily. He knew that he hadn't had to give Malcolm the nod for the solos, which irritated him.

'I'll have no truck with him, right. You heard that. Would you bleeding well believe it. He breaks into his missus's, ex-missus's house, helps himself to her stuff and gets away with it. Where's the justice in that, aye?' He was at the door.

'We don't know the circumstances, do we mate?' said Phil. 'For all we know she might be a nasty piece of work, like, and he was getting his own back for summat.'

'He will not be in my chuffin' band. End of. Even if it means there will be no band.'

'I understand, mate. Calm down.'

On their way down the stairs to the shop, Stan stopped outside a room from which the sound of a bass guitar could be heard. They listened to the riff being played, followed by a brief conversation, then by the same bass riff. Stan recognised it as the backing to The Cream's *Crossroads*. There was more conversation, along with what sounded like the packing away of the instrument.

'Did you hear that?' asked Stan. 'That is some playing, pure chuffin' rock bass. Pure Jack Bruce. I think I need to meet this bloke.' He knocked on the door and walked in, without waiting for a response. In the room stood a young woman of about twenty and a man in his forties.

'Can I help you?' the man asked.

'I hope so mate,' said Stan, 'I've being listening to your bass playing. Hope you don't mind, but we couldn't help it really. You can obviously play a bit, like. We're auditioning for a rock band, and just wondered if you'd be interested in auditioning for us. I'm Stan by the way, and this is Phil.'

'You're talking to the wrong person, Stan. This young lady is the guitarist, and very good she is too.' They exchanged introductions. The student's name was Angie. Completely wrong-footed, Stan did not know how to react to the idea of a female bass player, and was feeling slightly embarrassed. The young woman helped him out by shaking his hand.

'I could be interested, but only if you'll audition my friends as well. One plays the violin, the other plays the piano.' Stan wanted to ask *men or women*, but thought better of it. In the circumstances it was apparent that an audition there and then was not going to happen, so the young woman suggested that Stan could hear her and friends play at the university's R and B club, which would be meeting the following Wednesday evening in the Students Union building. It was only the second meeting of the new academic year, she explained, so there might be some new members who played something. From her accent Stan decided that she was a southern 'posho', and he wasn't sure that he fancied mixing with a group of poncy students. But Phil clearly had no reservations.

'We'll be there,' he said. 'What time, me duck?' She gave them the time and room name, suggesting that they ask at the entrance for directions. After giving them both the once over, she betrayed her own misgivings by saying that if they changed their minds she would understand.

Stan noticed a double bass propped up on a stand. 'And is that yours as well?' he asked.

'No. It's the shop's actually, but I do play it.' Stan asked if there was any chance of a quick demo. She obliged with thirty seconds of walking bluesy bass.

'Impressive,' he said. Minutes later, the boys were loading the van.

'Never thought I'd see the day you'd be so chuffin' keen to go into a place of learning. A bit out of our league, I would've thought,' said Stan.

'And young enough to be your chuffin' daughter. Nice pair, all the same. If they're all like her, you never know your luck. I thought you was a bit slow there, me old.'

'Randy old sod! I just hope your missus gives you a pass out.'

## Phil

Seems to me that guy has some issues. You can see the anger in him, bursting to get out. I would think he saw all kinds of stuff in Afghanistan, and who knows how that would affect him. Breaking up with his missus wouldn't have helped.

## Stan

So along comes this bloke, plays some great solos, writes his own stuff, has a half-decent voice, plays the sax to boot, but he's a total arsehole. A dickhead. What do you do?

Then this bleeding Angie appears playing Jack Bruce stuff almost as well as the man himself. And she's got mates who play. Hope they're not all as cocky as she is, so to speak. I could be fronting a girl-band.

So I'll get to see the Uni after all, though not in the way my old man would have liked. I did get some studies in, like, after I left school. Somehow. The schools in New Parks were pretty grim affairs that were built along with the big estate in the nineteen fifties. My Mum used to say that Leicester was in the dark ages, like, until the Labour Government of the sixties and seventies brought in comprehensive schools, and the City council decided to merge the boys and girls schools across the city. But the New Parks schools, right, were still separate sex schools when Phil and me were there, and in those days you could leave school at fifteen. Phil had struggled with the old reading and writing all the way though school, so he couldn't wait to leave. He went to work at the steelyard and worked there for forty years. He would flash his pay packet at me each Friday, right, and brag about the clothes he were going to buy and the motor bike he were saving up for.

I stayed on until I were sixteen, like, got a few CSEs and O-levels, and thought for a bit about going to college to take

HNDs. I was playing the guitar by now and getting quite good, so the music teacher was trying to get me to take an HND in music. But as I couldn't be doing with Phil waving his fivers in my face, I got a carpentry apprenticeship with a furniture making firm. I was good at woodwork at school and enjoyed the night school classes, learning to do proper woodturning and that. Once I had finished the apprenticeship I was on pretty good money, plus I could make a bit on the side too, doing jobs for mates and some of Mum's friends. She bought me a good second-hand lathe one Christmas and helped me to set up a workshop at the bottom of our garden. So when I got married I was able to knock up some decent tables and chairs, and put together a kitchen. I was seriously thinking about going it alone, you know, my own business, like. But the marriage went pear-shaped and I lost interest. In most things, not just the woodworking. About the only thing I kept going with was the guitar.

## Phil

School was a waste of time as far as I was concerned. I was standing at the gate cheering on the day they started to demolish the old boys' school. Two thousand and seven, I think. There were a few others there to watch. I remember one or two had managed to get into the building and came out with bags of old photos, books, registers and all kinds of crap. The place had obviously not been cleared properly, for that kind of stuff to be lying around.

# Eight

## Danse Carribe

The assistant in the music shop on London Road had suggested three people that Stan could contact for singing lessons. He chose the one who gave the first hour lesson free. She also had a sexy voice, either despite or because of her Welsh accent he thought, but the vision of loveliness he had conjured during the phone conversation evaporated the moment she opened the door to her Edwardian semi in Evington. After brief 'halloes' Stan followed her large figure down the hallway and into a room which he estimated to be twelve by fifteen feet, kitted out with a large keyboard which seemed to be connected to a computer and screen, plus alto and tenor saxophones on stands and two microphones plugged into speakers. During the introductions and preliminaries he imagined that she, Carla, would be quite attractive if she could lose a few pounds weight, and he was finding it difficult to not have his eyes transfixed on her expansive bosom.

After he'd explained his ambitions and reasons for wanting to have lessons, Carla asked him to sing something he was working on at the moment.

'What? Now?'

'Well that is what you're hear for, isn't it?' Carla asked, with no hint of sarcasm.

After discussing whether he should stand or sit, Stan decided to stand. They were only five minutes into his first lesson and he already felt completely out of his comfort zone. He found himself shuffling nervously, not knowing where to put his hands.

'Can I borrow a mic? Not plugged in like, just to hold. I'm not used to singing without one.' She obliged.

He announced that he would sing 'Still Got the Blues'. Carla asked if he knew which key it was in and did he need a starting note. Not really understanding much about the structure of music, he simply asked her to play a few notes until he was happy with one to start on. She told him it sounded like he would be in F major. Singing unaccompanied into a mic which wasn't plugged in felt unnatural, and he stumbled and forgot the words in a couple of places.

'Right. Well. Not bad. But listen, Big Man, you need to relax. I won't bite, OK. That's a promise. Let's work on the breathing for a few minutes, then I want you to have another bash at the song.' They went through a few exercises, which she wanted him to practise at home every day. 'Now let's have another go at the got the blues song, but this time aim your voice over my head as if there were an audience. And belt it out. Like this.' Stan ducked in surprise as her voice filled the room, the windows vibrating.

Second time through he did feel more relaxed, encouraged by the occasional smile and foot tapping from Carla. He could imagine the backing to the song playing along, and his timing improved.

'That's more like it,' she said. 'I think we've got some work to do, but you've definitely got something I can work with.' For the next twenty minutes or so they went through some scales, which again Carla told Stan to practise at home. She was positive and encouraging and Stan liked the way she called him 'Big Man'. He was beginning to enjoy his first ever singing lesson, until she told him that she was going to record him singing the Gary Moore song. Stan was impressed with the speed of her online research, which found a website that had the backing track to the song.

'We're in luck,' she said as she downloaded it. Carla then produced a microphone he hadn't spotted, which had a circular mesh attached behind it, making it look like an old fashioned radio mic. She then gave him a pair of headphones to put on, through which he could hear his voice and the accompaniment.

'This is just like in a studio, Big Man, so better get used to it.'

It had never occurred to Stan previously that he might go into a recording studio, but he could now see it as a possibility. They listened to the introduction a couple of times to make sure that Stan was confident about when to come in. Although it wasn't the karaoke version that Stan played along with at home, he knew the song well and the backing track was pretty accurate. He did not, however, enjoy the experience. He was disconcerted by the sound of his own voice. There were several times when his timing was out. Worse still, when she played the recording he realised there were times when he was out of tune, and even when he was in tune he didn't like his voice. He couldn't be consoled by Carla's assurances that first recordings were often like this and things would quickly improve.

'And actually, Big Man, it is a lovely ballad. For much of the time you were spot on and sounded good. I'll write down the website link for you. So you can download it and sing along at home.' He didn't let on that he didn't need it.

On his way home he sank into a depression. He switched on a table lamp in his living room, and with a bottle of Everards beer for company he reflected on the hour he had spent with Carla. For the first time he was experiencing doubts about his ability to sing with accompaniment, despite the time he'd spent singing along with backing tracks and the occasional karaoke night at the club. He slept badly, and his mood continued into the next day at work.

They were working their round in a leafy part of Glenfield, on a bright sunny morning, the air filled with birdsong. To start with, Phil accompanied the birds with tuneless whistling, but he had quickly sensed Stan's mood. Stan was 'winderin', as they had come to call it, the upstairs windows of the first house. Phil called up to him.

'What's up then, Barry Manilow? You're like a bear with a sore bum. Shall we have the radio on to cheer everyone up?'

'If you must. And don't bloody call me Barry Manilow.'

'Chuffin' Nora, you've got a right chin on this morning. What's up? Don't tell me. You tried it on with the music teacher and she sent you packing.'

'I wouldn't touch her with a barge pole. More your type, although she'd be a bit of a handful I'd imagine.' Stan stopped wiping, came down and walked over to Phil. He sat on the folding steps that Phil used.

'To be honest duck, I feel like a bear with a sore chuffin' bum after my lesson yesterday evening. I came away feeling about six friggin' inches tall. Do you know, she expects me to practise stupid breathing exercises and pulling stupid faces while I sing scales. Homework. At my age. When do I have the time? And then not only does she record me singing, she plays it back. It was total rubbish. I was out of tune, timing wrong. Just….'

'Otherwise it went well then, me old.'

'Tell you what Phil, there's no way I could stand up on a flippin' stage and front up a band. I'd be a laughing stock. I don't know what I was thinking about.'

Phil looked at his watch. 'It's ten o'clock, so let's have elevenses.' There was a bench in the garden where they sat in the sun with their coffee and biscuits.

'This is definitely not like you, Stan. I can see it weren't a good experience, but I thought you was a fighter, not a quitter. Only a few weeks ago you was singing at the club, knocking us all out. You don't suddenly become a crap singer. I think you need to stick with it and give this woman a chance. The chap in the shop said she was good, lots of people rate her, so she must know what she's doing. Stick with it, and you'll be fine.'

Stan mumbled words to the effect that they were falling behind with the work, and moved his ladder to another window. Phil turned the radio on. Radio two. He knew that Stan was not a Ken Bruce fan, so he hoped it would give him something else to complain about.

Later in the morning, Stan heard Phil talking to someone on his phone. As he came down the ladder for his lunch, Phil announced:

'Right, we're taking our snap round to Mandy's. I've called her and she's home from work, so we can have a chat about this singing stuff, see what she thinks. Let's get the van loaded and piss off. This lot can wait.' He saw the beginning of a smile cross Stan's face.

'So what it boils down to is this,' said Mandy, after listening to Stan's version of events the previous evening. They were sitting at the table in her kitchen, Stan's sandwiches as yet untouched, Phil's almost eaten. 'You were a bit nervous, you were being coached by someone you'd never sung with before and you were a bit out of tune. Oh and you don't like the sound of your voice, but who does? Like the sound of their own voice, I mean. So you're wasting your time and want to pack it in. Is that the lessons, or the whole idea of singing in a band?'

'Both. And there's the chuffin' homework to do, scales and stuff.'

'A few scales and exercises to practise. Listen Stan, nobody's going to hand things to you on a plate, as you ought to know at your age. Carla's a good teacher, and she wouldn't be asking you to practise at home if it wasn't going to improve your voice.' Mandy went on to explain that she'd gone through all this between the ages of eight and eighteen. Her parents had paid for her to have singing and piano lessons, and although as a rebellious teenager she had wanted to stop having them on a number of occasions, her mother persuaded her to persevere. Looking back, Mandy was glad that she had stuck at it. She'd enjoyed singing in choirs and a couple of bands over the years. She had the family's upright piano in her living room, which she still played and sang along to.

'The thing is, I'm fifty-five and I don't fancy ten years of practising scales and pulling stupid faces in front of the mirror. And no comment from you, mister smart arse,' he said to Phil, who was just about to remind Stan that he'd been looking in mirrors for fifty-five years.

At this point Mandy confessed to knowing Carla well and to having spoken to her the previous evening to ask how Stan's lesson had gone. Her response had been that although Stan had been understandably nervous, she could see that he had a natural voice and a good ear for music. Over the next few weeks he needed mostly to work on his breathing.

'So take my advice and stick with it, Big Man.' Stan grunted and picked up a sandwich. From time to time during the afternoon, Phil could hear him quietly going through what he assumed were musical scales.

The next challenge facing Stan was to enter the Students' Union building on the university campus. Phil had not been able to accompany him, saying only that he couldn't get the 'pass out', which Stan took to mean Phil and Jane had had a tiff. He was feeling slightly out of breath after climbing the steps leading to the huge glass fronted entrance of what seemed to Stan to be a new construction. I must get some exercise, he said to himself. He followed a group of what he assumed were students, all studiously focussed on their mobile phones, into the building. He was trying to blend into the environment and to act as if this were an everyday situation, but along with the silver hair, height and dress code, his starry-eyed gazing once inside gave him away. A porter spotted him and asked he could help, then directed Stan to the relevant meeting room two storeys up.

Apart from the furniture, the room was empty. He felt slightly relieved. After a quick look round Stan turned on his heels to retrace his steps, but bumped into someone on her way in, arms loaded and head down. After mutual apologies, he realised he was face to face with Angie, the bass guitarist he'd heard playing in the room above the music shop.

'Oh hi,' she said. 'I wasn't sure you'd come. On your own? Stan, am I right? There'll be others here soon Stan. They tend to arrive in dribs and drabs, usually about ten or twelve of us.

You could help me arrange the room a bit and carry a couple of amps and my bass in from the corridor. Sorry, I don't mean to be bossy, just that it's great to have someone here to help.' They moved tables aside, put chairs into an informal arrangement, and set up the amps and a couple of microphones, not that anyone would use the mics, Angie had said.

Stan chose a spot to sit where he hoped he would be inconspicuous, but Angie insisted on introducing him to everyone as they came in, explaining that he was an R and B musician looking for talent for his new band. Whilst on the one hand Stan felt this gave him some status within the room, on the other he felt like a fish out of water, surrounded as he was by people on the whole at least thirty years younger than him, some wearing rings on ears or noses or both, most looking as if they bought clothes from charity shops. He tried not to stare at the young man wearing make-up.

Eventually, one of the men spoke to open proceedings, which consisted of a welcome to four new student members, an unstructured discussion about previous meetings, the group's finances, a planned trip to a live music venue in Birmingham, and what music people had been playing or listening to. One of the group played two tracks from a CD by an artist Stan had never heard of. He thought the music was nothing special, but it was received well by almost everyone else in the room. Just when Stan was beginning to wonder whether he would be wasting an evening, Angie suggested that she and Tom play something they had been working on. Tom had a more mature look about him, Stan guessing he was about thirty years old. The man plugged an electric keyboard into one of the amps, then introduced the song while Angie checked the tuning on her bass guitar.

'This is a J.J. Cale song, *After Midnight*,' he announced. 'You'll have to tap along for the percussion.'

They played a four bar intro, then Tom started singing. He had a decent voice, which came across over the piano and bass despite the lack of microphone. Stan was trying to work out where he'd heard the name J.J. Cale recently. The piano part was a fairly repetitive sequence of chords, but Tom was clearly an accomplished pianist, which was confirmed by a short solo towards the end. Although Angie's bass line was straightforward, her timing and rhythm were perfect. They sounded good together and received whoops of approval from the small audience. Angie then suggested that Stan would like to hear Neil play, so could Neil come up and join them. To Stan's dismay, Neil was the one wearing make-up. He produced a violin from its case, then quickly checked that they were all in tune, making a corny joke about the well-known Chinese piece called 'Chu-ning'.

Stan had never heard of Andrew Bird, but apparently he had written and recorded 'Danse Carribe'. For this, Tom was on the guitar and, finger-picking, played the intro, accompanied by Angie on bass. Neil came in after a few bars, playing short riffs. Tom was doing the vocals again as he strummed along. After the gentle country-sounding pace of the first part, the tempo suddenly changed, signalled by some strident plucking on the violin strings by Neil, who then launched into a solo which had a real rock feel to it. Stan enjoyed the energy of the music and the playing, his feet tapping along with everyone else's. Must be their party piece, he mused. The violin solo was definitely the highlight, taking the whole piece to a different level.

When the applause died down, it was suggested that they all take a drinks break, which Stan would have welcomed. But at this point Neil wondered if 'our guest would like to contribute to the evening'. Did Stan sing or play himself? This completely threw Stan, who was inwardly cursing and outwardly blushing.

'Stan?' was all Angie said. After stuttering and stammering, Stan threw up his arms in submission. Now on the spot, all he could think of was the B.B. King song *Come Rain or Come Shine*. Borrowing Tom's guitar, he nervously twiddled with the tuning keys and played one or two chords as he spoke.

'Well, thanks for nothing. I really didn't know what to expect, like, when I got here. For a kick-off I never thought I'd be singing owt. And actually, after seeing these guys just now, I am not in the same league. Nowhere near. It's amazing that, well, tucked away up here in a little room in the Uni you can come along and hear that. I was gobsmacked, basically. So follow that, as they say. If any of you know this, please join in. Sing, play, clap hands, whatever, otherwise I'm chuffin' well on me tod.'

As the song moved along, Tom and then Angie gradually joined in as they worked out the chords and notes to play, which gave Stan a bit of confidence. After some decent applause he felt that at least he hadn't let himself down.

A break followed, three of the group leaving the room to fetch drinks for them all from the bar. Angie, Tom and Neil joined Stan to thank him for his contribution. Stan was complimentary about the quality of their playing.

'So you're trying to set up a band of your own then, Stan. Have you played in one yourself before?' asked Tom.

'Well, now and again.' Stan's reply was half true. They looked at him, waiting for more. 'Just a couple of times, to be honest, but enough to know it's what I want to do. I want quality musicians with me who want to be the best, and I reckon you could all have what it takes.'

'That's very flattering,' said Neil. 'Have you got anyone good lined up?'

Stan took a deep breath and told them he had a brilliant guitarist waiting in the wings, with lots of experience behind him, along with a young but gifted percussionist. The ex-squaddy and Phil's lad with OCD had suddenly been made fully paid up members.

'And what's your attitude to gays, Stan? How would you feel about one playing in your band?' asked Neil. They waited for a response.

After a pause that was slightly too long, Stan replied, 'It all adds to the mix to make it interesting. What matters is if they're good enough. How do you know I'm not gay?'

'Oh I know, all right. I saw the way you looked at Angie and the girls.'

Stan smiled, then explained that he had to go but would like to keep in touch. They all agreed to keep options open and that Stan would communicate through Angie. There were handshakes, then Stan drank his pint quickly and left. Once outside the building he exhaled and said out loud,

'Phil, where were you when I chuffin' well needed you?'

## Stan

'What's your attitude to gays?' he asks me. Fair question I suppose. Not one I've thought much about. I remember my Dad referring to shirt-lifters and queers, and Alf Garnett slagging off 'pufftas' on Till Death Us Do Part. At school the ultimate insult to any kid was to call him gay, although no one knew whether he was or not. One of Mum's councillor friends was in court once for what they called 'lewd acts' in some public toilets in town. It was all over the local papers and that was the end of him, like. But my attitude I suppose is each to his own.

I've had one gay experience, sort of. When I was a kid, about fourteen probably, I was out on my bike to see my mate Dave from school. His family had just moved to a posh house in Glenfield. He had a twin sister Dorothy, which was really why I went to see him. She was gorgeous. The trouble was she had a seventeen year old boyfriend who had a motor bike, right. He was earning good money somewhere, so I stood no chance. On the way, the chain came off the bike so I had to stop and fix it. I'd propped it up against a lamp post, like, and was down on the pavement sorting the chain out, when this bloke strolls up and offers to help. He stood there and held the handlebars to stop the thing moving. I'd soon got it sorted, got on the saddle and said 'Ta', like, but he didn't move, just kept hold of the handlebars. Then he asked me if I knew where he could get a wank, straight up. So I told him the best place would be the park. He would probably find a group of girls hanging about. I hoped that would get rid of him. *Do you shag them?* he asks. *Do you like shagging girls?* By this time he was stroking my thigh. He was quite a bit bigger than me. His breath reeked of booze, his hair was greasy and all over the shop. I remember he had on this long jacket... I said *Yes I do.* Would I fancy going with him to the park? *I'm on my way to a mate's and I'm late,* I replied. *How about tomorrow then?* he asked. I eventually agreed to meet him in the park at a particular spot some time on the Saturday, so he let go of the bike. Of course I had no intention, like, of going.

It wasn't until I got to the mate's house that I realised how shaken up I was. I told Dave the story and we came up with a plan. That Saturday, I was sitting on a bench in the place I'd agreed to meet this arsehole, thinking he wasn't going to come, but he did. I saw him walking up the path towards me and wave. His face was chuffin' beaming. So I got up and beckoned him, like, to follow me and I walked into some bushes. There was this open space, a clearing, where I stood as he got nearer. Dave was waiting in the bushes with a rope that was tied to a tree across the path, and he pulled it so it tripped the bloke up.

We jumped on him, tied his ankles together, then his wrists, whipped his trousers down and left him like that. He effed and blinded, but I just said, 'I'm fourteen, mate. You should be effing ashamed of yourself.' I would love to have been there when whoever it was found him.

## Phil

We had a blazing row, me and Jane. A real humdinger, you know. Never had one before and neither of us knew how it started. Just the usual sort of bickering, like. Where's the remote? Your turn to put the kettle on sort of stuff. Then pow, she really goes for me. I'm a lazy layabout. All those jobs need doing around the house and I'm sat on my arse. So I had a go back.

We were both shaken up, and just mooched around for a bit. It took a while before we could look each other in the eye and say anything. I did think about just putting my coat on and going to meet Stan. In the end we did sort of apologise. Kissed and made up, kind of thing, but God knows where it came from.

# Nine

# Black Magic Woman

On Friday mornings, between ten and ten forty-five there was a Rhythm and Rhyme session for parents and toddlers in a church hall off the Fosse Road. Stan discovered this when just before ten, on the way to collect a part for the van, he had to dash for the shelter of the porch entrance during a heavy shower. He was shaking the rain out of his hair when the entrance was invaded by adults accompanied by young children, who were either asleep in pushchairs, being carried, or managing to walk up the steps. As they made their way into the building, there were 'hallos' and hurried conversations about broken nights and first steps being taken. After a few minutes he could hear singing, and out of curiosity he ventured inside a little, leaving a trail of wet footprints, until he could just see and hear the adults and children. The song was 'Wind the Bobbin Up', with the adults doing the singing, a few of the toddlers joining in the actions, others crawling about on the central mat or in a couple of cases running around. Stan was more interested in the hall. It had seen better days but was a decent sized space, with a small stage at one end. What really struck him was the quality of the acoustics, which made him think the place had potential as a practice venue, if the hire price was reasonable. From his point of view it was certainly handily situated.

A voice came from behind him. 'Can I help?' He turned to face a man probably in his thirties, dressed in a jacket and open-necked shirt, holding a dripping folded umbrella. Stan could see immediately that the man was suspicious of Stan's motives for observing the group in the hall.

'Yes duck, you might be able to actually. Do you work here?' The man replied that he was the curate, which meant nothing to Stan.

'I was just sheltering from the rain and thought I'd have a quick shufty. They're having a great time. The thing is, I could be interested in hiring the hall and wondered who I should talk to.'

'Well, me actually. What would you want to use it for? The church has quite strict guidelines on what sort of groups can use it.' Stan hoped that the idea of two unemployed men, a teenager with issues, a war veteran and a couple of penniless students coming together to form a band that would perform in the local community might appeal to the curate's sense of public spiritedness.

'Well I have to admire your ambition and entrepreneurial spirit,' the curate responded. 'Until you manage to find your feet, I would think that a contribution to meet the running and heating costs of the hall would suffice. Say ten pounds per practice, up to two hours. How does that sound?'

Stan couldn't believe his luck, although he was at pains to point out that he would have to check that his colleagues could afford this. To the strains of 'Twinkle, Twinkle Little Star', he followed the curate across the hall to a small office, returning the wave of one of the toddlers and the smile of a grandmother. He was given a booking form, which three days later he had completed and returned. After several phone calls and emails, he had narrowed down the availability of his potential band members to a couple of hours on Tuesday evenings. The first meeting would be in the following week, to explore what songs they might be able to play together, and indeed whether there was enough in common for them to even contemplate going head. He had asked each one to bring along a couple of songs on CD to share, along with any sheet music they might have.

Phil suggested that Stan should meet Daniel and his mother beforehand, so it was arranged that he would accompany Phil on his usual Friday morning visit that week. 'But I'm not having some spotty-faced kid in my band,' Stan had reminded Phil, unsure that he had any alternative. 'Let's just wait and see shall we,' Phil had replied. Esther was clearly flustered as she led them into her living room. The reason quickly became apparent.

'Umm, this is Raymond. You've met him Philip, haven't you? I'm sorry, I'm terrible with names. Is it Dan?'

'Stan.'

'I'm pleased to meet you, Stan. Raymond was just leaving, weren't you, duck. He's very kindly fixed the handle on our bathroom door. Oh, he's also brought Daniel a couple of LPs. Or are they CDs?'

'Evelyn Glennie,' said Raymond, by way of explanation.

'Sorry?' said Stan.

'Evelyn Glennie. Extremely talented and totally deaf percussionist. I thought Daniel would appreciate hearing her play. Broaden his horizon, so to speak. She is amazing. You should listen to her as well, if you haven't already. Does it all by sensing the vibrations from the drums and cymbals, you know.' Phil and Stan quickly exchanged glances and brief smirks. His rather posh accent grated.

'Really,' said Stan. He could see that Phil was thinking the same. *Pompous prick.*

'Well, thanks for popping round, Raymond,' said Esther. He managed to look both sheepish and reluctant to leave at the same time. Esther succeeded in gently ushering him to the door as goodbyes were exchanged.

'Total nob,' said Phil, while Esther was still out of earshot. There was the sound of someone coming down the stairs, then a young person's voice. Daniel followed Esther into the room. He rather formally shook hands with Phil, then with Stan after being introduced, saying 'pleased to meet you' without making eye contact.

The four sat round the table in the kitchen, adults sipping cups of coffee, Daniel with a sparkling apple juice drink. Knowing the answer already, but not wanting to miss the opportunity to find out more about Raymond, Stan asked Esther if he was a friend. Blushing, she explained that they had become good friends since he'd moved from Manchester a few months ago. Broken marriage, fresh start, she added. Although he came across at first as being a bit stuffy, he was kind and generous. He was educated and very knowledgeable about music and art. He took her to concerts and the odd exhibition, not something she'd ever done before. Only last week they'd visited the New Walk museum, where she hadn't been for years, to listen to a string quartet and see an exhibition of war photography. And Raymond himself has been a choirmaster in a cathedral and the public school where he used to teach. Stan looked for Phil's reaction as she spoke, but his face was impressively deadpan.

Phil said, pointedly, 'But Daniel doesn't like him, do you, duck?'

Daniel looked impassively at the table top.

'I don't know why,' said Esther. 'He likes you and is always lending you CDs to record upstairs. I wish you would at least say hallo when he's here.'

'I don't dislike him,' said Daniel. 'I'd just rather spend the time in my room when he's here. I have homework and practising to do.'

'Philip's told Daniel all about you, Stan, and how you want to have a band that he might play in. You're really excited, aren't you, pet? He's been listening to a lot of seventies and eighties rock music on his computer. Is it by streaming, pet? Daniel's ever so clever with the computer, isn't he, Philip?' Phil confirmed that he certainly is.

'So what do you listen to, Daniel? Do you download or listen to radio stations?' Stan impressed himself that he could use the word download in this context.

'There are lots of radio stations. I think the best is Rockradio dot com. It's a website and you can connect to lots of different stations. Like Classic Rock. All the music is from the seventies and eighties, before I was born.' They listened politely for the next ten minutes as Daniel gave a detailed account of some of the stations he'd been listening to, Stan impressed as he recognised many of the band names, such as Deep Purple and King Crimson. Daniel's eyes never left the table top as he spoke. Stan latched on to the mention of Santana.

'That's an amazing coincidence, Daniel. *Black Magic Woman* is the Santana song I thought the band could try playing. Phil, sorry, Philip tells me that you can play the drum arrangement to a song once you've heard it, so does that mean you could do that for *Black Magic Woman*?'

'Of course. It's easy.

'Could you show me? I'd love to hear you play.'

'Not now. I don't play in the morning, in case the neighbours complain. I do my practising at five o'clock, after I get home on school days. You can come today at five o'clock.'

'We discussed this together, didn't we, pet,' said Esther, 'and Daniel would like you to come later on to hear him play the drums.' At this point Daniel asked if he and Philip could go and play football, which Stan took as his cue to say thank you and that he would be back later. He reminded Phil that they had an important lunch engagement at Ursula's place.

The traffic was moving slowly as Stan drove past the café. A crowd had gathered on the pavement and a van advertising itself as a BBC vehicle was parked a few metres away from the entrance. It was at risk of receiving the parking ticket which Stan imagined the traffic warden would take great pleasure in slapping on the windscreen. He found a space to park on a side street equid-distant between his house and the café. Two security men at the door asked Stan for some identification, also asking if they could do a quick body search.

'Are you expecting some trouble about the petition then lads?' he asked.

'Not at all,' one replied. 'We're just protecting one or two of the guests.'

Inside the café, Ursula was deep in conversation with a woman he recognised as one of the presenters from the East Midlands Today programme and a man he didn't recognise. A camera man and assistant stood chatting inside the doorway. Stan ordered a coffee and sat on a stool at the bar. Every table was occupied and the place was buzzing. The opportunity of appearing on TV had obviously been a great draw.

Stan spotted Colin, the newspaper employee who had offered to get in touch with the media to alert them to Ursula's petition. They exchanged waves, and Colin beckoned Stan to join him at his table. Stan was introduced to a young woman also sitting at the table, a journalist from the local newspaper who was covering the story.

'You've done well to get this lot here,' he said to Colin. 'Mind you, I suspect Ursula will be enjoying every chuffin' moment of it.'

'It's all about who you know,' replied Colin, 'and knowing how things work and people think. When we tell the stars and politicians that the cameras will be at a particular event, they're usually only too happy to be invited along. Sheer vanity.'

'So some big names are coming along, is that what you're telling me?'

'It's why I'm here,' said the journalist. 'Normally, a petition wouldn't attract much, if any interest, but if the Mayor and a couple of football stars are coming along it's a different ball game, so to speak.' She named the lady Mayor and the Leicester City manager and German player who were expected at any moment.

The journalist made notes as Stan explained how he knew Ursula and that it had been his and his friend Phil's idea to start the petition against the increase in rent. She asked Stan if he would be happy to have his photograph taken with Ursula, and his friend if he was coming.

'Happy to oblige,' said Stan.

'See what I mean?' said Colin, with a broad smile on his face.

'What?'

'Vanity.'

'Naah. Just doing my chuffin' duty.'

There was some commotion, as a big black saloon car pulled up outside. The TV camera crew quickly made their way onto the pavement, where a couple of press photographers suddenly appeared from nowhere. He could just make out the two security men standing at the back door of the car. The Mayor stepped out, greeted by a few cheers and the clicking of camera shutters. She waved and smiled, then the photographers and crew made their way into the café to film and photograph the Mayor's entrance and welcome from Ursula. The two were ushered to a space set aside for them to be interviewed.

Stan could see that Ursula looked happy and totally at ease with the situation. As the BBC presenter interviewed Ursula and the Mayor together, Stan recognised the City manager and player stepping out of the taxi cab which had pulled in behind the Mayor's black saloon. The scrum of snapping photographers and cheering on-lookers surged towards them, giving them no choice but to pose for the cameras and autograph anything members of the crowd could produce for the two to sign. Stan was sure that he saw one young woman present them with a marker pen and a pair of knickers. The first interview now completed, the football celebrities made their way to the café entrance, assisted by the two security men. They were greeted by warm applause as they entered, then escorted to meet the interviewer, camera crew and Ursula. The interview was very light-hearted, ending with an invitation from Ursula to her fellow countryman and his boss to stay and enjoy some dishes typical of the Palatinate. They politely declined, but at least agreed to sign the petition, which the Mayor had not done. As the signing took place in ceremonial fashion, Stan looked at his watch, wondering where Phil had got to, then caught a glimpse of him outside, making his way through the crowd, which was now thinning.

Stan stood up, to catch the attention of as many people as possible at the nearby tables.

'Hey! Look everyone, right,' he said earnestly, in the loudest voice he dared use without alerting Ursula and the rest of the group in the interview area. 'I need your help. Just for a laugh, like. See this bloke about to walk in, the short tubby one. Well when he walks in, yeah, could you all stand up with me and clap, cheer, whistle, whatever. I just want to see his face.' He sat down quickly, thinking he was about to make a fool of himself.

But his little plot worked. Phil walked in to a sea of smiling faces, whistles, whoops and applause. He looked behind him nervously, to see who it was for, then was suddenly surrounded by the camera crew and photographers, keen not to miss the opportunity to bring to public attention the unexpected arrival of this additional celebrity, whoever he was. Seeing Stan waving, he realised what was going on, suddenly warmed to the situation. He casually raised his hands to acknowledge the reception, smiling and nodding to the paparazzi before him.

A minute later, Phil and Stan stood either side of Ursula, having been coaxed by her to be interviewed in front of the television camera.

'I've always been a big fan of yours, pet,' Phil said to the presenter.

'What he means is he fancies you,' said Stan.

She smiled benignly, said she was very flattered, then asked Stan and Phil if they were happy to answer a couple of quick questions about their role in supporting Ursula. There was no need to be nervous, she explained. They should try and be as normal as possible. Ursula laughed at this. Stan and Phil were ready.

'So that was quite an entrance there, Phil. Do you always receive that welcome?'

'No, duck. The big man here was having a bit of fun, like, getting people to cheer me in. I'm just a regular punter, who enjoys coming to Ursula's café. I like that dress you're wearing today, by the way. Really suits you. Goes with your eyes.'

'Thank you, Phil. Flattery will…' Slightly flustered, she had quick second thoughts about what she was about to say. 'And Stan, I understand from Ursula that you and Phil here were instrumental in setting up the petition for Ursula, which has attracted so much interest and support.'

Stan stared at the microphone. 'Umm,' was all he could manage.

'Cut!' came the call.

The woman reached out and put her hand on his forearm. 'OK Stan, we can finish there if you like. I know it's a big thing to be in front of the camera. I still get nervous, believe me.'

'Sorry, duck, I don't know what happened. Just froze, like. But no, I think we should have another crack, if that's OK. Just give me a few seconds.'

'Fine. We'll go again from *Thank you Phil.*'

Once he started speaking, Stan's nerves settled. 'This woman is an example and inspiration to us all. She has worked so blooming hard to set this place up and make a go of it, we couldn't just let it fall by the wayside. So I'm dead chuffed, as I'm sure Phil is, that so many people have signed the petition. If you ask everybody here, like, they'll all tell you how welcome Ursula makes you feel and how good the grub is. So I hope this geezer, right, the landlord will have second thoughts about raising her rent, cos we would really miss this place if it was shut.'

'You should tell everyone about your new band, Stan,' said Ursula, catching him unawares.

'So yes, Stan, do tell us. What's the band's name?'

'Well, it's just something I've always wanted to do. It's early days yet, but I've found some useful musicians, so we'll give it a shot. We're keeping the band's name under wraps for the moment, like.' Stan hadn't begun to think of a name of the band until this point.

'Well I'm sure our viewers would wish you luck, whatever name you decide on. I worked on the local radio station here for a while, and I always tell my colleagues that in my opinion Leicester rocks.'

The excitement died down and the café gradually emptied, apart from the lunchtime customers. Ursula was able to give the boys a belated bear hug greeting, thanking them profusely for all their support. She was keen to show them the hundreds of names that had been added to her petition, which she would be handing over to her new landlord in the next day or so. She informed Stan that Leberknödel were not available today, as they had proved to be popular with the television team, and she hadn't had time to prepare any more. So like Phil, he opted for the all-day breakfast.

Stan briefly took Ursula to one side to ask if she had received any more visits from 'our footballing friends', which she hadn't. Interestingly, however, she had received a football signed by all of the team's squad, which she was free to auction to raise funds to support her cause.

'So that makes everything all right then, doesn't it,' said Stan cynically.'Just let me know if they give you any bother.'

Over lunch, Phil wanted to discuss his young team's football match coming up over the weekend. This was unprecedented. Phil had never discussed team tactics with Stan, who had once said that his best friend didn't have a tactical bone in his body. Even when Phil explained that the match was the first round of the county cup, Stan was still a little perplexed, until he was told that the opposition was the team run by Malcolm, Stan's erstwhile nemesis and potentially band member.

'There may be trouble ahead,' said Stan. He suggested that perhaps he shouldn't be one of the touch judges, to avoid any confrontation with Malcolm, but then had second thoughts, stating that he needed the exercise. He was having problems performing the breathing exercises recommended by Carla, who had in turn suggested that he needed to take up jogging or join a gym to improve his fitness. The previous evening, he had nearly passed out after ten minutes on a treadmill in the local gym, confirming his lack of fitness. Besides, there was no one else who would be willing to take the flag from Stan. They agreed that the best approach would be to have a friendly chat with Malcolm before the kick-off, to express their hopes that 'any aggro' could be avoided so that everybody could enjoy the game. Stan and Phil, exercising caution, would also encourage the parents of their own team to 'get their retaliation in first, if things looked like they were kicking off'.

Esther opened the door to Stan at five minutes before five o'clock and invited him in, explaining that he would be able to go up to see Daniel in five minutes. She had struck Stan as a very unassuming and warm person, who a lot of the time had a careworn expression that probably followed her everywhere. She was not unattractive, slightly built and a little taller than Phil. As they waited, Esther told Stan how delighted she was that Daniel might have the opportunity to actually play in a real band, rather than being stuck in his room playing along to music on his hi-fi or computer. Daniel would need a lot of understanding and patience from everyone. She asked that Stan and Philip keep her well informed in plenty of time about practice times and days and anything else that might happen, so that she could talk everything through with Daniel. Then there would be no surprises for him. She would take him along to wherever it was they were going to practise, a day or two beforehand, so that he knew what to expect. Stan responded with words of encouragement, although he felt that Esther's hopes were a bit premature.

As they talked, he could hear the sound of drums being played, though muffled as if coming from the house next door. He was led up to Daniel's room, where Esther pointed to a chair and then closed the door behind him. For ten minutes or so Stan watched and listened as the boy went through what he assumed were some pre-set exercises, using the full range of drums and cymbals, some played with brushes, others with sticks. Eventually the playing stopped and Daniel swivelled in his chair to face Stan, who at first was lost for words. Daniel waited for him to speak.

'That's impressive stuff, Daniel. And this is quite a set up you've got in here,' he said looking around the room. On one unit sat a computer and a number of electronic gadgets, with adjacent speakers. Stan asked what they all did, and nodded knowingly as Daniel talked about iTunes, streaming, iCloud, bubble, bridging, iPad, Spotify, Sonos, apps, and more.

'You must come and help me set something like this up in my house,' said Stan.

'Why?' Daniel replied. Stan was taken aback, but responded by saying that he would really like to know how to use modern music technology. It would be great if Daniel could help him.

'Well I don't know where you live, but Philip does, and he helped me to install everything in my room, so he could help you.'

'Good idea,' Stan replied, and then brought the conversation round to *Black Magic Woman*.' Daniel moved to his computer, explaining that he had downloaded the song from his favourite website, using some software to remove the percussion backing so that he had a recording of the song which he could play along to. He played the first few bars of the track, enabling Stan to hear what it sounded like without the percussion. Stan commented that he had no idea that it was possible to do this kind of thing.

'It's easy when you know how to do it,' Daniel replied.

A few seconds later the unmistakable guitar introduction to the song came across on Daniel's music system. Daniel quickly moved to his seat at the drums and slipped his headphones on. Before Stan could ask if it would be very loud and should he have a pair, the track was playing again from the beginning, and so was Daniel. The music and Daniel's percussion playing was loud but bearable. The arrangement sounded straight forward, but it was quickly evident to Stan that the boy's timing was immaculate. '*Shit. The kid's really rocking,*' Stan said to himself. Enjoying the song and unable to sit still, he got up and moved around to the music. Daniel seemed completely oblivious to anything but his drumming.

'That was absolutely chuffin' fantastic,' said Stan, as Daniel removed his headphones. 'You were spot on all the way through. Well done, mate.'

Daniel seemed slightly embarrassed by Stan's reaction. 'That was easy really. Philip said you wanted me to choose my own song for the first rehearsal next week, so I've done the same thing with this song. Would you like to hear it? It's by Radiohead, my favourite band. You must have heard it. *Lotus Flower.*'

'Uhh, yes of course,' said Stan, not wanting to sound out of touch. He wasn't a great fan of Radiohead. 'I know some of their stuff, but not this one. Must be new.'

'Not exactly. It's off their last album, which they made in two thousand and eleven. They're working on a new album, which I can't wait to hear. I've learned the words to this and can play along as I sing. On the album it's really only percussion and bass which play along.'

With the croakiness of having recently broken, Daniel's voice wasn't brilliant, but the percussion accompaniment was haunting. Stan was again impressed by the ease and confidence of the boy's playing.

'Chuffin' brilliant. I'm sure the others will think so too.' Pleased that Stan was enthusiastic about the song, the beginnings of a smile crept across Daniel's face. 'Perhaps you could bring it down on Tuesday,' continued Stan. 'Will you be able to record it onto a CD, like?' Daniel stared at him blankly. 'Soz. Silly question. Perhaps you could do me a copy as well, duck.'

## *Phil*

I can't see what Esther sees in that Raymond. He definitely gives me the creeps. Maybe it's all the cultural stuff. Concerts and museums and so on. Well I would have taken her to a concert if she'd asked me, although I'm not into that classical bollocks. I remember going to the New Walk museum on a school trip, like. I didn't think it were any great shakes. Maybe it's better now. Someone told me they've got a massive dinosaur skeleton on display.

Jane says we should get out more, instead of just watching TV or going to the club. Kit takes his missus to the De Montfort and stuff. They've seen Chuck Berry, Gerry and the Pacemakers, The Hollies. I mean, Gordon Bennet, all past it if you ask me. The club does me just fine.

## Stan

The way I froze in that friggin' interview, that's the big problem. Suppose I do that when I'm on stage with a band? I'd be a laughing stock. I was alright once I got going, but what's-her-name had to mother me before I could. And who would give Daniel all that patience and understanding his mother says he's going to need? Not me, nor that chuffin' squaddie either, for a start. Maybe that Angie. She likes to be in control, so she might be able to give it the 'big sister' treatment. Or Tom. But I'm sure we've all got enough on our chuffin' plate. And what was Phil bleeding well doing anyway, telling the kid he was going to be in my band?

One way or another, I don't see it happening somehow. They did show a bit of our interview on the telly though, including the bit about the band. But most of it was about the Mayor and the footie celebrities, obviously. I would just love to have been with Ursula when she watched it.

I was well impressed with Daniel's set up. Makes me realise I am so far behind the times. I've got a crappy old mobile phone that I can just about send text messages on, my ancient stereo system, plus an old laptop of Phil's which is so bleeding slow it almost ain't worth the effort . The best I can do is the gizmo that I can use to play my iPod through the amp. And then Daniel, with two clicks on his computer has downloaded, or streamed, whichever, the exact track he wants in about two seconds. It's amazing, really. You see people listening to music on their phones, taking photos, getting on the internet. And there's all them iPads, and tablets, whatever they are. What are they all about? I need to get up to speed.

# Ten

## Autumn Leaves

'Well who'd have Adam and Eved it?' Stan's mother Audrey looked around the old school hall, then continued. 'The last time I was in this room was over sixty years ago. Sixty-three to be precise. We used to have assemblies in here. Can you imagine three hundred and fifty of us squeezed in. And it was the gym as well. I used to do cartwheels, back flips and tricks on them parallel bars. You might not think it to look at me now, but I was good at gymnastics. And netball. If it was raining we would practise in here.'

They were sitting on a bench. On the walls around them was part of the exhibition about the excavations which led to the discovery of King Richard the Third's skeleton. Audrey had talked a lot in the past about her time spent at Alderman Newton's Girls' Grammar School in the late nineteen forties and early fifties. It was now the site of the exhibition. She had led Stan through the warren of nooks and crannies that had served as cloakrooms and even classrooms. The former science lab now served as a main thoroughfare. Audrey laughed as she recalled how she would be scolded for blowing down the tube of her Bunsen burner, causing the flames on others in the room to go out. A building across the road in St Martins, which had housed the dining room and library, was where she had been taught her favourite subject, domestic science.

'The Headmistress were dead strict. Miss Harrison. That's right. Miss Harrison. Woe betide if your hem was too high, or if you wore jewellery or nail varnish. But we loved her to bits. She were still Headmistress when the school moved up to Glenfield Road in '59.'

They moved to an area giving information about the 'Princes in the Tower', including an invitation to visitors to decide who was most likely to have had them murdered. Audrey read every sentence out loud to Stan, who made no attempt to stifle the yawns.

'So they don't really know who it was,' he said in summary, 'and for all we know they could have lived to a ripe old age.'

'Nah, it had to be him, Richard had them killed. They were ruthless in those days. I remember we did all this in our History lessons.'

Outside, they made their way across the former social services car park, where the skeleton had been discovered. They were able to see the exact site of the shallow grave through a glass cover.

'So the poor bugger was just thrown in there,' Audrey commented, 'all squashed up, like. And apparently, his feet were chopped off at some stage by some workman who had been digging here, who knows when. Amazing, when you think about it.'

Half way back to the exhibition entrance, Audrey stopped.

'Just think, Stanley. All them years ago when I played netball or ran around at playtimes with my friends, we would have been running across his grave, not knowing.'

Stan had to admit that it was pretty amazing.

They were asked to fill in a feedback form before leaving, which neither could bothered to do at first. Audrey did mention to the two members of staff at the desk that there were some factual inaccuracies about a couple of the rooms and what they had been used for in the days of the school. They would pass this on.

Crossing the road, they admired the statue of King Richard and then stood outside the gates to the cathedral. Stan knew what was coming.

'See that building there, Stanley?' She pointing to the large Victorian building a hundred metres to their left, now housing the Leicester Diocese. 'That was the boys' school where your father went. Of course, at home time there would be the chance to walk past the playground and catch the eye of any good-looking lad. That's what happened with me and him, then one thing led to another.... Anyway, let's go in shall we.'

Stan, Audrey, Phil and several of their friends had been amongst the thousands who had lined the streets of Leicester earlier that year, as the procession carrying the king's remains made its way from the University to the Cathedral. Stan swore that he could make out their group on the High Street when the event was shown on TV that evening, but the others weren't convinced. Audrey had complained that more local people should have been invited to the ceremony in the Cathedral, instead of 'all those poshos who just wanted to get on the telly and who will never set foot in Leicester again.'

Inside the Cathedral, they stood briefly in front of the tomb, a limestone block sitting on top of a dark plinth, on which were engraved the words *Loyaulte me lie*.

'Probably Latin,' said Audrey. 'I did a bit at school, but blow me if I know what it means. Come on, that's enough. Let's go and have a cup of tea.'

They found a deli-cum-café on the corner of Saint Martins and Grey Friars. Audrey made a bee line for a window table, calling to Stan to get her a chocolate brownie. He ordered tea and carried two brownies to the table. As he weaved between chairs, he spotted the back of a figure he recognised.

'Ma, do you mind swapping seats? You'll get the sun in your face there.'

'But it isn't shining.'

'It will be though. Go on, let me sit there.'

'Suit yourself.'

Stan had a clear view of Mandy, who was deep in conversation with a man he didn't recognise. As the waitress set the teas down on his and Audrey's table, the man got to his feet, put on his suit jacket, bent over towards Mandy to kiss her lightly on the cheek, then left. After spending a few moments looking thoughtfully out of the window, Mandy fiddled with her mobile phone. Stan realised his mother had been talking to him.

'Sorry, Ma....'

'I said don't let your coffee go cold. And if you're not eating your cake I'll have it.'

Audrey chatted away about the people who passed by the café, commenting on what they were wearing, or wondering where they were going in such a rush. It wasn't long before Mandy rose from her seat, put on a woollen coat and turned towards the door. She stopped in her tracks when she made eye contact with Stan, who waved and gave her a smile. She waved back, hesitated slightly and blushed, before walking over to his table.

He stood to greet her. 'Aye up, duck. I might have known I'd find you in a posh place like this.' *God you're gorgeous, he wanted to add.*

'Hello Stan. This is one of my favourite places. Fancy seeing you here. What brings you into town? And who is this young lady with you? Hallo. My name's Mandy.'

'Oh get away. I'm Audrey, Stanley's mother. I'm very pleased to meet you, Mandy. Are you going to join us? Pull up that chair for her, Stanley.'

'I can't stay, I'm afraid. It's back to work.'

'So was that work business just now?' asked Stan. 'None of my business, like ....'

'No. That was, umm, private business.' The tone made it clear that it was none of his business, but she had blushed again. 'A little bird tells me you've got a singing lesson this afternoon.'

Stan looked at his watch. 'Shit. Sorry Ma. I have. We'd better drink up so I can get you home.'

After dropping Audrey off, he made his way across town for the lesson, lost in thought as he drove. *Was the man an ex or current bloke, or something else altogether? Private business could mean he was a chuffin' lawyer or something. Why had she blushed? Embarrassed? Obviously. Must have been about me seeing her with this bloke, whoever he was. I were a bit embarrassed myself. I must have looked a right scruffy git in that café, jeans and baggy sweater. Maybe it was me that embarrassed her? Perhaps I should smarten up a bit. But I hate friggin' shopping.*

Parking outside Carla's house, he couldn't remember a thing about the journey.

'OK Big Man. On your feet and let's do some warm ups. Get those shoulders moving first.'

The vocal gymnastics she put him through during the warm up were just what he needed. She complimented him on having done his homework, then put him through his paces on *Still Got The Blues*. After some discussion they agreed on the Van Morrison song *Moondance* as the next project, focussing on the dynamics, which she had to explain as knowing when to sing softly or when to belt it out.

Stan was enjoying Carla's piano accompaniment and the way she was able to create exactly the right mood for whichever song they were worked on. After three lessons he was in no doubt that his singing had improved already. His voice felt stronger and his vocal range was wider. Carla was constantly praising his efforts, which helped his confidence to grow.

'OK Stan. What we need to do now is to get you out of your comfort zone, just a tad. Nothing too alarming, but I want you to think about having a go at something different to what you might normally try. Something which will give you a different challenge. Have a listen to this and see what you think.'

She played Eva Cassidy's version of *Autumn Leaves*. Stan was given the sheet music, so he could follow the lyrics.

'Who is the singer?' was his first reaction. 'Chuffin' lovely,' was his second. He had vaguely heard of Eva but couldn't remember ever listening to anything she'd sung. 'I know the song, like. My old Dad used to sing along with Nat Cole on his stereogram. You really think I could have a crack at this?'

'Why not? To make it work you've got to feel the emotion, tell the story, and although it's a very gentle song, there is some real work to do on the dynamics and breathing. Fancy a crack?'

'There's nowt to lose, so yeah.'

'Well, you're paying.'

Singing together, they took it a line at a time, until they had put together the first verse. The lesson finished with Stan singing the verse, Carla accompanying.

'Good start, Big Man. Take the script with you. I'll just quickly notate the chords for you.' She also showed Stan how to find a video on YouTube of Eva Cassidy singing the song.

He left feeling several inches taller than when he had arrived.

## Stan

It was great to see the old girl enjoying herself. The trip out did her the world of good, and she was as bright as a chuffin' button. Memory's a funny thing. One minute she can tell you everything about when she was at school, the next she can't remember where she's put her keys, or what day it is even. She enjoyed the bit of shopping as well, especially in John Lewis, spending like it were going out of fashion. It were a good job there were room on the bus.

There were always music playing somewhere in our house. Ma played the piano, the radio was usually on, radio one or two, occasionally radio three. My Dad's highlight of the week was Sunday evening, when he would play some of his fifties and sixties musicals on his stereogram. I am, or was word perfect on the songs of *Oklahoma* and *Oliver*. Ma's favourite on the radio were *The Jimmy Young Show*. He was absolutely bonkers. I can still hear her mimicking, *Orft we jolly well go*, or this character Raymondo's *And What's the Recipe Today Jim?*

## Phil

There were thousands and thousands at that procession which took the old King's body to the Cathedral. We were standing next to people from the States and Australia. I had no idea it were such a big thing really. It makes you wonder what will happen if City win the Premiership, which they might just do. Leicester would go berserk. Everyone would be out on the streets celebrating. But first things first. We have a big match tomorrow on the park.

# Eleven

# There May Be Trouble Ahead

*I*t was one of those weekends when all gardening and other outside chores had to be put on hold. It gave Stan the opportunity to use one of the few French expressions he remembered from the one holiday he'd had in France several years previously, and which had amused him: 'il pleut comme les vache qui pissent'. In Wellington boots and waterproofs, Stan and Phil huddled under an umbrella, as the few supporters from both teams arrived at the pitch on Western Park. The boys from both teams were warming up on the pitch and were already drenched to the skin. The rain had been falling relentlessly since the morning of the previous day, and balls being kicked from player to player were stopped dead by surface water on parts of the pitch. In recent weeks, Phil had been happy for one of the dads to lead the pre-match warm up, encouraging the boys to keep the ball on the ground and pass the ball to teammates in space, rather than kick the ball aimlessly towards the strikers. Pleasantly surprised at how well some of the boys could pass, Phil had basked in reflected glory as his team won the next three games in succession, moving into second place in their division.

'Not a day for the chuffin' passing game. Kick it long is what I would be telling them,' said Phil, almost shouting to make himself heard above the sound of the rain on the umbrella. 'Aye up, here's yer man.' Malcolm had finished his team talk and was walking off the pitch towards them.

'Stan. Phil. How's it going?' Malcolm surprised them both by offering a wet hand, which they shook in turn.

'All right me old, thanks,' replied Phil. 'It's a good day for ducks. You have to feel for these lads in this lot.'

Malcolm nodded in agreement. 'Just in case you were worried, after what happened last time, I've promised to be on my best behaviour today. I've told the lads to do the same.'

'That's good to hear,' said Stan. 'We was going to have a word, like. Maybe we could have a beer after.' He nodded towards the referee, who was talking to both sets of players. 'Ref reckons the pitch is just about playable, but if it keeps lashing it down he might have to call it off. We don't want lads getting hurt. Anyway, here we go. It's alright for you lot under your brollies. Just spare a thought for the rest of us braving the elements.' Stan jogged off, head down, wellies squelching, to take his place on the touch line. The water running off his waterproof had already soaked his jeans.

For the first few minutes of the game Malcolm stood next to Phil, the two sharing appreciation of the boys' efforts in the rain. As everyone had expected, the ball frequently stopped dead in mud or surface water. The determination from players on both teams to slide into tackles in attempts to win the ball caused anxious grimaces from Malcolm, Phil and dads on the touch line. Half way through the first half, the rain began to ease, then stopped, and the sun tried to break through the clouds. Umbrellas came down, waterproofs were shaken, and spectators found their voices. As the boys adjusted to the condition of the pitch, they realised that passing was pointless, so resorted to kicking long hopeful passes for their strikers to chase. This increased the possibility of the linesmen having to wave their flag because players had run offside. Stan had become accustomed to the banter from the opposition team's parents, which there was in most matches, even remarks which at times became personal. And as this game wore on, and parents became increasingly frustrated at the way the game had developed, predictably they began to vent their frustration towards the referee and linesmen. Two dads in particular, parents of boys playing for the opposition team, had begun to take exception to Stan's flag waving and shout obscenities at him. Stan did his best to ignore this and instead to focus on sprinting up and down the touch line to keep up with the play, pausing when he could to get his breath back. He noticed Malcolm talking to the parents concerned, who for a few seconds did much gesticulating and pointing at Stan.

'Sorry about those two clowns.' It was just before half time and Malcolm was standing next to Stan, having walked round the pitch. 'They get a bit excited about the offside stuff, cos their boys are the two strikers. Happens every week, so don't take it too personal.' Stan was about to reply, but there was a new anxiety in Malcolm's voice. 'Now what the fuck's going on?' The referee had blown his whistle for half time, and a scuffle had broken out amongst some of the adults on the other side of the pitch. Stan set off after Malcolm who had started to run towards the fracas.

Malcolm arrived to find that the two men who had been barracking Stan were rolling around in the mud with two fathers of boys in Phil's team. There was shouting and half-hearted attempts by the onlookers to intervene, but Malcolm suggested that it would be best to let them get on with it, as they would quickly run out of strength. Very soon he was proved right, and he stepped in to separate one pair, as Phil separated the other. Four adults, covered in mud from head to foot, were bent double in the centre of the group of players and adults, wheezing and occasionally pointing to nothing in particular, swearing at no one in particular.

'What seems to have happened,' said Phil, 'is that the two who were giving Stan some mouth had set off to have a go at him. Two of our lot tried to stop them and, well, you can see.' As the referee started to give the bedraggled foursome a dressing down, suggesting they take themselves home to shower or bath, Phil shouted an expletive.

'Can someone give me a hand? Stan's in trouble over there.' He was already running towards Stan, who was motionless on all fours in the middle of the pitch. He looked up as Phil and a couple of the dads reached him. He sat back on his heels, hands on his thighs.

'Are you alright, mate?' asked Allan, one of the parents. 'I'm a first aider so let me have a look at you. Just take your time.'

'Sorry about that,' he said. 'I missed the action. I just came over dizzy, like, and had to stop for a breather. I'll be alright – just attention seeking.' Allan asked if anything similar had happened before. Stan slowly got to his feet, as Malcolm joined the three other men.

'No, I feel fine,' Stan insisted. 'I'll be able to manage the second half, as long as everybody slows down.' Phil said he would stay on Stan's touch line to keep him company.

The rest of the afternoon passed relatively uneventfully. The weather continued to improve, although there was quite a strong breeze, which contributed to the only goal of the match. As a corner kick was floated into the penalty area by one of the Fosse Boys players, the ball was caught by a gust of wind. The goalkeeper jumped to catch it, only for it to bounce off his head and into the goal. Phil jumped for joy, hugging Stan and punching the air as if the team had just won the cup final. Stan smiled and said 'steady me old, you'll give yourself a heart attack.'

## *Stan*

Let me tell you about Niamh. It was a few months after I left school and had started the apprenticeship when this family, the Duffys moved in down the road. Irish they were. Things had kicked off in Northern Ireland, so apparently they'd left to get away from the bombing and other stuff that was going on. He was a nurse, which surprised me, especially as he was a big bloke, well over six foot. I didn't know you could get male nurses. His missus got a job a as a teaching assistant. They had five kids, so seven of them in 3 bedrooms. The eldest, right, were a girl about my age who I caught sight of once or twice, but she seemed to keep herself to herself. The other four were brothers, who liked to kick a ball about on the street or on the bit of common at the end of the street.

None of us had met or seen any Irish apart from on the telly, so obviously, like, people were curious. Kids would watch them playing and the brothers would shout *Are you playing or wha'?* After a couple of weeks there would be twenty or more chasing the ball. I was on my way home after work, stopping just for a couple of minutes to listen to the banter between the brothers. *So what're yous gawking at? You playing or wha'?* They ran rings round me for a few minutes, then stopped to chat, or rather to fire questions at me. *So is your mother the really nice lady lives at number thirty? What do you do then? Are you making anything now like? Have you a girl friend? Do you shag them? (From the nine year old.) Does your Mum know? Have you seen our Niamh? She's a looker now.* Their father called from the front door. *How're you, young fella? Are my boys being polite?* The boys were real charmers and everyone round us liked them.

## *Phil*

I bought a moped that year. 1977. You could ride one when you was sixteen, like, in them days, so a few of us bought one and hung about together on the estate. We probably pissed people off, bezzing around on these things, but we liked to impress the girls. Mostly, I liked to strip the engine down and put it back together again. Stan would sometimes come and hang about with us as well, but he weren't interested especially in the bikes, more the girls, and it really pissed me off the way some of them would flutter their eyelashes at him and start flirting.

Then I realised I hadn't seen him for a couple of weeks, right, and I heard the girls were saying he'd got a new girlfriend. The sister in the Irish family. Of course, I had to find out for myself, like, so the next day I went round. His Mum, right, said he were down the road, fixing some broken fencing for Mister Duffy. The next evening he was teaching the boys how to play French cricket. A likely story, I thought. He's got to be chasing their big sister. But I caught him in his workshop at home the next day. He swore blind he was just being a friendly neighbour. Then there was this big grin on his face. That girl is gorgeous, he said. But she was playing hard to get, always doing her chuffing homework.

## Twelve

# Further on Down the Road

Stan had asked Phil to accompany him to the church hall in time to set up before the others arrived. Not that there was much setting up to do. There were a couple of tables alongside one of the walls and a few chairs stacked in a store room. They had brought along a few cans of beer, tea bags and coffee, plus some nuts and crisps, to help break the ice. Phil couldn't remember the last time he saw Stan so nervous, as he fussed over where to place the table and chairs. He told Stan to relax, and suggested arranging things by a window where there were also two power points.

Daniel was the first to arrive, with his mother at precisely seven o'clock.

'Remember what we said, pet, won't you? And when you've done I'll be outside waiting in the car.' Esther kissed him on the cheek as she said goodbye, causing Daniel to turn his head away in embarrassment.

What did surprise Phil was how Daniel greeted the other potential band members, who all arrived shortly afterwards. Malcolm walked in first, followed by the university contingent.

'Hallo, I'm pleased to meet you. My name's Daniel and I'm the percussionist,' he said to Malcolm, holding out his hand rather stiffly. With a glance in Stan's direction and looking slightly bemused, Malcolm shook the hand and introduced himself. With increasing insurance, Daniel introduced himself in turn to the other arrivals. Neil was particularly warm towards him, saying, as he put a hand on each of Daniel's shoulders:

'I'm really pleased to meet you, Daniel, and I can't wait to hear you play. Stan tells me you're very good. You remind me a bit of my brother, who must be about the same age.' The boy looked down at the floor in embarrassment. By contrast, Malcolm was distinctly and conspicuously cool towards Neil, saying simply, 'Alright, mate?'

'Well done, Daniel,' Phil said quietly to him, as people were helping themselves to drinks a few minutes later. 'You've saved us a job there, mate.'

'It's what my Mum told me to do,' came the reply.

The group stood together in the centre, taking stock of the hall. 'It reminds me of the hall in our old primary school,' said Phil. 'The stage was just like this one. We did loads of class plays and Christmas stuff on it. Do you remember when we were two of the Three Kings, Stan? We'd be, what, seven, when we followed the Angel up the wooden steps onto the stage, you shouting out: 'Cor, I can see the Angel's bum, miss'. We couldn't keep a straight face all the whole way through.

You didn't half cop it from the friggin' teacher.' Everyone except Daniel laughed at this.

There was general agreement that, although a bit basic, the venue would be fine for practices. When Stan suggested that they get down to business and discuss some music, Angie asked if it would be a better idea to get to know a little about each other at the same time. She would like to know what instrument everyone played and what they liked to listen to as well. She was happy to start things off, as this was her idea. The others looked at Stan. 'Yeah, if you like.' Chairs were dragged towards the middle of the floor.

'So. I'm Angie and I play the bass guitar, or at least I'm having lessons, which is how I met these two.' She nodded towards Stan and Phil. 'I started off by playing the double bass in a school orchestra, which did mostly classical stuff, but there's no room for it in my flat so I thought I'd have a go at the electric. I enjoy all kinds of music, blues, jazz, indie, folk. The song I've brought along is by Finley Quaye, who you might not have heard of. It's called *Spiritualisation*, which I like because it's fairly minimalist but is driven by the bass and percussion, and really rocks.' Stan opened his mouth to ask what the word minimalist meant, but thought better of it. Angie put her CD in the player. She was right about the bass and percussion, but the more Stan heard the less he could imagine himself singing the song. He said so. Malcolm thought it needed some lead guitar to 'beef it up a bit'. There was plenty of scope, she said, for coming up with an arrangement that would include some, and also to suit Stan's voice.

'Tom's good at arranging, aren't you, Tom?' she said. Why don't you go next?'

'Fine, that is if that's OK with you, Stan,' said Tom. Stan gave a slight nod of his head and pulled a face which indicated his assent. He was beginning to feel that things could slip out of his control, if he wasn't careful, and wasn't too sure about when he should take his turn. 'Who's chuffin' band is it anyway,' he was thinking. 'Maybe I should save the best till last and go then.'

'Well, I'm Tom, in case you'd forgotten. I play the keyboard and piano, which I started learning when I was about seven. Oh, and the guitar a bit. In the sixth form at school I played in a little jazz band with a couple of friends, and got the bug, so to speak. Then at uni I met some lads who were keen musicians, and we had a lot of fun playing bluesy stuff. I used to do the arrangements, which might come in handy. I've been so busy workwise since uni that I haven't had the chance to get involved in anything since. Work still keeps me busy, but playing again would give me some sort of release, I hope.'

'So what do you do that keeps you so busy, Tom?' asked Stan.

'I work at the Glenfield hospital.'

'What, as a cleaner, nurse, or what?'

'As a doctor. What's called a cardiologist.'

'You're not like a GP then. So what do you do?' asked Phil.

'Surgery. I cut people open, sometimes their hearts.'

There was a few seconds of silence.

'It's alright,' he said. 'We sew them back together, so they're always fine afterwards.' There was muted laughter.

'Chuffin' nora,' said Stan. 'So we're alright then if anyone has a heart attack, like. Not that anyone is planning one. But you've got your black bag with you, and that.'

'It's in the car outside, if that reassures you all. Anyway, my piece is by Doctor John, appropriately enough. I love this version of 'Don't get around much anymore'. The piano in this gives it a real rocky feeling.' Everyone enjoyed listening to this, but again Stan said that it wasn't really the sound he had in mind.

'Follow that then, anybody,' said Stan, keen to move things along. 'Malcolm, what about you, me owd?'

'Well, I was wondering if young Daniel might want to tell us about himself.' All eyes turned towards the teenager, who was sitting in a foetal position, rocking slightly and humming something very quietly. Malcolm had mistakenly taken this to indicate boredom.

Phil cleared his throat. He explained quietly that Daniel sometimes finds these situations difficult. Although he was sure the lad would want to tell everyone about himself, he might not be quite ready yet. At this juncture, Neil spoke to Daniel, offering to sit with him and work out what he would like to say to everyone, perhaps when he was ready a bit later on. Would he like to do that? 'Yes, OK,' was the reply.

'Fantastic,' said Neil, and the two moved to a corner of the room.

The others looked at Stan, as if to ask 'What now?'

He suggested taking a break for five minutes to refill glasses or cups, or to visit the toilet. As they reconvened, Neil and Daniel re-joined the group, sitting adjacent to each other.

'Well, everybody. From what he's told me, Daniel seems to be a lot like my young brother. For a start they both like collecting things and both have unusual talents. Daniel has said he'd like to tell us all about these. Is that OK, Daniel?'

'Mmm, well I like to collect old blues singles. My Mum was going to throw away a load of my Dad's records when he left, but I said I'd like to listen to them first. I really liked the blues ones, with singers like Robert Johnson and John Lee Hooker.' As he spoke, he had his hands under his thighs and looked at the floor. When Neil asked him to explain how this got him interested in playing the drums, he said that when he asked a friend if he could have a go on his drum set he found he could remember the percussion arrangements of some of the songs he'd been listening to. His Mum bought him his own drum set, so now he can play along with songs that he likes. He listened a lot to Radiohead, and when Uncle Phillip comes to see him they sometimes listened to The Beatles and Rolling Stones together.

'So how does this work, Daniel?' asked Malcolm. 'Once you've listened to a song, you can remember the percussion arrangement and then play it from memory.' Daniel nodded. 'Well if you can really do that, that's amazing. Have you ever had any lessons?' Daniel replied that he'd had some lessons with his music teacher at school, who showed him how to hold the drumsticks and brushes properly, and also how to follow the music from a manuscript.

'I am in total awe,' said Malcolm.

'Me too,' said Angie, and Tom, who also said he would like to hear some of the records from Daniel's collection one day, if he could.

'Sure,' the boy replied, smiling, but still looking at the floor. Daniel's choice was 'The Bends', by Radiohead, which received lots of appreciation from Neil, Tom and Angie, less from Stan and Malcolm.

Stan pointed out that they needed to crack on, as they only had the room for a limited time. Hopefully they would all get to know each other better if the band came to anything, which inwardly he was beginning to doubt. As well as feeling that so far he didn't have much in common with the others, he'd also become anxious that his own choice of music wouldn't be heard. Malcolm was asked to keep it brief.

'I'll try, but I'll probably lower the tone anyway. I play the guitar, the sax a bit, and have been in a couple of bands, but that was before I signed up. I'm more of a classic blues and rock man, sixties and seventies stuff, Clapton and Led Zep kind of stuff. So this is a Clapton piece, which I like cos I can play it and it shows Eric's versatility.'

He'd chosen *Further on Down the Road*. Stan was the only one who showed any real enthusiasm.

Tom asked Malcolm which of the services he'd joined.

'Royal Marines. Afghanistan and stuff.' He looked around the group for a reaction. 'You'll have seen it all on the telly.'

'So while Tom here is trying to save people's lives, you were busy trying to kill some,' said Neil, with a wry smile.

'If I were you I'd stick to stuff you know about, College Boy,' replied Malcolm, angrily. 'You're probably too young to know what the Taliban were like, evil bastards who killed hundreds of innocent people. Our job was to see them off, then to train the Afghan army so that they could look after their own friggin' people.'

'Don't patronise me…' but Neil was cut off by Tom.

'So is that where you lost your leg, Malc? I spotted your limp, even though it's only slight, and I guessed it's a prosthetic. Am I right?'

There was a stunned silence, broken after a few seconds by Malcolm.

'I was lucky. Had it removed just below the knee. The bastards got us with an IRD – roadside bomb.'

'Was it bad?' asked Tom. 'I mean for the unit.'

'As bad as it gets, which is as much as I want to say about it.' He looked at Stan. 'I didn't come here for this, so let's move on, or you can forget it as far as I'm chuffin' well concerned. What about College Boy?'

'What about College Boy?' said Neil, bristling.

'Well, are you in the right place for a start? Isn't hiphop or jazz more your thing?'

Neil's voice rose. 'Why, coz I'm black? So what is it you don't like about me, Soldier Boy? The fact that I'm black or that I'm gay? Or both? Oh and throw in that I'm educated.'

The atmosphere had suddenly become tense. Daniel took himself into the corner where he'd been sitting with Neil a few minutes earlier.

'Jeez,' said Stan. 'I thought we were going to listen to some music and talk about getting a band together, not have a chuffin' barney. You two need to cool things down.'

'You're right,' said Neil as he stood up. 'And the only way I can cool down is to get out of here. I don't think this is going to work for me, so I'll get off home.' He started to move towards the door.

Tom looked across at Angie, shrugging his shoulders as if to say 'is there anything we can do?'

'You can't go!' shouted Daniel, who was banging his fists on his thighs. 'You can't go. If you go, I can't be in the band. And then my Mum would cry. And I want to be in a band.'

'Shoot,' exclaimed Neil as he sat down with a heavy sigh. After a minute or so, knowing that everyone was waiting for him to decide what he was going to do, he slid a CD into the machine, saying 'Well, at least you can hear the music I've brought along, so that you can see what you might be missing. It's an arrangement of an old Van Morrison track which I came across recently.'

Much to his surprise, Stan enjoyed listening to the female artist's version of *Tupelo Honey*. This song was on a Van Morrison album which he had played over and over when he had bought it in the seventies. The violin solo sent a tingling sensation down the back of his neck, so much so that when the track had finished he would have liked to hear it again. The soothing tone of the singing seemed to have a calming effect on Neil at least, and there were murmurs of appreciation from around the group. Malcolm, arms folded, made no response.

'Cassandra Wilson. Black American. It just shows what you can do to a song with a bit of creativity,' Neil said in response to Stan's question about the singer.

Not feeling optimistic, Stan played three of the five songs he had brought along, before pausing for some reaction. He had agonised over his choices during the course of the last few days, feeling as if he was choosing his desert island discs. He wanted to give a sense of what he would enjoy singing, without seeming to be too one-dimensional. First, Gary Moore's *Moving On*, followed by Santana's *Black Magic Woman* then Eric Clapton and B. B. King's *Come Rain or Come Shine*.

'That last song is just delicious,' said Tom. 'I loved it when you sang it for us at the uni.' Angie thought it was an interesting choice of music, but so far everything seemed a bit set in the seventies or eighties. She asked Stan if that was what he imagined his band playing.

After explaining his redundancy and current self-employment status, Stan said that it had always been his ambition to sing in a rock band, but until now hadn't found the courage to do anything about it. He admitted that most of the albums in his collection and most of the songs he could sing and play were from the sixties, seventies and eighties, but he was prepared to be open minded.

'But to be honest, I can't see it happening. I don't see how you can chuffin' well bring together a group of people to rehearse and perform together unless they like each other, as well as having something resembling the same taste in music. Am I right, or what?'

'You might be, Stan,' said Tom, 'but what might bring us together ultimately is the desire to be on stage performing. The challenge is to find the sound and the style that works for us. So why not give it a shot. Give it one rehearsal to see what we can come up with and take it from there. And what I can do, if you like, is try and come up with arrangements to suit the various talents here for, say, three songs, stick them on a CD and circulate them so that everyone can have a listen and a go at home. I've got a bit of time off this week, after being on nights. What do you think?'

'Well, first we should see if anyone else wants to carry on. Who doesn't?' They all looked at each other, to see who would be the first to put a hand up.

'I,' said Malcolm, arms still folded. 'I would first of all like to know what College Boy here does, when he's at work I mean.'

'For goodness sake!' exclaimed Angie. 'Can we show each other some respect. His name is Neil.'

'Sorry. Neil, would you mind telling the group what it is that you do for a living?' asked Malcolm, with mock politeness.

With apparent reluctance, Neil explained that he was Leicester born and bred, and worked as a lab technician in the medical research department of the university. His musical interest had been handed down from his grandparents, who had come over from Barbados in the early nineteen fifties to try and make their way as musicians. A really talented classical violinist, his grandfather found it difficult to break into the music establishment in England, but after seeing Stephane Grapelli perform in a club in London he became a jazz convert and formed his own combo. He worked on the buses during the day and in clubs at night. When he died he left his violin to Neil, who was already playing the instrument in one of the junior Leicestershire School Orchestras. He, Neil was a big fan of Andrew Bird, an American violinist. Like Neil, he was classically trained, but had branched out into rock and alternative music.

Malcolm gave a nod and a grunt, as if to say he was satisfied with what he had heard. Stan asked again if anyone did not wish to be involved, or should they 'give it a go', as Tom had suggested. Daniel continued to rock in his chair, but to Stan's surprise there were mutterings about giving it a go, nobody dissenting. They agreed to meet the following week for a full blown rehearsal, as long as Tom had the time to sort out arrangements for some songs to send out on CD.

## Phil

I just cannot see this friggin' lot getting on at all. I mean, Stan should tell them all to piss off rather than waste his time. One way or another there's nothing but trouble going to come out of it all. I can't see Daniel coping with all the agro, for a start. Those two, Neil and What's-his-name, mister Angry, took an instant dislike. He should stick with Tom and the girl, and have another go at finding some other musicians. They might be a bit too what-do-you-call-it, high-brow, but at least they're sensible and musical. Mind you, it was all her fault it kicked off. Did we need to know whether anyone was chuffin' well gay or not? Better to keep that sort of thing under wraps, in my humble opinion.

## Stan

We should have just gone straight into the music, like I suggested. I didn't need all that bollocks, nor did anyone else. Lesson number one is not to let that Angie push us around. There's plenty of time to get to know each other, like, if we want to. But now we have some right old stumbling blocks to get over.

If we do stick with it, Tom could be a real find, being good on the keyboard and at doing arrangements. He'll be useful to have around when there's any bother as well, keeping the peace or bandaging people up when there's any fisticuffs. The thing is, I've heard them and I know they can all play. The thing is whether they play together. I can't begin to understand what goes on in Daniel's head, but I do like the lad. He seems to have an instinct for who he can trust. Neil for one, obviously. The two of them clicked right off. So that could be a plus. He's a bright cookie that Neil, just a bit too quick to judge if you ask me. Take as you find, as my old Ma says. I'll do my best, but on balance I am not hopeful.

## Thirteen

## Blue

ack on the round which included Mount Pleasant, a few weeks since the first visit, there was very little of the usual banter between Stan and Phil. Apart from the odd comment about it being a 'rum do' and the sparks flying between Neil and Malcolm the previous evening, they preferred to talk in unusual detail about the work in hand, the weather, or the fact that some shops in Leicester already had Christmas displays up. Occasionally, one or the other would become lost in thought.

Mandy was hanging out washing as they pulled up and unloaded the ladders from the van. Perfect timing for coffee, she said, inviting them in. Stan remarked that she looked especially sexy in her house coat and marigolds. The discussion over coffee became almost an exercise in therapy, as the boys unloaded their thoughts and frustrations about the way things had gone in the church hall.

'So in a nutshell, Stan, you're stuck with a control freak, two blokes who hated each other at first sight, Kofi Annan and a lad with OCD. All the ingredients for a great story, it seems to me, so what more could you want. Plus some of them think you're a bit stuck in the past.' She paused for thought, before continuing. 'But seriously, you've got a challenging situation on your hands. Only you can decide if it's worth the effort.'

'That's just it. Is it? I just want to enjoy singing in a chuffin' band, but instead along comes all this friggin' crap before we've sung a bleeding note. And I hadn't really reckoned on all the arranging that would need doing. Maybe I should stick to winderin' and doing a bit of karaoke and open mic stuff.'

Mandy thought Kofi Annan's point about the others all wanting to be on stage playing could work in Stan's favour. From what Stan had described, she suggested there was certainly plenty of energy and creativity flowing amongst the various potential band members. It was a case of finding the way to channel this. A violinist in a rock band was unusual, let alone a female bass player. Having someone who could handle arranging music as well would be a real bonus. Stan's choice probably boiled down to singing the bog standard stuff that lots of bands do, or working with this group of people to find a sound that would make them stand out in a crowd. In her view there were some talented musicians around in Leicester who were stuck in run-of-the-mill bands playing the usual circuits. Stan should ask himself how ambitious he wanted to be. As for College Boy and Soldier Boy, whose names she couldn't remember, getting them up and playing together might be the best way for them to sort out their differences.

'Nothing to lose, apart from a bit of sleep. I should stick with it,' said Phil with his usual brevity, when asked by Stan for his thoughts.

'Thank you, duck,' Stan said to Mandy. 'I mean, helpful chat. We'll go away and ponder. Time to crack on and get some more winderin' done.' He let Phil leave the room first, giving him the chance to have a minute alone with Mandy. He moved his chair to be close to her.

'You know, duck, you are wonderful,' he said quietly. 'Are you sure I can't tempt you out for a drink?'

'Are you asking me out for a date? I said before that things are complicated at the moment, so don't say I didn't warn you.'

'Let me be the judge of that. So I'll take that as a yes. What are you doing tonight or tomorrow? I'll pick you up.'

Elbows on the table and hands clasped together to support her chin, she looked at him thoughtfully for a moment and then smiled. 'OK. I'd love to. Tomorrow works best, about seven. And I'll pick you up. I'd like to see where you live.'

'I'll warn the staff to expect you. Oh and there'll be no charge for the windows, duck. On the house, so to speak.' He resisted the temptation to kiss her, simply saying 'Chuffin' brilliant.' His face was beaming as he joined Phil to clean her windows. Phil sensed the change in Stan's mood, and guessed that he must have made some sort of progress in his pursuit of Mandy. The afternoon's pace of work was considerably quicker than the morning's.

Even so, Wednesday evening couldn't come quickly enough for Stan. The prospect of being with Mandy served as a distraction from the sense of limbo he felt he was in over the band. Whilst watching a European Champions League match on Tuesday evening and wiping down windows the following day, there were times when he realised he had been daydreaming for several minutes, picturing her face, her smile, the time she had sung at the club and the way she had walked towards him that evening. At times he also allowed himself to fantasise about the possible outcomes of the evening ahead, which he knew could be tempting fate. And going back over what she had said in response to his and Phil's frustration about how the band's first meeting had gone, he was struck by the fact that she seemed to care and the way she had presented the case for Stan to be optimistic about the way things could work out.

It had been some time since Stan had been on anything resembling a date. He agonised over what to wear from his limited wardrobe, before eventually deciding on the smart casual look, consisting of his best denims and newest shirt. Just before seven he was giving his shoes a polish to hide the scuff marks, when he heard the knock on his front door. Moving quickly from the kitchen, through the dining room and into the living room, he tripped over the flex to the still-cooling iron, crashed into the ironing board then banged his forehead on the edge of the small dining table. He swore as he checked his head for any signs of blood, which there wasn't, but he could feel the swelling beginning to rise. The ironing board was stuffed hastily and angrily into what he referred to as his 'shove-in' cupboard under the stairs. There was a second knock as he gathered the iron and its flex, which he placed this on to a kitchen worktop.

'Coming, duck. Shit!' he said as he fingered the bump, already the size of a golf ball. One hand was attempting to hide the swelling as he opened the door to Mandy, but he very quickly forgot about this. He stood open-mouthed as he took in the newly-cut hair framing her smiling face, the dark pink chunky sweater and tight fitting dark blue jeans.

'Well, I'm pleased to see you too,' she said with a touch of sarcasm. 'Are you going to invite me in?'

'Sorry, duck. I was er… well, you, um, you look chuffin'
gorgeous. Of course, come in.' He apologised for keeping her
waiting at the door, explaining that he'd had a little accident.
When she saw the egg on his forehead, she made him sit down
and asked if he had any ice. The nearest he had was a pack of
frozen sliced beans in the freezer compartment of his fridge.
As he gave her a blow by blow account of his collision with the
table, he soaked up the gentleness of her touch, along with her
subtle fragrance. Within five minutes the improvised ice pack
had noticeably reduced the swelling, but she insisted that Stan
keep the pack in place for a few more minutes. He watched for
any reaction as Mandy looked around his modestly furnished
living room.

'This is cosy, Stan,' she said, giving nothing away. 'And I
didn't realise you were an art fan. Is that a Picasso?' There was
a framed print of *The Old Guitarist* above the fireplace.

'Chuffin' expert, me. I picked that up at a car boot sale.
Couldn't resist it. I think it adds a touch of class, don't you?
Anyway, my little place does me just fine. You can have a quick
look round if you like.'

'Let's just sort you out first.' Gently removing the frozen
pack, now beginning to soften, Mandy examined his forehead.
With one hand Stan held her wrist, then putting the other
round her waist he half turned Mandy so that she sat on his
lap. Her mouth parted slightly as he gently kissed her. There
was no resistance so he kissed her again, first the lips, then
her eyes. She groaned slightly, tilting her head back so that he
could kiss her neck. Now superfluous to the proceedings, the
pack of beans fell to the floor. She put her arms around Stan's
neck, kissing first his forehead where the swelling had been
and then full on the mouth. Their tongues met. Stan explored
her lips, then her teeth, hardly able to believe that this was
happening. Then she pulled away.

'This isn't going to get us that drink,' she said.

'Maybe we can do that later. Right now there are other parts of me that need your wonder touch.'

'Yes, I've noticed.' He chuckled, then slid both hands under her sweater and lifted it over her head.

'You beauties,' he said, before softly kissing each nipple though her bra.

An hour later, Stan was savouring the moment, as they lay together in his bed. He held her close, caressing her back with his left hand, while she moved her right hand slowly up and down between his navel and chest. Joni Mitchell's *Blue* was on the CD player.

'I just love this album,' she said. 'You must have known.' After a long pause she asked, 'Stan, is there, has there been a Mrs Stan?'

He shifted his weight so that he leant on his elbow, his hand supporting his head.

'I'll answer your question if you'll answer mine.' She took up the same position so that they were looking at each other, noses almost touching. 'OK,' she said.

'You know we bumped into each other in the café, that day I was with Ma? Who was the geezer sat at your table? He left, then you got up to leave a couple of minutes later.'

'Ah. I'd wondered when you'd get round to asking.' She stroked his nose. 'Nothing to worry or be jealous about, Stan.' She seemed to have decided that was as much as he needed to know, but Stan pushed gently.

'I'll need a bit more than that. Was he a work mate, or what?'

Mandy sighed.

'That was my ex. My most recent, my second ex, to be precise. He isn't happy with the way the divorce is going. I've taken him to the cleaners basically, and he was, shall we say, pleading for me to take him back. He'd played away once too often, so I told him to get stuffed. So. What about Mrs Stan?'

Fair question, he replied, and yes there had been. Niamh. They were barely in their twenties when they married, after four or five years of courting. Teenage sweethearts. For several years they had lived in a council house, working and saving hard, planning to have a family but wanting to buy their own house first. Things were going well until she got involved in some American religious group, 'some sort of scientists', he said, and little by little they brainwashed her. Their relationship changed, he saw less and less of her. Their intimacy was replaced by her sullenness and the occasional rows. One day he got home from work to find Niamh waiting, bags packed, to say goodbye. She was, she claimed, going to devote herself to the church. He soon learned that it wasn't just his wife he'd lost to this organisation, but also their savings; nearly thirty thousand pounds. She had been persuaded to gradually transfer this money into an account in her own name. He had talked to a solicitor about taking the matter to court, but was told that this would almost certainly be throwing good money after bad. They divorced, and that was that. He hadn't heard from or seen his ex-wife since.

Stan lay silent for several minutes, eyes closed. Mandy stroked his hair, then his shoulder and arm.

'Stan, I had no idea. I'm sorry if it's brought back painful memories. What did you do?'

'This were nearly thirty years ago. It were tough and I didn't cope well with it. Nearly drank myself to death. But. What's the point, I thought. There's a frigging life to live. Phil and the others were great. You know. Rocks.' He paused. 'Like I say, I divorced her. The solicitor tracked her down, but I didn't want to know. The parents took it hard. Pleaded with her to come home. I think a couple of her brothers found her and told her to come to her senses, but she sent them packing.'

'And you've never found anyone else? In all that time? You must have had women chasing you, good looking, foot loose and fancy free.'

'Now and then, but no one that I was really interested in. Until now, that is. So let's change the subject. To ravishing.' He dived under the sheets to grab Mandy, who squealed with delight.

## Phil

Stan were love struck. He seemed to spend a lot of time hanging around with the boys, just to catch a glimpse of Niamh. Then one evening, one of the lads were caning it on his bike up to the shops where I was hanging out, saying there were trouble at the house and Stan needed me and as many as I could bring with me. His Dad had phoned the police but they hadn't turned up yet. There was six of us, like, so off we went on the old mopeds, the kid chasing after us.

It were almost like a scene from a cowboy movie. On one side of the street there was this gang from another estate, right, twelve or so, shouting and swearing, anti-Irish stuff, one or two chucking stones. On the other side were Stan and the boys with their Dad, using dustbin lids as shields. You could see one of the windows in the house had been broken. When they seen us slam on the brakes and run at them, like, they couldn't run away fast enough.

After that, you could see that it were getting serious between Stan and Niamh, and the other girls didn't get a look in.

## Stan

I'd just got home from work after doing a bit of overtime, when I could hear this racket going off down the road. There was this group of lads shouting outside Niamh's house. *Irish scum go home* kind of thing. I recognised some of them. A bad lot. I ran down and tried to reason with them, like, but they just said to fuck off. Then one of them chucked a brick through a window, and I could see it could get nasty. I stood at their gate and shouted at them to go home and leave the family alone. Mr Duffy and the boys came out and stood there with me. Some people were out in their front gardens watching, and started to boo the mob when the brick was thrown. I told the youngest brother, Paul where he could find Phil and to go on his bike out through the back garden and down the jitty. They backed off when Mr Duffy started to walk across to them. He's a big bloke, but he had to get back when they started to chuck stones.

They soon cleared off when they saw Phil and his crew. They would have known Phil. The Duffy boys started running after the gang, Mr Duffy and me joining in, like. When one of the gang tripped over, the boys were on him before he could get back on his feet, but Mr Duffy ran straight past him. I guessed who he was after, so I kept up with him.

The gang had stopped at a corner, right, probably cos they realised one of them had dropped behind, so the two of us were soon face to face with them. Some of them started to egg us on, like, and they came towards us, so just for a minute it was a bit scary. But they froze when they heard the mopeds coming up behind us. As they started backing off again, Mr Duffy charged at them and rugby tackled the leader to the ground, before he had chance to react properly. The rest of them weren't sure what to do at first, but they didn't have the courage to take us on, so scarpered.

There were cheers as we walked back to the house, Mr Duffy and me with this kid between us. Frog-marching is the word, I discovered later. At one point, right, the one who had fallen over in front of the Duffy boys went running past us, looking in a bit of a mess.

Mrs Duffy and Niamh came out and hugged the boys and their Dad. Mrs Duffy gave me a hug too. I got handshakes from Dad and the brothers, then Niamh gave me that gorgeous shy smile. I was in love from that moment.

The police came in two cars, and we all wondered whether they had been watching and waiting until it was all over before they decided to turn up. The kid was taken away, they took a few statements and off they went again.

I'd felt that maybe they were sheltering Niamh from me to start with, but now whenever I called she would come running down the stairs to say hallo. Soon we would have a chat, and that's how it all started. She needed a bit of help with some homework, which her Mum and Dad were happy about, as long as it was at the dining room table. And yes, I were able to give her a bit of help, with the maths anyway.

# Fourteen

# Some Kind of Wonderful

'Call it soft rock, if you like. I can't think of a better name, but there are plenty of bands playing standard rock stuff, some good, some not so good. I think what I'm suggesting will give us a lot more options in terms of choice of music and arrangements. What I've tried to do is bring in the violin to cash in on Neil's playing. I know how good he is and how really good he could be, and if Malcolm is anything like, then they'll complement each other and give us a great sound to work on.'

Tom had called Stan to ask if he had time to listen to the arrangements he'd been working on, before the CDs were sent out. Sitting in Stan's living room, they had listened to three songs: versions of *Tupelo Honey* and *Moving On*, together with one they hadn't heard at their meeting, Santana's *Love of my Life*. Tom thought that this would appeal to Neil, as the melody for the introduction was based on a piece by Brahms. When Stan said, without batting an eye lid that he'd heard of Brahms, as in with his mate List, Tom really couldn't tell whether or not he was serious. He went on to apologise in advance for the quality of his voice which he'd had to use on the recordings. He also warned Stan that the instrumental sounds were those available on the software he'd used, and didn't do justice to what they would come up with playing live. In each case they'd featured solos on guitar and violin, sometimes one instrument replying to the other, occasionally both playing together.

'Yeah I like these, Doc, and assuming everyone chuffin' well turns up, we should give them a go on Tuesday. But we don't want too much of this soft rock stuff. I mean don't we want to get the place rocking when we're playing.'

Tom had anticipated Stan's reaction, responding that it was a case of balance. 'How's this?' He played another track, not one of his own arrangements, but Doctor John and his band playing an upbeat version of a standard, *Don't Get Around Much Any More*. Stan wasn't sure about the spoken introduction – in fact he couldn't make out what was being said – but once the music started, he got up and bounced along to it.

'More like it!' he said, raising his voice. The saxophone solo prompted a discussion about the need to hear Malcolm play his sax, which they hadn't done. They agreed that Tom would include arrangements of all four pieces on the CD to send this out with copies of the sheet music.

'Thanks Doc,' said Stan. 'I appreciate you must be busy and that. Let me know if I can do anything.' Tom was about to ask Stan not to call him Doc, but inwardly shrugged, deciding that, in the context of the band, he actually quite liked the tag. He didn't realise that Stan had almost nicknamed him Kofi.

'No problem,' he said. 'It gives us all a long weekend to work on things and a chance to see how we do under a bit of pressure.'

The envelope arrived on Stan's doormat with the post on Saturday morning, two days later. By early evening, Stan certainly was feeling the pressure. He was pretty confident with *Moving On*, so decided to brush up on this first. This left him with three days in which to learn the lyrics, guitar riffs and chords to the other three songs; not something he'd ever had to do before. He tackled *Don't Get Around Much Anymore* next, on the basis that he enjoyed this more than the others and the key suited his vocal range. By eight o'clock he felt that he had more or less committed the lyrics to memory. Seeing the time, Stan felt drawn to the pint of bitter he could visualise waiting for him on the bar of the club. For no reason other than he fancied the idea, he decided to wear his cowboy outfit. He went through the rituals of his preparation, wondering what Mandy would make of it all. When she had told him that she would be singing with Chalkie's band this evening, he had felt desperately jealous of the band members, knowing they would be enjoying watching and listening to her perform.

For an hour or so at the club he sipped on his pint, preoccupied, which didn't go unnoticed by Jane. Commenting on his unusual reticence, she could only think that he must be in love. His failure to deny this was met by a long 'Ooooooh, he is' from her and Kit's wife Linda. At this point he knew that he had to see her. He walked quickly home, jumped into the van and set off for Syston, a large village on the west side of the city, where Chalkie's band was playing at a party being held in a school hall.

He parked the van on the roadside near the school entrance, wound down the window and listened. The sound of voices and laughter drifted across the car park, but there was no music. He decided to investigate.

The entrance door led into a small reception area, from where he could see a banner reading *Happy 60th Sandra* and had a limited view of people sitting at tables or carrying trays of drinks. It was clear that there was a sixties theme for the party dress, which for the women included mini-skirts, floaty dresses, hot pants and someone dressed as Cher, partnered by a Sonny. On the whole the men seemed to have made less of an effort. There were one or two in leather jackets and polo jumpers, an Elvis Presley, a couple with floral shirts with beads round their necks, plus a few non-descripts.

'Are you coming in or what, duck?' The enquiry came from a man sitting at a small table, presumably to collect tickets or payment from guests. He was of a similar age to Stan and wore a leather jacket and a Billy Fury hair style. Stan wondered whether the man would demand a ticket or payment.

'Err, yes duck. I'm with the band, the driver, like. I've just been out to the van.'

'Good band too. Perfect for this do, they are. They should be on again any minute.' He looked Stan up and down. 'Like the get-up, but I don't know if it's very sixties is it?' Stan suddenly felt conspicuous in his full outfit, including Stetson and replica six shooter.

'Wyatt Earp, duck. Don't you remember the TV series?'

'Before my time. And yours I would have thought. Anyway, come in if you're coming.'

To avoid being too conspicuous, Stan took his hat back to the van, then walked into the hall to the sound of the percussionist playing a short drum roll, and cheers welcoming the band back on to the stage. He headed to the hatch for the school kitchen, which served as the bar, asked for an orange juice, then, keeping low, headed for a chair he'd spotted in a relatively dark corner at the back of the hall.

At the moment there was no sign of Mandy. When the band struck up *Some Kind of Wonderful* it was Chalkie himself who sang. Guests quickly flooded onto the floor to dance, making it less likely that Stan would be spotted by anyone from the band. As the applause for the song died down, Chalkie asked everyone to welcome Mandy back on stage. She was wearing a full length black floaty dress, which swished gently from side to side as she moved around. Stan was instantly captivated. As soon as the band launched into *Da Doo Ron Ron* he was on his feet clapping, before he realised what he was doing then promptly sat down. Stan was envious of both the sound the band made and the way the people in the hall responded. Like them, he enjoyed every minute of the forty-five they played.

Their set finished, they were joined on stage by a woman dressed in a 'flower power' outfit, including headband and beads. He guessed this was probably Sandra. She thanked the band and hoped they would do one or two more sings for them. She then proceeded to announce the prize winners for the best dressed man and woman of the evening, as chosen by her 'spotters' dotted around the hall. The woman dressed as Cher was one winner. She went up to collect an envelope.

'For the men's prize, this goes to Wyatt Earp, who I believe is the band's driver.'

On his return from collecting a copy of The Guardian, Neil found his envelope containing the CD and sheet music in his mail box. He shared a rented garden flat just off Victoria Park. He loved the location in what he referred to as a 'Mumsy'

area, with its trendy coffee bars, hair dresser salons, soft furnishing and furniture shops displaying tables and chairs in the 'shabby chic' mode. Its proximity to the university was an added bonus. Inside, the large picture window at the front and the open aspect to the rear gave it a light, airy feel. Sitting in the front room in his favourite rocking chair inherited from his grandparents, he sipped coffee while flicking through the sports pages and then attempting the weekend quiz. The latter he regarded as a necessary form of masochism. In order for the weekend to be enjoyable his target each Saturday was to answer at least one of the generally obscure questions correctly. Just for a few minutes he ignored the realities of life. A couple had recently written in to the newspaper, proudly claiming that they had achieved their ambition of answering all fifteen questions correctly. These were people he felt needed to get out more. This morning he managed five, which was about his average, so he was feeling fairly optimistic about the day ahead.

A box room served as his music room/study, and it was here that he took himself next, with the intention of listening to the CD. He sat looking at it long and hard, reflecting once again on the events of the previous Tuesday. He had asked himself several times whether he really wanted to be involved in the project, given his reservations about the sort of music that was being talked about, but more especially the mutual dislike between himself and the guitarist. He enjoyed being and playing with Tom and Angie, so was drawn towards the idea of performing with them. For different reasons he was also intrigued by the prospect of Daniel being in the band, Daniel who reminded him so much of his younger brother, and with whom he felt he had made a connection.

He inserted the CD into his laptop, and listened through his headphones. Twenty minutes later, having played the four tracks through twice, his persistence with the weekend quiz was rewarded with a very positive feeling about the arrangements Tom had come up with. He tuned his violin, then for two hours he listened and played, experimenting with different sounds on the instrument, ending the session by cultivating a solo where this was played by the sax in the Doctor John song. He was beginning to think about his plans for lunch, but Neil knew there was something else he would also have to do.

It took him just a couple of phone calls to learn Daniel's home number and address. Thirty minutes after speaking to Esther he was standing outside the house, violin case in hand, knocking on the door. To his surprise Daniel opened it, and although there was the usual lack of eye contact, in his own way he was obviously pleased to see Neil, smiling and saying *please come in*. Esther's welcome was circumspect, something Neil had become used to on making first acquaintances. He tried to reassure her by explaining that he wanted to help Daniel overcome one or two problems with the CD that he had received. Esther appeared to be grateful, but pointedly reminded Daniel that she was taking him shopping in an hour.

Neil was genuinely envious of Daniel's collection of 45s. They listened to a couple of Daniel's favourites, *Apache* by The Shadows, and *Please, Please Me* by The Beatles. Surprised by the boy's choice, Neil asked him why he liked these tracks so much, to which Daniel replied that his grandfather had given them to him and had said '*You'll like these*'. They listened next to Tom's arrangements on the CD, and Neil asked Daniel what he thought about the percussion arrangements.

'Well, I'll practise them and I'll be able to play them.'

'What I mean is, Daniel, when you listen to a piece of music, what are you doing? Do you just focus on what the drummer is doing, which drum or cymbal he's hitting, or is it more than that? I tell you what, let's listen to just one again, *Tupelo Honey*, and see what we make of it.'

Daniel's face gave nothing away as the song unfolded, nor as it finished.

'What do you think of it, after hearing it again?' Neil asked.

'Mmm, it's a very nice song, fairly slow and easy. The violin sounds nice. It doesn't sound quite real, because the instruments aren't real. It's the software.'

'That's very perceptive. I agree. What about the percussion? What did you think?'

'Mmm, it's not difficult, the same beat and rhythm all the way through. It sounds a bit hard, I mean the drum is being hit too hard with the sticks.'

'That's fantastic. I can see what you mean. Would it work better with brushes?'

'It might do?' Shall I play it like it is on the CD?'

Daniel took his place at the percussion set, and after a bit of fidgeting he fixed his eyes on the snare drum, counted himself in then played the first few bars.

'Great stuff,' said Neil, clapping his hands. At his suggestion Daniel played the same few bars using just the brushes. This was followed by a thoughtful silence.

'Mmm. It doesn't quite work, does it?' said Neil. 'It loses that emphasis on the third beat in each bar, which drives the song.'

'I could use one stick and one brush, using the brush for the cymbal and the drum except for that beat.' Daniel demonstrated.

'Amazing! Perfect.' Neil clapped his hands again. Daniel gave a slightly embarrassed smile of appreciation. 'What about if I play the violin solo on my real violin, so you can see and feel the difference?'

'OK.'

After quickly making little adjustments to the tuning of the violin strings, Neil closed his eyes, started tapping his right foot, then launched into the sixteen bar solo. He waited to see if Daniel would give any reaction.

'Was that OK do you think?'

'It's different to the CD. It starts off the same, but you go much higher, and uh, yeah, it's better. I really like it.'

'I'm really pleased you think so. There are one or two bits I need to tweak. How about if we play together? You start off and just keep the rhythm going. I'll count myself in. OK?'

After a couple of bars into Neil's solo, Daniel stopped, saying with some urgency, 'No, that's wrong.'

'You're right. I came in too late. It should be on the second beat. Well done. Let's go again, from the top.'

They played it through. Neil gave a whoop of delight and they 'high-fived'.

'Pretty amazing for a first try. Let's give it one more go. Yeah?'

Daniel nodded. Neil then suggested that Daniel could invite his mother to come and listen to them playing together. After some reluctance, saying that his mother never comes into the room, except to tidy it, he agreed to go and ask her.

Daniel returned, followed shortly by Esther, a little breathless and looking slightly sheepish. Neil explained what they had been doing, stressing how helpful and positive Daniel had been so far, and invited her to make herself comfortable for the very short recital.

'I am so pleased you asked me to listen to you playing. I can't wait to hear the whole song now. You are both so clever. And you play the violin so nicely…. I'm sorry, is it Neil? How long have you been playing?' Neil gave a brief response, but turned the attention to Daniel, saying that he obviously has some good idea, which he shouldn't be afraid to suggest.

'I'm glad you think so. I'm very lucky to have such a talented son. Did you hear that, pet? Don't be afraid to talk about your ideas.' She paused before getting to her feet. 'Well, I'd better....' She gave Neil a smile which he felt held genuine thanks and a touch of warmth, enough to make him feel more comfortable about being there. For the next half hour Neil and Daniel listened to each of the other three songs, giving Neil the opportunity to show what his playing would sound like. He left feeling his mission had been largely accomplished, knowing that unless Daniel knew what to expect during the rehearsal in three days' time, there would be some difficult moments.

At around the same time as Daniel and Neil were giving their brief performance, Angie, Tom and Malcolm had also turned their attention to Tom's CD. Angie was playing along with the gentle bass arrangement for *Love of my Life*, continuing to work conscientiously on the pieces for the next couple of hours. Taking a break in his shift as duty doctor at the hospital, Tom had walked along to the visitors lounge in the cardiac unit, where a rarely used upright piano rested patiently in a corner. Here he plugged into his iPod and played along with Doctor John, oblivious to the small audience which had gathered at the doorway and just along the corridor, at the window to the room.

Malcolm had arrived home from his local, where he had been watching a lunchtime premiership football match with a couple of friends. The CD was on the worktop in the kitchen, where for a few minutes that morning he had agonised over what to do with it. The pub had offered the easy option as a delaying tactic. He re-entered the kitchen, took one look at the CD, swore at it, then picked it up and stuffed it into the waste bin, which received a hefty kick for its troubles.

On Monday morning there was much cupping of and blowing on hands at first, as Phil and Stan had their first experience of cleaning windows after a sharp frost. It was a beautiful, crisp early autumnal morning, with a bright blue sky, the low angle of the sun sending its light filtering through leaves in shades of gold, red, purple and brown, steam gently rising from pavements as they warmed. Here and there it seemed that coloured snowflakes were falling softly to the ground. Lifted by this and the knowledge of his date with Mandy that evening, Stan was in good voice.

'I've got a suggestion to make, my old' said Phil, when they stopped for their mid-morning break. 'I reckon it's time for you to catch up with the twenty first century. Here, get a load of this.' He produced his iPod, and headphones, from a jacket pocket and proceeded to give Stan a demonstration. As he listened to a track, Stan turned the iPod over several times then played with the controls.

'Unbelievable. The sound quality, it's like being in your own friggin' front room. So what music have you got on this thing?'

'Only the whole friggin' CD collection, like, plus stuff that we've downloaded. Daniel showed us how to do it all a few months ago. Me and the missus spent a whole weekend playing at it. Putting our music onto her laptop that is, right, then transferring it onto the iPod. Piece of cake once you know how. If you like, we could go and buy you one of those after work, then set you up with the songs you're learning, and any others for that matter. The world is …. whatever they call it. So tomorrow you can sing along with Tom's stuff and be word perfect for your first practice. Make a good impression. It's what all the others will be doing.'

He gave Stan a moment to digest the idea, then asked, 'Good idea, or what?'

Just at that moment there was a ping from Phil's phone. He read the text message from Malcolm. *Sorry, can't be doing with this band stuff, so am chucking it in. Problems with certain members. Sure u can find a guitarist.*

'Sorry,' he said to Stan. 'Just need to make a quick call. Won't be a mo.'

The late afternoon saw Stan set foot for the first time in a superstore of the new technologies, at the Fosse Park shopping centre. He stood open-mouthed inside the entrance, mesmerised by the array of signs and rows of high-tech equipment. An assistant asked if he could help. Phil had disappeared into the maze of aisles, so Stan asked to be directed to the iPods.

Phil was waiting in the aisle. 'This is what we need,' he said. Stan coughed when Phil told him the cost, complaining that it worked out at about thirty pounds per square inch. Nonetheless, he had become convinced that he should buy one. They wondered round the store, taking in the latest cameras, computers, printers, and televisions. At one point they stood facing a wall of large flat-screen televisions, all showing replays of Leicester City's match played at the weekend.

'Time to make a sharp exit,' said Stan. 'You could spend a friggin' fortune in here, very quickly. I'll have to go home and count the pennies, see if I can afford one of them new lap jobs.'

'I think you mean laptop jobs,' Phil corrected. They laughed.

In his living room Phil loaded Stan's new toy with Tom's CD, along with some of Phil's music, to get Stan started. Stan then had a couple of hours to work on the songs for the rehearsal. At home, he placed the iPod on his table. Apart from being given the odd suspicious glance, there it stayed as Stan inserted the disc into the CD player and proceeded to play and sing along with *Tupelo Honey*.

Later, Mandy was curled up against Stan, head resting on his chest. Both were naked and totally relaxed. They had quickly become overcome with desire and lust when Stan arrived to take her out. Her bedroom was as far as they got. She listened, smiling quietly to herself as Stan proudly told her of his latest acquisition that afternoon. Then he changed the subject.

'Know any decent guitarists? Available ones, that is. Phil told me just now that Malcolm had changed his frigging mind about being in this chuffin' band. I tell you, it's doing my head in, trying to work with these, these....'

'Prima donnas might be the best words to use, rather than those you're thinking of. Well, that's a shame, although I don't know how good he is. But you never know, he might change his mind at some stage. It depends how much he wants to play and whether or not he gets a better offer. Anyway, you can play can't you?'

'Yeah, but a second lead guitar would take the pressure off. Two guitars would be good.'

'Moan, moan, moan. I bet there's one thing you're better at than lots of guitarists out there.' He looked down at her. It was her turn to dive under the sheets, his to make the noises as they began to wrestle with each other.

'By the way,' she said, surfacing briefly. 'Is it you wears a Wyatt Earp outfit at your club?'

## Stan

For a couple of days, whenever I was in the house it felt like that chuffin' iPod was stalking me, taking the piss, like. Then Mandy spotted it and asked how long I'd had it. She had to remind me how to work it, then I was away, listening to it all the time, just like a friggin' teenager. We went online and bought a decent laptop as well. That's something I never thought I'd do. We should buy in shops, keep them going I've always thought. But the laptop was half the chuffin' price it was in that store, so I could just about afford it. Three days later it had come and Phil had helped me set it up. I still think it's amazing that I can carry my whole chuffin' record collection around in my pocket and listen to it anywhere. Apparently I can also get Paul Jones' rhythm and blues programme as a podcast now. A what?

## Phil

One. Stan gets an iPod *and* a new computer. Two. That Jamie Vardy scored to make it twelve in a row in Premiership matches for City. Three. City are second in the chuffin' league. I would never have thought them three possible, especially City being near the top, after last season. Claudio is the man for me, never mind Vardy. Not many thought he'd be any good as manager when he came. 'Mister Tinker Man' he was called at Chelsea, but he can't muck around too much with the City squad as they've only got so many good players. I know one or two people had a punt on City at a thousand to one to win the title.

# Fifteen

# Tupelo Honey

As the others moved around the small stage with a sense of purpose and anticipation, setting up and tuning instruments, Stan was a bag of nerves. Over the last couple of days he had convinced himself that he was going to make a fool of himself by trying to play along with a group of musicians who were far better than him, all of whom, including Daniel, were experienced in playing along with other musicians. It was one thing to mess about at home, he had said to himself, playing along with tracks on CDs, and to sing and play occasionally at the club. This was a whole new ball game. The prospect of being exposed by the extra expectation Malcolm's absence would place on him only served to increase his anxiety.

'We're missing Malcolm,' he heard Angie say. 'Has anyone heard from him?' Stan told them that Malcolm had decided to give the band a miss.

'No loss there, as far as I'm concerned,' said Neil. 'And it means more room on the stage.'

'The trouble is, duck,' said Stan, resisting the temptation to call him College Boy, 'we don't have a chuffin' lead guitar.'

'Well let's see how we go,' said Tom. 'The Santana song is the main problem because there's a lot of guitar, but let's worry about that later. Stan, you know the Gary number well enough to have a go I'd have thought. Neil's violin can take the place of the second guitar in the solos. And we can work on *Tupelo Honey* with you. The chords in *Don't Get Around* are straight forward and you're playing them anyway, so what's to worry about? And Neil tells me he's worked out a violin solo to replace the sax.'

After some shrugging of shoulders, Angie took control, directing everyone into a position so as to allow for some movement, with Stan standing self-consciously, centre stage, Tom sideways on to the left, so that he could see everyone. Instruments and microphones were plugged into amplifiers, Phil helped Daniel to arrange his percussion set.

Stan looked around the stage, a surge of adrenalin putting him on edge. His nerves got the better of him as twice Tom counted him in for *Moving On*. Both times he messed up his entry.

'Sorry everybody. I should chuffin' know this. Better if I count myself in.' Tom told him to relax. After playing the first few bars a few times, Stan regained some confidence.

'Come on, you can do this,' called Phil, from the back of the hall. 'This is not your chuffin' football team,' tought Stan. There was some nervous shuffling on the stage and nods between Stan and Neil. 'This time, shit or bust,' said Stan to himself. His entry was perfect, the first four bars of percussion and guitar holding together well. At the beginning of the fifth bar, Angie struck her first note on the bass. There was a loud bang and the hall was plunged into a silent darkness.

'Oh my God!' cried Angie. 'What was that?' There were a few expletives from the others. 'This just ain't going to frigging well work,' Stan muttered to himself

'We're doomed Mister Mannering, doomed,' Tom said out loud, in a mock Scottish accent, adding, 'are you there, Phil? Can you sort this for us?'

'Don't move, nobody,' shouted Phil, 'or you'll trip on the chuffin' cables. I'll fetch a torch from the van.' As eyes were adjusted to what little of the street lighting was filtering through a window, they could just make out Phil crash into a locked door, before finding his way out.

'Well, I thought those first few bars sounded very promising,' said Angie. 'I'm sorry if it's my guitar which has blown everything up.' Phil returned, quickly located the fuse box in a cupboard, then confirmed that the mains switch had tripped. After some detective work he identified the problem as a loose wire in the plug for Angie's amplifier, which he quickly sorted out. Angie took the opportunity to sidle up to Stan for a quiet word. She tugged his sleeve and tried to give him a reassuring smile.

'I can tell you're a bit nervous Stan, and I can understand why. You'll be fine. You know the song well, so relax into it. Like you did at the uni.'

'I'm trying to chuffin' well relax, but surrounded by you lot... This is all new to me, like.'

'Just close your eyes and focus on those first few bars before you start. You'll be fine.'

'You'd chuffin' well think so, duck. I've played and sung it often enough. Anyway, ta,' he said as she backed away, giving him another one of her smiles.

'Are you ready?' called Phil. 'Dadaa!' It took a few seconds for eyes to re-adjust. As they looked up they took in not the figure of Phil standing at the door to the fuse cupboard, but another, ghost-like, two or three steps inside the entrance.

A gasp came from Angie, and 'What the f...!' from Stan. A guitar case in one hand, an amplifier in the other, and what turned out to be a saxophone in a bag strapped across his back, there stood a slightly bewildered-looking Malcolm.

'Is this a game of murder in the dark, or what?' he asked. 'What's going on?'

'We'd chuffin' well given you up,' said Stan. 'I heard you'd stuffed the CD down the waste bin and wasn't coming. We was doing alright without you.'

Neil had become very agitated and jumped down onto the floor, baring Malcolm's way on to the stage.

'Why don't you crawl back under the woodwork? As Stan said, we were doing fine.'

'What, in the dark? It looked like it,' Malcolm replied sarcastically. 'Anyway, there was nothing on the friggin' telly, so I thought I'd come and see how it's going.' He squeezed past Neil, avoiding eye contact, and climbed up onto the stage, trying to make space for himself.

'Very persuasive, your lady friend,' he said. 'Came round Sunday morning with a sob story, then had me playing to her. And I played all evening after the football, all last night and this morning. I'd have been here earlier, but couldn't get the car started. You owe me for a taxi.' He grinned at Stan. 'Only joking.' Phil helped him to get set up then took his place at the sound mixer.

As the session progressed there was the occasional playing in the wrong key, missed cues and forgotten lines. But between these and the raised voices of accusation and counter accusation there was some accomplished playing, surprisingly constructive discussion during breaks, Stan began to feel that something was coming together, provided he could sort himself out. Phil and Neil had both feared that Daniel would not cope with the nature of a rehearsal.

'It's a practice,' he responded when they both told him how well he was coping, 'and I know that at practices people sometimes go wrong and make mistakes. That must be because they haven't learned their words or music properly, but I think they will eventually.'

Stan realised that Tom had achieved a masterstroke through his arrangements. This was by giving both Neil and Malcolm leading instrumental parts in more or less equal measure. In *Love of my Life* they shared the lead, and in one key part they played it as a duet, one playing a phrase and the other responding.

'You've nailed it. Great job you two,' Tom said to them, after the band had played it through for a second time.' Neil and Malcolm each grudgingly gave the other a nod of appreciation.

Among the lighter moments was the reading out by Stan of the spoken words to the introduction of *I Don't Get Around Much Anymore*, which he had written down on a piece of card. With the exception of Daniel, everyone fell apart with laughter. When Stan asked what the problem was, Tom suggested that he speak in his normal Leicester accent rather than in a New Orleans drawl. Everyone held their breath when Malcolm produced his saxophone, just as Neil announced that he had put together a violin solo to replace the sax.

'Sorry mate, but how was I to know you played the bleeding sax?' Stan and Tom exchanged looks then said in unison, 'You can both play your solos.' There were quiet sighs of relief.

'It'll sound twice as good,' Tom added. They played the song through a couple of times, Neil and Malcolm adding some improvisation so that their parts weren't too alike.

Malcolm played more than adequately and was complimented by everyone except Daniel, who looked unmoved by the experience.

'To be honest, I never thought we'd get this far, especially with the cock-ups I were making. Know what I mean?' said Stan, as they started to put instruments away. 'But for a first go, like, we weren't bad. So what do you reckon? Same time next week, for another go at it? I mean I'd like to. I were beginning to enjoy myself, even if I have got some work to do.'

Some were more enthusiastic than others, but they agreed to meet in a week's time. Tom produced a second CD with two more songs for them to play or sing along to: *Further on Down the Road*, to which Malcolm had introduced them at an earlier practice, and *Bless the Weather*, suggested by Stan. Tom explained that the latter was based on an arrangement of this John Martyn classic he had heard recently, which included a great sax solo for Malcolm.

Stan and Phil were the last to leave, Stan in a much happier frame of mind than was the case when they opened up. As they packed their gear into the van, Phil managed a few tuneless lines of *Moving On*, then Stan joined in as Phil mimicked his attempt at the Doctor John's New Orleans accent. They sang Queen's *We Are the Champions* very loudly on their way to The Brown Cow pub.

A week later they were back together in the hall. At Tom's suggestion the band played two songs straight through, ignoring any mistakes and without pausing for any discussion. Mandy, who had come along at Stan's request to give her assessment of the music, sat at the far end of the hall, listening to *Love of My Life* and *Tupelo Honey* for the first time. As the bass brought the latter to a gentle ending, she gave a loud whoop and stood up, clapping her hands above her head.

'That was just amazing, especially as this is only your second time together. The way the guitar and violin talk to each other in the first song is inspired. And I love what you've done with *Tupelo Honey*. There are some few rough edges though, as you'd expect. Can I make a few suggestions?' She looked at Stan, eyes narrowed, brow slightly furrowed; a look that signalled she was going to anyway.

'Go ahead, duck. The floor is yours, at least for a minute or so.' Stan had been given a huge lift by her reaction. She suggested they would have to invest in some better quality amplifiers, to improve the sound, and to work on the sound mixing to give a better balance, so that Stan's voice and the solos come through more clearly. Also they could take a leaf out of Chalkie's book, whereby at some practices he has each member taking turns to listen from the back of the room, to get a feel for the collective sound and how each instrument comes though.

The main problems arose from Daniel's increasing difficulties in coping with being in a confined space on the small stage, and with the regular stops when mistakes were made or specific parts of songs were played then replayed to achieve the desired sound. His reaction to the latter was either to hold his head in his hands and shout out something unintelligible, or to smash away on every piece of percussion randomly for a few seconds. Stan and Malcolm in particular became increasingly irritated with these outbursts. Neil's suggestion of agreeing to play a particular section of a song, so that everybody knew when to stop playing, seemed to solve this problem. However, Daniel's tendency to walk off the stage from time to time, saying 'I need space, I need space,' caused more frustration.

When this happened for the third time, Tom recalled seeing a band play a few months previously, in which the percussionist was playing to one side of the band and behind a tall plastic or glass L-shaped screen. He wondered aloud whether this was because the percussionist had similar issues to Daniel. Phil pointed out that if they did eventually start playing live gigs, Daniel was likely to find it difficult to cope with the proximity of noisy audiences in crowded bars or halls. Neil agreed. This prompted an angry altercation between Stan and Neil. Stan asked sarcastically why they didn't just play behind a curtain and put chuffin' earplugs on the kid. It was time, he suggested, to find someone normal who could just come and play instead of causing one problem after another. Neil took exception to this.

'Define normal then, Stan,' he challenged. 'We've all got our issues, but you're not talking about kicking anyone else out. Discriminate against Daniel and where do you stop? Do you just want a bunch of fifty something straight blokes?'

'Yeah, but…. Ah fuck it.' Stan had no better response, and walked out of the hall, muttering expletives. Phil looked at Mandy with shrugged shoulders and an open palmed gesture of exasperation. She went in search of Stan.

After a few minutes he'd calmed down sufficiently to walk back in, accompanied by Mandy. Daniel was now sitting on his stool at his percussion set, which had been moved onto the hall floor, a few feet from and to one side of the stage. Stan took this in, gently shaking his head.

'It's all part and parcel,' Mandy whispered to him. 'Just get up there and sing. You'll feel better.'

He stepped onto the stage, feeling the eyes of the others on him. He grunted an acknowledgement of the fact that he now had a little more space.

'OK. Let's get further on down the friggin' road, so to speak, shall we,' he said. 'Straight through if we can. OK Daniel?' The boy nodded. There was a collective sense of relief, and they were all pleased to be playing and singing again. The rest of the practice went relatively smoothly, finishing on a high note with *Don't Get Around Much Anymore*. There was laughter all round as Stan blundered his way through the last few bars, spoken in his broad Leicester accent.

By the end of the evening, the band felt they had established a repertoire of six songs, enough to be going on with. Neil, Tom, Malcolm and Angie each had an opportunity to listen to the band while sitting next to Mandy, who skilfully managed the ensuing discussions so that feedback wasn't taken personally and arguments avoided.

'How you react to feedback is important,' she said. 'Because you'll get lots of it, from your audiences, manager, studio bods, etcetera, mostly but not all of it constructive. And you can't afford to sulk every time.'

Tom raised the idea of hiring a recording studio for a couple of hours, partly with a view to producing a CD which they could circulate if and when they began to look for gigs, but also to gauge the quality of the music they were producing. When Stan asked whether they all felt ready to go into a studio, there was a cautious response from the others, who felt that they needed a few more practices under their belt. Stan replied that there was no rush, adding that they would need to start thinking about a name for the band.

'I've had one idea,' said Mandy. 'I was thinking about this earlier. The first time I heard Stan singing, he was wearing a cowboy outfit. So how about *The Cowboy Outfit*? As a name I mean.'

'Mmm, I don't know,' said Tom. 'It has certain connotations. I wouldn't want a cowboy outfit in the operating theatre.' He asked Stan what he thought.

'I were just thinking about what that presenter from the telly said at Ursula's café, when me and Phil were being interviewed. Leicester rocks, she said, and she were right. What a great name for a band.'

## *Stan*

They must have all been thinking *What's he doing? A total novice trying to get a band together, and we end up having to carry him.* Like I said, it's one thing playing around at home on your own, but there's nothing like playing with other musicians. Playing in the recorder group in primary school ain't exactly the best track record to have. But Neil and Angie are great. Loads of patience and lots of experience of playing in orchestras and stuff, with all them different instruments, which must be great. And I'm chuffin' panicking cos I've got to learn to play with five others.

Going back to Niamh, my Ma was dead chuffed when she got wind of the fact I was going out with her. Niamh had said one day would I like to take her to the pictures. So we went to see *Saturday Night Fever*. We really enjoyed it, especially Niamh. She let me kiss her, right, when we got off the bus. Told me how she used to go dancing regularly 'back home', and how much she missed it. The film had put her in the mood, so we found a disco to go to the next weekend. I was always like the other lads at discos, hovering at the side while the girls danced around their bags or cardies, diving in at the end for a smooch, right, but she was having none of that and insisted I danced from the off. And it was great.

Ma liked the family and thought Niamh was lovely. She would hint that I ought to marry Niamh, saying things like *I can see you two together*. It was different to being with any of the girls I'd been out with before, especially getting to know the family as well. Mr and Mrs Duffy would regularly remind me that Niamh was a *Good Girl* and say that they thought I was a *Good Lad*. I knew what they meant. They were wrong about me.

## Phil

It all feels a bit of a dog's dinner, as they say, the band and the practices. Stan is a bit stressed about it all. It's very unlike him to lose it. I think he's found it tough from the start. I was surprised he was struggling to play along with the others, but then again he hasn't really done it much before. Old dogs and new tricks, kind of thing. Good that they had a bit of a laugh though, about him trying to put on an American accent in that song. Name for the band? How about *A Dog's Dinner?*

## Sixteen

# All Along the Watchtower

One evening later that week, Neil also made his way along with a group of friends to The Brown Cow. The pub is a popular music venue, especially with the student population, who enjoy the eclectic mix of music on offer. The proprietors pride themselves on their ability to spot rising local talent as well as fairly big names. Keen to see the 1970s music-playing rock band due on stage this particular evening, Neil had made a point of arriving early enough to guarantee his entry, enjoy some beer and whatever food was on offer.

Along with many others, he and his group were already in party mode by the time the band started playing at eight. As they blasted out songs of Led Zepellin, Jimi Hendrix, Thin Lizzy and Deep Purple, the mood intensified, and Neil was carried along on the wave of enjoyment which swept through the audience. The title of their song just before the half time break was *A miss is as good as a mile*, and Neil shouted to his friends that unless he could get to the toilet soon, he would be missing by a mile. He managed to barge his way through the tightly bunched crowd. Fortunately for him the queue for the gents quickly shortened. He was still concentrating on buttoning his fly as he made for the exit, when he was sent crashing to the floor as a group of three men shouting loudly burst through the door.

'For fucks sake!' he shouted. Two of the three, both built like professional rugby players, helped him onto his feet, laughing as they did so. 'Sorry mate, but you need to keep your head up in these situations, I find,' said one, whose nose must have been broken at least once in previous skirmishes. 'I think you'll be OK.'

'Well look who it isn't,' said the third man, who had held back as Neil was being helped up. 'Fucking College Boy.'

'I might have known you wouldn't be far away,' said Neil. 'And I was just beginning to enjoy myself.'

'You two know each other?' asked the man with the bent nose.

'We have become acquainted,' replied Malcolm.

'Get a fucking move on,' shouted someone trying to get into the toilet.

'Good musician,' Malcolm continued. 'Watch it out there,' he said to Neil. 'It could get very noisy later.'

Back on the floor and amongst the heaving flow of bodies, Neil stopped to look for his friends.

'Funny smell round here, Carl,' came a voice. 'Are you getting it?'

'Fucking black, if you ask me.' Neil looked round to find four men looking at him menacingly. Each wore a black leather jacket and had hair slicked back.

'Sorry, have you got a problem?' asked Neil, not to any of them in particular.

'No, not at all,' said the first. He moved in close to Neil, so that they were almost nose to nose. 'But you have. Don't be here in ten minutes time. We don't like your sort here.' He turned to his three friends. 'Do we lads?'

'That's enough.' Two of the black-suited security men employed by the pub had quickly pushed their way through and moved between Neil and his confronter. 'Push off,' said one. 'Any problems from you lot and you'll be out of here, so move away.' At first, the leather jackets seemed to stand their ground, but after a few seconds they backed away.

Jabbing his finger in Neil's direction, their apparent leader said 'You'll keep,' as they melted away into the crowd.

The security man advised Neil to keep with his friends and try and tag onto a bunch of others as they left, and to avoid being the first or last to leave at the end of the evening. This lot hadn't been seen at the pub for a while, but they had a reputation of being a nasty bunch. Neil nodded and thanked them, before pushing his way through to where he thought he'd seen his friends.

He remained on edge during the band's second set, from time to time looking around for any sign of the leather jackets or slicked-back hair. He did catch a glimpse of Malcolm a couple of times, but not of the gang of four. The cheers and shouts for *more* as the band left the stage were rewarded with a rendition of *All Along the Watchtower*. Intoxicated by the atmosphere as well as the alcohol, Neil was in dreamland, playing air guitar and singing at the top of his voice, along with the many others. He and two of his friends watched the audience thin as they waited for the third to return from the toilet. Re-united and in good spirits, they weaved their way along the Welford Road, then a misty Victoria Park Road, occasionally bursting into song.

As they approached a dimly lit spot where the park broadened away to their left, they launched into the first verse of *All Along the Watchtower*. The singing came to a rapid halt when they were suddenly confronted by four figures which had emerged from the shadows to block their passage.

'Sorry lads, I don't think there is no way out of here,' said one. 'You, my black friend, should have pissed off while you had the fucking chance.' A flurry of kicks and punches sent the members of Neil's group shouting and sprawling, and Neil himself was quickly isolated and targeted. With no time to defend himself, a hard punch to the stomach was quickly followed by a punch to his head which knocked him to the ground. He instinctively covered his head with his arms, and grimaced with pain from the kick to his lower back. Bracing himself for the next one, he could hear loud voices and the sound of more punches and kicks hitting their targets, which he assumed were his friends. He could hear their groans and more shouting and swearing. This seemed to carry on for an interminable length of time, during which he began to think he must have been knocked into semi-consciousness. Why else couldn't he feel the kicks that must be raining into his body. In fact it continued for no more than about half a minute. The sound of people running faded. Then all he could hear was heavy breathing. It was suddenly very close to him. Slowly, he uncovered his face sufficiently to take in some of the scene around him. He recognised the face of the person kneeling close to him.

'Hello Neil, College Boy. You can come out now. Nice company you keep.'

Neil slowly sat up then got to his feet, brushing himself down. There was a swelling on his head, but no sign of it bleeding.

'Let's have a look at you then,' said Malcolm, putting his hands on Neil's shoulders and giving him the once over. 'You'll live. So will your mates. Lucky we came along.'

Malcolm and his broad shouldered friends had been not far behind Neil's group when they were assailed. They explained that they had previously run into Neil's attackers, who seemed to take pleasure in taunting anyone black or Asian, as well as gays and men who had served or were currently serving in the army. All former soldiers, Neil's rescuers had relished this opportunity of taking revenge for an attack on Malcolm and a former colleague outside a pub a few weeks ago, which had left his colleague needing medical attention for cuts to his neck made with a broken beer glass.

Apart from a few bruises which needed nursing, neither Neil nor his friends had been badly hurt. Hands were shaken and thanks expressed. They walked together for a few minutes, in conversation about the evening's music. His breath smelling strongly of alcohol, Malcolm put his arm around Neil's neck then gently rubbed his fist into Neil's chest.

'Look,' he said. 'I know we got off on the wrong foot last week. It was probably all my fucking fault. But you seem to be OK. I like the way you look after that kid on the drums, and your violin playing – well, awesome. Perhaps some time we could get together and work on some of those solos. Plus I write my own stuff. Be interesting to know what you think.'

Feeling a mixture of repulsion and intimidation, Neil replied cautiously. 'Yeah, that would be cool. I've got some ideas of my own as well. Let's see how it goes in the next couple of weeks.'

## Stan

Neil told us he had a run in with some bad boys. Sounds like they're one of the far right groups we're stuck with in Leicester. He had some proper old bruises, Neil. Maybe him and Malcolm will get on better. Ma had a couple of run-ins with one of these groups a few years ago. Some of the wazzocks, right, used to trawl round schools in the city where there was a lot of black kids, primary schools mostly. When the kids was out playing, like, these knob heads would stand at the railings swearing and shouting abuse, frightening the kids. Nasty racists and cowards is all they are. Probably unemployed, cos no one would have them. Anyway, Ma went along to one of their meetings to challenge them about this stuff. She took another councillor with her, a bloke, and gave them what for by all accounts. Apparently, they claim to 'put local people first' in all their crappy leaflets. 'So what are you doing targeting young local kids, who can't defend themselves?' she says. 'Shame on you.' I imagine it was a bit if a ding dong.

The thing about Leicester, one of the things I love about the place, is you can go into town and there'll be people from all over, meeting and chatting and that. Where else would you find market stalls selling fruit and veg from all over the world? You see masses of different spices, unusual fruits I can't say the names of, Polish food, jerk chicken form Jamaica. Et cetera. Jeans and T-shirts are dirt cheap as well. Alright so they're probably from some sweat shop, but good luck to them.

## Phil

My Mum and the old man used to argue about immigrants, colour and that. Her parents were definitly of the 'send them back where they came from' sort, and she inherited a bit of that. Dad would argue that we was all descended from immigrants at one time or another, so we all have the right to live where we choose, up to a point. He never explained what that point was. There was a group of kids at school, skinheads with tattoos, even though tattoos were against school rules. Trouble is you can't get rid of tattoos, so the school didn't know how to handle them. The thing is they caused a lot of bother about the black kids in school. There weren't that many in our area, which made it worse for them that was really. A couple of the skinheads were expelled, which kind of put a stop to the taunting and that. But you always knew trouble could be just around the corner.

We had a history teacher who one term was teaching us about the British Empire, and who would say things like 'the British civilised these countries'. I remember when one kid asked him why there are so many black people in our country. The teacher started to talk about the ship that brought the first ones over from the Caribbean after the war, cos the country was short of labour, like. Then he said the best thing that could have happened was if that ship had sunk, which caused a bit of fuss. When it died down I put my hand up, like, and asked him 'wasn't everyone in the room descended from immigrants somewhere along the line?' He didn't like that. Some of us are white British, through and through, he said. I don't know if word got back to the bosses, but he wasn't teaching at the school the next term.

# Seventeen

# Another Brick in the Wall?

*P*hil had his own unhappy memories of meetings at school involving himself, his parents and teachers, sometimes even the Head Teacher, usually to discuss his behaviour or truanting. As he walked up the path to the front door of Esther's and Daniel's house on this particular morning, he was not exactly looking forward to setting foot inside Daniel's school. Even though the circumstances were different, he would still be sitting opposite members of what he would have regarded as the enemy in his school days – a class teacher, Special Educational Needs Co-ordinator, and a deputy Head Teacher. Also there would be a woman he only knew of as

Sue, who supported Daniel when he was in school. Daniel liked and trusted Sue.

It was several weeks into the new school year. Daniel had been unhappy on the first Friday of term, because he and Phil would no longer be able to enjoy their Friday mornings together, but reluctantly went to school. He endured a difficult day, venting his anger and frustration by getting into fights with other boys and refusing to cooperate in classes. This set the pattern for the weeks ahead. He had become increasingly unhappy at school and difficult for the staff to manage. Yesterday, Monday, he had refused point blank to go into school, which meant Esther had to take a 'sickie' from work. He spent the day playing and rearranging his collection of old 45s, and reading the autobiography of Ginger Baker, the percussionist with the 1960s band Cream. The school had set up a meeting to discuss Daniel's behaviour, and Esther had asked Phil if he would accompany her and Daniel.

'Thank goodness you're here. He's had a right melt-down.' Esther closed the door behind Phil, who hung his coat on a hook in the hallway. 'He's calmed down a bit, but he's adamant he won't go to school,' she continued, 'even though all weekend he said he was looking forward to going. But Friday was a very difficult day for him, and for the teachers I would think. Perhaps you can talk to him.'

Daniel was sitting at the breakfast table playing with a Rubik's cube, which he often did when feeling stressed. 'Here's Phil, pet. I told you he'd come.'

'Aye up duck,' said Phil. 'It's good to see you, mate. How's it going?'

Daniel concentrated on the cube. 'Hallo Phil. I'm not going to school. I don't like it. The teachers always pick on me, and some of the other kids are horrible to me and say nasty things. Especially in games on Friday afternoons. And music is a waste of time. Most of the kids mess about and don't listen to the teacher.'

'Well, let's think about this for a minute, me old. First, we are going to your school for a meeting, aren't we?' Phil looked to Esther, who nodded in confirmation. 'And it's Tuesday, so there won't be no chuffin' games or music today. Anyhow, the point is to find out from your teachers what will happen on Fridays from now on. They know you don't like games, so I'm sure they'll have another plan. Second, you know we used to play football and have fish and chips on Friday, like, in the holidays. In fact, I was going to tell you that we could do that on Saturdays, that is if you'd like to.' As soon as he'd said this he regretted it. He would have to make up another lie to tell his wife Jane.

While Phil had been talking, Daniel had solved the cube and was now staring at the table, hands tapping the side of the seat of his chair.

'Promise me I won't have to stay at school today,' he said.

'It ain't up to me, duck,' said Phil.

'I want Mum to promise.'

'We talked about this, pet. Remember? What would happen if I kept you at home when there's nothing wrong with you?'

'You get into trouble with the police.' Daniel thought about this for a moment.

'Well promise we can play football and have fish and chips on Saturday.'

'Promise,' said Phil.

Daniel looked up at Esther and said he would go to school then. He in turn promised Esther that he would behave himself, wouldn't shout or roll about on the floor in the meeting.

Thirty minutes later they walked through the entrance to the reception area of Daniel's school, one of the county's academies. The building had only been open for fifteen months and the reception area, with its plasma screen showing photographs of students involved in a variety of activities, and water feature surrounded by large indoor plants, still had the smell of newness about it. They signed in at the hatch for the academy office and waited to be collected by a member of staff. Struck by how the smart appearance of the staff and students who passed through the reception area, Phil thought back to the scruffy little entrance area to his old school, where a grumpy secretary would deliberately keep parents and visitors waiting for several minutes before making them feel she was doing them an enormous favour by attending to them. There had been no doors which could only be opened after numbers had been punched into a key pad, and students and teachers had been predominantly white and predominantly scruffy.

'I know the codes for all of the doors,' Daniel announced. 'I've watched teachers going through and could tell which numbers they tapped. But they are meant to be secret, so I can't tell anybody.' Esther looked horrified. Phil smiled and agreed that it would definitely be best if Daniel kept that information to himself.

A woman came through a door marked 'Staff only', said hallo to Daniel and Esther and introduced herself to Phil as Ruth Jones, the school's Special Needs Co-ordinator. She led them to a small meeting room, in which two other adults were already seated and four empty seats. Phil and Esther exchanged looks before Esther said that it would be a mistake to even try to persuade Daniel to go into the room.

'I'd have thought that by now you'd all realise that Daniel doesn't cope with lots of people in a confined space,' she said to Ruth. Looking flustered and slightly annoyed, Ruth apologised for forgetting. After a short discussion with her colleagues, it was agreed that the meeting would be moved to an empty mobile classroom. By the time they were all seated the Deputy Head Teacher was already looking at his watch. He apologised rather tetchily for the fact that the room was not well heated, then looked at Phil.

'I don't believe we've met,' he said. 'You must be Daniel's father.'

Feeling awkward at having been asked, Phil explained that he was a friend of the family, who had asked him to come along because he had a good relationship with Daniel. Clearly unimpressed, the Deputy looked at Ruth with raised eyebrows, then went on to explain that the purpose of the meeting was to discuss a smooth return to school for Daniel, so that he would attend full time and the school could meet his needs. He handed over to Ruth and the third member of the school staff, Sue, who explained to Phil that she was a teaching assistant who provided specific support for Daniel and two other students.

Ruth explained that she and Sue understood Daniel's frustrations with school, and that they were trying very hard to help other teachers and the students to understand as well. There were several other students in the school who were like Daniel, very clever at some things, like Mathematics, but who find some things more difficult than most students. They had organised some training for teachers, and all of the students in years ten and eleven were reading a book titled 'The Curious Incident of the Dog in the Night Time' as part of their Personal, Social and Health Education. This had been written by a boy the same age as Daniel and who was like him in lots of ways. There were lots of interesting discussions about the book in lessons. Sue said that she felt sure this would help to stop the teasing of Daniel by some boys and girls, and there would be no need for Daniel to get into fights in games lessons or in the playground again. She then outlined plans for Mondays which they had discussed with Daniel, who confirmed that he liked the new timetable for Monday.

'Excuse me,' Esther interrupted. 'Did you say Monday? Why, has there been a problem on Monday as well? You haven't told me about this, Daniel.'

'You didn't ask,' he replied.

Ruth explained that Daniel had fallen out with the science teacher and went into a sulk for the rest of the afternoon. Fridays, she continued, would include the same lessons as before, Maths, English and Music in the morning and games in the afternoon. The mornings would stay the same, but Daniel would be in a different group for games, who would be going swimming for the rest of the term. Next term they'd be going to the gymnasium in the new sports centre.

'You're looking forward to that, aren't you Daniel?' said Sue. 'You'll be able to use one of those watches which send information to your computer so that you can keep track of your performance.'

'It will be better than playing football and rugby,' Daniel replied. 'I'll be able to measure how fit I'm getting. But why do I have to go to music? The other students mess about and talk all the time and don't listen to the teacher. So it's boring, except when he lets me go on the computer and keyboard, like mine at home.'

'Now listen, Daniel,' said the Deputy. 'You've heard how Mrs Jones and Sue have gone to a lot of trouble to make school more enjoyable for you, but you can't have it your way all of the time. We can't make any alternative arrangements for the music lesson. We just don't have the resources, in other words enough staff.'

'Well I won't go to music. I don't like it.'

'Now come on pet,' said Esther. 'You heard Mr Cooper. There's just isn't anything else you can do on Friday mornings.'

'I can stay at home.'

The Deputy looked impatiently at his watch again and stood up, saying 'If you'll excuse me, I have another meeting.' Daniel started to rock on his chair, holding his head in his hands and groaning.

'Oh not that again,' said the deputy.

'Before you go, can I make a suggestion, like?' asked Phil. He didn't wait for a reply. 'There is no point, it seems to me, in trying to make Daniel go to a lesson where he'll learn chuff all. I wouldn't want to, and I'm sure none of you would go on a course or owt if you weren't going to learn owt. Now, this young man has a special talent.'

'Mr Hickock.'

'Hiscox.'

'I think we should leave this to the experts.'

'Well if you'll just let me finish, right.' Phil had raised his voice and changed his tone, just enough to make his irritation clear. 'Is this meeting important or what? You've been looking at your frigging watch since we sat down.' He stared out the Deputy, who gave a heavy sigh and sat down. Phil continued. 'Like I said, Daniel has a special talent, well several actually, but one in particular. I wonder if you lot even know what it is.' They listened as Phil talked about Daniel's percussion playing and his practising with the band. 'What I was thinking, like, was what if I paid for a private teacher to come into school to help Daniel work on his drum playing. Could he do that as his music lesson, instead of going into some chuffin' room where kids are chucking things about and not paying any attention?'

For a few moments there was much staring at the carpets by the adults, as Daniel continued to groan. The deputy slowly got up from his chair, quietly excused himself, saying to Ruth:

'I'll leave that one with you.' He left the room. Daniel sat still and quiet, and there was an awkward silence for a few seconds. It was broken by Ruth's apology for the Deputy's departure, explaining that he really was very busy. She and Sue then discussed Phil's suggestion, agreeing that it was no different to the peripatetic music teachers working with other students in school. Ruth thought it was possible that the local authority's schools music service could provide someone. Enquiries would be made. When asked if he liked the idea of having percussion lessons in school, Daniel replied that he would, but pointed out that he was already quite good, and a teacher would have to be very good. He told them that the school's drum set wasn't very good, so he might have to use his own, which would then have to be brought into school. He asked where the lesson would be. It had to be somewhere where it wouldn't annoy teachers and their classes. All good points, Ruth commented, but she was sure they could all be sorted out.

'I'm reading about Ginger Baker,' said Daniel, as he, Esther and Phil sat drinking tea in the living room after arriving home. 'He also started playing the drums when he was fifteen, and when he was thirty years old he was already in the Rock and Roll Hall of Fame because of his playing with Cream. If our band is as good as Cream then I might be able to be in the Hall of Fame as well.' The others laughed, not mockingly, but in a way which suggested this was a worthy but unrealistic ambition. The big difference between Cream and Stan's band, said Phil, was Eric Clapton. The band doesn't have anyone who could be as good as Eric, he added.

'Not yet,' Daniel responded. 'But when I hear Neil and Malcolm play, I think that they could become very good musicians. But you have to do lots of practising.'

'Well, who knows? Who knows? I hope you're right, my old mate. We could all become rich and retire happy.' Phil looked out of the window just as the sun emerged briefly to light up the roses in the small front garden, before retreating behind the clouds.

# Phil

You could have knocked me down with a bleeding feather when Daniel told us he was reading about Ginger. I mean, reading? According to Esther the kid has never picked up a book to read in his life, other than to chuck it at somebody. So give him the chance to read stuff on computers and rock music. Maybe some number puzzle type things as well. Not by shoving the stuff down his throat, but by finding the right sort of magazines and books or whatever, and just have them lying around to pick up if he wants to.

The school's run by a bunch of wazzocks, if you ask me. It's taken all this friggin' time for them to realise that with the percussion Daniel's found something he's good at and enjoys doing. How many kids are going to have the chance to do that these days? Bleeding schooling gets in the way, that's the trouble. In my humble opinion, like.

# Eighteen

# First Impressions

Over the next few days Phil become increasingly frustrated with the fact that nothing tangible had come out of the meeting, nor apparent sense of urgency on the part of the school to move the situation forward for Daniel. As he worked away on the windows, he formulated a plan. He would offer a donation of a thousand pounds to the school, which would see off most of what remained of his redundancy payment. He would request that some be used to pay for a few lessons for Daniel, the rest to be put towards purchasing some percussion, supplementing the existing small set owned by the school. Phil would also offer to carry out the necessary work to soundproof whichever room was available for Daniel's lessons and practising.

After several attempts, Phil was eventually able to speak to Ruth Jones, the school's Special Needs Co-ordinator during a lunch break. He put his proposals to her. Rather than giving the enthusiastic response Phil had anticipated, she was non-committal, explaining that she would need to run the ideas past various people, and would get back to him in due course.

'Look,' he said, trying hard to not let his frustration get the better of him. 'I don't understand the problem. I could come in and do the work in no time at all, like, and give the school the money tomorrow for his lessons and some drums.'

Ruth patiently explained that there was a process to go through before this kind of thing could get the go-ahead.

'I know that Daniel is probably not all that important to you lot, but he's friggin' well special to me and his Mum. So unless I hear from you by this time tomorrow, I will be contacting the Chair of your chuffin' Board of Governors.' He had some vague idea that schools were run by an organisation which was called something like this. 'I've got his phone number in front of me,' he lied, 'and I will tell him what I think of the school's pussyfooting about. You've got my number, but in case you can't remember it, I'll give it to you again.' He gave the number. This was followed by a short silence, at the end of which Ruth promised to do what she could and would call him back tomorrow.

Cursing red tape, Phil switched off his phone and put it in his jacket pocket. Tempted as he was to explain the situation to Stan, especially when Stan commented on his lack of conversation, Phil realised that nothing might come of the whole business, so he did his best to push it to the back of his mind for the time being. They discussed team selection for the boys' next match, a 'six pointer' as Phil put it, against the club who were second in the table.

The following morning, Phil's phone rang while he was up a ladder wiping a window. In his anxiety to locate the pocket containing the phone, his sponge flew out of his hand and landed on Stan, working at ground level.

'Chuffin' Nora!' Stan shouted. He looked up in time to see Phil's phone following the path of the sponge, having slipped out of Phil's wet hands. Stan reacted quickly enough to catch it just above his pail of soapy water.

'Frigging dangerous things, mobile phones, especially in your hands,' he said. The phone stopped ringing. The missed call message told Phil that it was from the school, so he retreated to the van, tapped in the number and was relieved to hear Ruth Jones' voice. He apologised for having just missed her call.

'I've got some good news Mr Hiscox. I've managed to speak to the Principal, and we've identified a mobile classroom that could be used for Daniel to have lessons in and to practise. It's a little way away from the main part of the school, but isn't used at the moment, so it's ideal. We would need to see evidence that you're insured against public liability, which we would assume you are, given the nature of your business.' She paused, waiting for a response, which was not forthcoming. 'But as you would be doing the work on the classroom voluntarily, we will say that you've carried out the work as a member of the PTFA. The one condition is that you do the work at times when there are no students present on the school site. If you contact the premises manager, he will arrange access for you. The other great bit of news is that we've managed to track down a percussion teacher, who works for the local authority's peripatetic music service. The slight downside is that you will have to pay the full cost of the lesson at £30 an hour, as the school doesn't buy into the service.'

Phil didn't really understand what that meant, but he quickly estimated the cost of the lessons over a school term. There was a silence as he digested the whole of what he had just heard. The outcome was better than he had anticipated, although the cost of the lessons was more than he had bargained on, but he could work round it. He told Ruth that he appreciated her efforts and was really pleased with how things were working out. They agreed that the next step would be for Phil to visit the classroom, to enable him to work out what he would need in the way of materials, then for Daniel to meet the teacher, preferably accompanied by himself or Esther.

'I'll mash,' Phil called up to Stan.

'The smile on your face tells me either you're on a promise, or you've won the chuffin' lottery,' said Stan, as he sipped his tea. Phil explained what the call had been about.

'So you took the buggers on. I'm impressed, me old. Sometimes there's no holding you back.' Stan went on to offer what help he could give with the classroom, and thought that they would be able to persuade others in the band, Neil for instance, to lend a willing hand.

'Just one thing though, duck,' said Phil. 'Have we got any friggin' insurance, like? Such as public liability? And if not, should we have?'

'Well it ain't something we've talked about, so I would say no we haven't. And if one of our friggin' ladders should slip and land on some bugger's head we could be in trouble. So I guess we should get some.' Stan said he would sort it out. There was a club member who ran a small insurance business on the Ashby Road, who he was sure would give them a good price.

The following Saturday morning there was enough warmth in the sun for Neil to risk sitting at a pavement table outside his favourite café, which he believed served the best chocolate brownies in the world. He was enjoying one of these along with an Americano when he received two phone calls in quick succession. He was happy to comply with Phil's request to help with preparing the mobile classroom for Daniel to use. Reluctantly, he also said yes to Malcolm's suggestion that he came round to Neil's flat later that morning. Malcolm said he would appreciate Neil's input to a song he was writing. Although neither of them had forgotten the animosity there had initially been between them, the two had grudgingly developed a mutual respect for each other's playing. But Neil remained wary of Malcolm, and had avoided making too much reference to the evening on which Neil and his friends had been attacked on their way home from The Brown Cow.

Malcolm arrived carrying an acoustic guitar and a bag, from which he produced an eight track recorder and a laptop computer. Neil made coffee as Malcolm talked enthusiastically about his hopes for the band and the songs he was in the middle of composing. They moved to the living room. Neil sat back in an armchair, poker-faced with arms and legs crossed, Malcolm on the edge of his chair, ready for action.

'Chill out, mate,' he said. 'I ain't going to bite you. Have a listen to this. The sound quality ain't brilliant, but best I can do for the moment.' Malcolm had recorded the mixes he had made of himself singing and playing, with some added percussion. The four guitar chords which introduced the first song were quickly joined by clapping on every second beat, followed by percussion. Eight bars in came Malcolm's voice. The song had a strong insistent rhythm, which immediately had Neil smiling and tapping his feet. He was surprised to hear that what Malcolm was singing amounted to a protest song essentially about the way capitalism was ruining the environment.

'Great. Love it,' Neil said above the music. Malcolm nodded his appreciation.

'What do you think?' he asked when the track had finished playing. 'I've had this thing spinning round in my head for ages, but I've only recently managed to sort the frigging melody out. For the moment I've called it *We're All In This Together*. The recording's not great, as I said, and the whole thing's obviously still at the early stages. It needs a decent voice to really make it work, plus I want to bring in a keyboard sound. I think a violin solo could be the perfect finishing touch.'

'Well, where to start,' said Neil. 'You seemed so full of aggro when this band thing got started, I'd have had no idea you had this kind of stuff in you. Even from the laptop, you can tell it's got potential for a great song. I think Stan could do a good job on the vocals, and Tom will nail the keyboard into the arrangement. Sure, we can work on a few bars for the violin.'

'Thanks. I hoped you'd like it. And yeah, I was being a real arse-hole, I know, but I was a bit messed up. No excuses. But I'm getting things sorted, gradually.' He held Neil's gaze for just a moment. 'I'll sing you this next one, *First Impressions*, while we're in listening mode. It's a bit different.'

He picked up his guitar, checked the tuning, and played a couple of cords. He quietly counted himself in. Malcolm sang a much gentler love song, in which the singer reflected on the first time the couple in question had met. Neil closed his eyes, tapping the rhythm with the tips of his fingers on the arms of his chair.

'Wow! You really are full of surprises. Where did that come from? I mean, it's such a nice song and your voice suits it. There were a few quite high notes in there too, which you nailed. Can I ask is it based on personal experience, or what?'

'No not really. More on fantasy. I've added a bass and stuff to it in the mix I've recorded. Want to hear it?' Sure, Neil replied. Malcolm had added a keyboard and simple percussion, as well as the bass, and the acoustic was replaced by an electric guitar, which Neil felt worked well. After they had shared thoughts on how and where the violin might fit in, Neil made a plate of sandwiches, before they got to work on the arrangements for the two songs. In the two hours which flew by there was a level of collaboration which neither would have thought possible at the beginning of the day, each willing to accept ideas and criticism from the other. Having put instruments away, they finally sat down to listen to the results of their efforts.

'That was a good couple of hours work there, Malc. I don't know about you, but I can hear the band playing these two songs.'

'It seems to me, College Boy, that we could make a bloody good team. Which is amazing when you think about it. There is a website which you can use to actually write your composition for you from a recording. So I'll have a go at doing that and take the recording and music to the next rehearsal. I think it needs Tom to work his chuffing magic on the arrangements for us.'

In self-congratulatory mood they moved into the kitchen, where Neil washed the plates and mugs, Malcolm wiping them dry. They were quiet for a moment as they did so.

'I meant what I said about us making a good team. What do you think?'

'The new Lennon and McCartney you mean?' Neil was aware of Malcolm standing very close to him. He stopped washing and looked at Malcolm, who then put his hand on Neil's shoulder.

Malcolm said, 'No, I just mean you and me.'

'Now just sodding well hold on,' said Neil, pushing Malcolm's hand off his shoulder. 'Is this what it's all really been about? You making a pass at me?' He stepped away, wiping his hands dry on a towel. They looked hard at each other, both searching for an explanation. 'What the fuck is going on? First you obviously wanted nothing to do with me, couldn't cope with me being around, and now…. Are you gay, or just trying it on for size?'

'I…I'm sorry, I thought…' Malcolm backed away.

'Thought what?' asked Neil, angrily. 'I'm gay, and must therefore fancy a shag? Sorry, but it doesn't work like that.'

'I know, I know. Look mate, big mistake, OK. I shouldn't have come onto you. Can we forget it?' He paused, then looked towards the door way. 'I'll get my stuff together.' Neil watched him go into the hallway, then stood, hands on hips staring at the floor for a moment, before walking through into the living room.

'Look,' he said, his anger dissipating, 'just sit down a minute. I think you need to talk about this.' Neil sat on the sofa, while Malcolm put his guitar into its case. 'Come on,' said Neil. 'Help me understand.' Malcolm sat on the chair opposite, nervously clenching and unclenching his fists.

'How long have you known you're gay?' Neil asked. 'I mean, you certainly hid it well to start with. A few weeks ago you didn't have a chip on your shoulder, more a bloody great log. You were so full of anger, most of it directed at me.'

Malcolm gave a big sigh then looked at Neil. 'I guess I've been in denial, although looking back I've realised there were times when I had feelings for blokes. But in the bleeding army you do not give the game away, believe me. I gradually became more and more aggressive and angry, and people avoided me. Adjusting to Civvy Street has been really sodding difficult, and I was in a real mess a couple of months ago. One or two mates suggested I needed counselling for PTSD, so I went along. I still go and it's helped. But in the last few weeks…Do you know, watching you…. Seeing how you talk to people, how you handle young Daniel, how comfortable you seem to be with yourself, that's how I want to be. One thing the therapist has helped me to realise is that my issues were as much to do with my reluctance to admit my sexuality. And the way I behaved towards you I realise now was unforgiveable, but in a twisted sort of way, it was because I was attracted to you.'

'But you couldn't admit it to yourself. Or anyone else.'

'Exactly. Spot on. But I thought I was coming to terms with it, then I make a complete cock-up today. If you'll excuse the pun.' They were both silent for a minute or so.

'What I would say, Malc, is two things. First, don't assume all gay blokes fancy every other gay bloke. There will have been gay soldiers around you that you wouldn't have fancied for instance. Believe me, by the law of averages, there must have been. I don't fancy you. I don't mean that disrespectfully. You're just not my type. But now I know you're gay, I can help. Which brings me to the other point. There is a gay community in Leicester. There are places you can go to meet other gay blokes, which I can tell you about, then who knows. There are also dating agencies.'

'You see,' said Malcolm. 'That's just the point I was chuffing well trying to make. You are so bloody understanding and… I wish I could be. But look, going back to the music stuff we've been doing, we should try working together a bit more. You've got some good ideas, and today has been really creative. And I promise to stick to the music.'

Neil pointed out that there would be no other option.

The next time they were together was in the company of Phil and Stan, to assist in converting the mobile classroom into an improvised studio for Daniel. Neil's relaxed attitude helped Malcolm to feel comfortable about the situation, and catching Phil's eye, Stan winked and gave a nod in the direction of the other two, to draw attention to the fact that they seemed to be working well together.

Stan mentioned that he had looked at a couple of studios and booked the one he preferred for a day's session in a few weeks time. The band had continued to meet weekly for practices, and on a couple of occasions squeezed in some playing time together over weekends, although the pattern of Tom's shifts meant there had to be some flexibility on the evenings. This in turn led to difficulties with using the hall. On Mandy's suggestion she and Stan went along to a pub in the suburb of Wigston to enjoy a drink, but also to sound out the landlord on the possibility of the band using his large function room for practices. The room was rarely used during the week, so he was happy to give them use rent free, provided they spent a reasonable amount at the bar and also, if the band was any good, they played a couple of gigs at the pub for no fee. Stan couldn't believe his luck, especially as the pub served his favourite beer.

Phil had manufactured a two-piece L-shaped Perspex screen, held together in an aluminium frame, which he produced on the first occasion they used the new venue. Behind this they placed a slightly embarrassed-looking Daniel and his percussion set. Unorthodox as it was, there was a collective feeling that this might give the band an identity, if not a uniqueness. It helped that they had agreed on *Leicester Rocks* as the band's name, liking the double meaning. The idea of putting a CD together was spurring them all on, and they were able to play most of the songs in their repertoire straight through with confidence.

During a break, Tom, who had taken a few minutes out to listen to the band with Mandy and Phil, waxed lyrical about the quality of the music and the distinctive sound created by the combination of Stan's voice with Neil and Malcolm's playing. He was quick to add that the rhythm section made all things possible. As was the case whenever they stopped to discuss the session, several offered suggestions for widening the band's repertoire. Stan wanted to add *Walking By Myself* to their repertoire. From a CD she'd brought along Angie played *Midnight in the Oasis*, which was greeted with some enthusiasm. The lyrics, she pointed out, were such that it had to be sung by a woman.

'Well we'd better chuffin' well go and find one that can sing,' joked Stan. She cuffed him gently across the head.

'Cheeky sod. You've heard me sing before now.' She strode purposefully up to the mic and sang the first verse of the song unaccompanied. There were smiles and murmurs of approval.

'Like I said, we'd better go and find a woman that can sing,' said Stan. 'Only kidding, duck. I knew you could belt it out,' he added as Angie protested. 'I'd forgotten you've got a half decent voice. What do you think Doc? Can we do that one?' Tom said that he would work on it as his next project, then turned the discussion to the idea that they try coming up with their own songs rather than just perform cover versions. He waved the manuscripts and CD that Malcolm had given him, mentioning that he also had one or two things in the pipeline, then looked to Stan for his approval that Tom work on the arrangements and bring these along in the next week or two.

'Yeah, go ahead,' Stan said, 'But let's get this studio session out of the way first and not get ahead of ourselves.'

Daniel had his first couple of lessons in what he had named his 'Ginger Baker room', reflecting the fact that he was able to retreat to the room at lunch and break times and practise

Ginger Baker solos that he had seen and listened to several times on YouTube. Phil took the opportunity of an early end to the day's 'winderin' to meet Daniel at the school gates one afternoon.

'Yes, I'm sort of enjoying the lessons,' said Daniel in response to Phil's question, as they walked side by side. 'But I think Jonathon, the teacher is a bit surprised how good I am, and he might not be able to teach me very much. He has shown me how to hold the sticks and brushes in a more relaxed way though. Oh and how to position the drums and cymbals in a way that helps me play solos. The trouble is that some of the kids are being horrible to me, calling me 'a gimp', saying I'm getting preferential treatment and that they don't believe me when I say I play in a band.'

'We need to put a stop to that, me old. Your Mum should go in and tell your teacher, or tutor, whatever you call her.'

'No, I don't want my Mum to do that. It's telling tales, and I don't think you should tell tales.'

'OK. Any better ideas?'

'Well, I was thinking. What if we made a video recording that I could show them? Or maybe even post it on YouTube.'

'You'd have to ask Stan and the others, me old. They might not be ready for doing a video yet.' He was thoughtful for a couple of minutes as they walked. 'We could invite them to a practice, so they can chuffin' well see for themselves.' He stopped walking and looked at Daniel. 'Better still, we could take the practice to them. Hold it in school and let anyone that wants to come along.'

Phil had two obstacles to overcome to bring this idea to fruition. Persuading the band wasn't a problem, once he had explained the reason behind it. Stan had already indicated that he was happy for the band to play at the school. Tom enthused that as well as it being good experience for them all, they could use it as a practice for the studio session. The main difficulty for Phil would be having to deal with the school's 'bleeding red tape'. Ruth Jones sounded only too pleased to have to pass Phil on to the academy's bursar, who dealt with event bookings. After going through the booking and charging policies, the bursar was surprisingly sympathetic towards the idea of the band playing at the academy. There was just one date available in the run up to Christmas. This was for the smaller of the two halls, which could seat about one hundred and fifty. Phil had no idea how many would want to come along, but he reasoned that the kids would want to stand anyway, so if pushed came to shove, so to speak, they could fit more in.

With just a few practice nights to come before the band's first performance in front of an audience, Daniel hijacked the first of these by insisting that the band learned to play Cream's classic, *Crossroads*, so that he could play a Ginger Baker solo in front of the students. Stan quickly nipped the initial protests in the bud, saying they would give it a whirl for half an hour and see how they got on.

'Angie knows this one well, don't you duck,' he said, referring to the first time he had heard her playing at the music shop. Daniel proudly handed out the sheet music, then played the track on a CD player. Tom's keyboard wasn't needed so he was able to put together an arrangement as they went along. Angie picked up the bass part and Stan sang the lyrics and played rhythm guitar from the sheet music. Malcolm knew the song and guitar part well, so could improvise a solo, as could Neil on his violin. Thirty minutes became forty-five, at which point it was agreed that they would all work on the piece before the next rehearsal. They still hadn't heard Daniel's solo, but this didn't worry Daniel.

For the rest of the session the band focussed on the songs in their repertoire which they felt least confident about.

As they began to pack instruments away, Tom asked for a few more minutes to work on one more piece. He felt that the band had ten songs ready or almost ready to perform, eleven if they managed to pull off Crossroads. He had a suggestion for a possible twelfth, and proceeded to play a CD on which there was an arrangement of Malcolm's song, *First Impressions*. It was for the vocals and three instruments, keyboard, acoustic guitar and violin.

'It's a great arrangement, Tom,' said Malcolm. 'And yeah, we should do it sometime. But I don't think it's right for this gig. It's…I don't know how to express it.'

'Maybe it's a bit lovey-dovey,' said Neil, 'and I think Malc's right. His other one, what's it called? *We're All In this Together* would work much better. It's topical, and it moves along faster. The kids would love it.'

'The other thing is,' said Stan, 'that my chuffin' brain is hurting from learning all these songs. I don't know if I have the sodding space for another, especially one with big words. And with not many practice nights left, it's just pushing it a bit too far. But,' he added, 'if someone can send me the words and music, I'll see what I can do. After all, we are all in this frigging thing together.'

There were groans all round.

## Phil

Who was it said 'I love it when a plan comes together'? Might have been Winston Churchill. Or was it Hannibal in *The A Team*? The lad has practically got his own studio. If I had any money left I'd splash out on some recording equipment. All he wants to talk about at the moment is music and percussion. He's near boring the chuffin' pants off me. Still, it's great to see him walking around with a smile on his face.

## Stan

What made me say I'd got my own chuffin' song in the pipeline?
I have no such thing. It just feels like things are getting a
bit out of control. On the other hand it's great that there is
suddenly all this chuffin' creativity going on, all these ideas
flying around. Then Angie friggin' well caps it all by showing
off her bleeding voice. Just beautiful. And Malcolm doing the
Eric Clapton stuff on *Crossroads* almost like Eric was in the
bleeding room. I could become just a chuffin' bit part in my
own band, the way things are going.

# Nineteen

# Listen to Your Heart

Stan stood poised at the driver's side door, ready to take the van and equipment over to Daniel's school for the band's first gig. Phil was to meet him there to set up for the evening. He looked across to Mandy, who asked if he was feeling alright, as he looked 'a bit grey around the gills'. He admitted to feeling tired and asked her to drive.

'Look at me, Big Man,' she said before starting the engine. 'What's going on? You don't look too good.'

He told her about the pain and tightness across his chest, as if there was a bar there. He'd felt the same pain when he got out of bed that morning, but thought nothing of it. At some point it had worn off. He'd done his usual press ups and weight exercises after his breakfast. He had just become aware of it again.

'Bring him in. The doctor wants to run one or two tests on him,' was the response to her request for advice on what to do about a fifty-five year old man experiencing chest pains. Five minutes later they were back in the van, heading for his GP's surgery. 'Right, let's get you looked at,' Mandy said as they drove off.

He was seen by a doctor straight away. Stethoscope to Stan's chest, the doctor asked if he had ever been told about his heart murmur. Stan hadn't, but then again he couldn't remember when anyone had last listened to his heart.

Stan was ushered into a nearby room where a nurse stuck pads to various parts of his body. A wire connected each pad to a machine. The ECG test indicated that Stan had experienced a 'cardiac event'. Stan waited for an explanation. Instead, the doctor asked whether Stan had experienced any breathlessness, or any other pains. At this point recent events fitted into place in Stan's mind. The near black-out weeks earlier at the boys' football match; the times he had quickly become breathless when running along the touchline or carrying his ladder up hilly roads; the state of near-collapse he had reached two weekends ago after mixing the concrete for the base on which Phil would erect his decking; and the pain up his left arm he had felt yesterday. The previous evening he had helped Phil to load and unload the lengths of decking from the roof of the van, and he thought he must have stretched a muscle. He had read somewhere that heart attacks were often preceded by pains in the left arm.

In the car park, Stan swore loudly. Then, tears welling in his eyes, he phoned Phil.

'Look, me old. I might not be able to make the chuffing gig tonight. Apparently I have a dicky ticker, and, uh, they want me to see a specialist in the cardiac unit at the hospital.' He couldn't believe he had just uttered those words, and Phil told him to 'stop pissing about.' After a short silence he realised that Stan was actually not pissing about. Stan did his best to explain the events of the last hour, then said he would call when he had anything to tell Phil. But it was looking possible that the gig would have to be called off. The ensuing long silence said it all.

'Alright mate,' was all Phil could manage to say.

At the hospital an hour later Stan was told that he was being admitted for further tests, after a consultant, who had introduced herself as Val examined him and explained that his heart displayed all the signs of aortic stenosis.

'In plain English please, duck,' he said.

'Your heart has two valves which control the flow of blood. One of yours, Mr Booker, appears to be damaged, which is why you were feeling ill, so we need to find a bed for you in an observation ward for a couple of days, while we carry out one or two more tests, and give you some medication to settle things down.'

'So I could be out for the weekend?'

'We'll just have to wait and see.'

Stan was left to undress and change into a flimsy green open-backed gown. There was a wall mirror in the room, in which he admired his new apparel.

'Cheeky little number,' he said when he saw the rear view. 'I bet they get these as a job lot from Marks and Spencers.'

Mandy went to fetch a change of clothes and some essentials, also to put Phil and the band members in the picture. Feeling embarrassed and exposed in the gown, Stan was wheeled by an orderly through a maze of corridors to the ward. Sitting on the centre bed on one side of the bay of six, he surveyed his new companions. Two were reading, another watching the TV suspended on a metal arm attached to the wall behind his bed. A fourth was complaining to a woman Stan guessed to be a visitor that he was gasping for a cigarette, but the nurses had taken his from him. On Stan's right, an elderly man lay asleep, snoring gently with saliva dribbling from his open mouth.

'That's George,' said the patient in the bed opposite, as he put his book down and placed his spectacles on the bedside locker. 'He's off his trolley. That is when he's awake. What have they got you in for then, duck?'

'Dicky ticker, apparently.'

'Well that's what we're all in here for.' He gesticulated at the other patients in the side ward. 'This *is* the cardiac unit, after all. Anything specific?'

'Not yet,' replied Stan. 'They need to do tests and that.'

'They're pretty good here. Myself, I had a triple bypass three months ago,' said the man proudly, 'but things haven't settled down yet. They'll be moving me to the surgical ward in a bit.' Stan's eyes glazed over as the man continued to give a blow-by-blow, day-by-day account of his medical history. He had already nick-named the man as TBP. Stan nodded politely from time to time, as he tried to picture how Neil, Tom, Malcolm, Angie and Daniel had received the news about his illness. 'Well pissed off, probably,' he thought.

TBP eventually returned to his book. Stan exchanged pleasantries and names with the other occupiers of the side ward, except for George, still snoring. Gary, very tanned and obese, sitting topless on his bed, warned him about the dangers of becoming institutionalised. Sadiq, who had several family photographs squeezed onto his small locker, complained about the poor quality of the food. And Perry, wearing a red dressing gown and matching cravat (Posh Boy, thought Stan), removed the TV headphones and moaned about the cost of parking, although some of the nurses, he said, were *a bit of all right*. Stan then occupied his time trying to understand how the hospital's TV, phone and internet packages worked.

'Chuffin' Nora,' he said out loud to no one in particular when he saw the menu of prices.

'What, complaining already?' asked Mandy, as she placed a holdall on his bed. 'Well I hope these are alright for you.' She held up a bag from a shop on the Fosse Road he knew well. 'Jim-jams. Two pairs, cos I know you haven't got any to your name. Right trendy too.' She started to close the curtains around his bed. 'I just hope they're big enough. Let's get a pair on you so that people can stop peeking at your hairy arse.'

'Good thinking. It's a good job we've got these curtains,' said Stan as he removed the flimsy green garment and unwrapped one pair of pyjamas, 'otherwise everyone would be able to hear us. The last time I wore a pair of these, I was a kid. I remember there was a hole for getting your todger out when you needed a pee. Where is it in these?' He was standing in the trouser part.

'I'm sure you can work something out,' said Mandy. She pulled out his dressing gown from the holdall and tossed it to him.

'Hallo,' came a woman's voice from the other side of the curtain. 'Is it safe to come in?'

'Depends, duck,' replied Stan, 'on who it is and what you want. If it's my body, you'd better join the queue.'

'Ignore him,' said Mandy as she pulled the curtain back. 'Fancies himself as a bit of a Cassanova. But just in case, his body is spoken for.'

The woman, tall and thin, and wearing a yellow uniform, blushed, and said that she hadn't heard of Cassa-whatever-it-is, but was sure it was very nice. After introducing herself as Nora, she went on to explain how the meal system operated, and that as Stan hadn't been there at lunchtime to pre-order his evening meal, he would have to take pot luck. The choice was chicken curry, fish and chips or vegetable lasagne, followed by fruit or yoghurt.

'Any of those, or even all three would do me,' said Stan.

'It doesn't matter,' said Sadiq, 'they all taste the same.' The woman admonished him, disappeared briefly, returning with the tea trolley.

Mandy and Stan sat quietly, sipping their teas.

'This is a bloody turn up,' Stan said, quietly. 'I keep pinching myself to check this is really happening. I've no chuffin' idea really what the problem is, this aortic thing, or what they'll have to do to me, and I haven't seen a doctor or nurse since they wheeled me in here. All these blokes seem to have something or other wrong with their ticker. Mr TBP over there, for instance, had his chest opened up a couple of months ago for a bypass op, and he's still not sorted properly. God knows how this is going to pan out.' He looked searchingly at Mandy.

'I suspect, Stan, that they'll do a few tests, put you on medication then send you home in a couple of days. No one is talking about surgery, as far as I can see. So cheer up, Big Man. This place has a really good reputation. I'm sure they'll look after you. I should enjoy a couple of days of being pampered and you'll be home for the weekend.'

'That's what they said about the First World War. Look what happened there.'

'It was Christmas, actually.'

'What was?'

'At the start of the war, everyone was saying the soldiers would be home by Christmas. You can hardly compare your situation with the outbreak of war. For goodness sake, Stan, keep it in perspective. You're going to be alright.'

Mandy stayed with Stan through the evening meal, and for an hour or so afterwards. Stan thought the plate of fish and chips which Nora produced was passable. When he asked if he could have some more chips Nora was taken slightly aback, as no one had ever asked for more of anything in the seven years she had been serving food at the hospital. She did manage to bring him some more though.

Shortly after the meal a nurse appeared in the sideward, pushing a trolley containing a variety of jars. Her first stop was at George's bed.

'What have we got here then, duck?' Stan called. 'After-dinner mints? It looks like we get a choice. Myself, I prefer those square ones covered in dark chocolate.'

'Sorry, duck, but last time I looked there weren't any mints on here. I have got a few treats for you though, if you can manage to hold on for just a couple of minutes.' She exchanged a few words with George as he swallowed a succession of tablets which she administered.

'Now, duck,' she said to Stan as she picked up the clipboard at the end of his bed, 'Can you confirm your name and date of birth.'

'What, again? Can't someone just write it down, so that you don't have to keep asking me? Booker, May the eighteenth , 1961.'

'Thank you, duck. It's just our way of checking that we have the right patient in front of us. Doctor has prescribed some medication for you.' She laid out five different tablets on his tray.

'Well that's chuffin' news to me. And what doctor? I haven't seen one since accident and emergency this afternoon. No one has said owt about any medication.'

'Well, these have been prescribed for you, believe me. This one is a simvastatin, this one a beta-blocker, and….'

'Hold on a chuffin' minute. Do I have to take these?'

'Well, we can't force you to take them, Mister Booker, but as you have a heart condition the doctor has prescribed these. I would strongly recommend that you take them. Would you like me to ask the staff nurse to come and talk to you?'

'I just want to know exactly why I'm in here. Exactly what is wrong with me. You know. Someone to tell me.'

'All I can say is that the doctor doing the rounds in the morning will hopefully be able to tell you.' Hands on hips, she waited for a response from Stan.

Mandy broke the silence. 'Come on Stan, don't be so arsy. The nurse has lots of other patients to see. Take the tablets, and talk to the doctor tomorrow.'

Stan gave a sigh of exasperation. 'Give us that water, duck. Sorry, I'm not trying to be awkward. It's just all happened a bit quick, like. Know what I mean?' He swallowed the tablets, then turned down the offer of some medication later to help him sleep.

At this point Mandy told him that everyone in the band passed on their very best wishes and promised to visit him as soon as they could. Phil had told them that the gig would have to be cancelled. At first they had all accepted this, but after a few emails and calls to each other they had decided they would like to go ahead with the gig, in honour of Stan, as long as he gave his blessing. They reckoned that between them, and with a bit of help from Mandy, they knew the lyrics well enough to perform seven or eight of their songs.

'What do you mean, with a bit of help from you?'

'They've asked me to do the vocals on a couple.'

Stan closed his eyes and gently rubbed them with the thumb and middle finger of his right hand. Just a few hours ago he was on the verge of playing in his own band in front of an audience for the first time. Now he wondered if it would ever happen. His head was in a spin, with thoughts and images fading as quickly as they appeared. He imagined that he had been, maybe still was close to death. Then, that after some sort of surgery, he was never able to regain the strength to play and sing well again. On the other hand, he could see that he might make a full recovery and be fitter and stronger than he had been in the last few weeks.

Sensing the state of mind he was in, Mandy sat next to him, putting her arm around him.

'I'm sorry, Big Man.' Maybe it's not such a good idea. If you're not OK with it, that's fine.'

Reminding himself that he did not indulge in self-pity, Stan attempted to pull himself together. He gave her a big smile, hoping it looked genuine.

'Of course I am, duck. I'm chuffed to bits that they all want to go ahead tonight, so you'd better get your frigging skates on and get over there.' He reached out to stroke her cheek. He added quietly, 'just one thing though, Mandy. Well, two.'

'Yes?'

'I love you. And….' Mandy waited. 'Just don't sing so friggin' well that I can't get back into my own chuffin' band.' She laughed and hugged him tightly, saying that there was no way she could replace him, nor did anyone want her to. Stan's declaration of love had taken Mandy by surprise. Not knowing what else to say, she kissed him on the forehead, put her hand on his cheek, stood and walked away.

## *Stan*

Just shows, you never know what's around the chuffin' corner. Phil and his missus had both been saying I looked tired and drawn recently, and I noticed I'd lost a couple of pounds. Plus getting out of puff now and again, like at the kids' football. I just said to myself I'm nearing sixty and I'm not as fit as I was. I'd got on the weights, done a bit of jogging, even went swimming a couple of times, but I were still getting out of puff, not feeling any fitter.

The last time I were in hospital it were to have my appendix out. I was sixteen or seventeen. I'd been puking and crapping all night, and Ma had to phone for a doctor. This bloke, a locum, said it was probably gastric enteritis, and I should go to see my GP in the morning. A fat lot of good he was. Ma said I'd got appendicitis. She'd been watching this TV series *The Body in Question* and that week it had been about appendicitis. She reckoned my symptoms were just what they'd been talking about. She got the GP out and I nearly hit the ceiling when he touched the tender spot on my belly.

I were took to the Royal Infirmary, which is where in fact I were born. The junior doctor who put his finger up my arse to check it out couldn't have been much older than me. He did have his gloves on. When the consultant came along with his chuffin' entourage the next day, he explained that the young doctor had done the op and sewn me up, and were dead chuffed about the neat job he'd done. Which to be fair, it was. I struggle to find any sign of a scar these days. God bless the NHS.

## *Phil*

It were Daniel really. He went ballistic when I told him Stan was ill and we'd have to cancel. All the toys went out of the pram. I calmed him down eventually and said I'd talk to the others. He were obviously totally focussed on playing in front of the other kids at the school, so couldn't deal with anything else. Tom and the others were great. Stan would want us to do it, a couple of them said.

# Twenty

# We're All in
This Together

Christmas shoppers were out in force, Leicester City were playing at home, and it felt to Mandy that the city centre had become grid-locked. The traffic on the ring road had been moving at a snail's pace for a good twenty minutes and she began to panic that she would be late for the gig. Things were better on Abbey Lane and the Loughborough Road, but the next problem was finding a parking space at the school. Vehicles were being parked on the grass verge on the long driveway, the car park evidently full. She found a space for her Mini under a lamp post attached to which was a poster advertising the band's performance that evening. Head down into the wind and drizzle, Mandy scuttled along the pavement, weaving in and out of the students who she hoped were on their way to see the band.

The hall was beginning to fill as she walked in, passing through a group of adults on the door, who she assumed were members of staff. A few spotlights lit up the stage. Guitars waited on stands, the percussion set towards the back and behind the plastic screen. She found the band members in conference in a small room behind the stage, concerned faces turning towards her as she gave her apologies

'Great! You've made it,' said Angie. 'How is Stan? And is he OK about us playing without him?'

Mandy reassured them all that Stan was fine about it, then gave them a resumé of his first few hours in hospital.

'Worse things have happened at sea, as they say. And the Big Man wants us to enjoy ourselves, so let's do that shall we.' She could sense there was some sort of undercurrent. 'Everything alright otherwise?' she asked.

Neil explained that Daniel had been a bit concerned about the change in the line-up, which Mandy read as an understatement.

'But we've talked it through, haven't we mate, and we're going to be fine, especially as none of the arrangements will need to change much. We're going to miss Stan, of course, but Malcolm will pick up on Stan's solos. Are we OK about all this Danny?' Daniel nodded, to no one in particular.

They spent a few minutes talking through the set, which they would play straight through without a break. They agreed to have a bash at either *Crossroads* or *Midnight in the Oasis* as a finale, depending on which one felt right for the moment and provided things had gone reasonably well.

Tom would act as band leader, and they were to look to him as usual for the nod if unsure where to come in. Having poked his head around the back curtain of the stage, Malcolm reported that the hall looked pretty full. They realised that no arrangements had been made for them to be announced. Neil did a final tuning of his violin, there were some nervous high fives, and they were ready. Well, nearly.

'You know, these kids won't have heard any of these,' said Malcolm. 'It's not what they listen to. They won't mean a thing to them.'

'Well let's take the view that we're extending their musical education,' said Angie. 'Plus it's a live performance, which some of them will never have seen. So let's just enjoy it, shall we.'

It took a few seconds for the audience to register that the band were walking on to the stage. The ripple of applause grew, then as Daniel appeared, looking very sheepish, there was loud cheering and whistling. Daniel gave a hint of a wave, before making his way to his set behind the screen. Malcolm and Angie picked up their guitars, Malcolm taking centre stage. Mandy sat on a chair to one side, ready to join them after the first number.

'Hi everyone,' said Tom from the front of the stage, struggling to be heard above the continuing cheering. 'Welcome to the world premiere performance by Leicester Rocks.' He raised one hand as if to ask for quiet, and the noise abated.

'Unfortunately, our leader, Stan, can't be with us tonight, as he was taken ill this afternoon. So our performance is dedicated to the big man. I'm sure you'll join us in wishing him a speedy recovery. We're going to kick off with one of his favourites, a Gary Moore song, *Moving On*.' He took his place at the keyboard, then gave Daniel the nod to count them in with four taps of his drumsticks. Daniel himself came in right on cue, but nothing else happened. There were mystified looks from the others towards Tom, who quickly realised that they couldn't hear Daniel's count in above the noise.

'OK, on my count,' said Tom. They came in well enough to get away with it and were up and running. Malcolm was confident with the vocals, and everyone relaxed into the song. As the evening progressed, the applause was appreciative rather than rapturous. There were raised eyebrows and sighs of relief from the band members as each number came to an end, despite Tom's best efforts to gee them up. There was an element of uncertainty in some of their playing, which led to a collective feeling that they were going through the motions. Some students stood from time to time to capture photographs or video clips on their smart phones, but towards the end it was noticeable that many were becoming more focussed on their phones than what was happening on the stage.

Tom brought some bounce into '*Don't Get Around Much Anymore*', but this was enjoyed more by the band than the audience.

'OK,' he called to them. '*Midnight at the Oasis?*'

'Why not?' said Neil. 'Danny, are you up for it?' Daniel nodded vigorously. Tom announced that this would be their final song, before introducing the band members. There was light applause until he came to 'the one and only Danny Wilson', which brought much whooping and whistling, and a self-conscious smile from Danny.

*Midnight at the Oasis* was the one song which lent itself to dancing, and very soon twenty or so students were on their feet moving to the music. Solos from Tom, Malcolm and Neil went down well, but the best was yet to come. Neil gave way to Danny, who launched into almost ten minutes of a controlled percussion performance. The band members all walked off the stage to leave Danny well and truly in the spotlight. They could soon see that everyone on the floor was captivated. Danny was so focussed on his playing that he didn't notice that from halfway through, everyone in the audience was on their feet clapping. One by one the band members re-joined him for a repeat of the first verse, and he brought them in with impeccable timing.

Neil managed to coax Danny out from behind his screen.

'Come on mate, they want a proper look at you. You absolutely killed them with that. Great work.' Danny didn't move very far from the safety of the screen, but gave a hint of a smile and the shortest of waves in acknowledgement of the applause.

Backstage, he wouldn't be hugged but he did accept handshakes form the others, who were gushing with their praise. Tom summed it up.

'Danny, I reckon you saved the day for us tonight. That was just such a good performance, and the kids loved it. We were pretty average for much of tonight, but you've given them all something to talk about and remember, including your teachers.'

Malcolm turned from the bar and looked around. Mixed and same sex couples and groups sat in the booths or stood near the bar. Most were in their twenties or thirties but some looked older. There was a bit too much metal in noses and lips for his liking. He approved of the décor and furniture, which gave the pub a modern look. He recognised the Shaun Escoffery track playing.

'Just like any other pub, really,' he said.

'Well what did you expect?' replied Neil. 'The owners are normal, the staff are normal, the customers are normal. It's a gay-friendly pub. So what? Get that down your neck.' He handed Malcolm a pint of bitter.

As they walked out of the school hall, he had offered to buy Malcolm a drink at the city-centre pub, and to introduce him to one or two of his friends if they were around.

'I need a pint after that. Not my best playing,' Malcolm had said.

'Young Danny rescued us tonight. He's some talent.'

Now as they sipped their drinks, Neil drew Malcolm's attention to an email from Danny. It included a link to a Facebook posting by one of the students from his school, showing a video of Danny's solo. Moving to a relatively quiet corner, they watched it.

'Shit. Look at that,' said Neil. 'Over five hundred hits already. I wonder what he'll make if that.'

Neil knew a few people dotted around the main bar. He introduced Malcolm as they circulated. While getting in another round of drinks at the bar, Neil turned to see that Malcolm had joined a group he vaguely recognised but didn't really know. One of the group seemed to be hanging on every word of Malcolm's. He continued to watch, not taking the drinks over straight away. From Malcolm's gesticulations, Neil guessed that he was talking about his Afghanistan experience.

He squeezed his way across to the table and set Malcolm's drink down.

'Malc, mate, I've got to be up early for work, so I'll get mine down and shoot off, if that's OK.'

'Me too, mate, but I'll hang around a bit longer.' He introduced Jez, sitting next to him, who shook hands with Neil.

'Pleased to meet you,' said Neil. He didn't add *I've heard all about you. Just watch your step.*

'The pleasures all mine,' came the reply.

## *Phil*

The thing that struck me as the band was playing, was how many kids were on their chuffin' mobile phones. All the bloody time. Not phoning or owt, just fiddling with them. Tapping at them with their fingers, heads down. Fair enough, some took photos or videos. Angie explained it was FOMO. Fear of missing out, she said. Of what, I asked. Stuff like Facebook, what their mates are up to and that. Gordon Bennett. Sad gits. They'll see their mates the next day probably.

They might have been looking at photos as well, she said. Ones they'd just taken themselves, or had been posted on friggin' Facebook. A video of Daniel bashing away on that last number is on Facebook apparently, and has gone viral. I'm catching up with the lingo.

## Stan

Mandy showed me the video of *Midnight* and Danny boy's solo. The mobile phone doesn't really do it justice, but you could tell he was pretty amazing. The rest of the band sounded together as well. I didn't know what to feel really. Mandy reckoned they were OK, good in patches. She might have been under-playing it to keep me happy. Was I hoping deep down that they'd have been totally crap without me? I wouldn't admit it if I was.

# Twenty-One

# Now is the
# Cool of the Day

It wasn't until Friday evening, two days after being admitted into hospital that Stan was able to have a conversation with a doctor who told him the exact nature of his illness. The consultant had had to cancel his rounds of the ward two days running. Stan had been examined by another doctor on Thursday afternoon, who also used the term aortic stenosis for Stan's condition. She explained that in order to establish the seriousness of the situation she would arrange for an ultra-sound scan of his heart to be carried out that afternoon. Stan was in fact wheeled down to the diagnostic scanning unit twenty four hours later. It wasn't until he and Mandy went to see the staff nurse on the ward to explain their frustration about the fact that more than forty-eight hours after being admitted, no one had yet explained to Stan what exactly was wrong with his heart. He didn't want to have to wait until Monday.

'You're right, Mr Booker. You should have had a proper diagnosis from a doctor by now,' he said. I'll find someone.' Someone turned out to be a very attractive woman in a blue outfit which Stan had realised was worn by the doctors. Mandy watched Stan's face, seeing his jaw almost hit his chest as the woman approached.

'Mr Booker? Hallo, my name's Rachel and I'm the registrar for Mr James, who you'll meet on Monday morning.' There were handshakes as Stan introduced Mandy. Rachel produced the envelope containing the result of the earlier scan.

'I must apologise. You really should have been seen by someone before now.' She removed the scan result from the envelope. 'I've had a good look at this. Shall we all sit down?' She pulled a chair over from the adjacent empty bed and pulled the curtain screen around Stan's bed.

'I don't know how much you know about the heart and how it works, but I've brought this model of the heart, which might be helpful.' She pointed out the four chambers of the heart and the valves allowing blood to flow between them, explaining how they needed to open and close fully to allow blood to circulate properly. 'In your case, this valve here, the aortic valve is damaged and isn't opening properly after blood has been pumped through it, so some of the blood leaks back this way. So when we listen to your heart beat, we hear this leaking as what we call a murmur. Also the valve is narrowed, which is what the term stenosis means. Am I making any sense?' Stan and Mandy both nodded slowly, but with a look of puzzlement.

'So what can you do about it? Anything?' asked Stan.

'So. In your case the valve is very badly damaged and needs replacing. You're going to need surgery quite soon. We'll be able to take out the damaged valve and replace it with a new one.'

There was a pause. 'So what does that involve?' asked Mandy. 'Keyhole surgery?'

'No duck,' said Stan. 'I think she's talking about opening me up.'

'Yes, it will be open heart surgery.' She let this sink in for a moment. 'I'm sorry,' she added. 'But it's not as drastic as it sounds. The success rate is very high.'

Stan and Mandy looked at each other, both thinking about the likely implications.

'What I want to know is, does the food get any better and do I get to be washed and bathed by one of them lovely nurses?'

Rachel smiled then explained that Mr James, the consultant would say more about the procedure and timescale when he saw Stan on Monday morning. The medication Stan was on will have stabilised the situation. In the meantime, she would now arrange for Stan to be moved up to one of the cardiac wards, where he would be well looked after. But she couldn't make any promises about the food or the nurses bathing him.

Stan and Mandy sat in contemplative silence for a few minutes.

'Well, that's that then,' said Stan. 'Phil won't be able to do the chuffin' winderin' on his own, and the band'll be up the spout. But never mind! It'll soon be Christmas.'

'Now you stop that, mister glass-half-empty. That's not like you. And what makes you think you're so bloody indispensable?' She put her hand on his. 'Things will be fine Stan, you'll see.'

Stan mentioned that he was worried about his mother. He had tried to phone her a few times, but she hadn't answered his calls. Mandy told Stan that Audrey had a nasty cold and thought she should stay away from the hospital. But she had sent her love.

'Could you keep an eye on her for me, duck. Ask her to call me when she's up to it. She was a bit anxious, like, about this scan she's lined up for.'

They were interrupted by an orderly pushing a wheelchair into Stan's bay. When Stan insisted he could walk to the cardiac ward, the orderly told him that from now on he would be treated like royalty and be wheeled everywhere.

Later that evening, Stan met Harry, another patient in the six-bed bay, who helped Stan sort out the complexities of the TV and communication consul. They exchanged medical histories, Harry having been admitted after a two month wait for a mitral valve replacement, which was due to take place in a few days' time. In the morning they both flirted and enjoyed the banter with the team of women who changed their bed linen and brought breakfast. Having been invited by Harry to join him for elevenses in the hospital's coffee shop, Stan had to rest a couple of times on the way, feeling weak and breathless. Harry waited patiently until Stan was able to continue. They took their coffees to a table in an open area, from which they could see the reception desk, shop and café entrances. Harry commented on the high number of obese people who were toing and froing.

'It's always like this,' he said. 'And it's not just patients and visitors. Just look at some of the nurses.' Stan had to agree that there were a fair few people carrying a lot of excess flesh. He wondered out loud how some of the nurses would be able to react quickly if there was an emergency. He couldn't imagine some of them being able to run. Harry reached for a newspaper which had been left on the adjacent table. He gave a short laugh and showed Stan the headline.

## NHS CHIEF TELLS STAFF: JOIN A GYM

'Get this,' said Stan, pointing to a couple of women who he suggested could be mother and daughter. They were setting food down on a table just outside the entrance to the café. The elder of the two was in a wheelchair, and was reaching out for plates being passed to her by the younger woman, who retreated to the café interior, returning with another tray full of plates stacked high with food. When both were finally seated at the table, each had three plates in front of her, one of chips, another of pasta, the third of garlic bread. Both women were comfortably over thirty stone, suggested Harry.

'The one in the wheelchair must have been hoisted into it. I can't see how else she'd have got into it. What the hell is the café in a hospital doing serving this kind of food to people who are already obese? And it looks like they're expecting someone to join them, judging by the three plates at the side of them.'

They watched with fascination as the two women raced their way through their three plates of carbohydrates, then turned their attention to the other three plates, sharing the contents.'

'Oh my God,' said Harry. 'I don't believe it.'

'Chuffin' Nora. And it's not even eleven o'clock,' said Stan. 'What do you suppose they'll have for their main course?'

'More of the same probably. Or rice, followed by bread and butter pudding. I'm sorry Stan,' Harry continued. 'This is a bit of a hobby horse of mine. If you want to see fat people, go into a hospital, where they can buy junk food and sugary drinks. The hospital should put up a banner outside the café: FOOD FOR FATTIES. FEED YOUR ILLNESS.' He turned to face Stan. 'That's enough of that. What shall we talk about to cheer ourselves up?'

Music provided some common ground, although their interests differed. Harry was a few years older than Stan, and as a teenager his listening centred on the Beatles and Rolling Stones. They both enthused about the rock scene of the late sixties and seventies, but Harry's eclectic taste embraced jazz and classical music. More recently he had been listening increasingly to folk music.

'And,' he added, pausing for effect, to make sure Stan was listening, 'I'm a Morris Dancer.'

Stan spluttered into his coffee.

'Sorry,' he said. 'The coffee's chuffin' hot.'

'It's alright. I'm used to that sort of reaction, especially from friends and family.'

Stan then made the mistake of asking Harry to tell him about Morris dancing, confessing he knew next to nothing about it. Harry gave him a brief history of his village's team, then went on to describe the different dancing traditions. Stan made a pretence of listening, eyes slowly glazing over, until Harry began to talk about the music. The musicians accompanying Harry's team played accordions, melodeons, a violin and saxophone, a combination which intrigued Stan. He told Harry about his band, explaining that he was always looking for new ideas. They agreed to share their interests in music over the rest of the weekend.

They arrived back on the ward just as the lunch trolleys were being wheeled in.

'It's chuffin' Nora,' said Stan by way of hallo. 'Sorry duck. I've been saving that one up in case I saw you again. The nosh looks good.'

'And it's Mr chuffin' Cassanova. I sometimes do this ward as well. Enjoy your lunch, duck.' She placed his soup, sandwiches and pear on his tray. Stan sipped a couple of spoonsful of the soup, unable to recognise any definable tastes.

After the regulation nap between two and three o'clock Harry brought his iPad and iPod over to Stan. He proudly played a video clip on YouTube of his Morris team performing a couple of dances at a recent folk event. Stan couldn't stop himself laughing.

'I'm sorry,' he said, 'but I just had no idea what it would be like. I can't believe a bunch of old blokes would go round dancing, dressed like that and waving hankies at each other. No offence, duck. Each to his own, I guess. The musicians seem pretty good though.'

'The thing is though Stan, that if these old gits, and we're not all old gits if you look carefully, and we have a women's team by the way, if we don't go round dancing and playing these dances and music, they'll die out. They've been around for probably a couple of hundred years or more, and I think it's important we keep the traditional dances going. They're part of our heritage.'

'If you say so, duck.'

'Well that's what I think. And I'm not sure whether your punk rock and garage stuff will be remembered in two hundred years' time. Anyway Stan, keep an open mind on this stuff, especially the music. Good music takes its influences from lots from lots of things. I once heard someone say that all music can be folk music. It's all about the way it's presented.'

'Talking about which,' he added, 'I'd be interested if you've got any of the music you're banding is playing, on a CD for instance. And in return you can have a listen to the stuff I'm enjoying at the moment.'

Stan mentioned a DVD that the band had put together at a practice a couple of weeks previously, and would ask Mandy to bring one along for him. Stan's iPod did have a playlist of the band's current repertoire, which Harry was welcome to listen to.

As they exchanged iPods, Harry suggested some folk music for Stan to listen to. After a couple of tracks of one album, Stan called across to Harry to ask how he could get the music, as he could only hear singing. It's a cappella, came the reply, which didn't mean a thing to Stan. Just the voices in harmony, Harry explained. Stan flicked through the songs on the album.

'Roo dum dah, foddle riddle da, whack for me chuffin' riddle da,' said Stan quietly to himself, after listening to one track from beginning to end. He picked another, *Keep Your Distance*, at random from another album. Three men were singing in harmony, with clapping as the only accompaniment. He warmed to this and played it through a second time. He caught Harry's eye, giving him a smile and the thumbs up, to which Harry reciprocated, suggesting he was enjoying Stan's playlist. A second track, *Now is the Cool of the Day* also had minimal accompaniment, in the form of what sounded like a snare drum being tapped. Totally engrossed in the song, Stan hadn't noticed that the curtain had been drawn around his bed, or that there was someone standing by his side, until he felt a tap on his shoulder.

He unplugged the earphones then looked up to see a figure in blue scrubs and with a stethoscope around his neck.

'Sorry doc, I was well carried away.'

'Something worth listening to I hope, Mr Booker.'

'Oh, aye up Tom, I mean doc.' He sat up, smiling broadly, pleased to see Tom. 'Good to see you, mate. Fancy seeing you here. What's going on?' Then it dawned on Stan. 'Of course, this is where you do your stuff. Cardiac, and that.'

'Well yes, as luck would have it, Stan. Which means I can keep an eye on you. Are they looking after you? Everything up to your expectations?'

'So-so, on both fronts, I would say. No, that's not fair. It's definitely better on this ward, apart from the food. Not the world's best, shall we say. That Rachel, though, the blond doctor, is a bit special.'

'Ah, you've met the lovely Rachel. She's on the same team as me. We both have the same boss, and will probably be doing the rounds with the big man on Monday morning.' He had the clipboard with Stan's details under his arm. 'I see they've got you on a whole bunch of medication. Not sure you need many of these. I'll have a chat with Rachel and ask her to take a look. I shouldn't interfere. So come on. What were you so wrapped up in that you didn't notice me come in?'

Stan explained.

'Coope, Boyes and Simpson. Yeah, I've heard of them. They've won lots of stuff on the Radio Two Folk Awards. Can I have a listen?'

Stan suggested the two he had been listening to.

'Great harmonies.'

'That's what I think,' said Stan. 'I wouldn't have believed three blokes could make such a good sound without instruments to back them. It's got me wondering whether we can build some harmonies into our stuff.'

'Yeah, I've thought that, but I wouldn't know where to start in terms of the arrangements. We'd need someone who can put the harmonies together. To write them down as well. Anyway, food for thought. We might not be doing anything much for a while, till you're up and about.'

Tom asked if he could examine Stan, specifically to listen to his heart. He moved the stethoscope around Stan's chest for a minute or so, then sat back. He frowned, puffed his cheeks and breathed out of a corner of his mouth. He explained that these cases were seen on a regular basis on the ward, and Stan's was a real classis. The heart murmur was obvious, if you knew what to listen for. The scan showed the valve was in a poor state. What impressed Tom though was that to compensate for the gradual deterioration of the valve, the walls of the left ventricle have become thicker and stronger. With a new valve, he said, Stan would have a heart to die for, so to speak. Stan's worries were eased somewhat when Tom explained that this type of surgery was routine to the cardiac team, who had a very high success rate. He listened to Stan's chest again.

'To borrow one of your phrases, chuffin' Nora.'

'Well I'm so pleased that you're impressed,' said Stan, sarcastically. 'And talking of the devil, here is chuffin' Nora. Aye up duck.

Nora had drawn back the screen to reveal the lunch trolley. 'I hope you're behaving yourself, Mr Booker, or there's no lunch for you. The pasta is very tasty today.'

Tom took his leave, saying that he'd call in tomorrow and walk with Stan around the grounds if he felt up to it. Nora placed the pasta dish on Stan's tray, then watched, hands on hips, daring Stan to complain. Stan chewed with exaggeration, looking thoughtful.

'At least it's hot,' he said, then smiled at her. 'As, me duck, are you.' Nora blushed as she wheeled the trolley round. Stan was sure there was an extra wiggle or two in her walk as she moved away.

## Stan

What finally convinced me that things weren't right was the walk up to the café area with Harry. I felt weak and strange in a way I've never chuffin' felt before. What they do apparently, when they open you up, like, is take out this useless old valve and pop in a brand new all singing all dancing one. I had no chuffin' idea that this kind of stuff goes on. As Tom said, not too long ago people with this kind of problem would have died from it. When I told him my grandmother had died of a heart attack, he thought maybe she had the same issue as me. Or in my case it could have been congenital. I've been practising that word.

I'm dead glad that I met Harry. He's a character all right. Very knowledgeable about music. He was right when he says that there are so many different kinds of music to get into these days, but we have to hang on to our roots, which he reckons are in folk music. He says that in the olden days kids would learn the words and music from their parents and grandparents, and each region had its own traditions. Some of the folk bands around now have dug around and found some of these old songs. Harry has quite a lot of their stuff on his iPod, some of it a bit finger-in-your-ear kind of thing, which I can't be doing with personally. But according to Harry there are some great young bands.

I remember Ma taking me to see Steeleye Span at the old Haymarket theatre in Leicester, when I was about twelve years old. To try to broaden my outlook, she said. It didn't appeal then, but listening to it now, that folk rock sound is pretty cool.

## *Phil*

After being in that friggin' hospital a couple of times, I've decided it's time I lost a bit of weight. You can't help noticing the number of very large people there are in that place, some of them working there too. I mean, I look slim in comparison. You keep hearing stuff on the radio banging on about fat people with diabetes, or having heart problems, like, and when you see so many being pushed around in wheel chairs, it makes you think. Janey was telling me about this five-two diet thing. On the two days, you don't each much at all, which would be a bit of a chuffin' challenge, like, as I can't usually get to lunchtime without needing something to snack on. Beer doesn't help, apparently. Lots of calories in a pint, so I might have to cut down a bit. We'll see.

# Twenty-Two

# You Might Need Somebody

At two o'clock precisely, lights were turned off and screens were drawn on the ward for the obligatory one hour nap before visiting time. Stan couldn't sleep. Instead, in the relative peace and quiet his mind started to wander into possible scenarios which lay ahead of him. He decided he preferred to concentrate on the here and now, so explored the content of Harry's iPod. He was comforted to see names of artists he himself enjoyed, but there were many he didn't recognise, presumably folk and jazz musicians. He listened to those he knew and who suited the relaxed, slightly sombre mood he was in.

Phil appeared just after three o'clock, apologising for not having brought anything for Stan to eat, nor flowers, unsure whether they were allowed or not. He produced a book, *Beatles to Bowie, the Nineteen Sixties Exposed*, which Phil had been given as a Christmas present the previous year. He thought Stan would enjoy the photographs.

For ten minutes Phil flicked through the pages. 'Blimey O'Riley. Remember him? Remember her? Whatever happened to them? Jagger looked old even then. Mini-skirts. They didn't leave much to the imagination did they? Aren't hot pants coming back into fashion?' Stan would have liked to have been able to see the photographs himself.

'How are you, me old? Oh not too bad considering I've had a heart attack. What about you? Keeping alright? Things OK at home? Good. Well that's alright then.' Stan paused for effect. Phil still had his head in the book, apparently oblivious to Stan's sarcasm. After a judicious few seconds he closed the book and placed it on the bed.

'So how's it going then? Are they looking after you? What's the doctor saying about it all?'

'Nice of you to ask.' Stan summarised the events of the last couple of days. Over the next hour or so the conversation meandered between football, what to do about the window cleaning over the Christmas and New Year period, the direction the band was taking and the 'fitness' of the nurses. When they appeared to run out of things to discuss, a period of silence followed. Phil seemed distracted and reluctant to leave. Stan looked at some of the photographs in the book, but was unable to concentrate, so found a space for it on his bedside locker.

Phil broke the silence. He looked close to tears. 'I can't believe this is chuffin' happening to you, mate. It pains me to see you like this, in a hospital bed. I mean, you're never ill, always fit as a chuffin' fiddle, then all of a sudden they're going to cut you open, like.'

'You soft bugger. You'd think I was on death's chuffin' door. Tom was here just now. He says the operation is routine to them and once it's done I'll soon be fitter than ever. I'll be sprinting up and down that friggin' touchline on Sundays. So give over and cheer up. And look who's just walked in. Old Neil, so give him a friggin' smile will you.'

Stan wasn't quite expecting the hug and kiss on the cheek that he received from Neil, but almost managed to give the impression that this happened all of the time. The three of them tucked into the grapes and chocolates that Neil presented to Stan, along with a copy of *The Big Issue*, of which Stan pretended to be a huge fan and regular reader. Neil pointed out that Leicester Tigers were playing in a rugby match being shown live on the television in the visitors' lounge, to which they adjourned, joining in the vocal support for the team from other patients and visitors.

After a few minutes, Stan was suddenly overcome with fatigue. He gave his apologies and left Neil and Phil giving each other a concerned look. Back on the ward, he flopped down onto his bed and fell into to a deep sleep, during which he missed his evening meal and Mandy's visit. She sat at his bedside, tears welling as she watched him breathing, wanting to stroke his cheek. She read an article in the Big Issue about a newly opened hostel for homeless men and women in Leicester, as she listened to music on Harry's iPod. After an hour she left as quietly as she had arrived.

As they strolled together around the hospital grounds in the low afternoon sunshine, Stan was impressed when Tom explained that each of the doctors working in the cardiac unit had gone through rigorous training and examinations. Tom had come through the process a couple of years previously.

'So you have to keep taking exams, even after Uni?'

'Oh yeah! The training is tough and you don't get much free time. But it's worth it, in the long run.'

'I wanted to be a doctor when I were a kid. The parents were keen as well. My Grandad would say I could do anything I set my mind to. I were doing alright at junior school. In the 'A' stream and all that. Good marks in spelling and mental arithmetic. I were really good at the old times tables. But I fluffed the chuffin' eleven plus. I remember being a nervous wreck in school that day. Mum said it were because I wanted to be in the same school as Phil, who were in one of the duffers' classes. My old man just lost interest in me after that. He thought I were one of the duffers.'

'That's the problem with the exam system,' said Tom. 'Who knows how you're going to feel on the day?'

'The old git was probably right though. I'm fifty-five and cleaning windows. Not exactly a chuffin' success story, is it?'

'Well who knows, Stan? Maybe it's not too late. It's a funny old world.'

Stan was grateful for the quality of the training that night. He woke in the early hours, feeling the same pressure across his chest that he had experienced on the day he had been admitted. He pressed the button to call a nurse, who gave him a small bottle of something which she told him to spray onto the back of his tongue. This would enable his lungs to absorb more oxygen and the feeling of pressure would soon pass, she explained. She then went to find the doctor on night duty, and by the time he arrived the tightness in his chest had indeed eased.

After his examination, the doctor asked the nurse to arrange for an ECG and to let him have the printout as soon as it was available. Stan accepted the offer of some medication to help him get back to sleep.

He met 'the Big Man', Mr James, not long after breakfast. He wasn't physically large in any sense, but he was very self-assured and his entourage were obviously in awe of him. Stan was surprised to see Phil and Mandy alongside this group of doctors. They had phoned the ward to ask if it would be acceptable for them to be present when the consultant carried out his examination of Stan. The outcome was that Stan would spend a few more days on the ward, until it was clear that his situation had stabilised sufficiently for him to go home. There was a waiting list of a couple of months for the surgery that Stan needed, and during that time he would need to take things easy. Mandy said that she and Phil would watch every move he made.

This left Stan feeling oddly deflated, having mentally prepared himself for the prospect of surgery, wanting it to happen sooner rather than later. He didn't like the idea of having to idle his time away for several weeks, 'dossing around at home', as he put it. Mandy could see the positives it would offer Stan. He would be able to devote as much time as he wanted to his music, even have a go at writing songs. They could go for walks together. Stan just grunted in response, which she recognised as admission that she had a point.

At breakfast the following morning, Stan looked up from his cereal bowl to see Mr James standing at the end of his bed examining his chart. He was alone, wearing a dark grey suit, white shirt and red patterned tie.

'Good morning,' he said, looking up. 'I'm sorry to disturb you this early over your breakfast, Mr Booker, but I wanted to have a word.'

'Suright,' Stan mumbled back, his mouth full. 'No problem.' He pushed his tray to one side.

'After seeing on your chart what had happened during the night before last, I had a look at the ECG, which gave me some cause for concern. In short, we've had a cancellation, for reasons I don't need to go into, and we can operate next week. The day before Christmas Eve to be precise. What do you think?'

Although taken by surprise at this development, it took just a few seconds for Stan to reply: 'It's a no-brainer.'

The consultant gave a brief outline of what the surgery involved, then indicated that he would return in a couple of days to explain the procedure in more detail and to ask Stan to sign the consent form.

Half an hour later, surprised by his own sense of excitement, Stan was on the phone to break the news first to Mandy, then to Phil.

'Basically I think he was saying that if he didn't operate next week, I could snuff it quite soon,' he told them. He asked Mandy if she could bring in some more clean underwear and other clothes, and Phil if he could bring some pizzas if he was visiting that evening. He wasn't sure if he could face the prospect of hospital food for the next two weeks. When he asked after his mother, Mandy had said that she been to see her and that she was still quite poorly.

'The danger of being in this place for too long,' Harry said over coffee a couple of days later, 'is that you become institutionalised. Your life can revolve around the routine on the ward, so it's important, I believe, that you get out and do your own thing when you can.' This was Harry's last day on the ward, his heart surgery scheduled for the following morning. After a slow walk along the corridors, it being Harry's turn to need several stops to rest and catch his breath, they were sitting in the open area near the main entrance to the hospital.

Harry was staring at something in the direction of the entrance. 'Well bugger me!', he said as he broke into laughter. Amongst the comings and goings Stan made out two figures dressed in white, with coloured sashes across their chests and wearing panama hats. Then came the sound of melodeons and a violin playing, as the musicians entered, followed by a group of Morris dancers dancing their way into a space which had been cleared for them outside the café.

'This is my lot,' Harry explained. 'Perhaps come to wish me well, or say goodbye, I'm not sure which.' One of the two men who had entered as the advanced party came over to shake Harry's hand, and the two stood chatting as Stan looked on, transfixed by the intricacies of the dancing and waving of handkerchiefs performed by the eight men. A crowd had gathered, including nurses, doctors and other hospital staff, as well as patients and visitors. There was loud applause as the dance finished. One of the musicians, with a booming voice introduced the team, explaining that one of their team was awaiting heart surgery. He thanked the hospital authorities for allowing them to come and dance, and the doctors and nurses for doing such an amazing job. This brought loud cheers and more applause. They performed three dances, the last of which involved members of the audience joining in. Stan had to do a double take when he saw Ursula amongst the dancers. She was partnering one of the Morris men who was about half her size and in danger of being lifted off his feet as they swung round together.

He called to Ursula as she was about to make her way towards the corridor. They embraced.

'Steady now, duck. I'm about to have life-saving surgery so need to have some breath left.' He introduced her to Harry, who offered to fetch coffees while Ursula and Stan caught up.

'Well now I've seen everything. My favourite German doing some English country dancing. That were a bit of a chuffin' mismatch though. That little guy were lucky to come out of it alive.'

Ursula laughed. 'It was great fun. You should try it also Stan. But perhaps after your surgery and recovery.' She paused then took both of his hands in hers. 'Hey, I have some great news. The owner has said he does not need to raise the rent so much now. Just one per cent. Which is fine, so I am very happy. I really have to thank you and Phillip for giving me the idea of the petition. And of course I am now a celebrity. I've been on TV and everything.'

'That is chuffin' fantastic. I'm so pleased for you Ursula. What a chuffin' great Christmas present.'

Harry returned with the coffees, and Ursula produced a package from a small basket she had been carrying. She opened this to reveal a plum cake, a speciality, she explained, of the Palatinate, the region of Germany where she was brought up. It would go well with the coffee and was, she said, to celebrate some good news, which Stan briefly outlined for Harry's benefit. Smiles spread across the faces of the two men as they savoured the flavour and moistness of the cake.

'Best bloody cake I've ever eaten. Honestly!' said Harry. Stan went on to extol the qualities of Ursula's cooking, telling Harry he should visit the café and sample the Leberknödel. By the time Ursula stood up to take her leave, she had promised that she would bring them both some in three days time, by when Harry would be out of intensive care and on the recovery ward, hopefully getting his appetite back.

'That,' said Harry, as they watched her make her way to the exit, 'is a formidable woman.'

'I can't disagree,' Stan replied.

That evening, as Harry was wheeled away to a room where he would spend the night before his operation, Stan wished him well, promising to visit him and bring along the

Leberknödel,. He reflected how in the short time they had known each other, Harry had begun to open Stan's mind, particularly musically, and Stan felt he needed to broaden his horizons. Tom had possibly sensed this. He had left an envelope on Stan's bedside locker. Inside were three sheets of paper, on which were written the lyrics to 'Stand By Me', 'Lovely Day' and 'Bless the Weather', one with which he was already familiar. Also in the envelope were a mini iPod and a note from Tom asking Stan to memorise these lyrics and sing them along to the arrangements of the songs on the iPod, as the band had decided to work on these.

Over the next couple of days, between visits from various friends and band members, including Daniel and Esther, Stan was almost constantly plugged into the iPod. At first he had been singing along, but this began to irritate others on the ward, so he had to be content with mouthing the words. Daniel and Esther didn't stay for long, as Daniel was clearly disconcerted by the whole experience of being in the hospital. Stan, however, was able to ask him if he knew the new songs on the mini Ipod, to which his blustering response left Stan feeling bemused.

'Oh yes, of course I know them. I've been playing them. Actually, no, I didn't mean that. I was joking. I don't know anything about them. But maybe I will, now that you've mentioned them. Perhaps the band could sing them. Maybe we will. Umm. Sorry. No, is the answer.'

As promised, Ursula arrived with a large basket in which were foil trays filled with the promised hot food, along with a table cloth, paper napkins and cutlery. Her face beamed as she strode into the ward, waving at Stan when she saw him. She set the basket on the floor, and then froze when she saw Stan's face. He looked pale and distant.

'Stanley? Stan? Are you alright? You don't look well.'

He looked up. 'No, I'm alright, duck. I've just been to check where Harry is, and if it's OK to go and see him.'

'And?'

She knew from his face what he was going to say, before he spoke. 'He's dead, love. He didn't survive the surgery.'

## Stan

So that's that. Harry had really been looking forward to getting the surgery done with and going home. His face was a real picture when he saw his Morris dancing mates. So he won't be going home or doing any more Morris dancing, or passing on his little pearls of wisdom. I only knew him for a few of days, so I hate to think how much his friends and family will miss the bloke.

## Phil

I was actually scared of the idea of going to see my old mate in hospital. It were hard to look at him. And he did look a sight, like he'd suddenly aged ten years. When we was kids, he were the one that never seemed to be ill, whatever were going around. Chickenpox, flu, whatever. One year, we would have been eight or nine, there was some bug or other going round and there was a day when he was the only kid in our class to turn up for school. It seemed like he was indestructible. Hospitals give me the heebie-jeebies anyway, but when he chuffin' well told me what they would be doing to him, I nearly passed out. But like I say, the big man is indestructible.

## Twenty-Three

# To Live is to Fly

On the evening following Harry's death, Stan had felt emotional in a way he had never before, and in an A4 sized notepad in which he had begun to write lyrics for a couple of potential songs, he tried to express his feelings. What started off as a rant about life in general, developed first into a letter to anyone close enough to him who might read it, then into a soliloquy about the benefits of living life in the slow lane.

The letter, he realised after reading and rereading it, was a self-indulgent expression of self-pity. He thanked Phil for the comradeship, almost brotherliness, through their long friendship. He offered advice on how to bring the best out of Daniel, which included persuading Daniel and his mother that he should leave school at the end of the school year and try and find a college that would let him develop his special talent as a percussionist. His eyes welled as he told Mandy that he blessed the day they had met and cursed the fact that this hadn't happened until he was in his mid-fifties. Stan would have loved to have had children. In his view she would have made a brilliant mother. His children wouldn't have had to suffer the ignominy of failing the eleven-plus. They would have gone on to be talented and successful musicians, artists or dancers. He didn't stop to reflect that Mandy might never have wanted children herself, or that the topic was a sensitive one for any reason. Stan wondered whether there would have been children if his marriage hadn't broken up, immediately regretting what was a rare disturbance of something he had tried to keep buried deeply in his mind. It was at this point that he became aware that he was writing as if he would suffer the same fate as Harry. Telling himself to stop being such a daft bugger, he screwed up the pages and threw them into a nearby waste bin.

The following afternoon, guitar under his arm, Stan walked hand in hand with Mandy to the visitors' lounge. There she removed her winter coat to reveal a royal blue dress with a round neck and three-quarter length sleeves. The dress clung to the contours of her figure, causing a reassuring stirring of his loins, of which he informed her.

'I'd better put the coat back on, or I'll be accused of causing you to have palpitations.'

'Don't you dare, duck. When you've gone I want to be able to close my eyes, right, and conjure up the vision of your beauty. It's just what I need to cheer me up.' This had been her intention, he realised. He reached out to her and they clung long and hard.

'Any news on Ma?' he asked. 'I would have thought she'd have phoned me or something. Seems odd.'

'All I can tell you is that the doctor is looking after her, given her some medication and she should be on the mend soon. I'm sure you'll hear from her before too long. She knows you're on the mend.' Stan had rested his guitar on one of the armchairs. 'So come on, are you going to give us a song or what?'

Stan had spent some of the morning in the room experimenting with ideas for a twelve bar blues instrumental. He had forgotten how, in the nineties, he had enjoyed learning to play blues solos on his acoustic guitar using teach yourself CDs and trying to copy the playing of some of the accomplished guitarists. After a couple of false starts, he showed Mandy what he had been trying to do.

'Wow, Stan. That is amazing, and you looked like you were having fun. You should work on that.'

After visiting hours were over in the evening, he took himself back to the room and for an hour or so he had put together a piece he could play all the way through. The nurse had to drag him away to administer his medication. After breakfast the following morning, he retreated again to the lounge. Thankful that no one else was there, he played around, trying to improve some of his finger-picking of the chords.

'Bugger it,' he thought. 'Once through, cock-ups and all.'

As Stan played the final chord with a flourish, he was surprised to hear applause coming from near the door.

'Bravo,' called Tom. 'All your own work, or someone else's?' he asked as he walked across the room.

'All mine, me old. What do you think?'

Tom had enjoyed what he heard, and for the next few minutes he accompanied Stan's guitar playing on the slightly out-of-tune piano in the corner of the room, finishing with a short improvised solo.

'Oh man, that was great.' They high-fived. 'You've got something there Stan. We should work on it.' He looked up at the clock on the wall. 'Shit. Look, enough of this enjoying ourselves. Mr James is coming to see you anytime now, which is why I was looking for you.'

'This one is made from pig's tissue, and this from titanium,' the consultant was explaining a few minutes later. He had in his hand two heart valve replacements. He had also produced a model section of a heart. 'There are pros and cons for each. If we go for the pig tissue, it will function just as your heart valves should and no medication is needed. But the average lifetime is ten years, so at some point we could be looking at surgery again. On the other hand, this little chap here could go on forever, so you could live to a ripe old age and be as fit as a fiddle. The downside is that you would need to be on warfarin for the rest of your life.'

'So whichever, I ain't going to be one hundred per cent human. And warfarin, ain't that rat poison?

Mr James went on to explain that its main use has always been as an anti-coagulant, thinning the blood so that it doesn't clot. The body would try and reject the titanium valve, causing the blood to clot, which would be terminal. He added that the titanium valve cost three thousand pounds.

'On the National Health?' Stan quickly asked.

'Absolutely.'

Stan was able to handle the valves, appreciating the skill which had gone into the manufacture of something so small and yet so crucial for staying alive. He liked the idea of having an expensive bit of technology inside his body.

As if reading his mind, Mr James said 'There is a myth about warfarin that you can't drink alcohol if you're taking it. In fact you can drink as much as you like. But,' he emphasised, 'you have to drink the same amount every day. You could drink half a bottle of whisky, if that's your tipple, but you would have to drink that much every day.'

'So a blood clot won't get you, but your liver will.' After a pause, Stan continued,' I think I can cope with the drink side of it. Do me good to just have one pint a day, so I think we'll go for this boy.' He held up the metal valve.

Stan became aware of lights which alternated between bright and dim, and of dull murmurs which became voices.

'Stan. Stan. Can you hear me?'

His eyelids fluttered. He was able to make out Mandy to his right, walking alongside the trolley and holding his hand. Her face was beaming.

'Hallo darling. We're here.' He heard an 'aye up me old' and saw that Phil was walking along behind Mandy, waving slightly bashfully at him.

'Alright?' was all that Stan managed to say, in a weak croaky voice.

'Everything's fine, Mr Booker. You're out of surgery now. It's all gone well and I'm taking you down to intensive care.' He recognised Alison, the nurse who would be giving him one to one support.

'No, I meant Phil, my old mate there. Surprised he hasn't passed out.' He heard laughter.

He looked down at his chest and stomach, registering tubes coming out from various points, then drifted back to sleep. The next few hours were a blur, and he had no real sense of time. As he emerged from the anaesthetic, periods of involuntary groaning were interspersed with restless sleep. He was vaguely aware of a figure moving around him in the darkness, seemingly ignoring his pleas for water. Eventually he was able to sip from a small cup, aware that he was no longer groaning, there was light in the room and Alison was changing the drip bag on the stand beside the bed.

'Best cup of tea I've ever tasted, and in a proper cup,' he was saying a few minutes later. 'What's for breakfast?' He was finishing a bowl of Weetabix when Mandy and Phil came into the unit. They stood inside the door, assessing the situation.

'Stanley Booker, you are a sight for sore eyes. And in the circumstances we can forgive you the bad hair day,' said Mandy, who almost ran across the room to hug him. A pale-looking Phil stood at the foot of the bed, as if not knowing how to handle the situation.

'Chuffin' Nora!' he said. 'I've never seen so many blooming tubes attached to someone. So have you got one down there, you know, up your plonker?'

'I have, and there was one up my nose until a few minutes ago. Come here you daft bugger,' said Stan. 'Give us a hug. It's not often your best mate has heart surgery.' The two held each other awkwardly. As they parted, Phil managed to knock over Stan's fresh cup of tea, which spilt onto the plate of toast.

'Oh shit! Sorry mate.'

'You duffer. Clumsy as always. I was really looking forward to that.' He looked up and laughed, the others joining in. 'But in the scheme of things, it doesn't matter at all. Not one chuffin' bit.' Alison brought him fresh tea and toast.

That afternoon he was deemed well enough to be moved onto the recovery ward. Christmas decorations hung from the ceiling and over the entrance to the six-bed bay, and the sound of carol singing carried through from a radio somewhere. He reminded himself that it was Christmas Eve. Alison handed Stan's records over to the Staff Nurse standing at the bedside, who introduced herself as Tracy. Alison wished Stan a speedy recovery and a happy Christmas, adding that she would come and see him in a couple of days to check that he was behaving himself. Stan asked for a kiss and hug, but had to settle for a light peck on the cheek and a handshake as he expressed his thanks.

'Now then, duck,' said Tracy as she tucked in the sheets. 'I have an important question to ask you. Would you like me to order a Christmas dinner for you? Roast turkey and all of the trimmings. Had you remembered that Santa's coming tonight?' Stan sensed the woman's natural assertiveness, but warmed to her strong Leicester accent.

'Well duck, that's two important questions. Yes and no, in that order. I stopped believing in Santa yonks ago, and suggest you do the same. The whole chuffin' Santa and Christmas thing is the biggest con trick adults have ever played on kids in my view. We give them all this crap about him and his elves and reindeers, Santa comes down the bleeding chimney, even if it's blocked up cos there's central heating, then one day the older kids get it and spill the beans to the younger ones. How friggin' cruel is that?'

Tracy stared at him in disbelief, hands on hips. 'Well bah humbug. Don't you go spreading these nasty rumours on this ward. The shock might be too much for some of them. And when Santa appears tonight with your presents I'll make sure he wakes you up, so you can say hello and share a glass of sherry. Happy Christmas, Mr Booker,' she said as she walked away.

He chuckled. 'I'll look forward to meeting him. Happy Christmas.'

There were two empty beds in the bay. Stan wondered who had last been in them, what had become of them and who would be in them next. He reflected that Harry would possibly have been in this part of the ward. None of the doctors or nurses had been willing to discuss what had happened to Harry. Stan understood why.

He slept for most of the afternoon and evening, disturbed only by nurses doing their 'obs', emptying his urine bag, or administering his medication, and the arrival of his tasteless afternoon tea. He had become very aware not so much of his heart beat but more of a gentle thudding in his chest, a new sensation which he guessed he might have to adjust to. Through the night he dreamed that he possessed powers of levitation and could fly. After swooping down through a long canyon and gliding across sunbathed fields of grass, he awoke and became aware of fluctuations in his heart rate. He was sufficiently concerned to call a nurse, who in turn fetched the doctor on duty for the ward. The doctor checked Stan over, attached a saline drip to his arm then gave him a very salty solution to drink, which he said would settle things down. Stan read his name badge.

'So where are you from Zahid?'

'Leicester,' Zahid replied, without looking up from Stan's record sheet.

'Oh. OK.'

'What about you?'

'Yeah. The same. Leicester.' He wanted to add 'I thought it was chuffin' obvious,' but thought better of it. He had been at school with children of Asian descent who had arrived from various countries. Their kids would have been born here, he realised.

'My parents and grandparents were kicked out of Kenya in 1969, if that's what you meant.'

'No. No. It's not. Which school did you go to?'

'Spencefield. What about you?'

'Uhhh, New Parks Boys,' replied Stan.

'Other side of the city then.'

'Yeah, you could say that. In more ways than one.'

'Anyway, things should settle down now, Mister Booker, but call me if you are concerned.'

'Thanks doc. Thanks for sorting me out.'

## Stan

I remember as a five-year-old looking out the bedroom window on Christmas Eve, waiting to catch a glimpse of Santa on his chuffin' sleigh. Dead excited I was at bed time, after putting the glass of sherry and a couple of mince pies out on the hearth, along with some carrots. 'Mustn't forget the reindeer,' Ma had said. 'How does he manage to get down this chimney?' I asked. 'Using his magic,' said my Dad. 'How does he manage to get to leave presents for all the kids in the world?' Same answer, but he only visits kids who have behaved. After what seemed hours of looking out of the window, I eventually slipped into bed and was just drifting off when I heard my bedroom door creek. In pops my Dad and he leaves something against the end of the bed. I knew what it would be, but checked anyway that it was a stocking full of presents. I became one of those kids who knew there wasn't really a Santa, and told the other kids.

## Phil

Last Christmas, yeah, there were some blokes down at the club saying they'd bought this and bought that for their kids. Laptops, iPads, play stations, TVs for their bedrooms. All expensive electrical stuff, right. And these were mostly blokes that couldn't afford it on what they were earning, or were even on the dole. 'You've got to let the kids keep up with the latest gadgets,' they'd say. Or worse still, 'anything for an easy life, to shut the little buggers up.' You'd see kids playing up, throwing a wobbly, like, in front of everyone in the shops if they couldn't have what they wanted for Christmas. Their mates had it, and it was advertised on the telly, I want it, kind of thing. Embarrassing, it were.

## Twenty-Four

# In the Bleak Midwinter

Christmas Day, mid-morning. *So where were the presents and stocking?* Stan asked himself, inwardly chuckling. *Santa my arse.* He was sitting naked on a stool, enjoying a shower in a wet room just along the corridor from his bed. After breakfast, his catheter and drip had been removed, a physiotherapist had shown Stan how to get in and out of bed then accompanied him on a short walk. Warm water was now washing over his body, and he felt he had never enjoyed a shower so much. That was until he reminded himself of the occasion he and Mandy had showered together after making love. Feeling a bit more human, he started to sing *Lovely Day* to test his memory of the lyrics. He had to fill in with some la-la-las in the second verse.

'So what's going on?' he asked the nurse escorting him back to his bed. Patients and staff were making their way from the bays and along the corridor to the open area next to the nurses' station, where a Christmas tree had been erected. She replied that it was bit of a surprise for the patients, who were all in for a real treat. Stan dumped his towel and toiletries and the nurse pushed him along in a wheelchair to see what was going on. Patients sat and staff stood, waiting for a couple of minutes until a group of about twelve doctors and nurses walked in and organised themselves in front of the tree, in a way that suggested to Stan that they were going to sing. Before they did so they were joined by five others all dressed in Santa costumes, waving and ho-ho-hoing, which raised a few chuckles. They took their places at the back of the group.

One of the doctors in the choir produced a recorder and played a single note, the signal for them to launch into a version of 'While Shepherds Watched' with the chorus of Sweet Chiming Bells. It was sung in harmony, and Stan realised he was smiling along with everyone else, appreciating the quality.

'Thank you,' a voice was saying, in response to the applause. Stan strained his neck to see the speaker, who turned out to be Tracy, the nurse who had chastised him for not believing in Father Christmas. 'Welcome to our little Christmas morning soirée. We call ourselves the Glenfield Singers, and get together a couple of times a year to sing on the wards here. We like to think that it cheers everybody up, and who knows, it might speed up your recovery. This Christmas we're honoured to have been joined by Santa and some of his helpers, who have a special song for us in a few minutes. We are going to sing four more carols for you, before we move on to the next ward. You'll know them all, so sing along if you want, or just mime. That's OK. Some of us do. This is my favourite, an arrangement of *Hark the Herald* known as *Curly Hark*, which is popular up north in Sheffield and Derbyshire.'

This was followed by *The Anger Gabriel*. Stan quietly hummed along, trying his best to join in the bass line. Three of the Santas then stepped forward. One carried a guitar and sat on a stool, a second produced a violin. The guitarist played a four-chord introduction to what the violinist revealed was *In the Bleak Midwinter*, as he played one verse of the melody. Stan was slightly surprised when the vocalist turned out to be a woman, and he felt there was something vaguely familiar about her. He really liked the sound they made together, applauding enthusiastically at the end of the carol. *Gaudete* followed. At its conclusion those that could, which included Stan, just about, stood to clap and cheer.

Stan would have liked to talk to someone in the choir about the music and singing, but its members quickly broke up and moved on, apart from the Santa figures who were in a huddle next to the tree. He thought about going over to them, but was ushered away to join the procession back to beds.

From his bed he heard a slight commotion and looked up to see that the five Santa figures seemed to be heading his way. They stopped at the end of his bed, where one picked up the clipboard holding Stan's chart, so Stan assumed that they were a group of doctors, or doctors and nurses, despite a couple of 'ho ho ho's.

'So you're not heading off with the others then, doc?'

The one holding the clipboard looked at the others. 'Is it time to fess up?' They each removed their beard to reveal the smiling faces of Tom, Angie, Neil, and Malcolm, and also Daniel, who Stan was most surprised but at the same time delighted to see. After some laughter and more ho-hoing, Stan complimented them on the quality of their singing, in his own awkward way thanking them. He was fighting back the tears. Tom had persuaded the choir to accommodate them at the last minute, and after joining one rehearsal, the band members met a couple of times to make sure they could sing the various parts. They had all enjoyed their first experience of singing in harmony. Each presented a small gift to Stan, which with a little help he ceremoniously opened. Tom produced another which nurse Tracy had said was from the real Santa. Stan unwrapped a Scandinavian style woolly hat which he dutifully put on. He sang the praises of the hospital staff.

'And get a load of this,' he said, revealing the dressing running down over his scar.

'Gordon Bennet!'

'Ah, shit!'

'You poor man.'

Daniel quickly looked away and reached for a chair.

'It's hard to believe, ain't it. It's sore, like, and it chuffin' well aches across here, but I'll be fine. Small price to pay really. They've said with a bit of physio I should be out in a week at the most. I have to show that I can manage up and down stairs on me tod, like, and work on me breathing.' They spent a few minutes discussing what Stan could remember about the lead up to and recovery from the surgery. Keen to know as much detail as possible, Daniel was obviously happy to hear about what Stan had gone through, as long as he didn't have to see any physical evidence.

Tom asked Stan to make sure he learned the lyrics to the three songs he had been given, adding that they would be back in three or four days to test him out. Stan asked what the big deal was about these songs, to which Neil replied that they hadn't just been sitting around picking their noses while Stan was in hospital. The band had a gig lined up and needed Stan to be ready.

Stan was motivated by this news, and by the time Mandy visited him on the day after Boxing Day, he was able to walk around the ward and a little way up and down the corridor, a circuit he managed twice during the day. There had also been plenty of time for him to work on the lyrics, and finding the visitors lounge empty, he used Mandy as an audience and sang quietly to her.

'One thing I've noticed already,' he said, 'is that when I take a breath it lasts a lot chuffin' longer than it did before. I can take quite a deep breath if I take it carefully.'

'Well I am so proud of you Stan,' she said, planting a kiss on his forehead. You are doing so well. Which is just as well, because I think this gig might be coming up quite soon.'

'Best be ready then, hadn't I. Only one problem though, duck. I haven't been since before my op. I mean I am very, you know, constipated. I've been trying, but it just isn't happening. Even after the enema which the nurse gave me up me jacksie. And it's no laughing matter,' he added, as Mandy started to chuckle.

By the day before New Year's Eve, Stan was feeling stir crazy. He was becoming stronger and more independent each day, able now to walk up and down stairs and from one end of the hospital to the other unaided. Desperate to know when he could go home, he had been told that this could happen that afternoon, but his blood test results hadn't come back in time. According to Tracy is was all about his INR, or International Normalised Ratio, which was a way of checking that the warfarin was effective in preventing his blood from clotting, as long as he took the correct dose every day. Once the blood tests showed that his INR was within the necessary range in three consecutive tests he would be given the all clear to be discharged. He was fed up with the day to day routine, his uncomfortable bed and the poor quality food. This was apparently brought over from across the Midlands, already prepared, so by the time it had been warmed through and wheeled on a trolley to the ward it had become fairly tasteless. Phil and Mandy had brought sandwiches and pizzas on the previous two days, which the three had shared in the visitors' lounge, and he was pleased that today he and Ursula were able to have a teatime meal in one of the cafés.

He told her about his constipation and how Tracy had found the solution.

'It was one of the friggin' drugs they'd put me on. She changed it after she'd spotted it on my medication list, right. So this morning, alleluia! Mind you, duck, it was chuffin' painful. I thought I'd given birth when I looked at the size of the thing in the toilet pan. Anyhow, it's sorted and we're almost back to normal.'

'Well that's just what I need to hear when my food is about to arrive. But when you get home, Stanley, you must come and have some of your favourite food at Ursula's. On the house. There is one condition though.'

Stan's ham, eggs and chips arrived, shortly followed by a Panini for Ursula.

'And what's that, duck,' he asked, as he squeezed brown sauce over his chips.

'That you bring your band to play in the restaurant sometime. I'm sure it would be good for my business and also help you to get known a little better.'

'Oh it's a chuffin' restaurant now is it? Does that mean I'll be paying restaurant prices?'

'I was just practising the word really. Ursula's restaurant. Or Restaurant Ursula.' She could see that Stan wasn't too impressed. 'Maybe it will stay as a café.'

'If you keep it as Ursula's café, duck, I'll check it out with the band. How's that?'

He enjoyed being with Ursula, and he suspected that she was pleased to be able to escape from the café. While she seemed comfortable in his company, he was content to mostly sit and listen as she talked easily about her plans for the café, how she loved living in Leicester, at the same time missing her home town. He was disappointed when it was time for her to leave.

'But see you later then,' she said, as they kissed goodbye.

'Later?'

'Err. Well I mean in the next few days, when you get home.'

Stan was back on his bed in time for the post tea-time issue of medication. Shortly afterwards one of the nurses appeared at the entrance to the bay to announce that there would be some musical entertainment starting soon in the visitors' lounge, for those that fancied it. She didn't say what sort of music would be played. Mandy then appeared pushing a wheelchair up to his bed.

'Right then, Stan, I fancy a bit of a sing-a-long or whatever it is, so jump aboard and we'll go along shall we?'

'Hallo to you me duck too. Do I have any choice? It doesn't like it.'

Leaving the wheelchair in the corridor, they walked into the lounge to find it set up with about thirty chairs in rows. Facing them were two stools, a few music stands and instruments, which included a double bass, violin, acoustic guitar, keyboard and an interesting percussion collection. There were no mics or amplifiers, so with the exception of the keyboard it was going to be an acoustic set. They sat on the front row. Stan became curious as to what to expect as the room quickly filled with patients, nurses and a couple of doctors, some having to stand. There were several disappointed faces looking through the window from the corridor.

Tom then appeared, but instead of finding a place amongst the audience, he stood in front of them and asked for their attention.

'Good evening everyone. I was afraid that we might be struggling a bit for room, but never mind. I'm sure there will be many opportunities for you to see our little band playing in and around Leicester in the months ahead. We call ourselves Leicester Rocks, and here they are.' There was some gentle clapping and curious stares as Tom was joined by Neil, Malcolm, Angie and Daniel, who took up their instruments and places.

'There is just one more member to join us. Well two actually.' Looking at Stan, he said, 'Your face is such a picture Stan, if only you could see it. This stool is for you, so please come and join us. The other's for Mandy.'

Stan looked at Mandy and said quietly, 'I don't know if I can friggin' well do this. I'm not ready for it. I look and feel a right scruffbag.'

'Nothing new there. Come on, just have a go. We'll sing together, and if you can't manage it just leave it to me.'

'What are we singing anyway? Oh, I get it. Those songs doc left me to learn, like.' He slowly rose to his feet, looked at Tom, muttering 'you bugger' at him, then walked over with Mandy to take their places on the stools. Over the applause he recognised the voice calling out 'come on Stanley.' He looked across to see Ursula standing near the door, Phil next to her. The two then scampered across to take the seats vacated by Stan and Mandy. Arms folded, they looking as pleased as punch. Stan gently shook his head, as if in disbelief at their cheek.

'So you're all in on this then. I apologise for this everyone. I've been well and truly dropped in the s h one t.' He looked around at the band members. 'Nice touch guys. I appreciate it, so let's give it a chuffin' whirl. *Stand by me* first?' There were nods from the band. Angie played the double bass introduction, Daniel accompanying on a pair of cymbals on a stand with a foot pedal. Stan realised he had missed the cue as Mandy started to sing, but joined in on the second line, albeit gingerly. He managed to increase the volume for the chorus, feeling only slight discomfort, and grew in confidence. Some of the audience were singing along.

As the audience clapped and cheered enthusiastically at the end of the song, Stan turned to smile at Neil and the others, nodding in appreciation. As they got into *Lovely Day*, he realised that the choice of music had been deliberate, that he was basically singing to Mandy. So he found himself looking at her as they sang.

He let Mandy take care of the long note on the '*day*', lasting seven or eight bars. The chorus for *Bless the Weather* confirmed his thoughts.

Phil having returned to the wings, Stan enjoyed watching and listening to the band from his seat, as they performed three more numbers. Mandy's silky voice, with its touch of huskiness, fitted in well. He pushed to the back of his mind the thoughts he had of the potential tensions that might arise if she one day joined the band.

As the applause died down, Stan stepped forward.

'I'm not really, like, an emotional sort of bloke normally, but at the moment I'm actually feeling a bit choked. It was only a couple of weeks ago, right, that the surgeon basically told me that if I didn't have this surgery, the old ticker would pack in, sort of thing, and that would chuffin' well be that. I know that some of you, like, have also had life-saving operations. So I just want to take this opportunity to say a big 'thank you' to this lot,' he said, pointing at some of the staff. 'The doctors and nurses, who have looked after us all so well.' There was more clapping and cheering. 'Mind you.' He paused. 'No, probably best if I don't mention the food.' A few laughed.

'Then this chuffin' lot come along and do this for me. If I'd gone home today like I was hoping, I'd have missed this. I can't help wondering, mind, if one of them made sure I didn't go home. We only got together, like, a couple of months ago, and I was on my way to our first gig when I had to make a diversion to my GP. Now here we are, so does this count as our first gig?'. He wiped away a tear. 'But to the lovely Mandy and my mates in the band, well, what can I say?'

As he and Mandy hugged, they were joined by all but one of the band members for a collective huddle. Daniel stood watching, not knowing quite what to do. As they broke up, Stan beckoned Daniel over. 'You and I could hug, Daniel,' he said quietly to him. 'But only if you want.'

'Yes, I'd like that.'

'You did really well tonight, my old,' Stan said as they embraced. 'In a small room, lots of people, like.'

'I told myself I could do it, because it wasn't for long. I really concentrated on the music and only looked at the band.'

'Good for you. Good for you.' Stan looked around for Phil and caught his eye. Still close to Daniel, he pointed at him, and smiled and nodded at Phil.

As the room gradually emptied and the band began to collect their things, Ursula stood in front of them, hands on hips.

'That was great, guys. Remember to ask them, Stan. Gig. At the café. Tschüss.' They watched her go.

'Assertive, or what?' said Neil.

Stan walked back with Mandy to his ward. One or two patients were asleep, others were watching TV or reading. It was past visiting hours.

'I'd better get going,' she said quietly. 'But there's something I've been meaning to tell you, so sit down and listen.' She read the look on his face. 'It's alright, I'm not leaving you or anything like that. But it is bad news I'm afraid. You're Mum has had a fall and is in hospital. The General, not here. They suspected a broken hip at first, but nothing's broken.'

'Shit. So what happened? Why is she still in hospital?'

'Well. She was in the supermarket when she fell, and couldn't get up, so they phoned for the ambulance. This was the day after you were admitted here. The hospital X-rayed her chest as well as legs, to check there were no broken ribs. There were no broken bones, but they have discovered a growth. She has a massive tumour apparently. Lung cancer, basically, which is much too advanced for the doctors to do anything about.' She paused and squeezed his hand. 'I'm ever so sorry, Stan.'

'Did they say how long she's got, like?'

'A few weeks, at the most.'

Stan sat staring at nothing in particular, with his hand to his face, thumb on his cheek, forefinger stroking the end of his nose. 'Poor old girl. You know, she was going to have a scan after she'd complained to her chuffin' GP about pains in her shoulder. Not that it'd have made any difference.' He blew through puffed cheeks. 'So I'd better go and see her, asap. Have you been? Is she in a lot of pain?'

'Me and Phil have popped in a couple of times. She was asking after you. Pain wise, she's on morphine. But when you go in, be prepared for a bit of a shock. She's not very with-it, and does look very poorly.'

She got up to leave. 'There's a slightly funny side to the whole story though. Guess where she was when he had her tumble. Which aisle.' Stan shrugged his shoulders. 'Appropriately enough, by the spirits looking at the whisky bottles.' They laughed together.

## Stan

I thought she had a few years in her yet. Just goes to show, you never know what's around the chuffin' corner. I reckon she must have had some sort of sense that she was near the end somehow, which would explain why she'd cleared out a load of stuff over the last few months. She's been my best mate, my teacher, my bringer-down-to-earth, whenever I got a bit cocky, like. After Niamh left, she kept a close eye on me, knowing that the black dog wouldn't be far away. We've had some laughs as well. Capsizing our rented canoe on Rutland Water when we got into a part where the waves came over the side. Christmas party games with the family were hilarious. There was one we called the humming game, where you had to hum the tune of a song to your team, for them to work it out. I only had to look at her when she started humming and I would always crack up at the face she pulled. When Halloween became popular she would dress up in a witches outfit, blacken up a bit and take her teeth out. When she opened the door cackling to the kids, they would scream and run away. They'd creep back later and ask her if she was a real witch. They would ask trick or treat, and of course it would always be treat. She offered a spoonful from a jar of what she claimed was jellied spider, or something. We laughed when they ran away again.

When Harry went, I honestly thought it could be me next. It wasn't exactly a case of my life flashing by me, like, but I did do a lot of thinking. And as I've said many a time, too much thinking can be bad for your health.

## Phil

You rarely see the big man getting emotional, but you could see what it meant to him having the chuffin' band there and being able to join in, like, just a few days after his op and everything. But his Mum's situation is a killer. So to speak. Just hope she can chuffin' hang on in there till he can get to see her.

When we'd got through all the Christmas stuff, mince pies et cetera, the missus suggested I start the diet. She was practically giving away the Christmas cake, knowing how much I love it. It wasn't so much suggesting as blackmail. Diet, sex. No diet, no sex. It's going to test the old staying power. Monday and Thursdays are going to be diet days, and I've done a Thursday. Porridge for breakfast, some fruit for a snack, then nowt till the evening meal – a beetroot salad with some ponsy cheese. And plenty of water. I was so friggin' hungry by bedtime. First thing in the morning I was on the old scales. They seem to be stuck on fourteen stone four pounds.

# Twenty-Five

# Journey's End

The funeral was held two weeks later.

Stan had visited Audrey shortly after leaving hospital, and the sight of his mother sitting up in her bed, waving and smiling at him as he walked into the ward had stayed with him. 'She'd been waiting for you, duck,' Mandy had said. 'She must have known she didn't have long.' He managed two visits. On the second, she was asleep or unconscious, but at one point sat bolt upright, eyes wide open, uttering nothing more than a gasp, before falling back onto her pillows as if nothing had happened. It was obvious to Stan that her presence on the open ward was causing distress to other patients, so he asked whether there was somewhere she could be moved to, out of sight. After a break for a cup of tea, he returned to find that she had been moved to a private room just off the ward. Audrey's condition had deteriorated, he was told, and she had been put on a respirator to help her breathe. He sat and talked to her, about his childhood memories, things they had enjoyed doing together, how proud he was of her, even though she was 'a bit of a duffer'. After an hour he left, but not before he leant over to kiss her cheek and whispered, 'I love you Mum. It's time for you to let go. It's OK.' He sniffed and held back the tears as he walked out of the room. He had debated with himself whether to wait around in the hospital, or go home, choosing the latter, not knowing for sure when the end would come. The call came just after he had walked through his front door, so back he went.

A short piece appeared on the front page of the local paper, announcing her death, a lengthier one inside acknowledging her contribution to public life, particularly as a councillor. There followed several letters of tribute. Even so, Stan was amazed at the turnout. He stood at the entrance to the chapel to welcome what he had imagined to be the dozen or so that might come along to the funeral. One of the first to arrive was the mayor, with whom he had a long conversation as car after car dropped off others who had come to pay their respects, causing a queue to develop behind him.

The previous evening, Stan had shared with Mandy the eulogy he had written for his mother. She suggested some minor alterations, as they sat up in her bed.

'It's hard, aint it,' he said. 'Trying to fit in all the chuffin' things you want to say when you only have a few minutes. There's all the stuff I remember as a kid. then there's the questions I'd always wanted to ask her. Like why did she only have one kid? Did she really love my Dad?' He propped himself up on his elbow, looking her in the face.

'There could be a few people there tomorrow, I guess. I'll be shitting bricks talking in front of them all.'

'You'll be fine. It's a real shame people don't get to hear the lovely things being said about them at their funeral. Don't you think? This is lovely Stan, and your Mum would have loved to hear it or read it. We all ought to write or say our goodbyes and these, what do you call them? What's the word? Tributes will do. We ought to let the people we love know how we feel about them and what lovely memories we have of them, before they pop their clogs.'

He leant over and kissed her lightly on the lips, stroked her breasts then moved down to kiss them, feeling her nipples harden under her nightie.

'I know what I'd say about you. Soft lips, great to kiss. Perfect tits...'

'Just stop there, mister. I can see where this is leading and I'm not sure you're up to this just yet.'

'Let's see about that.'

Now, as he stood in front of the gathering, he was surprised at his lack of nerves. He took in the expressions on the sea of faces looking up at him, which ranged from anxiety from those that knew him well to bemusement on the part of those that didn't. A few smiled encouragement. He thanked the vicar for his kind words, then thanked them all for coming, saying how gratifying it was that so many had turned up to pay their respects. He promised to mind his 'p's and 'q's, as she'd be sure to be watching. He fidgeted with the sheets of paper in his hands, but decided he would look at them only if he got stuck.

'So the old gal has definitely gone. I suspect, like, that some of you are here just to make sure, perhaps a bit worried that she might come back to haunt you. Serves you right.' A few more were now smiling. 'Audrey Mary Booker. I am so pleased and privileged to say that she was my Mum. She'd always been there for me, you know. She was one of the most principled people you could meet, right up until the last minute. She passed away, like, in an NHS hospital, when she could have gone private. She was in because she'd fallen over reaching for a bottle of her favourite Glenfiddich. She'd rather it was after putting down an empty one than reaching for a full one, but there you are.

'Mum had lived in a council house all her life. She didn't believe in private ownership. She never wanted anything what she would call flash. She would send me back to the shop if I came home with any clothes which she thought were too fancy, and when Dad came home with a Jag he'd bought second hand she went ballistic. She wasn't having that parked outside our house. Either it went or he went. It took a while, but eventually he did, sadly. One day, the mayor sent a car to fetch her for something or other. She gave the driver a tenner and caught the bus.

'She would say "Big car, small brain. And judging by the number of posh German cars and four-by-fours in the car park at County Hall, some councillors seem to have a problem." There was a rumour that one of the councillors was having to take Viagra to save his marriage. Excuse my French here. "He's always full of s h 1 t, that one," she said. Now he won't know whether he's coming or going". He waited for the laughter to subside.

'She were in her element travelling on the old bus. She would talk to anybody and everybody. It were her way of finding out what people think, using it to hold court, sort of thing. And the passengers treated her like a celebrity, royalty, almost.' He paused. 'She didn't suffer fools though, did she?'

'I always admired her for the way she managed full-time work, plus being a councillor and a Mum. She was dead organised. Like we knew what day of the week it was by the meal on the table at tea time. Tuesdays it was cauliflower cheese, bacon and tomatoes, every chuffin' week. She kept me on the straight and narrow, made sure I kept me head down at school and stuff. One day, Phil – where are you mate? You'll remember this – Phil and me went back to our house after a dead boring day at school, effing and blinding about everyone and everything. Ten or eleven we'd be. "Right. I've heard enough. Stop bloody swearing." OK it was funny, but she insisted that in our house, and if we knew what was good for us, outside the house as well, that we could use the words 'chuffing' and 'frigging' whenever we wanted to swear. Dad had to agree the same, so as to set an example. And it's still 'chuffin' this and friggin' that', ain't it Phil?

'She would put her hands over my ears whenever we went to a footy match at the old Filbert Street and the language were a bit ripe, shall we say. This was in the days when Jimmy Bloomfield were manager, and the great Peter Shilton and Frank Worthington were playing. Remember? FA cup semi-final, 1974. She took me there. What an experience. Liverpool had Kevin Keegan, John Toshack and all those. She was a season ticket holder for over fifty years, even when City were in the third division, whatever they call it now. She was still taking an interest up to the day she died. Some of you will know that she liked to have a bit of a flutter, and she put £10 on City to win the league at the beginning of the season, at five thousand to one. It was last season though, not this unfortunately. Now she won't get to see her beloved team win the league, as we know they will.' There were sounds of approval.

'She had an interesting theory as to why City are doing so well. Nowt to do with Claudio or teamwork, she said. It's divine intervention. When I asked her what she meant, she told me it was because City were the first to cough up when the Richard the Third lot were asking for money.

'Audrey loved this city, and would be dead chuffed about the way it's getting a bit more recognition, like. You'll have all heard her banging on about what a great place it is, how much is going on with everything the different ethnic groups bring to the place. She was the best mayor we never had, which I reckon some of you know. I think she never quite forgave them who couldn't quite bring themselves to vote for a woman, but she shrugged her shoulders and got on with it.

'She had her faults, like all of us, but she was kind and generous, always had time for people who knocked on her door or stopped her in the street. Her memory was going a bit near the end, and we didn't realise how poorly she was. But she kept her sense of mischief, and she was still crafty enough to send me off with a shopping list when we got to the supermarket, while she went off in the other direction with her real list, which included the bottle of malt. I am going to miss her to bits.'

Stan thanked them again, and gave them directions to the working men's club for the wake. A few of the Tory councillors even made their way over.

*Stan*

Enough said.

# Twenty-Six

# Kind Hearted Woman Blues

wo days later, Stan was pleased to be back in the van for morning coffee with Phil.

'Do my friggin' eyes deceive me, or have you lost a bit of weight?' Stan had asked as they stood looking at each other over the roof of the van.

'Quite possibly, duck. It's all the extra work I'm doing while you swan around going to the chuffin' gym and stuff.' Phil was persevering with the five-two diet, pleased to have lost a few pounds. For the first time in his life he was thinking about his food and drink intake, and was trying to cut down on the carbohydrates, including beer, limiting himself to two pints on any given day. Most days he had been successful, but he found it hard at weekends. Recently discovering that there were such things as alcohol-free beers, he had found one German version to be very acceptable.

Stan was accompanying Phil on one of their rounds, to see his latest equipment in action. This included a brush on an extending aluminium pole, with a hose connected to a drum of water in the back of the van, all designed so that one person could clean windows on the first floor without having to use ladders. 'What's more, my old,' he had said, 'it uses deionised water, whatever that chuffin' well is, from that machine so that when it dries there are no friggin' smears. So it cuts right down on the time, like, so I can be in the pub for lunchtime. Bob's your uncle. You'll have to come and have a butchers at the deionising kit I've got at home. It's taken over the friggin' garage and the missus is not happy.' Stan promised to pay half of the cost, provided it lived up to Phil's claims.

Phil was obviously proud of his new system, and as well as being impressed at how well Phil had mastered the equipment, Stan was also pleased that his friend had shown some initiative. Because it could be another four or five weeks before Stan could start work again, they had discussed employing someone in the short term to keep the business going, but Phil had insisted that he could cope on his own. Stan was attending weekly sessions with a physiotherapist, religiously doing the exercises set for him as homework. He had also joined a cardiac rehabilitation class at the hospital, which involved ball games and a circuit of exercises. Amazed at how quickly he felt he was getting back to fitness, the sight of his scar in the mirror served as a reminder that he shouldn't rush things. Even so, he closed his eyes and smiled as his mind went back to Mandy's bed earlier that morning. She had been rubbing a brand of baby oil into his scar daily, to reduce the redness and help the healing. Within a couple of minutes they were making love properly for the first time since before he had been admitted to hospital.

Phil's voice cut into the moment.

'Oi! Romeo! I know that smile. A mucky one, if ever there was. As I was saying, what about asking my misses if she can get us some business cards done at her place, like, so that we could pop them through people's letter boxes or hand them over. I reckon with this contraption, right, we could take on more work when you're back on the grove. Maybe we could buy another.' Stan thought that business cards were a bit poncy. The next thing, they would be working in suits and ties, he suggested, but agreed that they should have some printed.

A mobile phone was ringing.

'That yours or mine?' asked Phil.

They both searched frantically through pockets. Stan found his. 'Not mine,' he said.

'Shit, mine's on the wall.' The ringing had stopped by the time Phil located his phone.

'Esther,' he said, shrugging his shoulders in a way which suggested he should call back, which he did.

'Aye up duck.' As he listened, he sat down in the passenger seat, his smile turning to a look of concern. 'Slow down duck. What time was this? Are the police still there?' He looked up at Stan, shaking his head and mouthing an obscenity.

'Of course I can. Just sit tight. I'll get over as soon as I can.' Phil hit the dashboard hard with his fist.

'That bastard. I knew there was something about him.'

'The suspense is killing me. What the chuff's going on?'

Phil explained that the police had raided Esther's boyfriend Raymond's house at five o'clock that morning. Evidently, Raymond had previously been imprisoned for possession of indecent images of children on his computer, so after being informed of his presence in the area, the police had gone to his house with a search warrant and had taken away his laptop and tablet. To make matters worse, after learning of his friendship with Esther, they had knocked on her door, then insisted on taking away any computers that there were in the house.

'So poor old Daniel has had his two computers friggin' confiscated. You can imagine the chuffin' state he'll be in. Anyway, I need to get round there sharpish. I'll drop you off. No reason why you should get bogged down with this.'

'I was thinking that it might be helpful if there were two friendly faces, especially for the lad. But whatever you want, like.' They drove to Birstall together.

Esther burst into tears as soon as she saw Phil, who gave her a long hug before they moved into the living room. Stan tried to be as unobtrusive as possible.

'I'm so sorry. It's such a bloody mess,' she said.

'It's not your fault, duck, so come on. Where's Daniel? School?'

'He's upstairs, very upset about what happened. He wouldn't go to school.' She wiped her eyes on a tissue. 'That policeman. He was a brute, a right nasty piece of work. Said Raymond was a dangerous person. Strikes me he's the dangerous person.'

The story was that following his release from a six month gaol sentence, Raymond had moved from Birmingham to try and start a new life. Esther had met him at a choir concert at the local church, and he had managed to charm his way into her life. He was honest enough to tell her about the court case and imprisonment. One of the terms of his release was that he agreed to a supervision order, which stated that he had to have a supervising person with him whenever he was in a situation in which minors were present. The police had become involved because he had sung in the local church choir at the recent Christmas service. The vicar was pleased to have him, especially as Raymond had experience of directing choirs. What he didn't know about was Raymond's conviction as a paedophile, until Raymond told him. The vicar consulted the diocese, who were happy to allow Raymond sing at the service as along as his supervisor was present.

'So who was the chuffin' supervisor?' asked Phil.

Esther hesitated. 'Me.'

'Chuffin' Nora, Esther,' said Phil, with a mixture of despair and anger.

'Well he wasn't doing anything wrong. As far as I could see someone has to support him. He's done his stint in prison, so I think he deserves a chance.'

'Once a paedo....' Phil cut himself short.

'Anyway, it seems that someone on the diocese board shopped Raymond to the police, who were soon onto him.'

'And what about Daniel?'

'He never touched him, if that's what you mean. He's never touched any kids as far as I know, only kept pictures of them.'

'Exactly. As far as you know. But you can't know for certain. And you trusted this slimy git.'

For a couple of minutes there was only the sound of Esther's sniffing, nose blowing and heavy sighs. She then seemed to gather some inner strength.

'I was always sure to be around whenever I knew Daniel was in the house. Like I say, someone has to stand by Raymond if he's going to sort his life out. His family won't have anything to do with him. And do you know what? He hasn't actually done anything wrong. He just wanted to sing carols in the church service. Alright there were a few kids there, but so were their parents and so was I.'

Stan broke his silence. 'Where is he?'

'Who?'

'Yer man.'

'I don't know. And I don't want you two going anywhere near him. Leave him alone.'

'Shall I pop up and see Daniel and have a chat?' asked Stan. Esther gave her nose another good blow.

'That would be nice. I'm sure he'll be pleased to see a friendly face. But I doubt he'll be very communicative.'

'Actually, I'll go up if that's alright,' said Phil.

'Yeah. Sure. In that case I'll make my way home. I'll use the bus. I need to catch up on a couple of things.' He slipped his coat on and said goodbye. At the door, he stopped and turned.

'Just a thought, like, but by my reckoning this chuffin' copper mightn't have had a search warrant for this place, in which case he had no right to take any computers. You might want to think about that, my old.'

'Good point, mate. We should be able to find out which nick he's from. I'll get onto it.'

'Yeah, but go carefully. I know you, you'll go in all guns chuffin' blazing and make things worse. It needs a bit of what's-a-name....'

'Diplomacy?' suggested Esther.

'Exactly. Anyway, see you. Take care, Esther. We'll see you're alright.' She thanked Stan and he left.

'One thing we might think about, duck, is making a complaint. You know, to the police about that chuffin' copper, especially if he has barged in here without a chuffin' search warrant.'

'I've written it all down Phil, on that pad over there.' She pointed to her sideboard. 'But I don't want to make things any worse than they are already, so we'll see how it goes.'

'Well, something to think about. I'll nip upstairs and see how he's doing.'

As soon as Phil started to go upstairs he could hear the tapping of Daniel playing quietly on the percussion set in his room. Opening the door slightly, he was surprised to see the boy sitting at the set, headphones on and plugged into his iPad. He was playing softly with his brushes to keep the sound down to a minimum. Phil stood at the door, enjoying the opportunity to watch Daniel totally absorbed in the music, deftly using all parts of the kit. At the point at which the track he had been listening to seemed to have finished, Phil knocked on the door.

'Aye up. Your Mum said I'd find you up here, me old. How's it going? She said you were upset after what's happened, so I thought I'd pop up, like.' He walked over and sat down on the spare chair, as Daniel removed the headphones. He swivelled round to face Phil.

'I was a bit cross and upset at first. The policemen were very unkind and rude to my Mum, and they took both of my computers away. But I knew you would come and help to cheer Mum up. They didn't take my iPad, by the way. And,' he added with emphasis, 'I get to miss boring Geography, and practise instead.'

'So you're coping alright?'

'Well the other thing is, I realised that the police shouldn't have taken my computers without a search warrant, so if I go round to the police station they will have to give them back to me.'

'We've just been talking about that my old. We could go round to the police station together if you like, see what they have to say.'

'That would be really exciting. I've never been into one before.'

'They're nothing to write home about, I can tell you, so don't get too excited. But one condition – you go into school this afternoon.'

'It's Art this afternoon, which I like.'

It didn't take Phil long to track down which station they needed to go to. Standing at the station door, Phil was nonplussed to find it closed and that there was a security system to negotiate.

'Thankfully, I haven't been to one of these for a year or two, like. You used to be able to chuffin' just walk in. Sign of the times, I suppose. There is a chance, my old, that one or two people in here might recognise me from a few years ago.'

'Why, do some of your friends work here?'

'Not friends exactly. More acquaintances.'

Expecting to be treated as a suspect and to be kept waiting for hours, after half an hour or so they were on their way out, carrying Daniel's computers. They had been met by a woman Sergeant. After listening to Phil and Daniel's explanation of what had happened earlier, claiming that the policeman didn't have a search warrant for his house, she invited them to take a seat while she looked into it. She also arranged for them to be brought cups of tea. Phil's response to the courteous treatment was to say 'I'm sure it was just a mistake. I mean them taking the laptops, not bringing the friggin' tea.'

On her return to her desk, the sergeant informed them: 'It seems there has been a mistake, as you said Mr Hiscox. Someone will bring Daniel's computers to return them within a few minutes.'

The few minutes turned out to be thirty, which Phil saw as the police trying to make a point.

'Well at least one good thing has come out of this chuffin' mess,' he said, as they walked back to the van. 'Here you go, duck.' He handed the two laptops to Daniel.

## *Phil*

What I'd like to know is what did these perverts do in the days before the chuffin' internet? They must have had to pass round their dirty photos, or something. There are so many of them, and they're not all blokes neither. There were a couple of women in the news who were taking photos of young kids in the school where they were working. It seems to me that the world has become a more dangerous place cos of the friggin' internet. You can find out how to make bombs, terrorists can keep in touch with each other, kids are being brainwashed and turned to terrorists, celebrities and politicians get all sort of shit thrown at them on the internet, especially women. Paedos go on this dark internet thing, which I don't get, spreading their nastiness. It's like no one knows how to stop it all.

## Twenty-Seven

# Fields of Gold

*E*yes closed, moving gently back and forth on Neil's rocking chair, Stan listened to the song playing on the sound system. Steeleye Span's *Gaudete*. He remarked that he had been to see the band with his mother in the old Haymarket Theatre when he was in his early teens.

'Sounds great,' he said, as it finished. 'A bit religious, though. It's not really what I want to be doing.'

'That's not the point, Stan. You wanted to know how harmonising works, so this might help us. Bear with me, OK.' He passed some sheets of music to Stan. 'This is the manuscript for their arrangement of *Gaudete*. There are several arrangements around, but they all follow the same principles. Are you OK following this? I assumed you can read music.'

'I learned a bit, like, with Miss Banner back in junior school when she taught us the chuffin' recorder, so I can follow a melody alright. Well sort of. I have to work it out. It's not like I can look at it and play or sing straight away, sort of thing.'

Neil showed him how the music for the four singing parts was written down. He played the melody on his keyboard while Stan followed the written music. After working on the melody and baseline for a few minutes, they were able to sing the two parts in harmony.

'That sounds so cool,' said Stan. Neil then played the piano accompaniment to a choral arrangement of *In the Bleak Mid Winter*, which Stan had so enjoyed hearing the choir sing in the hospital.

'Yeah, I could pick out the parts there,' said Stan. 'It's like in the chuffin' band, when you have to be listening to what everyone else is doing, as well as your own stuff.'

'Exactly. So if you really want to get us doing some harmonising, we could do it. It doesn't have to be as complicated as four parts, either. Lots of bands just use two or three. Simon and Garfunkel made a chuffin' amazing sound with just the two of them.'

'As I was lying around, like, in hospital, I listened to all sorts of music, and did a bit of thinking. That can be a bit friggin' dangerous, or it can be a good thing. But I just thought that we could aim to be a bit more ambitious, a bit more .... What's the word?'

'Sophisticated?'

'Yeah, that'll do. Sophisticated. Know what I mean? So that we don't end up sounding like any old band. We do make a good sound together. Your violin, Angie's bass and her singing, even if I do take the piss. They're all good. But there's loads of good bands out there trying to make it. We need something to give us a bit of an edge. Now I'm not chuffin' saying that singing harmonies is the answer, but it could be another bow to add.'

'You mean string. Another string to our bow.'

'Alright, smart arse.'

'I kind of think you're right. At the same time, it doesn't mean we should be trying to write and play our own stuff all the time. You can be creative with covers as well. Have a listen to this Stan. I love it.'

A choral a cappella arrangement of *Fields of Gold* came through on his sound system. When it had finished, they sat in silence for several seconds.

'That is hairs on the back of your neck stuff,' said Stan. 'You see, it's not something I would normally listen to, but who would think that someone would come along and do such a great job on Sting's song.'

'I was thinking we could take that and develop it. Have some accompaniment, probably Tom on the keyboard, throw in some solos. I had a play around earlier on.' He picked up his violin, quickly tested the tuning then played. There was some improvising, but it was clearly an interpretation of the song.

Stan applauded. 'Amazing. You can almost hear the piano and guitar solos as well.'

'And the double bass. You wouldn't need any percussion. Going back to Daniel, and what's happened to him and his Mum, is he going to be alright to play with us still, do you think?' Stan had called each of the band members to put them in the picture about the police visit a couple of days, so that they could be prepared for any reaction from Daniel. He replied to Neil's question by explaining how well Daniel seemed to have coped so far, and seemed to be as enthusiastic as ever about playing with them.

'So that Sting track; could we do it?' Stan asked.

'The solos and accompaniment, definitely. The challenge is in the vocal arrangement. But no reason why we couldn't crack it. What we need, though, is someone to work with us on the harmonies. Like a choir director. I have just the person in mind, and if it's alright with you, I've asked her to come along tomorrow night to our practice. Well, Tom did actually. As luck would have it, she's available.'

'Oh right,' said Stan, taken aback. 'Anyone I know.'

'Possibly.'

Tom walked into the practice room accompanied by a woman, both in waterproofs, hoods up, leaving a trail of rain drops behind them. Stan was grateful for the opportunity to break off from the heated discussion, in danger of becoming a full-blown row, he and Malcolm had been having about the plan for the evening. Malcolm was complaining that they should have talked about the whole idea of having a practice devoted to 'ponsy singing'. 'I joined this band because I want to play the guitar, not for any harmonising bollocks,' he had said.

'Yeah, I can see your point, mate,' Stan had replied, quickly losing his patience, 'but we do have a plan, Neil and me, which includes some playing. And anyhow, if we had had a chat about it and it had come to a chuffin' vote, you'd have lost, so we'd be here anyway. So stop being so friggin' mardy.' He refrained from adding 'and grow up.' Now Neil, Angie and Stan, who had put his arm around Daniel's shoulder before he could react to the argument, stood and faced the advancing couple, while Malcolm sat long-faced on the stage, barely acknowledging their presence.

Tom and the woman removed their waterproofs. She was wearing jeans and a sweater. Tom took her coat, as he said,

'Well here we are. You've all met Staff Nurse Tracy.' Greetings were exchanged, then Tracy turned to Stan.

'Well, it's Mr Humbug,' she said, with a hint of surprise in her voice. 'You're looking a lot better than when I last saw you.' Stan was aware that he must have been staring at her for a few seconds. The penny had dropped.

'I'm sorry love, it's a…, umm, you….' he spluttered. 'I've only seen you in a nurse's outfit, like. Yeah, I'm loads better. Fighting fit, almost, which is just as well with some of this lot.' For her benefit, Stan explained everyone's role in the band, coming last of all to Malcolm, who gave a gruff hallo, barely making eye contact.

'Do I detect a reluctant participant?' she said. 'From what I can remember, you have a really good voice, which came through strongly when you sang with our choir. I won't bite, honest.' Malcolm ran his hand down his face, then managed a half-smiled. He said he was fine.

'Now,' she said, addressing them all. 'I want to say first that I'm more than happy to be here to help out, but I am not a professional. I have directed the village choir where I live, as well as the hospital choir, so I do have some experience. And we'll do what we can. From what I've heard already there are some good voices here, and as you all play instruments, you'll be used to listening to each other, so I've been looking forward to this.'

She outlined her plan for the evening, checking that the band were happy with it. This included time to help with anything the band particularly wanted to work on. When asked, Daniel opted to watch from the side, rather than join in the singing. Over the course of the next hour our or so, Tracy led them through some vocal exercises and scales, before moving onto some short songs in harmony. This involved assigning each person a part. They had all heard Daniel singing along with them quietly from the side, at this point Tracy suggested to him that the band would sound even better if he joined them. They clapped as he took his place, and were rewarded with a self-conscious smile. Malcolm's surliness and reticence gradually disappeared, as Tracy consistently praised them collectively and individually. Stan was to remark later to Tom that 'she had us eating out of her hand. We'd have done anything for her.'

'I think you're ready to have a go at this, one hopefully you'll all know well,' Tracy handed out a songbook, asking them to find *Danny Boy*. Tom accompanied on the piano as she sang with them in unison, before working on the harmony, again giving lots of praise and encouragement. Before breaking for drinks, they sang through the whole song just once. She stood at the back of the room, listening, just as Mandy had encouraged the band to do when they first started to practise together

'Absolutely amazing. You should hear yourselves. After just half an hour on that one piece, you sound so good. Alright, you wouldn't be ready to perform that in public just yet, but even so. And you are such a pleasure to work with. None of the chuntering and grumbles I would get from one of the choirs.' Neil replied that having a great teacher helped.

After the break, Neil and Stan introduced the idea of working on an arrangement of *Fields of Gold*, and explained their thinking behind it. He then played a recording of the same choral version that he and Stan had listened to the previous day. A silence followed, while they each considered their reaction. This was broken by Tom, who thought singing this was out of their league and wasn't sure that it would fit in with what they had been doing so far. Malcolm shared this point of view, whilst Angie said that she would love to be able to perform it.

'But we can make it fit our style,' Neil responded. We have kind of developed a sound without talking too much about it, and it can be really good. For me it's a case of do we just carry on meeting to practise, just seeing where it takes us, or are we going to get out there and show what we can do? I..' Stan interrupted.

'I ought to say something, as it was my idea, like, to have a go at this stuff. Like I said to Neil, there's lots of chuffin' bands trying to make a go of it and hoping for a break. There's also them bands what just want to do gigs. Parties and stuff. Is that us? Or do you want to aim for... I dunno. Being on the radio, doing albums and stuff?'

'But Stan, don't...' Tom tried to interject.

'Just let me finish, me old. Even without all that 'what's the point?' bollocks, like Neil says we can make this *Fields of Gold* chuffin' well work for us. Neil, mate, will you just give us a flavour of your solo, yeah? Then if you'll bear with me, like, Tom, let's see if you and Malcolm could pick it up and ad lib a couple of solos. If you know what I mean. The key is C, which should help. Just give it a go. Alright?'

'Suppose so,' said Malcolm. Tom nodded agreement. As Neil plugged the violin in to his amp, he asked Stan to play back the recording as far as where the line which included the song title was sung twice. From there he played sixteen bars, nodding to Tom that he should be ready to take over. Tom played a couple of chords to feel his way into the tune, then produced something which was a bit more strident than Neil's playing. Malcolm picked up on the tone of Tom's playing at first, then brought it back to the more gentle feel of the song.

'Hang on,' called Angie, as the others started to break into applause. 'I've got it.' She had quietly retrieved her double bass from its large case and quickly checked the tuning. She made her own contribution, finishing with a flourish which brought her to the D note on which the vocals would come in.

There were smiling faces all around. 'Absolutely, chuffin', friggin' amazing,' said Stan, who couldn't stop clapping, until Tracy walked over and stood next to him.

'You have got some very talented musicians here, Mr Humbug,' she said. 'It's such a lovely song. Let's start working on it while there's a bit of time left. We could certainly get as far as where the solos might come in.'

'I agree. It is a lovely song,' added Tom, 'and yes we have some talented musicians. But let's just have a reality check, before we get too carried away. Some of us are in demanding full-time jobs, me for one, and if we're talking about looking to do more than the odd gig, and maybe a bit of recording, I don't think I could make that commitment.' Smiling, he added, 'Not unless you can guarantee me stardom.'

'Stan, what are you hoping for exactly?' asked Malcolm. 'Like I said earlier, I came along so that I could have a go at playing my guitar in a band, not too worried about where it led to.'

'And so did I my old, to start with. But A, I didn't reckon on having such a, um, good, group of people together, making such a great sound. And B, I don't want, like, to be cleaning windows for the rest of my life. Yeah, to start with I thought 'let's see if we can get something together and take it from there. See if I can do it in a band as well as plugging away at home, like.' So I dunno. Granted, winderin' doesn't compare with doing heart surgery and suchlike. Maybe what we do is chuffin' well sort out a couple of gigs, see if we can pull it off on stage.'

Angie and Daniel also had their say. Daniel suggested that the band needed to set up a website, as well as Facebook and twitter accounts. 'Are you offering?' Neil jokingly asked. Much to everyone's surprise, he answered 'Well, yeah, I could do it, with a bit of help. And don't we need a manager? I thought all bands have a manager.'

The consensus was that Stan would talk to Ursula about playing a gig at the café, as she had requested, while Neil and Angie would explore the possibility of playing somewhere at the university. The idea of a website, using social media and looking for a manager, would be explored further down the line. Tracy agreed to come along to the next practice to work on *Fields of Gold* and anything else she could help with, dismissing the offer of being paid, 'unless you can guarantee me stardom.' To finish the evening on a high note, they enjoyed a twelve bar blues-rock jam.

Later, Stan was on a barstool at the club, Phil to his left, each with a half-drunk pint. Stan summarised the outcomes of the evening for Phil's benefit. Phil appeared to be deep in thought, hardly acknowledging what Stan was saying.

'Everything all right, my old?'

'Sorry mate. Yeah. Well, no. I was intending to get along to watch you lot tonight, but I got into a bit of a row with the missus.'

Stan waited, sensing there was more to come. Spotting a bulging hold-all on the floor beside Phil, he asked, 'Going somewhere?' Phil looked down at the bag, as if only just noticing it.

'Oh, that. Yeah, I could be.' Stan waited again. Phil looked at him, eyes glistening. 'She's kicked me out. Told me to eff off. Once and for all, she said.' Stan looked at him in disbelief, but could see he wasn't joking.

'What? So what the chuff's got in to her, then? Was this on the cards, like?'

'You'd better bleeding well ask her. To start with it looked like things were going to work out differently, sort of thing. We had a bit of a kiss and cuddle on the sofa, which hasn't happened in a while, and I suggested we might go upstairs, like, you know how it is. Then she started with the usual *not-in-the-mood stuff, got-a-bit-of-a-headache crap*. So when I said it had been a long time since we'd done any of the old in-out stuff, she went ballistic. I was never home, never showed any interest, blah, blah, blah, and when I did the old spark had gone.' He paused. 'Then something made me ask: *Was she seeing someone?*' More ranting. *So are you?* I asked. *Might be*, she said eventually. Then she had a go at me. She's seen an email from Daniel on my iPad. Who was he? So I told her. The whole lot, you know, me and Esther. And that bastard paedo. So here I am. The kids don't know yet. At least, unless she's told them, like.'

Eyebrows raised, Stan gave a long, slow breath through puffed cheeks. 'Holy shit,' he said. 'What a chuffin' mess, all round. I'm really sorry mate. So who's been giving her one then? Any ideas?'

'She wouldn't tell me. Just a guess, but once or twice I've passed Kit's car as I've turned into our road, and wondered what he was doing round our way.'

'Crafty sod. So what are you going to do? Presumably you've got your toothbrush in that friggin' bag. If you need somewhere to get your head down, you only need to ask.'

'Well I was hoping I might cadge a bed at your place for tonight, like, then take stock tomorrow, see what I can find.'

Stan quickly tried to assess where that would leave his arrangements with Mandy, but could foresee no problems in the short term. 'Yeah, absolutely. What are mates for? Stay as long as you need. Within reason like. One condition though. No farting at the meal table.'

'Fair enough.'

'Nor picking your nose. And come to think of it toe nails clippings go in the bin.'

'Right. So that's three conditions.'

'I think you'll find it's one A, one B and one C. And there could be D, E, F and G if necessary. But I'm sure we'll get on just fine, me old.'

## *Phil*

It feels like I'm staring into a deep dark pit and I can't see the bottom. Even when I was seeing Esther, like, I never stopped loving Jane, never imagined I would leave her, or she would leave me. But looking back, the old spark hasn't been there for a while. We weren't having sex very often, which was the excuse I gave myself over the Esther thing. So I ask myself, how long has this thing with this bloke, who I reckon is Kit, cos it seems to fit, how long has it chuffin' well been going on?

On that first night at Stan's I didn't really sleep. My mind were just wandering backwards and forwards. I'd never thought about getting married or having kids. Especially having kids. They were both her ideas. *Do you love me?* She asked me at the end of one date. Caught me on the hop a bit. *Yes*, I said, supposing that I did. *Well why don't we get married?* I remember the look she gave me, straight into the eyes. Sort of daring me, like it were a conspiracy or something, to catch everyone out. *And have kids. I'd like two.* I couldn't think of a reason to say we shouldn't do either, except I'd never thought about it.

She was a natural mother, you could tell from the minute she found out she was expecting the first. The kids were her whole life, and she gave them so much love. She could forgive them the sleepless nights and the chuffin' tantrums, and would calm me down whenever I had a rant about them. She would always say to the kids how important the family is, would tell them all the time that she loved them, and they would say they loved her back, until they reached the age when they decided it wasn't cool.

Lying there, I admitted to myself that I might have done better, like. I could never quite bring myself to say I love you too. *Yeah, me too,* I would say. I could've tried to change the odd nappy now and then. I did read them bedtime stories when they were little, until the books got a bit too difficult, like. And I did enjoy playing with them on the old Lego and other construction stuff.

Fuck.

## Stan

We was all a bit surprised when Phil told us he was getting friggin' married. *She must be up the duff,* a few said. I would have said that he wasn't the marrying kind, like. I don't know why. His face was a picture as he walked down the aisle with Jane. She was beaming all over, and old Phil looked a bit overwhelmed by the whole church and wedding suit thing. It was probably the only time I've ever seen him in a suit. No, I tell a lie. He wore one at my wedding. We were each other's best man. Ever the romantic, he took her to Blackpool for their honeymoon. Apparently it rained most of the time. He took her to the boxer Brian London's night club one night. I can just about remember him boxing in the sixties. One of the old slug-it-out brigade. Of course, Phil knew all about him. Brian was one of his heroes, so he was over the moon when he got to shake the bloke's hand at the club. Seems Phil was about to get into a spot of bother, and the big man had to step in.

I always thought that they chuffin' worked as a couple. Looked after their kids well, worked hard, played hard and that. After a while you couldn't imagine them apart.

# Twenty-Eight

# We're Going Wrong

Radio two's breakfast show was playing on the second morning after Phil had moved in, as it had on the first. 'I hate this bloke,' complained Phil, over his bowl of Cheerios. 'Smarmy git, if you ask me.'

'Well you'd better get used to him, my old.' Stan spread marmalade onto a slice of toast.

'And do we have to have this poncy brown bread? I'd prefer white, especially for the sarnies. I'm sure you used to eat white. Getting a bit middle class in here, ain't it?'

Stan was slightly taken aback. 'Well you know where the chuffin' shop is, my old.'

'And can we have some marmite in for me toast?'

Stan bit his lip. 'I tell you what. I'll put a sheet of paper over there, right, on the worktop for a shopping list, and anything you want bung it on the chuffin' list. OK?'

'Fair enough. We'll split the cost after you've done the shopping, shall we?'

'Or you could chuffin' well do it. By the way, have you seen my magazine? Guitarist. I bought it yesterday, but can't see it anywhere.'

'Oh, err, I was doing a bit of tidying up, and might have put it into one of the drawers in the other room.' He caught Stan's look of bewilderment. 'Well, you're an untidy git, so I was just trying to help a bit, you know in return for....He looked around. Your shoes are by the back door. Oh and I put all the cloths under the sink, and your....'

'Hang on, hang on. Just a chuffin' minute.' Stan walked over to the back door and collected two pairs of shoes. He stood at the table and held them up. 'Now look my old, I know you're trying to help, like, but the last thing I need is someone going round tidying up after me. I want things where I left them so I can friggin' well find them, not to have to hunt around.' He sat down and sipped his tea. 'And since when have you been so friggin' anal, anyway?'

'Well, it's just....'

'And you snore for England,' said Stan. He got up and left the room, returning with his magazine. He pointedly opened it and slowly turned the pages.

'So what's in the sarnies today then?' asked Phil.

'I'll let you decide. They're your sarnies,' Stan replied without looking up. 'Might be a new experience for you I guess.'

'Yeah well, once in a while....I'll see what's in the fridge.'

In an attempt to lighten the atmosphere, Stan offered to get some fish and chips for their tea, but he felt a sense of relief when Phil declined his invitation to join him at Ursula's for lunch, on the basis that it was too far from Oadby, where he would be working. Stan was hoping to arrange a date for a gig at the café, as well as to enjoy Ursula's company.

Breakfast time was similarly fractious the following day, each coming up with petty complaints about the other. By the end of the week Stan decided to avoid the niggles by getting up earlier and finishing his breakfast before Phil appeared. Phil seemed not to notice, and Stan sat in his bedroom reading and listening to the radio until Phil called up that he was leaving. The evening meals were less of a problem, as both had the story of their day to share, but Stan began to tire of Phil's boasting about the 'fit birds' who brought him tea or coffee, obviously wanting to chat him up, and 'probably more'. So on that Friday evening, he and Mandy drove out to a country pub for a bite to eat, leaving Phil to his own devices. The conversation soon got round to a discussion about Phil's situation.

'You have to try and see things from his point of view though, Stan,' said Mandy, after he had summarised the week, including the low-level bickering. 'He must be feeling pretty shitty about things, and wouldn't have imagined a week ago that he would be dossing in your place. Believe me, it's difficult to cope with being kicked out of your own home. I went right off the rails for a while. Phil's lucky to have a close friend to rely on.'

'Yeah I suppose so. It's a slightly weird friggin' situation for us both. I've known him for years, like, but we've never been under the same roof together, having to share space and stuff. But it's like I'm seeing a side of him I don't bleeding recognise. I don't want to lose him as a mate.'

'It sounds like you both need a bit of space. You've got a key to my place, so why not spend a few nights with me and leave Phil to it? I know it's early days yet, but have you had any sort of chat about what he might do? You know, about what's going on with Jane, or where he might live if she won't have him back.'

'I thought I'd leave it till he brings things up, like. It ain't really my area of speciality. I'll perhaps give him a couple of weeks before I suggest it's time he started to look for somewhere more chuffin' permanent.' He sipped his beer thoughtfully. 'What I could do, right, is suggest we have a pint and watch the City match tomorrow at the club. And I haven't seen his boys play for a while, so maybe I could do that on Sunday.'

'You're coming to our gig tomorrow evening, as well. What more could you want? Your weekend will be complete.'

'Oh I can think of one or two more things to fit in, so to speak.'

'Said the bishop to the actress.'

The match kicked-off at lunchtime. Leicester City, riding top of the Premiership, were playing away to Manchester City. Talk in the club, as across the city, was of Leicester possibly going on to win the Premiership title. When they walked through the door into the main bar, Stan and Phil sensed the air of expectancy and excitement. The large room was already packed, thirty minutes before the kick-off, several members clearly the worse for wear after drinking on empty stomachs. Stan and Phil pushed their way through and bought beer, cobs and pasties at the bar, before making their way over to the TV area with the large screen on the wall, where they chatted with friends and acquaintances for a few minutes. There were several rows of seats, most of which had been taken. Resting his drink and food on a window sill, Phil dragged over a couple of bar stools. They sat at the back, precariously placing plates and glasses on the floor and on their knees.

'I have never seen this place so buzzing,' said Stan.'Imagine this lot if Leicester chuffin' score first.'

'Yeah. Hold onto your pints. Two one the Foxes, I reckon, the way they're playing.' The teams were walking out side-by-side onto the pitch, and the cheering and whistling in the room was deafening. A number of people were chanting 'Come on you Blues.' The Leicester team was in fact playing in black shirts and shorts, their away strip. This, in Phil's opinion, made the team look more menacing than usual.

Three minutes into the game Leicester scored, and there was mayhem in the clubroom. Every person immediately rose from his or her seat to roar approval, glasses rising with them, which gave the contents upwards momentum. Hair, shirts and jeans became soaked, but no-one seemed to mind. This was repeated whenever here was a shot on goal from a Leicester player. Consequently, there was a constant flow to and from the bar for glasses to be refilled. One supporter, returning to his seat carrying two full pints of beer, slipped on the wet floor, raising a cheer almost as loud as the one accompanying the goal, as the contents were spilled over those within range. There was some respite at half time, during which chairs were moved aside as a vacuum cleaner mopped up most of the slops from the floor.

'Cracking game,' said Phil.'The Man City defence look shit scared whenever Leicester attack, especially when yer man Vardy gets the ball.'

'Absolutely,' Stan replied. 'But Mahrez is the man for me. Class player.' He paid the barman for their drinks. 'I tell you what, my old. I don't fancy getting any wetter than we are already. I reckon there's more chuffin' goals to come, so let's hang about at the back for a bit and see how it goes.'

Just as in the first half, Leicester City scored a second goal three minutes after the restart, resulting in an equally enthusiastic response in the room. After the third goal, people were standing on chairs, star-shaped, arms aloft. Others were running around in a state of delirium, while one old man in a wheelchair temporarily forgot his disabilities, stood up to dance a little jig, before collapsing back into his chair. Phil and Stan looked on in amusement. When the excitement had died down a little, they smiled at each other and raised their glasses.

'You have to chuffin' well pinch yourself,' said Stan. 'This time last year we was all saying they'd be relegated.'

'I just hope my lads are watching. You can't beat team work.'

'Me too,' Stan thought to himself. 'And good coaching,' he said out loud. Phil gave him a questioning look. 'From your lordship, obviously,' Stan added.

The final score was three goals to one, and the noise level remained high as many stayed behind to celebrate and re-play the game in their drunken conversations. Stan and Phil found a relatively quiet corner, from where they looked on for a couple of minutes. Stan suggested that they go back to his house to change into some dry clothes, adding that Phil was welcome to put any laundry into the washing machine. He explained that he would be out for the evening at Chalkie's band's gig. Phil had no particular plans, saying he would probably return to the club for a bite to eat, see who was around and 'just go with the flow.' Aware that Phil and Jane would normally be out with a group of friends on Saturday evening, Stan wondered how Phil would cope, but this didn't prevent him from announcing that he would be spending the next few nights with Mandy.

Phil stared into his half-empty glass, gently swirling the beer around. Loneliness seemed to envelop him.

'But I'll be there in the morning, mate. Big game isn't it?'

'Quarter final,' replied Phil. 'The County provide the touch judges as well as the ref, so you'll be able to pick up some tips.'

'Cheeky git.'

The Peter White Band, otherwise known as Chalkie's, was playing at a wedding anniversary celebration in Markfield, a few miles from Leicester. Stan made himself useful, taking any light equipment he could carry in from Chalkie's van on to the stage of the hall. As the band tuned up and sorted out the sound balance, he waved or gave thumbs up from the back of the hall on the couple of occasions that he caught Mandy's eye. He had accompanied Mandy on a couple of the band's gigs previously, but oddly, for the first time and for reasons which he couldn't identify, he began to feel a bit of a spare part, especially when the band disappeared to the room allocated as their dressing room.

The band were going through their usual repertoire, which was received well enough, but Stan felt that Mandy's performance in the first half was a bit flat. She acknowledged this herself at the interval.

'Chalkie's not too happy either,' she said. 'So I'd better gee things up.'

'Anything I can do?'

'A hug and a kiss might help, Big Man.' He duly obliged.

There was much more sparkle to her singing in the second half, which he suspected was more down to the gentle bollocking he knew Chalkie would have given her.

'Don't wait up for me,' she said, after the last of the band's gear had been safely stowed away in the van. 'It'll be nice to have a lie-in and a snuggle in the morning.' The post-gig meal and drinks were strictly for the band members, so he knew he had no right to expect to be invited. But, as always, he felt disappointed.

Stan had difficulty getting off to sleep alone in her bed. He found himself glancing at her bedside clock at ten minutes to one and again at two thirty. Eventually, he was aware of her creeping quietly into the room, undressing and slipping into the bed. He grunted in reply when she whispered his name, but gave no further response, and was soon asleep.

Sunlight streamed through the kitchen window, as he made a pot of tea just before nine in the morning. He placed a cupful on her bedside table, leaned across and kissed Mandy on the forehead, announcing 'tea up'. It was her turn to grunt a reply. He read the Leicester City match report in her Sunday morning newspaper, then looked around the room, wondering what to do next.

'Aye up, pet. Don't let your cuppa go cold.' She turned to face him, slowly opening her eyes. He always found Mandy particularly attractive when she was in this drowsy state in the mornings, and felt his loins stir. She mumbled something which he interpreted as asking for the time, which he told her.

'I have to be out in an hour or so. Phil's chuffin' team's playing and I said I'd go along, so I'd better show willing.' He leaned across, kissed her cheek and licked her ear. 'But there's plenty of time for umm, you-know-what.' Mandy slowly rolled over on to her back, then turned to look at him.'

'Maybe later, Stan. I might have more energy then. You go off and give Phil a bit of support.'

'Oh, OK. I just thought....' He picked up the paper and pretended to read the front page.

'It's upside down,' she told him.

'What? Oh.' Feeling jilted, he climbed out of bed, put on the dressing gown she provided for his use, then made his way over to the door, intending to shower.

'Stan, don't be like that.'

'Like what?'

'Sulky.'

'I'm going for a shower. What's sulky about that?'

She emerged in her dressing gown as Stan was finishing his breakfast. After making herself another cup of tea, she bent over Stan, put her arms around his neck and gently nibbled his ear.

'Let's not start behaving like we were married, Stan. It's been great so far, but try not to get miffed when you can't have your wicked way.'

'You don't make it easy though, duck. I spent the whole friggin' evening lusting after you while you was on stage, and again while I waited in bed for you to come home. No wonder I had such a chuffin' hard on this morning.'

'Naughty. Well it can keep till later, aye, chuck.'

'I'll hold you to that.' Stan put on his coat and kissed her goodbye.

On the park, the teams were warming up for their match. As Stan approached the pitch, he could see no sign of Phil. 'Come on you old bugger,' said Stan to himself. He walked past the group of parents.

'Where's your mate then?' one asked. 'This is no ruddy good. A big game and he's late. Sets a bad example to the lads.' Stan explained that he had no idea, but was sure Phil would be along. He walked some way along the touch line, putting some distance between himself and the disgruntled fathers. The one that had complained about Phil's lateness walked on to the pitch and gathered the team together. As he spoke, the referee blew his whistle and called the captains of the two teams together. There was still no sign of Phil. He tried to call him, without success.

Fosse Boys started the game well, and the parents and supporters of the opposition soon began to express their frustration with their own players. This increased as Phil's team scored one and then quickly added a second goal. Adults, who Stan assumed were mostly parents, aimed abusive language at their own players, the referee and linesmen, until the referee decided to go over and ask them to stop swearing and shouting abuse.

'Poor kids don't stand a chance with this lot on the touch line,' Stan muttered to himself. He decided he'd had enough. Turning to walk away, he caught sight of Phil jogging towards the pitch. Stan walked across to intercept him.

'I know, I know,' Phil called as he saw Stan approaching. 'I'll get it in the neck from that lot, so I don't need your chuffin' tuppence worth as well.'

'You'd better make it a good one, me old. They are not happy. One of the dads got them started, sorted them out, like. But at least the boys are winning, so they might have cooled down a bit. Two nil.'

'Moz's dad I expect. I thought he would. Good start, two nil. I'd better show my face.'

Stan half turned to go, then stopped. 'You don't have to tell me, but just out of interest, like, what friggin' well kept you.'

Phil smiled sheepishly. 'Well I pulled, didn't I. The old magic charm still works.'

'You what? More likely you were rat-arsed, along with the unfortunate woman probably. Anyone I know?'

'Possibly. Rita. Used to work at the hairdressers.'

'What, Meter Maid? Used to charge by the hour? Last I heard she had a bloke in tow.'

'Did have, but he ditched her. So we sort of consoled each other.'

'I bet you chuffin' well did. And where did this consoling take place?'

Phil hesitated then looked towards the pitch as he said 'Your place.'

'I knew it. Shit, Phil. It is not a friggin' knocking shop. Any more I need to know before I piss off?' Phil avoided his angry stare. He knew he should apologise, but held back.

'I'll see you later,' Stan said, and walked off. Phil called after him, but Stan kept going.

'Shit!' said Phil. He turned towards the pitch in time to see his team score a third goal.

## Stan

Funny how when you've known someone most of your life, like I have Phil, then you realise there's another side, probably several sides to them that you don't know at all. I know what makes him tick when we're out together, how to wind him up and that. We have lots of stuff in common through school, mates, socialising and so on. But where does this domesticated stuff come from? I never imagined him being so bleeding anal as he clearly is.

Nor can I imagine him as a lover. Come to think of it, nor would I want to.

## Phil

I'd been looking forward to having Saturday night out with the lads. It'll be like the old days, I'd said to myself. I hung about in the club after the game, but most of the lads I knew went home to their missus and the place emptied. I sat quietly supping as it began to fill up again around sixish, when the footballers rolled in. I know one or two of the older ones, like, and had a bit of a chat. But the young uns can't hold their beer and were soon rat-arsed and noisy as hell. I went to the chip 'ole, then slipped into the local on the Fosse Road. Again, full of kids really, but I had a pint. Out of nowhere pops Rita. She used to be one of Stan's admirers when we was kids. I did get to snog her once or twice back then, but that was it. Only this time she came on to me like, so I thought if she's interested, why not. We kept the small talk going for a bit, had a few laughs, but we both knew where it was going. I suggested getting a takeaway, from the Chinese on the corner. We ended up taking it to Stan's cos it was nearer, and I figured probably a lot cleaner than her place might be. The food was still in the cartons in the morning. Rita nearly tore my clothes off. But I couldn't get it up – the old brewer's droop – and she was soon snoring. So was I.

## Twenty-Nine

# The Payback

At least the band practices were going well. A date had been arranged for them to play at Ursula's café, which gave an increased sense of purpose in the way they approached their singing and playing. Having become a de-facto vocals coach, Tracy came along whenever her shifts allowed, suggesting ideas for the arrangements of some of their songs. Phil and Mandy were also in regular attendance, and Mandy and Tracy clearly enjoyed each other's company. Whichever combination of the three was present made a noisy appreciation society from the back of the hall, clapping and cheering enthusiastically. A few customers and staff members of the pub sometimes crept in to join them.

Stan had been filling his days as best he could by doing his physiotherapy exercises and working on a couple of songs he was trying to compose. He had worked out the lyrics, melody and chords, but the putting together of an arrangement was new stuff for Stan. Neil had spent some time showing him how to use some software to do this, but he found it painfully slow going. He was always pleased to see the time approaching one o'clock, when he would walk to Ursula's for some lunch. They'd come to an arrangement whereby Stan would pay her for the meals once he was back at work. 'But let's see,' she had said. If Ursula wasn't too busy, she would join him for a chat. On one of these occasions, she raised the subject of Phil's situation. She wondered if Phil might be interested in moving into the room above the café, which had been a bed-sit but was presently used for storage. Stan asked to have a look. The room was a reasonable size, with a shower and WC off the entrance corridor.

'We could get this tidied up,' said Ursula. 'Most of the stuff is empty boxes. The rest I could find a home for. It would do both of us a favour, or is it all three of us? Phil would be independent, this place would be cleaned up and tidied, which I've been meaning to do for ages, and you would have your own place to yourself again. Plus having someone in here would make me happier about the security, which has always worried me a little bit. What do you think?'

'You are so right, duck. We could soon get rid of this lot, add a lick of paint for you and tart it up a bit. And Bob's your uncle.'

'Sorry? Who is Bob?'

That evening, Phil and Stan ate together for the first time in a while. Exchanges between the two had become brief and matter-of-fact, but when Stan phoned him during the afternoon there was some banter about Phil's day at work, which encouraged Stan to suggest they shared a take-away meal later on, providing that it wasn't one of Phil's dieting days. It wasn't. Despite everything, Phil had managed to persevere with his diet, and he was pleased that most of his acquaintances were noticing that he had lost weight. Neil had asked whether he had a target in mind in terms of the amount he wanted to lose. This made Phil think for the first time about what he wanted to get his weight down to. In the back of his mind was the possibility of reducing it to twelve and a half stone, representing a loss of almost two stone. But today he fancied an Indian take-away.

'You get the food in, like, I'll buy the beer, and we'll split the chuffin' difference,' said Phil. 'I'll be with you after I've been round to Esther's.' He was calling in on Esther almost daily to see how she was.

'So any sign of that chuffer Raymond?' asked Stan, as he served the food onto the plates. Phil explained that Raymond had returned to Birmingham, although he still seemed to be renting the house in Leicester. Esther was in touch with him. Apparently Raymond had received a summons for a trial at the Leicester Magistrates court, sometime soon. She wouldn't tell Phil the date. The conversation got round to Stan's lunch at Ursula's café. He mentioned the bedsit, wondering whether Phil might want to take a look at it.

Phil put his fork down and looked hard at Stan.

'Oh I get it. The two of you, right, have come up with a cunning plan. You're trying to friggin' well farm me out so that you can have your chuffin' place back. My company not good enough for you then? Or what?'

Stan held both hands up. 'Her idea, not mine. You can chuffin' well stay here as long as you like, I've told you that, my old. But just have a think for a minute, will you. We've been getting on each other's friggin' nerves, and I'd hate to see us fall out. The café is handy for the club, like, easy to get into town, you'd be able to come and go whenever, and well, whenever a chance comes along, you know, if you pull, like….'

'You've got it all bloody well worked out, haven't you?' Phil picked up his fork and they ate in silence for a few minutes.

'I suppose I could go and have a shufty,' Phil said eventually, with an air of resignation. 'You've seen it I suppose. What is there?' Stan described the layout of the bed-sit and explained that there was a bit of clearing out needed. He collected their empty plates together.

'I know it's a tough friggin' time, mate, but I think this could be a good move. Gives you more independence, like.'

'And you get your place back to yourself, which I understand you would want. So I'll go and see Ursula tomorrow if I can.'

Phil was deep in thought while Stan cleared the plates and cutlery from the table. 'Any chance you and Jane might get back together, like?' he asked as he sat down. 'Have you heard from her, or been in touch?'

'She's tried to phone me couple of times, but I've just chuffin' ignored them. That so-and-so Kit has kept his distance ain't he. No sign of him. Knows I'd deck him, probably.'

Having slept on it, Phil saw the move as a good idea, and became a co-conspirator in his expulsion from Stan's house. The following weekend saw him, Daniel and Stan clearing Ursula's rubbish from the bed-sit. As they gave the walls and woodwork a coat of paint, Ursula sent up a regular supply of tea, plum cake, Brotwurst and cheeses. Listening to the radio commentary of Leicester City's win against Norwich City also helped them along, and Fosse Boys' victory on Sunday morning put Phil in an even better mood for the afternoon.

That Saturday morning, while Stan and Phil were clearing the room, Neil paid Malcolm a visit. Neither Malcolm nor Tom had been at the practice during that week. The band knew that Tom was working a late shift, but Malcolm simply hadn't turned up, and hadn't responded to phone calls or text messages from Neil and Stan over the next couple of days, asking if he was OK. Stan complained that he always felt that Malcolm was not one hundred per cent reliable, and that at some point he would let them all down. The practice had been very low key, leaving Stan feeling frustrated and despondent.

Neil knocked on the front door to Malcom's small semi. From the untidy state of the borders around the small uncut lawn, it was obvious that Malcolm was not a gardener. Neil knocked a second and then a third time. He was just about to turn and walk away when he heard the rattle of a chain on the inside of the door. Malcolm took one look at Neil and walked back inside the house, without speaking. He'd left the door open, which Neil took as an invitation to go in. He stepped over the mess of shoes, coats and bags on the floor of the small hallway and could see Malcolm looking out of the window from a chair in his kitchen-dining room. Neil walked through the door. There was a smell hanging in the air, which he recognised. In addition to the unwashed plates, cups, pots and pans were stacked up in the sink and on the worktops, there were piles of newspapers and food cartons alongside empty beer bottles and cans on the kitchen table. Neil dusted the crumbs from the one armchair and sat down. Neither spoke for a minute or so.

'Do you want to talk about it?'

'What's there to talk about?' Malcolm replied.

'Well you tell me, mate. This is not the house of a happy person.'

He waited, but got no response. He managed to find a couple of mugs, decided the kettle was clean enough to fill with water and switch on, then used the boiling water to clean the mugs before making two black coffees. He found a bag of sugar, but the milk in the open carton on the worktop was rancid.

Neil was half expecting to hear stories of flashbacks to the fighting in Afghanistan, and of colleagues dying from battle wounds. Malcolm picked up his mug of coffee and stared at it, turning it slowly in his hands. Neil noticed that his knuckles looked crusted with scabs.

After a couple of minutes, Malcolm looked up. 'I'm sorry mate,' he eventually said. 'Things are pretty shitty at the moment.' He put one hand to his forehead to shield his eyes, and his face crumpled as he fought back the tears. Neil waited patiently.

'That arsehole. That effing arsehole.' He sniffed and sighed heavily. 'Things were going great, you know, with that bloke you've seen me with. I thought we had a good thing going.' He closed his eyes, still fighting back the tears. 'But the bastard was just stringing me along. Told me last weekend that he was bored and wanted to move on. I was a bloody fool. Couldn't see what was going on. Let's do this. Let's do that. Let's get the beers in. Let's eat there. Let's....And always me paying. Then last weekend I was skint.' He wiped his eyes with the back of his hands.

'The worst fucking thing. The worst was that he called me a cripple, that he'd only slept with me out of pity and curiosity.' He paused and looked at Neil. 'I lost it at that point.'

'In what sense?'

'I gave him a bloody good hiding. I could have killed him. Told him if I saw him again I would kill him.'

'Right. So your hands....'

Malcolm held his hands up and inspected the knuckles. 'Yeah, well. Small price. They were a bit sore, that's all. Anyway, I spoiled his looks for a while.'

Neil asked Malcolm why he hadn't called him. Malcolm shrugged his shoulders and said his phone was switched off. It was obvious to Neil that Malcolm wouldn't have been in to work, but he asked the question anyway. Malcolm had called in sick. Neil then sat and listened as Malcolm opened up. This was the story of his life, he said. Whenever things were going well, something happened to screw things up, and it was usually his own fault. He talked at length about his childhood and school days. Male friendships usually ended in acrimony. Girlfriends always drifted away after a few weeks. He became 'Johnny No-mates'. He underachieved badly in his exams, when he, his parents and teachers had been so hopeful of him going on to university. His grades would have got him in through the clearing process, but he felt a sense of failure. He did at least manage to get a job in a music shop, which gave him the opportunity to become knowledgeable about guitars, and also to improve his playing. He got on well with the girl, a sixth former, who worked at the shop on Saturdays. But the shop wasn't doing well. When it went out of business, he drifted from job to job until he took his father's advice and went along to the army recruiting office. The recruitment officer saw something in him and persuaded Malcolm to sign up. The army had been the best thing that happened to him. He'd kept in touch with the girl from the music shop, and on one occasion when he was home on leave they decided to get married. But he quickly realised that it wasn't going to work. Then he was caught up in a roadside bomb explosion. His wife couldn't cope with the situation when he came home, and left him. His life turned upside down again. This time the band had saved him, showed him he could still play a bit.

Neil waited a few moments until he was sure there was no more to come, at least for the moment.

'And you certainly can play. I don't think any of us had an inkling how much the band means to you. It would be a total waste if you gave up now. For all of us.' He watched and waited as Malcolm got up to find some kitchen roll to wipe his face and blow his nose. Neil felt it was time to be assertive.

'So are we going to sort you out, or what? You can stay here and wallow, or get a grip.'

Malcolm breathed out through puffed cheeks, as he looked around.

'Shit. I'm sorry you had to walk into this lot. It looks like one of those squats.' He sighed heavily. 'If I knew where to bleeding well start, I'd try and pull my finger out.'

At Neil's suggestion, Malcolm went upstairs to shower and change into some clean clothes. Neil wondered if the house was just as untidy and messy upstairs as down. He looked around, with the intention of starting to clean the place up, but, like Malcolm, he didn't know where to begin. Instead, he used his phone to research local cleaning agencies. He called one, and was given a quote for a one-off thorough spring clean. He arranged for this to happen on the following Monday, adding that he would call if there were any changes to the arrangements, by which he meant that Malcolm wouldn't go along with the idea. Neil then phoned his sister.

'Right, mate,' he said when Malcolm re-appeared, looking better for having shaved, showered and changed into some relatively clean clothes. 'You look one thousand times better. What I need you to do is pack a bag with clothes and stuff for a couple of days. We'll drop it off at my place and then go and have some lunch. I'm staying at my sister's for a couple of days. My partner's away, so you can use my place. And why not bring a guitar with you.' He explained that he had arranged for the house to be cleaned top to bottom, unless Malcolm had any objections.

'Oh mate,' said Malcolm, as he broke into tears. Neil reached out and held him in his arms.

Stan's first job on his return to work on Monday morning was to collect a box of business cards from Phil and Jane's house. Both he and Phil had received a text message from Jane to say that the cards were ready for collection, and that she would leave them inside the back porch for one of them to collect. He found the box on top of a shoe rack. As he turned to leave, there was the sound of a key turning in a lock. The back door opened.

'Hello Stan.' He had expected Jane to be at work. She was certainly dressed for it, in high heels, dark blue skirt and jacket and light blue blouse. They exchanged pleasantries. Stan saw that despite the makeup she looked tired and drawn.

'How is he?'

'Phil? Hard to say, duck. He's been all over the place, proper messed up, like. But he's hanging on. Probably doing better now that he has his own place.' He explained where Phil was staying. 'How about you, duck? How are you doing?'

She smiled weakly, shrugging her shoulders.

'Oh, you know. Alright. They gave me a bit of a promotion at work, which is nice.'

'That's great. Congratulations.' He wanted to ask how things were between her and Kit, but felt she was pointedly avoiding mention of the subject.

'Anyway, must go, duck. I'm running a bit late. Good to see you looking well, Stan.' She opened her mouth as if she was going to say something else, but turned to go back inside the house.

'Yeah, you take care.' She had already locked the door.

Stan drove slowly along Mount Pleasant, looking for Phil. He loved this particular road, not just because Mandy lived here, but because it was relatively quiet, the trees either side adding to the sense of peace. The cherry blossom glistened in the morning sun, drops of water falling from the leaves as the overnight frost melted. He smiled to himself as he recalled the soaking he had given Mandy and Phil the day before. He had been 'test-driving' his new equipment on Mandy's windows, as part of the process of proving to Phil and Mandy, as well as himself, that he could manage the physical side of the work; the carrying of ladders and buckets of water. Mandy had not previously seen the extended poles which enabled Stan to clean the upstairs windows from ground level, and burst into laughter as she compared them to the size of Stan's penis, joking that he needed to go on a course of Viagra. When Phil joined in the banter, Stan turned the hose on the pair.

He found Phil a few doors up, ringing a chamois cloth over a bucket.

'How's it going, my old?' asked Stan as he got out of the van. Phil turned off his radio.

'I was just thinking, like, as you drove up, that with two of us on the job we're going to finish early, especially with this new chuffin' system.'

'Well, hey presto,' said Stan. 'That's bleeding obvious. The devil makes work for idle friggin' hands, so we need to drum up a bit of business. Ain't that what these cards are about?' They discussed when and where they should distribute the business cards, agreeing to use the time freed up during the next few afternoons to target the areas where they already had rounds and were known. Stan didn't like the idea of getting into 'patch wars' with rival cleaners in other parts of the city.

Phil was gladdened by the sound of Stan launching into 'The Wind Cries Mary' as he set to work a couple of doors away, and smiled when he caught a glimpse of Stan playing air guitar to the solo. He thought that perhaps they wouldn't be working much quicker after all.

An hour later, they were having elevenses in the van. Stan mentioned that he had seen and spoken to Jane, telling Phil about her promotion.

'So the missus is doing alright then. That's good,' said Phil, staring into his mug of tea.

'Well, I dunno. Hard to tell, but she weren't exactly brimming with happiness, if you ask me. She didn't mention Kit, and I didn't ask. Have you heard ought? Rumours or ought?'

'Nope.' Phil finished his coffee and without a word got back to work.

That afternoon, they pushed cards through letter boxes of houses in this district, receiving promises of work from people they spoke to in their driveways. Encouraged, they drove to Aylestone Park, pulling in close to the county cricket ground on Grace Road.

'Did you see what I think I just saw?' asked Stan as they pulled up. 'Just back there.'

'No, what?'

'Some geezer up a ladder, cleaning windows.'

'Well, could be he lives there.'

'That blue van with the ladder on the roof might give a chuffin' clue, though.' The van was parked fifty metres down the road. 'Let's have a shufty.'

'Suppose he is a winderer. What do we do, then?' asked Phil as they walked along. 'There's nothing to stop him, is there? I mean, is it a case of who's first? First come, first served, like.'

Stan stopped walking, and they faced each other.

'But we can find out what he's friggin' well up to,' he said. 'If he's trying to barge his sodding way in and take over our sodding work, we need to know, like.' He carried on walking, Phil struggling to keep up. 'Let's just check him out.'

As they reached the end of the short drive way in to the semi-detached house, they could see that there were in fact two men, who had taken down the ladder and were just preparing to move on.

'Aye up, me old,' called Stan to the nearest one. 'Have you got a minute, like?' The man looked up.

'Shit!' the man said. Stan and Phil stopped dead in their tracks, surprised to find themselves almost face to face with Kit.

'Fuck. What's he playing at?' said Stan.

'Aye up Stan, Phil. Fancy seeing you here.' Kit tried hard to hide his surprise and embarrassment.

'Yeah, just fancy,' said Stan. They were now standing just a couple of paces apart. Phil came alongside. 'What the fuck's going on mate?' asked Stan.

'Everything alright, Kit?' called his colleague, who was a few yards back, reeling in a hose.

'Fine, Mel. These are a couple of old mates. The ones I helped out.' This had given him time to think of his response to Stan's question. 'We're just doing a favour for an old customer, like. Old bloke, can't get up the ladder himself these days. You know how it is.'

'Come on, Kit,' said Mel, as he approached. Mel, who looked to be in his mid-thirties, was thin and wiry, with short spikey hair, and wore a short-sleeved Leicester City top, which revealed the tattoos on both forearms swearing allegiance to the club. 'We ain't got all bleeding day. We need to get going if we're going to do them others this afternoon.'

'You lying toad,' said Phil, who moved too quickly for Kit to avoid the punch. Stan had anticipated the likelihood of this happening, and was happy for Phil to land the one punch, but then stepped in to prevent any more, holding Phil firmly around the chest.

'What the fu....' cried Mel, in a high pitched screech. Kit lay on the ground, putting his hand to his bleeding nose and looking at Phil in disbelief.

'Just back off, mate,' said Stan. 'This is personal between these two.'

'Too fucking right it's personal. I could kill the bastard. First he shags my missus, now he's trying to stuff us. You bastard arsehole.' Phil struggled to get out of Stan's grip. Stan's chest was aching, and he wondered how much longer he could hold Phil.

'That's enough, Phil. Hold still. There's no chuffin' point in getting yourself into trouble.' Stan turned to Kit. 'As for you, you total wanker, what's this all about? Ain't they paying you enough on the post, or what?'

'Give us a hand, mate.' Kit reached out to Mel. He slowly got onto his feet, but was bent double, catching the drops of blood from his nose into a none-too-clean-looking handkerchief.

'They're laying off, ain't they. Last in, first out.' His voice had a new nasal twang to it. 'This is just to tie me over for a bit. I were going to tell you, like, but….'

'But you couldn't chuffin' well be arsed,' said Stan.

'What, like you was going to tell me you was shagging my missus,' said Phil, who had calmed down sufficiently for Stan to release his grip, and was dusting himself down and straightening his shirt sleeves. Stan rubbed his chest to relieve the aching.

'The thing is,' said Mel, standing in a challenging pose, arms folded. 'As I see it, we have a perfect fucking right to clean windows wherever we bleeding well like. You can't stop us. Market bleeding forces, ain't it. I mean…' He stopped as Phil took a step towards him.

'Just shut your hole. Or you'll get some of the same.'

'Phil. Alright. Leave it, mate. Leave it.' Stan put an arm in front of Phil to block his path. He looked at Mel. 'Normally, you might be right, my old, but this isn't normally. What I suggest you and this piece of shit do is find other parts of the city where there must be plenty of winderin' to do without upsetting us. Now I believe you was packing up to go.'

Stan and Phil stood to one side and watched as the other two collected their things together, loading them onto the ladders for ease of carrying everything in one go, one at each end. As they neared the gate, Kit asked Mel to stop for a moment. He turned awkwardly to face Stan and Phil as he spoke.

'One thing you should know. I ain't seeing Jane. Haven't for a couple of weeks. We had a row, like, and she told me to piss off. It don't change what happened, but thought you should know.'

Stan and Phil both stood hands in pockets, looking around, as they waited for the emotions to subside.

'And it's only my first day back,' said Stan. 'Can't chuffin' wait till tomorrow.'

'All in a day's work, me old.'

They walked towards the gate.

'That was some chuffin' weight in that punch. Glad it wasn't me on the other end of it.'

'I was holding back, believe it or not,' said Phil. 'Perhaps as well.'

## Phil

Would I have her back? Would she have me back? Hearing him say they'd had a row and hadn't seen each other for a bit gave me a real lift, so obviously I would have Jane back, if she'd have me. I guess we'd have a few things to sort out, and would have to sit down and talk. That's the stuff I don't do well. Never have. I know it's a bloke thing. My Dad was just the same. Probably my Granddads as well. If there was a row over anything at home, no one would talk about it. Things just simmered away, until maybe they were just forgotten about, or no one could remember what the disagreement had been about. You copy what your parents do, don't you. I never saw mine hold hands or kiss properly in front of me, and my grandparents certainly never did. The one thing I've noticed about Neil, whenever he's turned up with his partner, is that they don't hold back. They're very touchy-feely. And so are Mandy and Stan, come to think of it. Very different to how he was with Niamh. Maybe I need lessons.

## Stan

I was chuffed to bits to be back at work. I can't believe how quickly I've recovered, like, just a few weeks after the old surgery. Everyone has been amazing. The doctors, nurses, the physio. Can't fault them. I'm off nearly all of the medication and have been signed off by everyone. I can live with being on warfarin and the blood tests. A small price to pay. I won't miss having to go to the bleeding hospital though. The parking's a bleeding nightmare. I don't get why the NHS aren't running the car parks and making the profits, instead of some private firm? Seems bloody stupid to me.

# Thirty

# Moving On

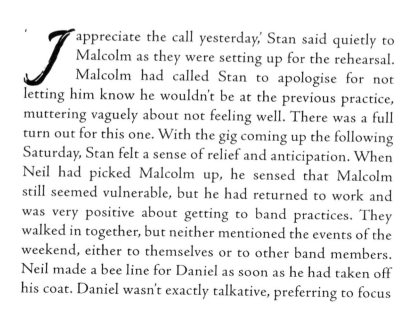

'I appreciate the call yesterday,' Stan said quietly to Malcolm as they were setting up for the rehearsal. Malcolm had called Stan to apologise for not letting him know he wouldn't be at the previous practice, muttering vaguely about not feeling well. There was a full turn out for this one. With the gig coming up the following Saturday, Stan felt a sense of relief and anticipation. When Neil had picked Malcolm up, he sensed that Malcolm still seemed vulnerable, but he had returned to work and was very positive about getting to band practices. They walked in together, but neither mentioned the events of the weekend, either to themselves or to other band members. Neil made a bee line for Daniel as soon as he had taken off his coat. Daniel wasn't exactly talkative, preferring to focus on setting up the percussion set, which Neil read as him wanting to be left alone.

The usual group of onlookers had congregated at the back of the hall, including Phil, Mandy and Tracy, along with Axel, a friend of Tom's, who had brought along his sound mixer with a view to showing Phil how to use it. Stan and Tom had agreed that the cheap and cheerful one that Phil had been using was not really up to the job. If Phil was able to master Axel's machine, the band would fork out for a new one between them.

Once they were organised and ready to start, they quickly discussed the set they would be playing at Ursula's café, which they would be running through in the practice. They were confident about most of the songs, but Stan and Tom felt that the very first number, appropriately with the title *Let's Get The Show On The Road*, needed tidying up. Most of the ideas for the lyrics and music of the sixteen bar rhythm and blues song had come from Stan, of which he was immensely proud. Neil had put it down on paper for him.

Several bars in, just as Stan started to sing his first line Tom called out and stood up.

'Hold it! Hold it!' He clasped his hands on top of his head and breathed out through puffed cheeks. 'Right, we're all over the place with that at the moment, including me.' He walked round to stand in front of the group.

'We need to get this right from the start. If we do, the place will rock. It's got real drive. But most of us came in late, as if we're terrified of it. Daniel, what I need you to do is count us in on the sticks. One, two, three, then bass, percussion and Malcolm come in on the fourth beat, absolutely together.'

It took half an hour of stopping and starting before they were able to play the song straight through without any hitches. Of the ten they were practising for the gig, they had three left to work on when Phil burst in through the door at the back of the room, after taking a call on his mobile phone. Beckoning to Stan that he needed a word urgently, he was clearly agitated.

'You are not going to friggin' well believe this, mate. This thing about bleeding Raymond is all over the front page of the Evening Gazette. Photos, the lot. He was in the magistrate's court today and found guilty of breaking whatever it was.'

'Some sort of chuffin' orders,' said Stan.

'Yeah, them. Esther is in a real bleeding panic, like, as you'd expect. Word's got round somehow that she were friendly with the pillock, and there's a crowd of youths outside her house. I need to get round there, before it gets nasty. She's called the police, but no sign of them yet. But what do we do about the lad?' They thought for a moment.

'Let's ask Neil what he thinks,' said Stan. He walked across to the stand in front of the band, all of whom were looking on anxiously, sensing something was amiss. 'There's a bit of bother, that's all,' said Stan. 'I'll fill you in in just a mo. Neil, mate, could Phil and me have a quick chat. Phil needs a bit of advice.'

'Sure.' Neil stood his violin on its rest, and walked over with Stan. They put Neil in the picture.

'Hard to tell how he'll cope with this,' he said. 'But I'd be inclined to give him the full picture, so that he knows what to expect when he gets home. Tell him he needs to look after his Mum, and that the police are on the way to sort things out.' Phil was happy to go along with this.

'He's going to worry about his percussion set, though,' added Neil. 'Tell him that we'll pack it up and take it home for him.'

'We're just going to take a short break,' Stan told the others, trying to appear relaxed. Phil came over and offered Daniel a mint sweet. He took Daniel to one side, with Neil in support, then explained what was happening at the house.

'Your Mum says she needs you at home to give her support, so we'll both go over, shall we mate? Neil and the others will bring your kit home, if you're OK with that.' Phil held his breath.

'We'd better get over there then, as quick as we can,' said Daniel.

'Good lad.'

As soon as Phil and Daniel were out of the room, Stan explained the situation to the others, suggesting that in the circumstances he ought to get across to Birstall and help out.'

'Well, I'm with you as well,' said Malcolm.

'There's strength in numbers,' added Tom. 'I'll ask the landlord to lock this place up until we get back, but just to be on the safe side take your instruments with you and stick them in the boot of whichever car you're in. I'll take care of Daniel's stuff, if someone can give me a hand.' Angie offered.

Stan had to park the van several doors down from Esther's house. Turning into the street, they could see that a crowd of twenty or so had gathered. As they got out of the van they could hear the aggressive chanting.

'Paedo! Paedo! Paedo!' This was coming from a group of mostly young men and teenagers, but it included a couple of women. As Stan, Phil and Daniel approached, they could see something being thrown at the door of the house. The contents of an egg dribbled down from the pane of glass.

'Shit!' said Phil. 'Where are the bleeding police? Daniel, I need you in the house to look after your Mum. Go! There's a good lad.' They watched as Daniel hurried along the pavement then up to the front door. He turned briefly to take in the scene before going in, opening and closing the door as quickly as he could. This was accompanied by boos from some of the crowd. The chanting changed.

'No paedos in our street! No paedos in our street.'

Phil and Stan pushed their way past a couple of women, who each stood with a young child on either side.

'Oi, watch where you're going,' called one. They ignored her and pushed on until they were in front of the middle part of the low wall between Ester's garden and the pavement. They stood side by side, arms folded, facing the crowd, which had grown in number. Some were curious on-lookers, but there was no doubting the potential for malicious intent from a section, some of whom had covered their faces with scarves. Phil raised his arms above his head.

'Now listen. You've had your fun, made your point, now clear off. The coppers are on the way, so if you don't want to end up in the nick, I should go home.'

'What the fuck's it got to do with you?' one of the young men shouted back. 'There's a fuckin' paedo in this house, and we want him gone.'

'Our kids aren't safe while this bleeding pervert's here,' called a woman, to shouts of agreement.

'Hold on. Just chuffin' well hold on,' Phil shouted back. 'The only people living here are a mother and her son. You lot are standing outside the wrong fuckin' house. And anyway, the bloke you're after has long since cleared off.'

There were calls of derision. As the chanting restarted, Stan nudged Phil and pointed to a raised hand holding a piece of brick. Nearest to the man with the brick, Phil pushed his way through, shouting 'Fucking put that down!' The arm was pulled back, about to hurl the brick towards the house, but Phil was quick enough to be able to reach out with one hand to pull the offending arm down. Then with the other he knocked the man to the ground with a hefty blow to the face. Phil retreated sharply to take his place beside Stan. Then as he realised that Neil was also standing next to Stan, he could see lined up along the pavement, confronting the crowd, were Malcolm, Tom, Angie and Daniel, who must have been watching what was going on from the window.

'Nice one Phil,' said Neil.

'Anyone else want a dose of the same?' Phil shouted, fists clenched, adrenalin surging. For a moment, it felt as if the crowd had begun to close in on them, but at the sound of the siren of an approaching police car, the pressure eased and the gathering began to disperse. The man who Phil had hit to the ground was on his feet, using the scarf half covering his face to gingerly wipe away the blood coming from his nose. He took a step forward and glared at Phil, jabbing his finger as he spoke, threateningly.

'You'll keep.' As he moved to walk away, Phil stepped in front of him to block his path.

'Let's have a look at you, me old.' He pulled the man's scarf down to reveal the face of someone in his early twenties. 'Right, now I've clocked you, if I see you anywhere near this house again, I'll give you a fucking good hiding.' He pointed to Daniel. 'This lad lives here with his mother. The paedo bloke lived down the road and has cleared off. Got it? Now you piss off.' The man shrugged his shoulders, grunted, flicked his head upwards as if to half nod, then walked away. Phil watched him go for a few seconds before turning to walk to the house. With the exception of Tom, who had intercepted the two police constables to explain what had been going on, the band members had bunched together, with Angie at the front. They smiled and clapped hands.

'I do like an assertive man,' said Angie. 'Good for you, Phil.'

'Remind me to never get into an argument with this man,' said Neil.

Malcolm added, 'Mate, you are awesome. You faced the whole bloody lot down.'

'Let's get you and Daniel inside, in case the police start asking questions,' said Stan. As they walked towards the front door, he added, 'That's twice in a couple of days. You've clouted someone, I mean. Best not make a habit of it.'

'No danger. It's all under control.'

As Stan closed the door behind them, Esther rushed over to hug Daniel, chastising him at the same time for daring to go outside, although her tone of voice suggested she was proud of him for putting himself in harm's way to protect her. She was clearly shaken and upset, understandably, and Phil felt her body trembling as they embraced. After hugging Stan and thanking them both, she sat down on the sofa, then burst into tear.

'That was the most terrifying experience I have ever had,' she said, between sobs. 'If you hadn't turned up I don't know what might have happened. And where were the police? And what if they come back?' She was rocking back and forth, wringing her hands on her lap. Phil sat next to her, looking slightly awkward.

'I don't think they'll be back, duck, now that the police have turned up.'

As if on cue, there was a knock on the door. Daniel opened it to find himself facing one of the police officers, who asked if he could come in.

'Well you took your bleeding time,' said Phil.

'Phil, pet. It's OK.' Esther put her hand on his forearm. 'I'm sure they got here as soon as they could.' The officer apologised for not arriving sooner, explaining that there had been a major incident in the city centre. He asked a few questions, starting by requesting the names of everyone present. What time had the disturbance started? Was Esther or anyone else hurt in any way? Did she know the cause of the disturbance? Had she recognised any of the people involved? Was there any damage to the property? Would she like to speak to a woman PC? Has she anyone to call on for support? Esther held herself together, giving matter-of-fact answers which seemed to satisfy him.

'We'll keep a patrol car close by for as long as we can, Mrs Wilson, in case anything kicks off. But hopefully, now that they've let off a bit of steam they've all gone home.'

'But what about the chuffin' Gazette, putting that stuff all over the front page like that,' said Phil. 'Can they just do that? I mean, isn't there some privacy thing to stop that happening.'

'Afraid not, sir. The local press usually have a reporter in court, in case there's anything worth printing. And paedophiles raise everyone's emotions, as I'm sure you're aware.'

Esther accepted Phil's offer to camp down on the sofa for the night. As Stan left the house, he was surprised to find Malcolm sitting on the wall. Apart from the police car parked a couple of hundred yards down the road, there was no-one else about. Malcolm was choosing his moment to carry Daniel's percussion set in to the house, after helping to unload it from Tom's van. Stan helped him carry it in. There was an awkward silence as they stood facing each other in front of the house. Stan had glanced at his watch. The pubs would still be open and he almost suggested they went for a drink, but thought better of it.

'Well, an unusual ending to the practice,' said Malcolm.

'Dead right it was.'

'Look, umm, I just wanted to say. We've had our ups and downs, especially early on, but I hope we're OK now. I'm still trying to sort myself out.' He looked down at his feet, before continuing. 'But this band, we're going to be great you know, if we keep it going. I'm looking forward to our gig, and to meeting your friend, what's-her-name.'

'Ursula.'

'Yeah, Ursula. Should be good.' He wanted to tell Stan how much the band meant to him, how much he admired Stan's playing, how much Neil's support had mattered. Stan could see that he had more to say, but was struggling to get it out.

'Tell you what,' said Stan. 'Fancy a quick pint?'

'Why not?'

## Phil

Turns out that most of what the Gazette printed was lifted from the police website, almost word for word like. Daniel had got on to the website and showed me. So some arsehole had tipped off the chuffin' newspaper. There's also some friggin' nasty, evil stuff on Facebook which we had a look at, most of it total bollocks. These duffers weren't hiding their feelings at all, and let the whole world know. Makes me glad I don't do Facebook.

## Stan

It were only a small crowd outside the house really, but makes you realise how chuffin' scary it could be facing a mob out of control. There's no way of knowing what sort of shit might come out of it. I just hope that the sight of us and the police turning up is enough to stop owt else happening. But you can understand how people with kids would feel about having a chuffin' paedo living in their neighbour. You don't want any chance of one getting anywhere near your kid. One thing the copper told us was that the local police should be informed whenever a convicted paedophile turns up in their area, and this didn't happen. I dunno who's supposed to do the informing. And this is so that they can, as he put it, manage the situation. One copper's idea of managing it then, was to put the bleeding media onto it.

## Thirty-One

# Say You Love Me

'Thanks everybody,' said Stan. 'I hope you've enjoyed the show so far. I'd like to introduce the band.' He kept it simple, giving the name of and instrument played by each one. During the huddle just before going on, Neil had asked who was going to introduce the songs and the band members. It wasn't something they had thought about. The floor seemed suddenly to have captured everyone's interest, until eventually Stan realised that they were all looking to him to do the honours.

'Chuffin' Nora,' Stan had responded. 'What would I say? I mean, it's not something I've ever had to do, like.'

'Just tell them who we are, what we play, maybe where we're from, what we do. Try and make it amusing if you can,' offered Neil. 'As long as you don't go too far, like.'

Stan thought for a moment, looking slightly sceptical about the prospect, then stood up as if to face the audience with an imaginary microphone in one hand.

'Our bass guitarist is also known as Bossy Nickers, cos she's the one that keeps us in order. From some posh place down south and studying micro something or other at the Uni, Angie Coleman.'

'Hey! Less of the Bossy Nickers. Where's that come from? And I do not come from some posh place. It's bloody Leamington.' Stan said he would have to think again about that one.

'OK. How about this for Malc? Our very own war hero, who survived the bombs in Afghanistan, and is an expert in unarmed chuffin' combat. So we daren't turn him down at the audition. And his guitar lessons are beginning to pay off. Malcolm Dunne.' The others looked at each other, Neil, Tom and Daniel worrying what Stan might come up with for them.

'On reflection Stan, mate, I think maybe just stick to our names and what instrument we're playing, if that's OK.' Tom spoke for them all. It was agreed that Stan and Tom would share the announcement of the songs.

As Stan went through the introductions proper, there was enthusiastic applause for each band member. He came to Daniel last of all, allowing himself a little more elaboration.

'Last but not least, the boy genius on percussion, who, in case you were wondering, plays behind the screen to keep the girls away. All the way from Birstall, Daniel Wilson.' Surprisingly, Daniel responded to the whistling and cheering with a brief wave.

They were half way through the set, which had started with *Let's Get the Show on the Road*. The polite clapping which had greeted their arrival was replaced with smiles and chatter of appreciation as Stan and the rest got onto their stride.

Tom gave them all the thumbs up as they finished the song, and there was a collective sigh of relief that it had gone well. It was the guitar and violin solos of *Love of My Life* which really turned heads and literally brought people in off the streets. Passers-by began to poke their heads round the door, several squeezing their way in when they saw that there was standing room at the bar, where it quickly became three deep. Concerned that things might be getting out of hand, Ursula decided to stand at the door to prevent any more coming in. For the twenty or more congregated on the pavement, it was a case of pressing their noses against the window as they tried to get a better look at what was going on. The extra staff Ursula had employed were kept busy plying those inside and out with sandwiches, soft drinks, coffees and teas.

Esther, Mandy and Phil had been given pride of place at a table in the centre of the café, although Phil spent most of the time next to Axel at a table to one side of the bar, watching as Axel made adjustments to the sound mixing. Tracy was working her shift at the hospital. Ursula and Esther had quickly warmed to one another when they were introduced that afternoon. They had walked arm-in-arm as Ursula showed Esther round her domain, the two exchanging life histories, in particular their experiences of recent years, with a shared empathy. The evening was a welcome break for Esther, who had found life difficult to cope with in the previous few days. Phil had continued to sleep overnight on the sofa. On the morning after the noisy gathering outside the house, Daniel had become withdrawn, refusing to go to school on the grounds that in the crowd he had recognised two 'nasty boys' from his school, and he didn't want to get into trouble. Esther had made a call to the school, during which she passed the phone to Daniel, saying that Sue, his support teaching assistant would like to talk to him. Sue tried her best to reassure Daniel that the boys he had seen outside his house would be spoken to and warned to keep away from him. Daniel insisted that he would not go to school that day, but that he would the following day as long as Phil accompanied him to the gate. This presented a problem, as Esther was determined that she would go to work as usual, rather than shut herself away at home. So it was that on that day Daniel accompanied Phil and Stan on their round, helping out where he could and enjoying the banter. His verdict on the day was that it had been fun and interesting, but he didn't see any career prospects in the work. His return to school had so far met without incident.

Now, as the band took a short break Esther had abandoned her seat to provide reinforcement behind the bar and in the kitchen. Stan had assumed that during the interval the band would gather together to discuss how things were going, but apart from Daniel the others quickly dispersed to find and talk to people in the café that they knew. Daniel sat in front of his percussion set, gently rocking, so Stan found a stool which he slid across the floor to sit on, next to him.

'Right, me old. The others all quickly buggered off, so what shall we do? Seen anyone you know to go and talk to?'

'No. I'd rather sit here anyway.'

'OK. Can I get you a drink? Tea, coffee, soft drink?'

'I'm fine with my water, thanks.' Stan folded his arms and looked around the room.

'I think it's gone down pretty well, like, so far. They seem to like us, anyway. What do you reckon?'

'Some of it has been good, but some has been not so good.' Daniel went on to list the missed entries, late starts and wrong chords he had noticed, all of which had completely passed Stan by. He was impressed that Daniel had been able to register these mistakes, while seemingly giving a faultless performance himself. Stan suggested that the band had been nervous to start with and that mistakes were bound to happen.

'Yes, I was a bit nervous, and made a couple of mistakes in the first song,' admitted Daniel. Stan thought about asking him to mention the mistakes at the next practice, but felt that it would be better for morale if they could bask in the relative success of their first gig, assuming that the second half of the set went as least as well as the first.

Before trying to summon the band back to their instruments, Stan drifted away to Ursula's office for a quiet moment alone. He closed his eyes so that he could focus on his heart, which was thumping away reassuringly consistently. *Every day a bonus*, he thought. Back in the café, he stood at the mic to call the band up for the second half. As they picked up and checked the tuning on their instruments, the audience returned to their places, although Ursula had to intervene at one table, where a group who had been outside were attempting to claim the seats of those who had occupied them before the break. Ursula calmly managed to find seats for the interlopers.

As this was happening, a woman made her way over to her stool which was at the wall opposite to the entrance. She wore dark glasses and kept her back to the band, moving quietly and without fuss. She could have been in her forties or fifties, and although dressed casually, the designer clothes, elegantly styled hair and subtly-applied makeup suggested that she took care over her appearance. She removed a smart phone from her handbag and held it on the wall-mounted bar in such a position that she could take photographs of or film the band performing.

Their arrangement of *Don't Get Around Much Anymore* brought the smiles back to faces and had feet tapping along. But it was the combination of and interplay between the two guitars and Neil's violin in the quieter songs towards the end of the set which excited Stan. These included *Still Got the Blues* and *Come Rain or Come Shine*, plus compositions by Neil and Malcolm. Neil played with an intensity and feel for the music that Stan did his best to replicate, sensing that Malcolm was responding in the same way. As Stan played the riff which brought *Still Got the Blues* to an end, Phil, Mandy and Ursula stood to applaud, as did the woman with the dark glasses, forgetting herself just for a moment before she promptly sat down again. Within seconds, she was on her feet again, to join in the standing ovation. For Phil and Mandy, it was a case of knowing that the weeks of practice were paying off, and a shared pride in seeing their friends perform well.

The band had managed to work some harmonies into some of the songs. For their encore they sang *Fields of Gold*. The intro was slower than they had practiced, which led to a nervous start to the vocals. The harmonising worked well, but there were mistakes in the solos, and although there was strong applause again, there were looks of disappointment amongst the band. They had only to look at each other to acknowledge that it had been one song too many.

Later, the café empty of customers, the band sat together in a corner near the bar, in exhausted, reflective silence, some sipping on beers which Mandy had produced before taking her leave, needing an early night but also appreciating their need to be by themselves. Phil was nowhere to be seen, so Esther took a taxi home, after asking Neil if he would arrange one for Daniel when he was ready.

'You'd think we was at a funeral,' said Stan.

'Too right,' replied Neil. 'Come on everyone. Daniel, I thought you were amazing tonight, I really did. Well done, mate.' He offered his hand to Daniel, and they shook. Daniel managed 'Thanks,' after catching Stan's look which warned him off saying anything critical. For the next few minutes the compliments flew around.

'When you consider where we were when we first got together,' said Tom, 'that was a great start. And let's hope it was only a start. Let's see what happens.'

'Anyone know if any press people were here?' asked Malcolm. Stan replied that Ursula had mentioned getting in touch with the local paper, but wasn't sure if she had.

'We need to find ourselves a chuffin' manager,' said Malcolm.

There was muted agreement, but, suggested Tom, this was not a subject to be discussed at that particular moment. As they collected their belongings, they agreed to meet as usual for the next practice. Stan was about to leave when Ursula emerged from her office.

'Fancy a night cap, Stanley, before you rush off?'

'Well, just a quick one, duck.'

She closed the door behind him, collected two glasses from her desk and walked over to him.

'Schnapps. Home made by my father. Try it.' She handed him a glass. 'Prost!'

'Cheers. Prost.' Stan sniffed the clear spirit. 'There's a fruit there.'

'Plums.' The room was darkened, and music was playing quietly from a CD player on her desk. Stan thought he could hear muffled voices from the first floor flat. They both drank. The warmth quickly spread through his chest.

'Gordon Bennett. That's fiery!'

'Do you like it? Drinking it in one go is the way.' She demonstrated. He copied, gasping hot fumes when he'd emptied the glass.

'That, as my Mum would say, will put lead in your pencil.'

'If you're a good boy, you can have as much as you want.'

She was standing right up against him, unbuttoning his shirt. She then ran her hands over his chest. 'I've never seen your scar, Stanley, until now.' She kissed it then ran her tongue along its line. He stirred.

'Oh shit, Ursula, duck. This is very tempting, but….' She kissed him lightly on the lips, pulled her top over her head, then pushed her breast against his.

'Tell me about this lead in your pencil, Stanley. Is this what I can feel down here?' She stroked his groin then turned her back to him. 'Help me with this please Stan. My bra.' He unhooked it. She turned to face him and took a step back. He sighed with pleasure.

'They are beautiful,' he said.

'I hoped you would like them. You see, you don't know what you've been missing. This might be my only chance, so please, tonight, hold me, make love to me. Then I will be able to say I made love with a rock star.' He laughed.

'We've a long way to go yet, Ursula.'

'Maybe. But just for tonight, say you love me.'

## Stan

It's been what? Something like seven months since that first time we all got together. Looking back, it's chuffin' amazing we ever got going at all. But maybe, just maybe, we might have something. As Tom said, let's see what happens. One thing I have realised is that you learn a lot about yourself in this kind of situation, like. Apart from the fact that I had a dicky ticker, I mean. You have to stick at something and work at it if you really chuffin' want it, especially when things get a bit tough. I wouldn't have said I necessarily had that in me before. There has to be a bit of give and take. Being seen as the leader doesn't mean you should expect to have things your own friggin' way.

And it pays to listen to what people have to say, share ideas and that. It all sounds bleeding obvious when you say it, but I've never really had to take this kind of stuff on board before.

A big plus is that my playing has got a whole lot better. A combination of watching and listening to Malcolm, as much as I hate to admit it, and to Chalkie's lot as well as getting down to the practising. The old voice has got better too. I always thought if you wanted to sing you just bloody sang, you just needed to have the voice. I would never have believed how much difference a bit of coaching could make, like.

There is still this nagging doubt. It's always there, you know. That I'm not really good enough, never have been. The others are carrying me, sort of thing.

## *Phil*

If I'm not mistaken, Ursula pulled. And so did I. So did I.

## Thirty-Two

# Still Got the Blues?

few evenings later, Stan and Mandy were sitting at Stan's small dining table, sharing a beef casserole which had been simmering in his slow cooker since breakfast time. The cooker was a present from Mandy, who said it would help improve his diet. The accompanying recipe book was full of ideas for healthy meals which didn't take long to prepare, so 'you can say goodbye to take-aways and fry-ups, and have proper meals ready for you when you get in from work.'

'That's as may be, duck, but not a chuffin' word to my mates, or they'll accuse me of having gone middle class.' Stan had used it on most days over the last two weeks. Without actually admitting that he was enjoying his new diet, he had proudly displayed his prowess with meals such as lemon roast chicken, a pasta bake and beef stroganoff. He had got up thirty minutes earlier than usual to prepare the casserole. Mandy had duly complimented him on the quality of his cooking, jokingly asking him if he was enjoying his new status.

'As what?'

'A member of the middle classes. You'll soon be drinking broccoli smoothies for breakfast.'

'Sounds good. Have you got the recipe?' They laughed. 'Actually, I can't think of anything less chuffin' appetising. Makes you fart, broccoli, according to my mum, which is probably why the old girl never served it up.'

This was the first time they had been able to spend more than a few minutes together since the gig in Ursula's café. Reality quickly set in for everybody concerned, not least that it had been their first gig, they didn't have a second lined up, plus they all had day jobs. As a talking point it had slid down the list. Over the weekend, Prime Minister David Cameron had announced that there would be a referendum in June on whether the UK would remain in or would leave the European Union. More importantly, Leicester City were still on track to win the Premiership title after beating Norwich City. Both topics were being discussed widely, including between rival supporters of the boys' football teams on Sunday afternoon. Phil's team, Fosse Boys were also looking likely winners of their league after another victory.

Stan and Phil had a brief conversation about the referendum during the morning, but as soon as it became apparent that Phil might be in favour of the country leaving the EU, Stan changed the subject. Surprised at how emotional he himself felt about the idea, he could see that any exchange on this with Phil could become heated, so was best avoided if possible. He had already seen interviews on the TV showing that families were divided on the issue, and he now found himself facing the person he was closest to, wondering how they would both react if they had differing views. Each had avoided commenting on the topic when it was mentioned on the TV news, or bringing it up in conversation.

'So, do you think Ursula enjoyed the other evening? Do you know if she made much?' The questions were fair enough, thought Stan, but he still wished she hadn't asked them. What had happened between him and Ursula had been nagging away in his mind, filling him with a sense of guilt. *'She came on to me,'* he had said to himself. *'In the circumstances, it would have been rude not to.'* But it had made him reappraise his relationship with Mandy. He had strong feelings for her, and believed they were reciprocated. He felt comfortable in her company, able to talk openly in a way he hadn't with anyone for a long time. Since his marriage broke up, or even well before that. And the sex was great. But there were still mysteries in her life, about which he had never quizzed her about, nor had she offered any information. Not, he reflected, that he had any entitlement. They were relevant all the same, in his view. What did she get up to on the nights she sang with Chalky's band? And what about her previous relationships? Two marriages had gone pear-shaped, he knew, the second seemingly because the man was an alcoholic. But Stan was wise enough to know that there were two sides to every story.

'It's not really my business to ask,' he replied. 'But you would chuffin' well hope so. The place was full and she and the staff worked bloody hard. And good luck to her, anyway.'

Mandy gave him a look which suggested she and Stan were sharing a crafty secret.

'You like her, don't you Stan? Oh it's all right, I don't mean in a sexual way. She's not your type. But she fancies you like mad. You must know that, surely?'

'I don't know. I doubt it, really. She flirts a bit, but then she does with other customers.' He kept his eyes on his food.

'What do you suppose would happen to her after the referendum, if we vote to leave the flipping EU?' This wasn't the question he was anticipating, but he was partially gratefully for the change in topic of conversation.

'I've no bloody idea, nor I think do the chuffin' politicians. It's all about immigrants, whatever anyone says, and at the end of the day, she's an immigrant.'

'At the same time, though, there are British people living in Spain and France, and other countries. Germany included. It's not that simple, is it?'

'Exactly.' He sensed they might be of the same opinion, so he asked outright. 'Do you think we should leave? The EU, I mean.'

'Do you?'

'No way. It would be friggin' stupid to, if you ask me. Which you just did.'

They were interrupted by a loud knock on the door. He didn't move.

'What about you?'

'I agree. Now see who's at the door.' Another loud knock.

'Whoever it is, they're not afraid to let you know they're there.'

A woman stood at the door step. She was slim, attractive, wearing jeans, an expensive-looking waterproof and a woolly hat, cream with a white bobble. A leather handbag was strapped over her shoulder. She looked at him through designer spectacles. There was something familiar about her.

'Hello Stan.' She smiled nervously. He stared back at her.

'Sorry, duck. Do I know you?'

'It's been a long time, but yes.'

At the sound of the light Irish brogue, the sense of vague familiarity turned to recognition, which was accompanied by a flood of mixed emotions. He swept a hand through his hair, staring in disbelief.

'Chuff-in'-No-ra. Niamh. What the fuck are you doing here?' Stan and his ex-wife were both transfixed for a moment, each remembering the circumstances under which they last spoke.

'I was just passing, and thought....But if it's not a good time....'

'You were just passing,' he replied, with a hint of anger in his voice. 'Well, duck, you should have kept going.'

'You're right. This wasn't a good idea.'

'Stan, why don't you invite her in.' Mandy could not help overhearing the doorstep conversation, and was standing at Stan's shoulder. 'I should go. The house needs tidying. You two will have a lot of catching up to do.' She stepped forward. 'Hallo Niamh. I'm Mandy. I was just going. Stan will make you a cup of tea, won't you love.' She disappeared back inside to collect her coat and bag. Stan was dumbstruck. *Thanks a friggin' lot*, he thought. Mandy squeezed past him, making a point of kissing him on the lips and thanking him for a sumptuous meal.

'Call me later,' she said, and was on her way, heels clacking on the pavement.

Neither Stan nor Niamh moved or made eye contact.

'I'm sorry to land on you like this,' she said. 'I had no way of contacting you, otherwise....' She looked down the road. 'I've parked a couple of doors down. Do you think it'll be alright there?' She was referring to a shining silver BMW convertible.

'As long as you're not staying long.' This was tantamount to asking her to step into the house, but he wavered. Did he need this added complication to his life? Did he really want to invite into his house the woman who deserted him all those years ago, leaving him all but destitute? What's more, he had just lost the evening he was going to spend with Mandy. With a sigh of resignation, he ushered her in.

'Tea? Coffee?' Whatever he was having, she replied. He left her standing as he went into the kitchen. She was still standing inside the front door when he returned with two mugs of tea.

'Still have yours black?' he asked.

'You remembered.' She looked around. 'Is it alright if I take my coat off? I promise not to stay long.'

'Might as well make yourself at home.' He waved an arm as if to say sit down, make yourself comfortable. She sat on an armchair, leaning forward, knees together, arms on her thighs, hands clasped tightly. Sitting back on the sofa, his crossed legs outstretched, arms folded, Stan looked first at the carpet then at Niamh, finding it difficult to believe that she was here, in his house.

'Your friend seems very nice,' she said. 'Mandy, isn't it?' He nodded. 'You haven't changed much, Stan. As handsome as ever. A bit greyer, but then aren't we all.'

'You've changed though, duck. I mean look at you. You look… well you're obviously doing alright, driving around in a Beamer. Must have set you back a bit.' He added pointedly, 'I could never afford anything like that.'

'It's a company car actually, but I ….' She looked down at her feet. 'And yes, I'm doing alright, as you put it. What about you?'

'I muddle along, like.' He felt too embarrassed to elaborate. An awkward silence followed.

'So come on, Niamh. Why are you here?' He was struggling to keep a calm steady voice. He sat up straight, giving her a hard stare. 'I mean, over twenty five years ago, like, you pissed off, leaving me with virtually nowt; now you just turn up out of the friggin' blue in your flash chuffin' car. Was you just passing, or what? Thought you'd drop in for a friendly chat, like?'

'I know, I know.' She stood up. 'I'm sorry, maybe this wasn't a good idea. I should go.'

'No. You chuffin' well sit down,' he said firmly, raising his voice slightly. 'I want to know. What made you come?'

She remained standing, folding her arms, and looked him in the eyes. 'I saw your band the other night. I'd asked around after you and learned you would be playing at the café. It was good to see you still have your favourite guitar.' He said nothing, his eyes following her as she walked around the small room. She looked out of the window. It had started to rain.

'You were good, Stan. I mean good. The band, too, especially considering it was your first gig.' She sat down again, on the edge of the chair, leaning forward, with a sudden eagerness and confidence in her demeanour. 'It was a bit rough around the edges at times, but I loved the violin and the way it complimented the guitars. And the kid on the drums – a bit geeky, but he would go down well with the younger audience.'

'So what? Like you're an expert and should know?'

Niamh looked down at her hands, then back at him. 'It's part of what I do. Talent spotting, if you like. Look,' she said excitedly. 'With the right support, I think your band could go places. Sorry if that's a bit clichéd, but from what I saw you could be really good.' She paused, weighing up what to say next.

'I went to the café this morning, and met Ursula. We had a really useful chat. Just for ten or fifteen minutes or so, but I learned a lot in that time. She obviously thinks the world of you. *My hero*, she called you. She told me about your heart operation, Stan. And your redundancy. You've done amazingly. I mean, it must have been tough to go through all that and still make a real go of things.' Stan opened his mouth to tell her to stop patronising him, but she quickly cut him off.

'Let me finish, Stan. Please. Ursula also told me that the band doesn't have a manager. This is where I could come in.' After rummaging around in her handbag, she handed him a business card. 'This is us. I mean who I work for. Artistic Management Services. AMS for short. We do a whole range of things: organise concerts and shows, exhibitions, project management. The whole lot. Including managing actors, artists, bands and so on. So what I'm coming to is that as you don't have a manager, then I could do it for you. And not through AMS. I'd do it for free.' She looked at him, bright-eyed and expectantly. 'What do you think?'

Stan scratched the back of his head and looked out of the window at the rain, now coming down heavily.

'What do I think?' He stood up and looked at her, his anger coming through as he spoke. 'Unbelievable. Un-be-lieve-able. After what happened, you expect me to let you back in to my life, so that what? You can manage my chuffin' band? Out of pity, or is it guilty conscience? How do I sell that to the others then? Oh, guys, this is Niamh. She pissed all our money away when we were married. She's feeling dead guilty, so she wants to be our bleeding manager. Then we can earn shed loads, and it will all be safe in her bleeding hands.' He paused, then added through gritted teeth, 'so what I think, same as what they would think, is on yer bike. Or rather your flash foreign car.' He walked to the door, opening it slightly. Seeing the hardness in his face, Niamh's eyes welled with tears. She picked up her waterproof and handbag and walked across the room. As she came close to him, the tears were rolling down her cheeks.

'Listen Stan, I'm not going to go, not just yet. I want, I need you to hear what happened.' She went back to her chair. 'You might want to sit down,' she said.

Feeling slightly foolish holding the door open, Stan closed it and reluctantly returned to the sofa, muttering under his breath.

'I can't change what happened, Stan, and I don't expect you to forgive me. But believe me, I am so, so sorry for what I did and how it must have hurt you.' She found a tissue in her handbag, and wiped her eyes. The poise and self-confidence she exhibited so far had evaporated. He waited, as she tried to gather herself back together.

'I was such a fool. You're probably thinking I told you so, which you did.' Stan listened patiently and with increasing intrigue as she told her story. Niamh had been persuaded to move to Sussex, where the religious organisation she had become involved in had its headquarters. She had been promised work there. Initially, she was given menial and administrative tasks to do, until she had 'proved her worth'. In lieu of the payment she had been expecting, she was provided with basic accommodation in a run-down hostel. The pastor who acted as her supervisor gave strict instructions not to mingle or socialise with people other than those within the organisation.

To start with, things went reasonably well. She received positive feedback about the quality of her work and how much it was valued. She was told that she could expect better things. It wasn't long, however, before the pastor asked her for money to 'support the charitable work of the organisation', which apparently was short of funds. It was difficult for her to refuse, and it wasn't long before the next request was made. The pastor became a regular visitor to her apartment, at first to discuss the organisation's principles and work, as well as, in his words, 'to offer pastoral support' should it be needed. Then the requests for sexual favours started. Niamh politely refused these, but after the third time of trying and being refused, the pastor became aggressive, threatening to deprive her of her privileges, which she took to mean her job and accommodation. By this time, she had just over a few hundred pounds left to her name, so when, the following day she received a letter from the head of the organisation asking for a further contribution of five thousand, she had to reply that she didn't have the means. Her situation then quickly deteriorated. In a follow-up letter she was told that unless she could provide continued support for the organisation, her services would no longer be required. She was given seven days notice to either cough up or leave her 'prestigious' post and accommodation.

Niamh didn't know who to turn to or where to go. Her parents had disowned her, she was sure that Stan wouldn't have her back, and was on no more than speaking terms with colleagues within the organisation, who would in all likelihood disapproved of her perceived lack of support. So she packed her bags and left, taking the train to London to look for work and somewhere to live.

Things quickly went from bad to worse. She found a cheap hostel, which she imagined being for the short term until she sorted herself out, but on the first day the room was broken into. Everything she had was stolen, apart from the clothes she was wearing and a few pounds in her purse.

'I hit rock bottom, Stan. For three weeks I was homeless, sleeping rough, eking out my last few pounds. The only consolation was that there were people even worse off than me. In that short time a whole new world opened. I met people who had suffered nervous breakdowns, teenagers who had left home, men who had left their homes and families. Plus musicians, bankrupts, people who had been bankers or teachers. All, for one reason or another, had taken a wrong turn or life had just been cruel. There were some nights when I was given a bed in one of those temporary shelter homes. It was only ever for one or two nights, but I met someone who saved my life. Changed my life, in fact. The kindest person in the world, at least to me.'

Emily, a volunteer in the Shelter hostel had befriended Niamh and taken her under her wing. She had been homeless herself after running away from home as a teenager, to escape an abusive step-father. Her elder sister had tracked her down and helped her get back on her feet, to the point at which Emily was renting a small flat in Islington, from where she was running a business selling jewellery online. With the business doing well, she needed someone to work for her. Niamh was offered a job, plus the use of a sofa until she could afford her own place.

'Over the next few months Stan, we became close. I mean very close.' She looked at him, as if to say 'do you get my drift'. 'We were earning a lot of money quickly, which meant we were able to buy a flat together. And, you know, we were like....a couple.' He looked blankly at her.

'Do I have to spell it out to you?'

'What?' The fog seemed to clear. 'You're telling me you're a les. You're gay, you mean?'

'Like I said, she changed my life, in more ways than one.'

Stan picked up her business card which was on the table and studied it. He saw the letters CEO after her name. He wasn't sure what they stood for, but could guess what they meant.

'You're not just any old bod working for this lot are you? You chuffin' well own it.'

Niamh explained that she and Emily were joint owners of the business, although they no longer lived together as a couple. Speaking excitedly again, she told Stan that there were lots of opportunities out there for the band if they wanted them badly enough. As examples, she explained that there were a couple of festivals coming up in the summer for which they were still looking for bands, and she knew of a TV company which was looking for a resident band for a chat show that was at the planning stage. If *Leicester Rocks* were interested, they could go along for an audition.

'But first we need to get you some more live-on-stage experience, as well as generating a following. There are...'

'No no no no.' Stan waved his hands animatedly. 'Just wait a friggin' minute. You're getting way ahead of yourself.' He was on the edge of his seat, their knees were almost touching. He sighed and looked at her.

'Look, Niamh. I know you think you're being helpful, like, but listen, duck.' He searched for what he wanted to say. 'Right, first off, you've seen us play just the once. You know naff all about us. What they're all like, what they do, what they want. I don't even chuffin' know what they want. All we've done so far is try and enjoy playing and singing together, and try and get a bit better. Most of the others, no, all of us do stuff full time, either working or studying, like. You know? We have a doctor, for god's sake, a technician, and so on. What you're talking about sounds like a full time bloody commitment. They won't want to walk out on their jobs, will they? It ain't like we've thought about it seriously.'

'Well, put it to them Stan, get them thinking about it. There are loads of bands which are part-time professional and make a go of it. Give it a whirl, and who knows what could happen?' She paused, then added, 'Who was it said *we're a long time looking at the lid?*'

'Now that is naughty.' It was an expression his mother often used. 'All I can say is I'll think about it, duck. Just now it feels like a whirlwind has swept in.'

The topic of conversation changed to Stan's mother, and they discussed the part she had played in bringing them together. Stan described the last few months of her life and the funeral, after which Niamh felt it was time to leave. At the door she turned to him.

'Get a manager, Stan. I would understand if you didn't want me, but find someone who would look after you.'

He stood looking at the door after she'd left, wondering whether he had just dreamt what had happened. He plugged his guitar into his practice amp and started to play the intro to Gary Moore's *Still Got The Blues*, but a few bars in he had a change of mind. He swapped the electric guitar for his steel strung acoustic, then launched into Dire Straits' *Ticket to Heaven*.

## Stan

I don't really have the words to describe how I felt when she came in and sat on my armchair and started talking. At first it was like having a chuffin' ghost in the room. Later, there was that smile and glint in her eye, the sound of the Irish lilt, and for a moment I thought I might fall in love with her all over again….

But Christ, no. Please no.

Her parents took it real bad when she pissed off. Upped sticks and moved to somewhere on the west coast of Scotland. Place with the football team. Stranraer, that's it. I always thought it were Stranraer Nil. They had family there. Last I heard they moved back to Northern Ireland after the Good Friday thing. I wonder how much they know about what happened to Niamh, wandering the streets and that, losing everything. If I believed there was a God, I'd say he was getting his own back. Or maybe he doesn't think like that. Perhaps he was showing her a different way, starting from rock bottom, knowing what it is to have nowt.

Here's her chuffin' business card. Niamh Duffy. CEO. She changed her name back then. According to their website, this AMS has some big names signed up, and some big events. Stuff at the O2 and that. Shit, she must be loaded. But would I trust her? It is all about trust.

## Thirty-Three

# Ticket to Heaven

'id-morning tea break in the van. No biscuits, so they had a short argument about whose turn it was to buy the next packet. Phil gave his view on City's home game the previous evening, for which he had managed to get a ticket. City could only manage a draw against West Bromwich Albion, which in his opinion had put the dampers on their chance of winning the Premiership title.

'Great if they did win it though,' said Stan. 'Think what it could do for the local chuffin' economy.' He was thinking of his own economy in particular.

Phil got his news in first, announcing that he and Jane were getting back together, and he would be moving back into the matrimonial home at the end of the week.

'Presumably, she wants to get rid of any frigging trace of Kit's being there, like,' he had said. When they bumped into each other at the café on Saturday evening, Jane had asked him if they could have a chat after the gig. One thing led to another, and although he had tried playing hard-to-get, she ended up staying the night. Stan had smiled to himself as he thought about what had been going on in Ursula's office, at probably around the same time.

'She finally came to realise that Kit is a total arsehole, on which we are in full bleeding agreement.'

'Well, that's great. I'm dead chuffed for you both,' said Stan. 'I'm sure she's fallen for the new slim-line version of Phil, which was only a matter of friggin' time.' He screwed the cup onto his vacuum flask. 'But actually, me old, I think I can probably top that.' He looked straight ahead, with a wry smile on his face. 'In fact, I'm still not convinced it friggin' well happened. Go on, guess. I'll give you twenty questions.' After five questions – female? (suspecting a woman was involved), age?, young or old?, blond or brunette?, did he know her? – Phil gave up in frustration.

'Piss off. I hate this twenty question lark. Just bloody tell me, won't you?' Stan teased him with a few titbits, before telling him about Niamh's visit and the discussion they'd had. Phil sat in stunned silence.

'Well fuck me backwards with a banjo,' he said eventually. 'Right. So she pissed off, saw off most if not all of your money, decided she was a lesbo, got stinking rich, thinks she can worm her way back into favour by becoming the band's friggin' manager. You did say no, I take it?' Stan thanked Phil for his in-depth analysis, adding that he was keeping his options open.

'Well, I wouldn't touch her with that banjo,' said Phil. They both laughed.

At the practice that evening, only band members were present, all keen to discuss the performance in Ursula's café. After five minutes of everyone trying to talk at once, Stan put his hands in the air and asked them to stop. Far better, he felt, to put their energy into getting set up and playing a few songs. Tom agreed, asking if they could make time for a look at a new piece which he and Angie had been working on. They sang three of what was becoming referred to as their usual set, then spent some time on the new piece.

Angie introduced this. She had this idea, she told them, for a song about those people living on the breadline, and to which she had given the title '*Just About Managing*'. With Tom accompanying on the keyboard, she sang it all the way though. There was applause all round, followed by silence, as they looked at each other to see who was going to comment first.

'I need to hear it again,' said Neil, 'but first off, I loved the melody, and the lyrics are full of poignancy. Very political.'

'Damn right it's political,' said Stan. 'I don't necessarily mind that, like, but it's not something we've done or talked about.' Neil reminded him that they were already singing *We're All in this Together*. 'What I don't chuffin' want,' Stan continued, 'is for us to go down that road. You know, like doing protest songs.'

'No-one's saying that Stan,' replied Angie. 'I just had this idea going around in my head, and had to get it out of my system. We could always work on it and tone it down a bit. Tom?'

'My view is that the melody itself has a lot of potential, I mean in terms of what we can do with it. We could do a great job on the backing, and there's scope for some great solos. I think kids would love it, too. But I'll also say that there is so much material for songs like this. Songs with a social and political message. The rich get richer, the poor get poorer type of thing. Our politicians are making such a cock up of things.' Tom looked around. He could see that he had given them food for thought.

'But let's just see what we can do with this.' After he had explained his ideas for an intro, they got to work.

At the break, they shared their thoughts about the gig, agreeing that each should give one positive comment and one about any room for improvement. There was a lot of positivity about the overall sound, praise for individual contributions, and general enthusiasm for performing at another gig soon. It was generally felt that they needed to sharpen up on entries, both with vocals and instruments, although Tom pointed out that most mistakes were only noticed by band members. He again raised the issue of having a manager. Most felt that they weren't yet in need of one, but if they got to the stage where they were playing gigs frequently, they should look around for somebody.

'What about you Stan?' asked Neil. 'You've said nowt on this.'

Stan hesitated. He had hoped the subject wouldn't come up. Even though it had, there seemed to be no sense of urgency. Despite that, he couldn't help himself.

'Well, as it happens, I have been approached by someone offering to take us on.' He stopped there, hardly believing he'd said it.

'Well, go on,' said Angie. 'Don't leave us dangling in suspense.'

'I wasn't going to mention it, cos I don't think she's the right chuffin' person.'

So he told them about Niamh, including a summary of their conversation the previous evening. For reasons he wasn't quite sure about, he didn't mention that she had squandered their savings all those years ago, or why, saying only that they had drifted apart and decided to get a divorce. But the overall effect was that he had generated some excitement.

'Well, you dark horse.'

'I'd no idea you'd been married, Stan. You kept that quiet.'

'Wow. So she could get us on the telly and playing at festivals.'

'If she'll do it for free, it's a no-brainer, surely.'

'She really thinks we're good then?'

Typically, Tom was more reflective.

'Hold on a bit, guys. Let's not get carried away. First, we need a reality check. We've played one gig. We struggle to get everyone to practices, because of work and other stuff. What Stan's ex is talking about is light years away from where we are. Second, we need to know what we'd be getting involved in. What's her organisation's reputation like, and no offence intended Stan, but what sort of track record does Niamh have?'

'I agree, mate. We've got a long way to go yet. I've no chuffin' idea about whatsit, AMS. I'm just telling you what she told me.'

'I'm looking at the website now,' said Neil, who had his smart phone out. 'Fuck me. They've got some serious people on their books. Solo artists, bands, actors.' He named some. 'I'm looking at reviews. Lots of positive stuff.' He passed his phone to Daniel. 'Have a look yourselves. They seem to be the real McCoy.'

Angie, Tom and Malcolm were soon looking at the website on their own phones. For a couple of minutes there were only background sounds. The hum of conversation coming through from the bar. A dog barking nearby. Some light traffic.

'Well, I for one would like to meet what's-her-name, Niamh,' said Angie. 'Is that Irish? Anyway, it wouldn't do any harm to hear what she has to offer, and we don't have to commit ourselves or anything.'

After some discussion and agreement that they would not be swept along by promises of riches, there was a consensus that Stan would get in touch with Niamh to arrange a meeting at the Stonemasons Arms on Welford Road at three o'clock the following Saturday afternoon. The venue was chosen on the grounds that, relatively speaking, it was neutral territory and the evening match between Watford and Leicester City was being televised, so those that wanted to could stay on and watch it on the pub's TV.

'Well, I only hope to God you know what you're frigging well doing,' commented Phil the following morning. Sitting in the van and unscrewing the tops of their flasks, he and Stan had taken shelter from the rain.

'So they're prepared to frigging well trust the woman?' Stan didn't respond, and looked straight ahead.

'You did tell them?'

'What?'

'That she took all of your sodding money.'

'Well, umm. Not in so many words.'

Phil sighed in exasperation. 'Well for fucks sake. They need to know, me old. I mean….'

'Yeah well, I've given it a bit of thought, like. It was a long time ago Phil, mate. We've all chuffin' moved on, like. Niamh wouldn't have got to where she is now, with her business, like, if she was, well, if people didn't trust her. Know what I mean?'

'Be it on your own head.' He passed Stan a biscuit. 'Chocolate gingers. Cos you're worth it.' Phil dunked his in his coffee and took a bite, which left a ring of dark chocolate around his mouth.

'To change the subject, you know it's that arsehole Raymond's appeal today in the Crown Court.' Stan nodded in acknowledgement. 'Esther's taken the morning off work to be there. His solicitor woman thinks he'll win.'

'Oh yeah?'

'Yeah. And that bastard copper, you know, the one who took the computers away. Well he's been pestering Esther trying to get more stuff about Raymond out of her, but she says she doesn't know any more than she's told him. What he told her though was that Raymond was originally done for having loads of CDs that had thousands of photos of kids. I mean, the mind boggles. What do these fucking perverts do with these photos? Where do they get them?'

'Well they probably play with themselves, like, trying to get it up. And I think if you know where to go, who to go to, like, you can buy this stuff or download it from websites. Has he got any family?'

'Apparently. I don't know what exactly, but they want nowt to do with the tosser. You can understand why, can't you? I mean. They should castrate these bloody perverts. That might stop them.'

'The trouble is, my old, that there are thousands of them out there. Probably several living on your estate and you don't know it. And they're not all blokes. There was that case not long ago of a couple of women who worked at a school, took advantage and took photos of kids naked when they was changing for PE. Mandy's take on it all is that most paedos were abused themselves as kids, and are.... What's the word? Damaged, I suppose.'

It had stopped raining, so they got back to work. Later, as they were packing up for their lunch break Phil received a phone call from Esther. For several minutes he listened, nodding and occasionally asking her to 'say again'. The upshot was, he told Stan, that the court had upheld Raymond's appeal on the basis that he had not broken his control orders at any time, and he was awarded several thousand pounds compensation and costs. The police and crown prosecution service were given a 'proper roasting' by the judge for improper conduct and wasting everybody's time and money. The new case which the 'nasty copper' had put together was thrown out as well. Raymond was returning to Birmingham, so Esther doubted whether she would see him again.

'Somehow, I don't think that's the frigging end of it,' said Phil. 'Not for Esther. She's had it tough because that arsehole got into her life, and because of what's happened, the looks she gets from people and everything, she doesn't feel bloody safe. So where's the fucking fairness, I ask you? She was just trying to help the prick get his life back together.'

'I don't know, mate. It isn't fair on her. We'll just have to look after her.' After a pause, Stan added, 'Suits you, by the way.'

'What?'

'The chocolate lipstick. It could catch on.' Phil wiped his mouth with his sleeve. He was lost in thought for the rest of the day, and barely spoke.

On Friday, they knocked off for the day at lunchtime and headed for the café. Ursula called from the kitchen when she heard their voices at the bar, then rushed out to greet them. Phil was given the usual bear hug, but she stood on tip toe to kiss Stan on each cheek. She chattered away as she led them to a table, mostly about the complimentary comments people had made about the band. Stan ordered the special of the day, saumagen with sauerkraut and mashed potatoes. Phil was going to have the same until she mentioned that the meat, onions and spices were cooked in a casing of pig's stomach. Instead, he asked for the all-day breakfast.

'Boring old fart,' said Stan. 'The human race wouldn't be where it is, like, without taking chuffin' risks.'

'What, like dropping fucking atom bombs on the Japanese? Or electing that pair Cameron and Osborne?'

Stan laughed. 'I was thinking more on the lines of City signing Claudio frigging Ranieri. Or the university lot digging up that car park to see if Richard the what's-his-name's skeleton was there.'

Phil was looking inquisitively at him. 'It seems to me, like, that something must have changed.'

'Like what?'

'You chuffin' well tell me. I get the usual bleeding squeeze from Ursula, but you get the gentle peck on the cheek. So what's that all about?'

'I'd say she was just being careful about the old chest wound. You know, from the surgery.' Stan replied. But his face had reddened, and he couldn't help the half-smile.

'I think not, me old. You should see your friggin' face. The word *guilty* is written all over it.' Phil leant across the table, grinning. 'You've been giving her one. Am I right, or am I right? You randy old git.'

'Randy old git yourself. What was you up to upstairs on Saturday night then. You wasn't friggin' well playing cards, was you?'

'Could have been. Strip poker, like.' They both laughed.

'Good to see you two are happy,' said Ursula, approaching the table with their meals. She set the plates on the table.

'We was having a serious discussion about the pros and cons of risk taking, duck,' said Stan.

Ursula looked first at Phil, then Stan. 'Well, that is a serious topic for lunchtime, for sure. On balance, I would say that risk taking definitely has its benefits. Enjoy your food, guys.' She gave Stan a warm smile then walked back to the kitchen. Stan took a deep breath as he looked at his plateful of saumagen, then blew out through puffed cheeks. Picking up his fork, Phil was about to say something, but Stan cut him off, pointing his finger at Phil as he spoke.

'Not another chuffin' word. Eat.'

As he walked into the relatively quiet Stonemasons' Arms, Stan hoped he had arrived early enough to be the first, but Neil and Angie were sitting at a corner table, deep in conversation with Niamh sitting opposite them.

'Shit,' he said to himself. He walked across to say hello, offering to buy drinks. Their glasses were still full. He returned from the bar with a pint of bitter. The obvious place to sit was next to Niamh, but he was reluctant to do so. Seeing his hesitation, she patted the space next to herself and invited him to sit there. Stan guessed from their faces that he had interrupted a conversation which they were reluctant to continue in his presence. He noticed that Niamh had dressed down for the meeting. She was wearing no makeup, there was no sign of any bling, and her jeans and top were low key. Nothing suggested she might have been the CEO of a successful business, apart possibly from her obvious self-confidence. He had to admit to himself that she had aged well and looked very attractive. Sensing the awkwardness of the situation, Neil started to tell them a funny story. By the time he'd come to the punch line, Daniel, Esther Tom and Malcolm were standing near the table, all apart from Daniel joining in the laughter.

'Just got the tail end of that, Neil,' said Tom. 'Very good impersonation and French accent. You ought to think about a career change.'

'Does that imply I'm crap on the violin then?'

'No no no. Definitely not. And you must be Niamh,' said Tom, looking at her. They shook hands and he introduced the others with him. Drinks were ordered and fetched from the bar, then they were all seated, some on the bench seat, the rest on individual chairs which they had drawn up. Esther explained that she wouldn't be staying long, and that Neil had offered to take Daniel home.

They looked at each other, wondering who was going to take the lead.

'I guess I should kick off,' said Stan. 'We've asked Niamh to join us cos she has offered to manage the band, daft as it may be. And they, well I guess we all, Niamh, wanted to have a chat and umm, well what?' He looked at the others for help.

'Just get a sense of what you could do for us,' said Malcolm.

'And how far you think we could go. Being realistic, that is. You know, given what we all do and that,' said Angie.

'OK, well I can do all that, of course. And let's get this straight to start with. I won't ask for any sort of remuneration, apart maybe from some expenses.'

'Yeah, I was wondering about that,' said Malcolm. 'Why is that? What's in it for you otherwise?'

Niamh hesitated and looked at Stan.

'I don't know how much Stan has told you. About me and him, I mean.'

'They know, duck. That we was married, drifted apart and divorced.' His look suggested that was all they needed to know.

'Right. So let's just say it's for old time's sake. I owe Stan a big favour, and this would be my way of repaying him. Plus, you know, I get a real buzz out of seeing any talent reaching its potential.'

Niamh outlined the role she would play and how it might develop, depending on how successful the band became, and how far they wanted to go in terms of becoming semi-professional or fully professional. There was a stirring amongst them at the mention of the word professional. She was effusive in her praise for what she had seen and heard, and delighted in the fact that such a talented group of musicians had joined Stan and were bringing out the best in him. She had always known that Stan had a good voice and could play the guitar a bit, but he'd never had the confidence to go out and perform, except down at his club occasionally.

The first step, she said, was to generate some local interest in and support for the band, to develop a following. To that end, she had come to an arrangement with the owner of The Brown Cow in Leicester. She asked them whether they were interested to hear it. Neil, Tom, Malcolm and Angie looked towards Stan, nodding heads but careful not to look too enthusiastic.

'That look like a yes,' said Stan

'Well, as you might know, he likes to support and develop local talent, so what he has said is that if you're as good as I've built you up to be, and no pressure there at all is there, then he would give you a couple of slots on one of his band nights. If that works out, he'll give you the following two weeks, which could be near the top of the bill.' She paused to let the information sink in.

'So when would all this happen?' asked Malcolm.

'This could be changed if you wanted, but the first gig would be early next month. I know that you have work commitments to work around, and at the moment the guy can be flexible, but at some point he will need some definite dates. So I think you should go away, have a think, talk at your next practice perhaps, and see where we are with dates. I don't need to be at the gigs, but I will be if I can be. What I would like is to be at your next practice, if that's OK. Just to get a feel for how they work.'

In the discussion that followed, Neil, Malcolm and Tom expressed concerned at the pace at which things seemed to be moving, as did Stan, but Daniel seemed unmoved by this. Angie had become very positive and enthusiastic about the possibilities. They eventually agreed that at the next practice they would try to sort out dates on which they could play at The Brown Cow. The next few days would give them a bit of thinking time as well.

Niamh asked if they would like to hear about the icing on the cake.

'There is a festival in June at which one of the bands we had penned in has withdrawn. It's out in the sticks, in Derbyshire. It's been running for a few years now and has become really popular. All the artists do rhythm and blues or rock stuff, so it's very focussed. Which means your audience won't be there hoping to catch some garage or boys band. They'll be appreciative. So there's an opening, if you want it.'

By this time the pub was beginning to fill, and the preamble to the match between Watford and Leicester City had begun on the TV. Tom, Neil and Stan brought refills from the bar, enough for two rounds, along with a selection of cobs. Phil had joined the group, having squeezed in on a small stool which looked slightly vulnerable. Niamh almost screamed with delight at the sight of him, and reached across the table to give a sheepish looking Phil a hug and kiss, telling him that he looked great. There were three TV screens in the pub, one to the right of the group giving them a clear view of the screen. There was a loud cheer at the kick off, and even louder oohs and aahs when City missed an early chance to take the lead. Stan was half watching Niamh, who wore a rather bemused look.

As people continued to come through the door, the pressure on the backs of Tom, Phil, Daniel and Malcolm was such that they decided it was more comfortable for them to stand. With the excitement, conversation was almost impossible, apart from between those immediately next to each other. The score was nil-nil at half time, but few seemed in doubt that the eventual result would favour the City team. Niamh got up to leave, making her apologies. Before Stan had the chance to decide how he should say goodbye, she had kissed him lightly on the cheek, saying she would be in touch and would see him at the next band practice. He caught Phil's eye, and they raised their glasses to each other.

There was pandemonium in the place after one of City's star players, Riyad Mahrez scored early in the second half. Even Daniel managed a broad smile and high fives. For several minutes the windows vibrated to the sounds of cheering, singing and chanting that followed the goal. The tension built towards the end of the match, so when the referee blew the final whistle there was a sense of relief, not just in the final result, but also in the knowledge that beers could be bought and toilets could be visited.

'Five points clear,' Phil shouted to Stan, as he held up the five digits of his right hand.

'Did you enjoy that then, duck?' Stan asked Angie, who had moved close to him.

'Amazing. I'm really glad I stayed to watch the match. I don't really follow football, but I can see why everybody in Leicester is so excited. And do you know what, Stan? It was so nice to have everyone together here. I mean the band. There could be exciting times ahead, don't you think?'

'Who knows? We'll just have to see how it goes. We'll need a bit of hard graft and a bit of luck, just like City.'

'Oh come on, mister glass half empty. But I suppose you're right.' She said her goodbyes and joined the steady trickle of those leaving. Phil and Stan were soon the only ones left at the table. Phil pointed out that there was another big game the following morning, as the boys were playing in the semi-final of the cup competition. Stan had been looking forward to his first runout as linesman since he had come out of hospital. He asked Phil what his game plan was.

'Same as usual,' he replied. 'These days I just say go out and enjoy yourselves. I don't bother with all that tactical bollocks.'

'What, like you used to, not?'

'Oi! Just be careful. Right, another pint? Your round I believe.'

## Phil

Well I only hope Stan knows which chuffin' side his bread's buttered on and doesn't mess things up with Mandy. I mean there's Ursula and now Niamh in the picture. I was surprised to see him sitting next to Niamh. There they were, together, like, almost as if nothing had ever happened. He's a different bloke since Mandy came along. Like he has something to live for again. I thought she was a bit out of his league at first, kind of thing, but just shows first impressions can be wrong.

My advice – keep your dick zipped up, me old. Otherwise, how does that song go? *There May be Trouble Ahead.*

## Stan

There is only one thing better than watching a match live in a packed pub, and that's being at the game. Trouble is, it's so chuffin' expensive these days, at least thirty quid to go and watch. Twice that for one of the top teams, like. There's too much friggin' money in the game. Why should those big girls blouses be paid seventy, eighty thousand plus a week, when the average bloke earns twenty a year, if he's lucky?

But I was glad that Angie enjoyed watching City. She's a smashing kid. You can tell she's been well brought up. Kind, polite, considerate and that. She can stamp her feet when she wants to, mind, and is a bit of a bossy nickers. What I like though is how positive she is. Always looking on the bright side, always sees the best in people. Talented too. I'd be dead proud if she was my daughter.

# Thirty-Four

# Dream on Dreamer

The semi-final match was a game of two halves, as they say. Phil's team stormed into a three-nil lead in the first twenty minutes. As Phil gave his half-time team talk, the boys were so excited they basically took no notice of what he was trying to say. It took Stan's booming command to shut up to get them to listen. Unless they calmed down, he added, they could still lose the match. Concentrate, keep it tight, was Phil's message. He said it four times, hoping it would sink in. Five minutes into the second half, the goalkeeper lost his concentration as the ball was floated into the penalty area. Unchallenged, he allowed the ball to slip through his hands and into the goal. His fellow defenders vented their fury, and from then on the lad had the jitters every time the ball came near him. His nervousness affected the whole team, pass after pass going astray. A sliced clearance from a centre back went straight to an opposition striker, who had a clear run into the penalty area and scored. Somehow, they managed to hold onto a one goal lead, defending desperately, but the equaliser came ten minutes from the end. Five minutes later the referee awarded a penalty to the opposition, despite a blatant dive from their striker.

Stan ran behind the goal to talk to the goalkeeper, as the opposition celebrated the referee's decision.

'Listen son. Kyle, isn't it? You've played a blinder all season. You don't suddenly become a crap goalie. Now, you know what Kasper Schmeichel does when he's facing a penalty?'

'Yeah. He stretches his arms up, so that he looks really tall.'

'Let's see you do it then. It also makes you a target and makes the goal look smaller. Another thing. Stand just a bit to your left so that the right side looks inviting, then just has he runs up step quietly into the middle and dive that way. Got it?' The lad nodded. 'Good luck.'

Kyle did as Stan suggested. The penalty shot was not far to his right and he was able to save it. As the opposition players froze in disappointment, all bar one of his own team rushed to pat him on the back. Kyle spotted the one hovering near the half-way line. His kick bounced perfectly in front of the striker, who, with a clear run on the goal, calmly rounded the goalkeeper and side-footed the ball into the net. The final whistle was blown two minutes later.

After the celebrations had calmed down, a beaming Kyle walked up to Stan, who was walking the perimeter of the pitch, collecting in the flag posts.

'Thanks mate. That was the best bit of coaching I've ever had.'

'It's Stan. Shows how much notice you friggin' well take. Anyway, like I said, you don't suddenly become a crap goalie. You still had to save it and you did, so well done. Give me five.'

The match had been played on a neutral ground, which in this case belonged to a prominent semi-professional club that played in the top Leicestershire league. It had two small stands and railings all the way round the pitch. The county Football Association had provided all of the match officials, so Stan had been given the job of first-aid man come physio, which basically meant he ran onto the pitch whenever one of the team appeared to be injured, bucket of water in one hand, first-aid box in the other. He would apply the magic sponge of cold water to the offending knee or ankle, or on a couple of occasions use a painkilling spray, followed by a pat on the back of the injured player. Stan was able to do his job unmolested by supporters of either side. Better still, he realised that he was feeling fitter than he had for some time, able to run about without becoming breathless or any other problems.

'That chuffin' Kyle,' said Phil later, as he and Stan enjoyed a quick celebratory pint in the club. 'He put the shits up everyone in that second half, going from hero to zero and then back to hero. I'll never know how he managed that save.'

'Perhaps his guardian angel was looking after him.'

'I didn't know you were a little blondie. So cute.' Mandy was sitting on the sofa of Audrey's apartment later that afternoon, looking through some of the photograph albums Stan had found in one of the wardrobes, while Stan carried boxes of Audrey's belongings into the living room.

'How old are you there? Three? Four?' Stan looked over her shoulder.

'Probably four. I just about remember that. My aunty Joan's wedding. I was page boy.'

After weeks of prevarication, Stan had got round to the task of sorting out his mother's belongings. In the immediate aftermath of her death he was slightly overwhelmed by the whole business of sorting out his mother's estate. He had met with the solicitor who Audrey had asked to be the executor of her will. The man, a second cousin of hers, worked for an established Leicester firm that had dealt with the family affairs for many years. The legal world was totally alien to Stan, and the meeting was the first time he had been in a solicitor's office.

Audrey had left some money to her favourite charities, but the bulk was left to Stan. He was pleasantly surprised to discover that her savings and cash assets amounted to almost one hundred and fifty thousand pounds. What he hadn't known was that she had also owned the three bedroomed semi off Glenfield Road where her parents had lived. Stan had always assumed that the house had been sold after his grandfather had died in the nineteen eighties. It was currently being let to a young couple.

'Crafty old so and so,' he had said. 'I had no chuffin' idea.' He did the sums. If he sold the house he would be comfortably off, beyond his dreams. There were other options, which for the time being he kept this all to himself.

Stan knew that his mother had become something of a hoarder as she grew older, so was not surprised to find boxes and suit cases crammed into cupboards and wardrobes in the apartment. These were full of family photos and paraphernalia, including those photos, letters and bank statements which had seemed to have disappeared recently. But he hadn't been prepared for the fact that in the attic of the semi was a treasure trove of documents, newspaper cuttings and more letters she had kept, many of them covering her time as a councillor, some even going back to her childhood. She appeared to have kept every letter she had ever received.

There were also suitcases full of clothes, including artificial fur coats and dozens of skirts and dresses. What he was going to do with them, he had no idea. He felt it was going to take months, even years to go through everything else, if he could be bothered. It occurred to him that the charity shops would be interested in most, if not all of her clothes, but it didn't seem right to Stan to just give her stuff away.

Stan took down the few framed photographs and prints from the walls of the living room and bedroom. He arranged them in boxes which he had brought along for the purpose. The last photograph he came to was of the bowls team for which she had played, and as he tried to squeeze it into a box, he noticed a piece of paper which had been attached to the back with Blu-Tack. He removed it, then sat down in the armchair to look at it.

'Well bugger me. She kept that quiet.' He stared disbelievingly at the small piece of paper.

'What's that?'

'Oh it's nothing much really. Just something the old girl'd lost, and it was stuck behind this old photo.'

Stan was looking at a betting slip, dated August the previous year. She had staked ten pounds on Leicester City to win the premiership. Stan did the mental arithmetic. He folded the slip and put it in his wallet, then stood up, muttering quietly to himself. *Chuffin' Nora.*

'So, me old, supposing you won the lottery. What would you do with it?' asked Stan. It was morning coffee time in the van. Football had been the only topic of conversation so far. They had attacked the windows with gusto and worked a half hour longer than usual before taking the break.

'Just goes to prove that productivity always improves if the local team is doing well,' Stan had said. 'Had there been football in his chuffin' day, like, I'm sure Karl Marx would've had something to say about that. Who benefits most? The workers or the frigging capitalist owners?

'Where does that put us then, mate? We're self-employed, own our own business like, so where do we fit in?' asked Phil. Stan thought for a minute.

'It's a different ball game, when you think about it. In Marx's day, there probably weren't too many self-employed. Maybe stonemasons, smithies and the like. The workers were poor, the owners rich. There's inequality today, but the workers have a much better standard of living than in those frigging days. There were nowt like the National Health Service or pensions, or owt, and there was a lot of bleeding slums. There's a lot more filthy rich people today though. Them what hides their dosh in offshore accounts, the bastards, not paying their taxes. Did you know that the richest ten percent in this country own more than half of the total wealth?'

'Yeah, yeah, yeah,' said Phil, slightly irritated. He had heard it all before.

'Anyway, to answer your question, a lot more people have had to become chuffin' well self-employed cos they've had no alternative. And in the gig economy they get bleeding well ripped off. You know, delivery drivers, taxi drivers and the rest. Like I say, it's a different sort of model to what Marx was talking about.'

'So the short answer is you don't frigging know where we fit in.'

'No, that's not what I'm saying,' replied Stan, getting slightly flustered. 'We're workers, like, who've had to adjust to the way things are. To be fair, we are in a bit more control than some.'

'What, cos we can charge what we decide and knock off when we bleeding want?'

'Precisely.' This one-sided discussion had led to Stan's lottery question. Phil asked whether Stan had had a winning ticket. Stan said he was just thinking out loud. If Phil had won, not millions, but say a couple of hundred thousand, what would he do with it? Phil's reply was that it was a pointless discussion, as he never bought a lottery ticket, and wouldn't be anytime soon.

'No, nor me neither. But just suppose for a moment. Would you pack in this lot, for instance, or buy a bigger house?'

'You'd have to frigging well work, wouldn't you? I mean, if you live the life of Riley, what use are you to anyone?'

'But window cleaning? Come on, wouldn't you do summat else?'

'I really dunno mate,' said Phil after a moment's reflection. 'But here and now, we need to get back to it.'

Stan was understandably preoccupied with the idea that he could, at some time in the not-too-distant future, become relatively wealthy after inheriting from his mother's estate. Asking himself whether or not she had done him any favours, one minute he was all for giving most of it away to charity, the next he imagined himself sunbathing on a golden beach, beer in hand. He was able to distract himself by focussing on the lyrics of the latest song that he was trying to put together, the theme of which was the rich get richer while the poor get poorer.

## Stan

Life's a lottery, full stop. When you see them people in Syria, say, being bombed, kids being killed or losing legs, and those poor starving buggers in Africa, well not just Africa is it, you have to wonder what they've done to deserve it. And what that ISIS lot are doing to people as well. Bastards. And all this stuff is usually cos one power mad arsehole is in control, encouraging the raping and pillaging, so he can get rich on the back of it. It's all about chuffin' power. Same in this country. Although at least we don't go chopping people's heads off or dropping bombs on them. But it's all about power. You go to one of the posh fucking public schools, then Oxford, and you're in. If you go into politics, it's cos you want the power. If you get a top job and have shed loads of money, it gives you power. The more they have the more they want. This Brexit stuff is all about power. You watch. The Tory party will pull itself apart, cos they all want a slice of the action, the bigger the better.

Take two kids. One born into money, which gets you a big house and that, the best education and then the best jobs, so more money for his or her kids, and so on. The other born into poverty, possibly just the one parent struggling on benefits, poor living conditions, poor diet, bad health, crap school probably. Don't both of those kids deserve the same chances? I read about a good idea somewhere recently. If money, property and everything had to be handed to the state and couldn't be passed on to your kids when you die, one way of giving all kids the same chance in life would be to give each one an amount of money when they were born, which would see them through until they had finished college or whatever and had got a job. Something like that anyway. You could see what might happen though. Money-grabbing politicians would want to get their hands on that money and use it for other stuff, pet projects and that. Or greedy parents would swindle their own kids out of the money.

Rant over. Sorry.

# *Phil*

I wonder if Stan remembers a friend of ours who won on the lottery not long after it started. He and his missus won about half a million I think. Well they didn't have a friggin' clue what to do with it. They'd never seen that sort of money, and there was no one to give them any advice. Either that or they didn't want any. Of course they all say it won't change them, they'll still go to work and live the same life. Will they fuck. These two blew the lot eventually, fell out along the way, then got divorced.

I don't know where Stan was coming from, but I wouldn't want to suddenly have loads of money. I'm happy as I am thanks. Mind you, if someone bought a lottery ticket for me and it won the top prize or something, I would donate it to Leicester City in exchange for a place on the board. That would shake them up a bit.

## Thirty-Five

# Be Careful
# What You Like

S tan arrived early for the practice to make sure the place was fit for use and to set up his own gear. Hoping also to have some time to practise on his own, he was slightly annoyed to realise, as he walked towards the door, that he wasn't the first to arrive. Neil and Malcolm were in animated discussion about a new song they had been working on, and barely acknowledged Stan as he placed his guitar and amp near the stage and shouted hallo. He didn't want to disturb the creative flow of ideas which he assumed was going on between the other two. The room was fortunately clean and tidy, so with the intention of waiting quietly for them to finish, he grabbed a chair but wasn't given the opportunity to sit on it.

'Maybe Stan can help us out,' Neil was saying. 'What do you say, Big Man? We could really do with you playing the chords while we have a crack at some solos. We're calling this *Be Careful What You Like*'. They talked Stan through and then demonstrated the first part of this new song. After a quick practice run through the chords, he was able to play along with them up to the point where the solos would come in.

'Righto, so this is a song about social media, yeah? Not that I know much about it, but why would anyone want to chuffin' well listen to a song about social media?' Stan asked.

'You'll need to listen to the lyrics all the way through when we're done,' Neil replied. 'But basically it's about the way that the people behind Trump....,'

'And the Russians,' Malcolm cut in.

'Yeah and them. The way they and Trump's lot have got loads of people working for them just to target Facebook users with loads of fake news stuff. And they know who to target by looking on our accounts, seeing what sort of posts we click the 'Like' button for. So if you or I were to have read and liked a post that was racist or right wing in some way, we would be targeted with ads and fake news to try and influence how we'll vote. It's all about algorithms.' He paused, taking in the glazed look on Stan's face. 'Sorry, it's a bit technical, but that's what's going on. I'm guessing you don't use Facebook yourself.'

'Sorry mate, no. You lost me on posts and accounts, like.' The other two laughed. 'What? Oh yeah. Like. It all sounds a bit political to me, like, and you've heard me before on that. But the song rocks along, don't it. The way it starts off pretty fast and then gets faster, sounds good, like.' He looked at them. 'Too many likes around here. Maybe I should stop using that chuffin' word, or somebody will start sending me fake ads and stuff. Let's get on with it. Who's doing the vocals by the way?'

Neil and Malcolm looked at each other and then at Stan. Malcolm spoke for them both.

'We thought you'd be perfect for this, Big Man. You'd bring out the anger that's in the lyrics. But see how it goes, yeah? We'll carry on for now, until you're ready to step in, like.' Stan groaned quietly, but didn't disagree with the idea.

They discussed how the solos would come in and how the accompaniment would work, then played it through from the beginning.

'That's a fucking blast,' said Malcolm. 'That'll work alright.' They turned towards the person clapping and whooping just inside the doorway. Niamh walked towards them.

'I love the sound of that, guys. Something new you're working on?' Neil explained that it was at an early stage, but thought it 'had legs'. Niamh wondered when she might be able to hear the finished product. Rather than reply to this directly, Stan suggested that they concentrated mostly on the new stuff they were coming up with, as Niamh was reasonably familiar with what they had played so far. Tom wanted to spend time on Angie's song *Just About Managing*, so they would both be happy with the idea.

There were nods and sounds of agreement from Neil and Malcolm, and Niamh was happy with whatever they decided. Expressing concern that Daniel could be the stumbling block, Neil suggested that they kicked off the practice with a couple of their 'usuals', then digress from there.

The others arrived shortly afterwards. As they were setting up, Stan put them in the picture regarding the plan for the evening, then announced to everyone that they would warm up with *Fightin' Hard* and *Moving On*.

'Tell us when you're ready, Daniel mate, then play us in. Okey dokey?'

*Fightin' Hard* started well enough, but there were a few jitters, and things ground to a halt when Malcolm was late coming in for his solo. Re-starting, they managed to play both songs straight through without any hitches, although Stan pointed out that neither was totally up to scratch. Tom then handed out copies of the score and lyrics for *Just About Managing*, which they worked on section by section. Progress was slow, and Daniel became increasingly frustrated with the stoppages. The fact that no one as yet knew the lyrics didn't help. However, they persevered, eventually managing to play and sing it through from start to finish.

'Work to do, everyone,' said Tom, who promised to do his best to send arrangements for all of the new songs on a CD by the end of the week, using pigeon express so give them time to learn their parts and the lyrics for the next practice.

Neil had a whispered discussion with to Stan about the best way to continue, as Daniel was beginning to moan and had become very fidgety. They agreed that they should revert to plan A, and forget the new stuff for the moment, otherwise they would lose Daniel. The drinks break which followed gave Neil the opportunity to sit and chat with Daniel about the music they had been listening to recently. Consequently, Daniel was much more relaxed as they played *Still Got the Blues*, and for the rest of the evening they were able to focus on specific parts of their repertoire which were in need of improvement.

Despite some chuntering that it was all getting a bit serious and pressurised, they were able to fix two additional practice dates, meaning there were five in total before the first gig at The Brown Cow. Niamh didn't seem too concerned about the lack of progress that evening, but advised on having as much original material as possible. 'Originality stands out,' she had said. 'But obviously only if it's any good. And yours could be.'

'Sorry duck,' Stan said to Niamh after the others had left. 'That didn't go to plan, as you could see. We have to work around the kid sometimes. At least we have a target date to get sorted by, but we'll have to pull our fingers out.'

'Let's say you've got your work cut out.' She paused then added, 'I understand Daniel's difficulties Stan, and why you would want to include him, but he does seem to present a bit of an obstacle to progress for the moment. Have you tried any other percussionists, looked around at all?'

'To be honest, no duck, we haven't. The thing is, he's good, as you've seen that yourself. I've had my issues with him before now, but as Neil would say, we all have our problems.'

'But Daniel has specific problems that are affecting the band's progress, which could well get in the way later on. It might be worth seeing who else is out there.' Stan thought for a moment.

'Do you know, duck, it really surprises me to hear you talk like that. When you were dead on your chuffin' feet, someone gave you a chance and stuck by you, yeah? I reckon everyone in the band would want to stick by the kid. There might be some ups and downs, like, but he'll come good, and we'll all be the better for it.' It was Niamh's turn to think for a moment.

'I consider my wrist duly slapped. You're right, Stan, I should know better.' She smiled at him, a twinkle in her eye. 'Another thing, before we head off. The music and all that is your domain, so I'll try to stay out of it unless you're making a real balls up of things. But I have one or two suggestions about how you present on stage, if that's OK. You know, the picture you want your many future fans to take away with them. Do you want to hear them? It's been a long night for you.' Fire away, he replied. She asked if there had been any discussion about who stood where on stage. There hadn't been really, Stan replied, although it was assumed that he normally stood centre-stage.

'You know, Big Man – is it alright if I call you that? – you know, we could carry on this conversation over a drink. That's if you want.' Stan recognised of old the twinkle in her eyes.

'I tell you what, duck,' he said after a quick assessment of the possibilities, 'I'll pass on that tonight. We've an early start, like, so why don't you send your ideas in an email and we'll take it from there.'

'Of course. No problem.'

Stan gathered his things. As they said goodbye in the car park, they could both sense the uncertainty as to how they should part.

'All things considered Niamh, best keep things on a business footing, aye?'

'Oh I agree absolutely.' Nonetheless, she stood on tiptoe and kissed him gently on the cheek. 'I'll be in touch.'

Mid-morning break next day, coffee in mugs steaming, as was Stan. There had been five minutes of heated discussion about what had recently been daubed as *Brexit*. Phil wanted his country back like it used to be. He had nothing against immigrants, he wasn't a racist, but a lot of them only came to the country for the welfare benefits. And they're the chuffin reason we don't have enough houses, you can't get an appointment at the friggin' doctors, some of them are criminals, people smugglers. He was in La-La land, Stan had told him. How far back did he want to go, then shout stop the chuffin' clock. The sixties, fifties, war time? It wasn't going to happen. Most Europeans came here to work, and lots have raised their families here. Do we kick them out? Did he know that most immigrants were from outside Europe, that if it weren't for immigrants our NHS would fall apart? Phil came back at him. What if they do come here to work? Ain't that the problem? There are some places where you can't get a job cos the bleeding immigrants have taken them all. Such as? asked Stan. No reply.

'Look mate,' said Stan. 'We'd better keep off this chuffin' subject, otherwise we'll fall out. Best agree to disagree, like.' He opened the window to let some cool air in to the van and to help him calm down. He changed the subject.

'Niamh was at the practice last night. It didn't go too well, like. Danny boy had one of his moments. Not his fault, really. Last minute change of script, to suit bloody Niamh, but it didn't work.'

He went on to explain that she had half-suggested that the band find a new drummer, but Stan had put her right on that one. Good on you, Phil said.

'And then, would you Adam-and-Eve it, she gives me those 'come to chuffin' bed eyes' like she used to, and suggests we go for a bleeding drink.'

'You what? I friggin' told you she was bad news, mate. You didn't sodding well listen.' He put the top on his flask. 'You should ditch her, if you ask me. Interfering cow.'

Stan didn't respond. They got back to work, Stan quietly trying to get the music and lyrics to *Be Careful What You Like* sorted in his mind.

## Stan

Jesus. Suddenly everything seems so bleeding complicated. It used to feel like I got up, went to work, enjoyed the banter with the lads, like, had a couple of pints down the club, maybe three or four on pay day. I never had to think about money, cos I had enough to not worry, like, and now it looks like I'll have more than enough. Occasionally I'd come across a woman I'd fancy and she fancied me, and we'd be alright for a few weeks or months, but nothing serious. Now and then I'd go and watch a City match or the Tigers, but tickets are like chuffin' gold these days. I was quite happy whiling away the time at home on the old guitar, sometimes wondering 'what if....'. Phil's lads lost more games than they won, which meant he'd be like a bear with a sore arse for a couple of days. Now it feels like we're on a bus which won't stop, and I don't know where it's going.

## Phil

Politics has never been my strong point, but the trouble with Stan is that he's never chuffin' well taken me seriously, in my view. Never accepts that sometimes I'm right and he's wrong. Nowadays, like, you can be in a shop, or in a doctor's surgery, standing at the gate outside Daniel's school, or just walking down the chuffin' street, and you will hear any number of different languages. Don't seem right to me. Come over here and you should learn to speak English, if you ask me. Otherwise how can we understand each other? I don't know where it's all going.

# Thirty-Six

## Fighting Hard

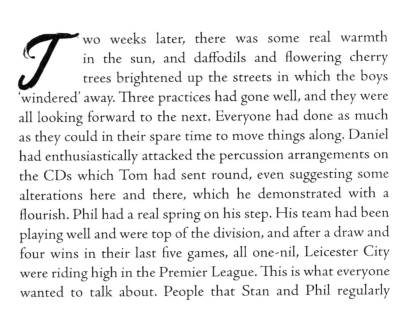

Two weeks later, there was some real warmth in the sun, and daffodils and flowering cherry trees brightened up the streets in which the boys 'windered' away. Three practices had gone well, and they were all looking forward to the next. Everyone had done as much as they could in their spare time to move things along. Daniel had enthusiastically attacked the percussion arrangements on the CDs which Tom had sent round, even suggesting some alterations here and there, which he demonstrated with a flourish. Phil had a real spring on his step. His team had been playing well and were top of the division, and after a draw and four wins in their last five games, all one-nil, Leicester City were riding high in the Premier League. This is what everyone wanted to talk about. People that Stan and Phil regularly saw on their rounds but could rarely draw into conversation, were now only too keen to stop and sing the praises of players and manager, each of whom a few months ago were largely unknown except to the regular match-goers. Becoming slightly paranoid, Stan would check every morning that his mother's betting slip was still in his sock drawer.

Niamh had been away on business, citing the potential collapse of the signing of a major star, and had missed the first two of the practices. Stan suspected her absence was tactful. It felt to him that it had lessened the pressure on the band, and there was a consequent surge of creativity. She crept in unnoticed halfway through the third practice, standing behind Phil, who had more or less mastered the subtleties of the sound mixing. Axel stood next to him to help, if asked. Niamh made her presence known as they produced a rousing finale to *Where Did it all Start*, another of Neil and Malcolm's creations. As they saw her walking towards them, the mutual praise and back-slapping came to a gradual halt.

'Hi guys. That's one I haven't heard before. Original, too. And do you know what? You've really nailed that distinctive sound. You've obviously been working hard.' Looking relaxed and smiling, she stood next to Neil. 'So has Stan been cracking the whip?'

'You could say that,' replied Neil. 'Stan and Tom together. But we're enjoying it, I would say.' There were nods and sounds of agreement. Niamh looked from one to the other as she spoke. She warned them not to become complacent, suggesting that with two sessions left before their gig, the next one should effectively be the last practice. They should treat the one after that as a dress rehearsal. It would be a good idea to try and drag some people in to watch them if they could. Friends and family, customers from the pub, or just pull them in off the street if necessary.

'So play it as if it was a gig itself, like?' asked Stan. 'It would go down well with the landlord, as we sort of promised him our first gig would be here.'

They discussed publicity. Angie would sort out a poster and email it for everyone to print off and put up wherever they could. She suggested they would do well to get twenty people coming.

The one blot on the landscape was Esther's situation. Despite the result of Raymond's appeal, she was still receiving unwanted attention in the form of insults from mainly young men in her neighbourhood. This was always late evening as they wandered past the house, probably, she thought, on their way home from the pub. Things came to a head very recently, when a brick was thrown. If it was aimed at the window it missed its target, as it thumped against the front door. She had just gone to bed and so was awake at the time. Fortunately, the sound hadn't woken Daniel. If it had, his likely reaction would have complicated the picture even more.

Esther related all this to Phil over the phone the day after it had happened. She was clearly near her wits end, and now felt so unsafe in her home that she was going to look for somewhere else to live, probably away from Leicester. She asked Phil to promise not to mention anything of this to Daniel until she had thought things through and talked to her sister, who lived in Leamington Spa.

Mid-morning break in the van next day. 'Can't lose Danny boy, can we. We need a plan,' said Stan after Phil had outlined the situation. 'Presumably this all happens at the weekend when these arseholes are tanked up.'

'Bang on, mate. Friday or Saturday, sometimes both, when they're on their way home. It's likely to be some of them that was outside the house that night it all kicked off. There's one wazzock I'd definitely recognise.' Phil suggested there were two pubs that were the likely drinking holes of the group concerned. They decided to try and enlist Malcolm's support, and invite him to join them for a drink the following Friday. He returned their voicemail message later that day to say he would be available.

They almost literally bumped into the likely suspects on their way into the first of the pubs.

'That'll be them,' said Phil. 'Use the other door.' He'd recognised one of the five men who were on their way out. In the shadow of the doorway, they watched as the group made their way to the other pub fifty yards down the road.

'No panic,' said Stan. 'They'll be there a while yet. We can wander over later and have a gander. Let's get them in. My round.'

They drank slowly, two pints each over the next hour and a half, and another one after relocating across the road. Whereas the first pub had been relatively quiet, they were welcomed by the stuffy warmth of the crowd in the second. The drinkers were mostly men and women in their twenties, some possibly early thirties, and there was a sense of the large majority knowing each other. A wide screen TV featured a rugby match involving Leicester Tigers, but apart from a group watching with craned necks from their table directly below, it was for the most part being ignored. Phil, leading the way through the crush and feeling slightly out of place and conspicuous, spotted the men they were looking for waiting to be served. Seeing that there was an open serving area, the main bar on one side and the lounge on the other, they backtracked to use the side door which opened directly into the lounge, which itself was busy. They managed to squeeze onto some barstools in a corner, which provided a vantage point for Stan to be able to see the comings and goings at the main entrance. Stan and Phil found it frustrating to be looking at an empty glass for more than two minutes, let alone twenty. They settled for a round of soft drinks and bags of nuts and crisps. Being sober will give us an advantage if things get going, Malcolm had said. Huddled in their corner, and battling against the increasingly noisy atmosphere, they conversed on topics ranging from Malcolm's new male friend to their favourite films. Phil and Stan had just about contained their laughter as Malcolm explained why he loved *The Sound of Music* so much.

'Finish it later, me old. Looks like we're off,' said Stan. They waited a couple of minutes before following their quarry. The five had become three, as the group split up at a junction a few yards down the road, shouting and swearing as they went their separate ways. Stan, Phil and Malcolm kept well back as the other threesome meandered their way along the pavement, swearing at a man across the road whose dog was barking at them, then asking two young women walking arm-in arm in front of them if they wanted to make love, but rather less politely. They laughed as the women started to walk much faster, their heels clattering on the pavement.

As they neared the turning which would take them past Esther's house, the words *paedo* and *paedo lover* could be heard clearly amongst the continual stream of foul language.

'Leave twat features to me,' said Phil, 'then by all means pile in if you need to.'

'Use that street light by Ester's house to our advantage, and we'll just hang back a bit,' Malcolm suggested. 'We'll see them, but they will only see shadows.'

The abuse aimed at Esther and Daniel started.

'That'll do,' said Phil. He stepped forward, calling out, 'Oi. Shit-for-brains.' The abuse stopped and the men turned towards him. Phil had stopped within a few feet of them.

'You what? Who the fuck do you think you're talking to?' The man speaking was the one Phil had had a set to with outside the house previously.

'You, you dim-witted arsehole.'

'I remember you, you cunt. You're another fucking paedo-lover. So what? You going to take the three of us on, then?' He stepped menacingly towards Phil.

'If I need to, but you'll do.' He moved to provoke a reaction from the men facing him. Shit-for-brains took a wild swing at Phil, followed by an attempted kick.

'Is that the best you can do?' asked Phil, and knocked him down with one punch to the face. As the other two moved in, Stan and Malcolm appeared at Phil's side. Malcolm intercepted one who was aiming a kick at Phil, and who in a split second had joined his friend on the ground.

'OK, OK.' said the third one, with his hands up in self-defence against Stan. 'I get it.' Malcolm in the meantime had rolled Phil's victim onto his back, stood with his good foot on the man's chest and extracted a wallet from whichever pocket it was in, and then did the same to the second, all in about ten seconds. He quickly looked through the wallets and found what he was looking for.

'Driving licences and bank cards.' He handed them to Phil.

'On your fucking feet. Come on, get up,' said Phil. They did so, slowly, taking in the three standing in a triangle around them.

'I told you last friggin' time, but you didn't listen did you?' He threw the wallets and cards towards them, scattering them on the pavement. 'We know where you live, and who you are, arsehole. So if we get any wind of you lot bothering this family again, we'll be fucking after you.' He jabbed his finger at the face of their leader. 'And we'll give you such a fucking lamping, you won't walk for a month.' He stepped back a couple of paces. 'Now I want to hear it from you. Promise me and my friends here very nicely that you will leave this good woman and her son well alone. Then we'll all be on our way.' He paused. 'Well come on.'

'Yeah, OK,' said one.

'OK what?'

'Promise.'

'Promise what. For fuck's sake. Let's hear it properly.'

There were mumbles from all three to the effect that they promised to leave the woman and boy alone.

'Now piss off,' said Stan, not wishing to be seen as an innocuous accomplice.

'I think they got the message,' said Malcolm, as they watched the men shambling off, heads bowed.

'I had hoped they'd put up more of a frigging fight though,' said Phil.

Without explaining the means, the following day Phil told Esther that she should receive no more of the abuse or threats that she had been experiencing. He reiterated this the next day, after checking that there had been no incidents during the night. Esther promised to allow some time before making any decision about whether to move or not.

## Phil

It were great to see Stan's reaction when he thought we might lose Daniel. Stan probably doesn't realise it, like, but the kid has changed so much in the last few months, and a lot of that is to do with being in the band and the boost that it's given him. Whenever I call in these days, he's so chuffin' keen to show me new stuff he's worked out for the backing. It means nowt to me really, in terms of the music. I can't tell the difference, except for in Daniel himself. He still has his moments, the odd paddy, like when something is done differently or there has been an unexpected change in routine at school, say. But he does seem to cope better. He smiles more, sometimes when you wonder what there is to smile about. I love it when he repeats a joke he's heard at school or on the telly or radio, and you must know he doesn't quite get it. Like the old one he came out with the other day. *What's the difference between a bad shot and a constipated owl? No idea, I lied. The bad shot shoots but can't hit.* I laughed and then had to explain it to him. And he's listening to a whole range of stuff. Jazz and classical, as well as pop and rock. Stuff from the fifties and sixties, as well as modern. He'll jabber away, on the likes of Keith Moon, Buddy Rich, and others I've never heard of, and of course his favourite, Ginger Baker. He plays these long solos, which tend to bore me after a while, and I doubt whether he notices that I've left the room.

It would be so bad for him if they had to move out.

## Stan

As someone on a kid's TV programme used to say , *I love it when a plan comes together.* Only recently I realised that it's not just me but everyone else in the band is really fond of the kid. Seeing him struggle with whatever goes on his head sometimes, and staying with it. Of us all, I would say he's got the most talent. Possibly as much as the rest of us put together. Well, maybe not including Neil. Respect.

# Thirty-Seven

# Somewhere Over the Rainbow

🎸

Arriving together, Ursula, Esther and Mandy had been hoping for a front row spot, but were surprised to find the room almost full. With Ursula leading the way they managed to squeeze into a space near the front and to the left of the staging, but they would have to stand. It was the sort of modular staging used by many schools, and had been borrowed from Daniel's. On each side sat the speakers, one to the left, two to the right, and on the stage instruments rested on stands, watched over by microphones. Somebody had had the presence of mind to place a row of chairs, marked 'for band use only', in line with Daniel's screen, about five meters in front of the stage to give the band some room to move about. Even

396

so, it was hard to see how the band would not feel cramped in the space they had. Some fifty people were squeezed into the remaining two thirds of the room. They included a mixture of Daniel's fellow students, regular customers of Ursula's and some from the pub, members of Chalkie's band, friends of band members along with a few from the club, and others there just out of interest.

The atmosphere was one of anticipation mixed with curiosity. Mandy caught Chalkie's eye and gave him a wave. She saw that behind him, at the back of the room another smaller section of staging had been erected for Phil's benefit as sound-mixer-in-chief, with Niamh standing on one side, Jane on the other. Then to their left she could make out the tall figure of Stan coming through the door from the bar, followed by Tom and the others. They had earlier retreated to the empty lounge bar to gather their collective thoughts, and now made their way to the staging, some with nervous smiles others with deadpan faces. There were hallos here and there as they squeezed past people they knew.

Stan stopped to wait by the staging until they were all together.

'Right you buggers. Ready? Well chuffin' well look ready. Smile.' He looked at their contorted faces. 'On second thoughts, you'll scare the shit out of them. Let's go.' They did their best to show a spring on their step, waving as they made their way to their respective places. The applause was muted at first, becoming more enthusiastic as people put their drinks glasses between their feet, and friends shouted encouragement.

Although the staging was only thirty centimetres high, Stan seemed to tower over everyone as he stood at his microphone. He wore black denims and a light blue T-shirt with *Leicester Rocks* emblazoned diagonally across the front. He held the gaze of the audience for a moment, as if to dare them not to enjoy the music they were about to hear, then simply said 'Hallo. Thanks for coming.' After checking that everyone was ready, he nodded at Daniel to count them in.

The intro to *Let's Get the Show on the Road* was flawless. A wave of confidence swept through the band, which carried them through this and the next two upbeat songs, *Moving On* and *Be Careful What You Like*. There had been some discussion about whether or not the latter should be included, but Neil and Malcolm had been persuasive, stressing that a dress rehearsal was about ironing out any problems. There were one or two minor hitches, in the form of cues being missed, noticed only within the band, and there was a collective sigh of relief mixed with pleasure on the final chord.

There was a pause for breath, during which Stan introduced the band members, keeping it simple. On keyboard, the amazing Tom Plumley, the boy wonder on percussion, Daniel Wilson, et cetera. Hoots of appreciation from Daniel's following. They slowed the tempo with *Love of My Life* and *Still Got the Blues*, then changed the mood with *Fighting Hard*. On the final chord, Stan looked up to see Niamh smiling and waving, then giving two thumbs up. Stan announced a ten minute break to replenish glasses.

'Everyone OK?' he asked, looking around the band. There were smiles and nods. 'Still happy with the set for the second half?' More nods. They had another eight numbers lined up, plus the possibility of an encore. Tom sloped off to discuss the sound balance with Phil, at which point Mandy appeared with a tray of drinks.

'I know it's thirsty work up there, so thought you'd appreciate these.' She set the tray on the stage. She turned to Stan. 'Hi Big Man. It's going really well. Sounds great from back there. But try and relax a bit, Stan. Maybe ask Tom to do a bit of the talking, so it's not all from you.'

'So what're you saying, duck?'

'Nothing, Stan. Don't get me wrong. But if you just shed a bit of the load, I think you might enjoy things a bit more. I don't think you've smiled yet.' She stepped up onto the stage and kissed him. 'But whatever. It's your show. I love you. See you later.'

It was clear that there were more bodies on the floor after the break, as people who had been drinking in the bars had come through, and with them the extra noise brought on by a few pints of bitter. When asked by Stan, Tom said he was happy to kick off the second half. He started to introduce *Walking By Myself*, when he was interrupted by calls of 'Cut the chat and get on with it', and 'Just fucking play will you.' Heckling was something they had yet to experience. Tom and Stan exchanged looks, which both suggested they ignore it and carry on. Unnoticed, Phil had quickly appeared at the side of one of the hecklers, a young man in jeans and T-shirt, who was clearly the worse for wear. Phil muttered something to him.

'You what? You and whose fucking army?' the man shouted. Others around him tried to calm the man down, and seeing he was outnumbered, he called out 'You're a shit band anyway. You are. Don't know why we fucking bothered.' He and his friend made their way to the exit door, shouting and swearing as they went, followed by Phil. To quell the buzz of excitement in the room, Tom called to Stan.

'Let's just play it.' The unsettling effect of the minor disturbance was clear, as they gave a stuttering and lacklustre performance of the song.

'Right you duffers,' said Stan as he turned to look at them. 'Let's hope we've got that out of the system. Change of plan. Let's give them *Fields of Gold*, show the buggers how good we are. OK? Happy, Angie?' Perfectly, she said. 'Malc?' He was ready. They took their places centre stage.

It was just Angie on vocals and Malcolm accompanying on guitar at first. On the appropriate line Tom, Neil and Stan joined in the harmony, and Stan felt the shiver go down his spine. Instruments and percussion came in, and there were solos form Neil and Stan, none of which broke the spell and gentleness of the arrangement.

There was almost total silence in the room for several seconds as the last chord faded. As soon as one person started to clap, others quickly followed and the applause, cheering and whistling grew to a crescendo lasting a good half minute.

'Good call, Stan,' said Tom as things settled down again. 'Shame we can't stop there and go home.' He gave brief introductions to the two songs that were about to follow, explaining that *We're All in This Together* and *Just About Managing* were their own little stab at how the country was being run. *Come Rain or Come Shine*, which was a recent addition, *Bless the Weather, Where Did it All Start?* and *Don't Get Around Much Anymore* completed the set and were well received, to the extent that there were shouts for more. *Midnight on the Oasis* was their encore. Daniel was under strict instructions to restrict his solo to one minute and to watch Tom for the signal to play the rest of the band in. It was more like two minutes before he eventually looked up at Tom, but nobody really minded.

'So how does Chalkie deal with arseholes who give you a bad time at a gig?' Stan asked Mandy. They were walking arm in arm in Beacon Hill Country Park. A cool wind was blowing, and they were grateful for their woolly hats and windproof tops. The breeze at least kept the clouds away, giving them clear views towards Loughborough, the rural landscape of

Nottinghamshire and Lincolnshire beyond. Behind them stood the beacon and the rolling countryside of North West Leicestershire.

Mandy tried to reassure him by saying that thankfully, it doesn't happen a lot. The culprits are nearly always men who have had a bit too much to drink. The best way is not to get drawn in and to play through it. Let the security people deal with it. That's assuming there are some. The other night had just been unfortunate. Stan shouldn't worry about it.

They walked on, comfortable in each other's company, and not feeling the need for unnecessary conversation. A pair of ravens flew overhead, clonking, and seemed to point the way to some rocks which offered shelter. In the rucksack which Stan carried was a flask of tea, some biscuits, and a blanket which Mandy spread across a reasonably flat rock to keep their backsides from getting cold. Stan filled two mugs with tea.

He had been waiting for a suitable moment to tell her about his inheritance and discuss what he might do with it, and this seemed to him as good a time as any.

'So what would your friend Karl Marx make of it, I wonder. If you sold the house then, how much would it fetch? Any idea?' About two hundred and fifty thousand, he told her.

'Chuffin' Nora! As you would say. I see your problem. When you haven't had more than a few pennies to rub together, and suddenly you have a very lot, what do you do?'

'The solicitor bloke says there'll be some inheritance tax to pay. About sixty thousand. That's what really pisses me off. The idea of friggin' George Osborne getting his hands on my old Ma's money.'

'But I thought you were all for wealth distribution?'

'Yeah, but, when she's paid taxes all her life, like, chuffin' well worked hard and saved hard, and that, why should her money be taxed again.' He realised immediately that he had fallen into the trap, and they both laughed. As the solicitor had also suggested, Mandy thought Stan should hang on to the house, and continue letting it. He could always move in at some point in the future. But the income would add to his pension, and he would be pretty comfortable in his old age.

'A place like that would be too big for me on me tod, like. And I'm happy where I am anyway.' He realised how that little statement had sounded, and wondered what Mandy had read into it. They hadn't at any point discussed what the future might hold for them as a couple. On reflection, he regretted what he had just said.

'I'm sorry duck. I didn't mean…It must've sounded like….'

'Like I didn't fit in the big picture, is that what you mean?' She waited. 'So, do I Stan? Fit into the scheme of things for you?' Stan briefly met her gaze and then turned away.

'At this moment I wonder where I've been, who I've been for the last thirty bleeding years. It's like the time's just gone, I've nowt to show for it. Wasted years. Then you came along, and all of a sudden, like, stuff happens. My life opens up, no, a new life even, opens up in front of me, and I could make something of it.' Now he turned, and their eyes met. 'But the reality is I am still just a friggin' window cleaner. Nothing more. So you tell me. Where do you see yourself in the big picture?'

She put a hand firmly on each of his shoulders and gave him a gentle shake.

'Listen Stan. For a start, corny as this might sound, it's not what you are but who you are that counts. You clean windows, I work in an office. So what? I think we've been good for each other. I know you've been good for me, made me do a stock take as well, if you like. You are warm, kind, giving of yourself, funny, fun to be with.'

'Don't forget great to have sex with. Oh, and about to become loaded.'

'Great to have sex with. And talented in more ways than you know. Seeing you on that stage with Neil and the others, it's like, how can I put it, it's so bleeding obvious that it's what you should be doing.' She still held him by the shoulders, and they were smiling at each other.

'Don't stop,' he said. 'I'm enjoying this.'

'And so you should be. But in answer to your question, I want us to be in the big picture together, whatever that means.'

He took her face gently in his hands and kissed her on the lips.

'Me too,' he said. 'So that's settled. Let's walk.'

For the time being there was no talk of living together, or any other way of being closer together. There was just small talk, Mandy resting her head against Stan's arm as they walked. The conversation took a different turn as they started the drive back to Leicester.

'Going back to this money,' said Stan, 'I look on it as a bonus, like. I wasn't expecting it, and I'd have been fine without it. So I was thinking I'd like to use it to help people. Young kids in particular, in some way.'

'That sounds good, duck. Any ideas?'

'Only about doing something to help kids who want to do something musical. Like learning an instrument. I dunno. Maybe it's just pie-in-the-sky stuff. I'll have around about a hundred thousand in cash, like, when all's said and done, as well as the house.' Mandy sat quietly in thought for a few minutes.

'Just thinking out loud a bit, the studio where Chalkie's band sometime rehearse has come up for sale. Supposing you bought that. I don't know what they want for it, but we could find out easily enough. Supposing you bought that and paid for kids to have lessons there. You could let other musicians use it, like Chalkie and anyone else who wants to hire studio time, so you might cover the costs of the kids' tuition.'

Stan glanced at her.

'It's worth looking at. What an excellent chuffin' idea.'

Mandy phoned Chalkie to ask for the studio owner's contact number then called her. Mandy asked the woman to confirm that the studio was in fact for sale, and enquired about the asking price. She received a lengthy reply. A meeting was arranged for the evening of the following Monday.

'How much does she want?' asked Stan. Around two hundred and twenty thousand, she told him. For several minutes there was the sort of silence that comes with disappointment. It was worth going to see the place, Stan suggested, to get a feel of what he might get for his money. But he would have to look around for something he could afford.

'Early days yet. It'll be a month or two before I have the dosh,' he said as they pulled up outside Mandy's house. 'Are you still on for cooking dinner tomorrow?' She was, as long as Stan kept the evening free. Stan was planning to spend the day, Sunday, brushing up on the lyrics and music ahead of the gig at The Brown Cow during the week. He had given his apologies to Phil for not being able to run the line in the morning, and he would catch up with City's afternoon match against Southampton on Match of the Day.

It was around five thirty when Stan played the introduction to *Come Rain or Come Shine* on his guitar. He ignored the knock on the door, and heard Mandy shout that she would get it. He sang the first line, becoming aware of some shuffling behind him, but carried on. By the third line, he realised that he was being accompanied. He stood and turned as he continued playing. Standing inside his front door next to Mandy were Malcolm, Neil and Angie, all of whom took over the singing. They had to make room for Daniel, as he knocked and was let in, and also, just in time to join in with the last line, in entered Tom. Stan played the finishing cameo solo with a flourish. They all clapped. Mandy had arranged the surprise get-together, and prepared a meal that could be eaten off plates on laps, given the size of Stan's kitchen table. Chairs were quickly produced from various rooms, and they sat down to talk football, which was on everybody's mind, even Angie's, who despite her apparent disdain for the professional game was being swept along by the euphoria caused by Leicester City's extended good run of results. She admitted to having a slight crush on Kasper Schmeichel. Malcolm raised a laugh by naming two players on whom he had a crush. Drinks were served and a toast was made to City's one-nil win that afternoon which put them seven points clear at the top of the premiership, and to Phil's team who had also won their match and led their division by the same margin.

The dishes were stacked in the kitchen sink, and they settled down for a jam session. Tom would play Stan's keyboard, Neil and Malcolm had brought violin and acoustic guitar respectively, and Angie had with her a second hand acoustic bass guitar, recently acquired. Daniel, who was happy to join in with the spirit of the evening, had brought his snare drum and brushes. One rule was stipulated and agreed. They could play and sing anything as long as it wasn't one of the band's pieces. Malcolm set the ball rolling with *The House of the Rising Sun*, and an eclectic mix of twelve bar blues, pop, rock and folk followed, including the folk ballad *Black is the Colour* sung by Angie, without accompaniment. *Wow* was the collective reaction, and Tom wondered if they could work out an arrangement that would work for the band in the future. There was also much appreciation of Stan and Tom's playing of the twelve bar instrumental, as yet with no title, which Stan had put together when in hospital.

The approach of ten o'clock, and Tom's need for an early night after a long weekend at the hospital, led to the gradual breaking up of the evening. Malcolm played a stirring rendition of *Somewhere over the Rainbow*. You never cease to amaze me, said Neil. For the finale, Tom coached them quickly in the harmony for the short chorus of *Goodnight Sweetheart, Goodnight*, which he played and sang.

Before anyone made a move to find their coat and other bits and pieces, they sat and looked around at each other in a moment of quiet reflection on an evening well-spent. Stan couldn't quite bring himself to give a hug to the men as they started to leave, instead offering his hand to Neil, first in line, who said 'Come here you daft bugger. Male hugs are OK.' Hugs followed for the others, and Angie planted a kiss on his lips.

'Right, mister. There is washing up to do.'

'Leave it, Mandy,' replied Stan. 'It can wait till the morning. The washing up fairy might even come in the night.' He walked over to her and picked her up in his arms, as if to carry her over the threshold.

'I've got a much better plan.'

'Which I suspect means going upstairs. Two conditions,' she said, putting her arms around his neck and kissing him. 'One, you put me down and let me walk up those narrow stairs, you daft so-and-so.'

'Two?'

'You bring me hot chocolate and a ginger biscuit after.'

## Stan

One of my earliest memories is sledging on Beacon Hill. My parents would always refer to that winter as The Big Freeze, when everything stopped. The trains, the buses, the electric some of the time. I found a couple of photos when I was going through Ma's stuff. There's one of me looking as happy as Larry on the sledge, balaclava round my head, scarf blowing in the breeze. The other one was a group photo, which had my mum's parents on it. I just about remember them. Grandad had a fag in the corner of his mouth and wore a cloth cap. He won the Victoria Cross for some battle in Africa and came home a war hero. He chained smoked all his adult life apparently, and apart from in the war he worked down the mines. His chest was in a bad way and I remember he would have these massive long coughing fits which made him go red in the face. He tried to stop smoking after the doctor told him it was killing him. A few months after he retired early cos of ill health, he died of lung cancer. I was six. I don't think there's anything about lung cancer running in the family.

The other thing I remember from that year is watching City on the telly in the FA cup final against United. My mum and dad bought their first telly specially. United won of course, but there was still a big party afterwards. We had a houseful. Grandparents, uncles, aunties, cousins. And the way City are playing this year, we might be having a party too.

## Thirty-Eight

# We Are the Champions

The morning after the first gig at The Brown Cow.

'Pass the biscuits, me old. Good choice, chocolate gingers.' Stan took one before passing the packet to Phil.

'Went well last night, I thought,' said Phil. 'Cracking night in fact. Was you happy with how it went?'

'Overall, yeah.' There was a weariness in Stan's voice.

'Marks out of ten? I'd give it nine myself.'

'Eight, probably.'

'What was the best bit for you then? What was the best song? I really liked *Moving On*. The whole chuffin' place was rocking.'

'Yeah, it was OK. Malcolm's solos for me. He was great, all night.' Stan looked thoughtfully out of the window.

'Yeah, suppose he was.' Phil had the usual thin chocolate moustache, after dipping his biscuit in his tea. 'I'm beginning to enjoy some of your new stuff. You know, *Just About Managing* and that. I need to hear songs a few times, like, before they grow on you, sort of thing. Know what I mean?'

'Absolutely.'

'Good chuffin' atmosphere as well. Seems to me the crowd there know good playing when they friggin' well hear it. Very respectful, I thought.' Phil became animated. 'Except for that arsehole and his mates, standing near the stage, getting in Neil's chuffin' face, like. Nasty sort, racist bastards. Good to see the security guys in there sharpish, told them to piss off.' He looked at Stan, expecting a response then waved his hand in front of his face. 'Are you with me, mate?'

'Sorry, mate. I am absolutely fucked after last night. Yeah, he had bother from them a few months ago, he said.' He sipped his coffee and resumed his focus on the open sky.

'Daniel did well. Not sure we could have friggin' well said that a few months ago. Place like that, a bit cramped and packed out. Yeah, he did cope very well.' He studied Stan's reflection in the windscreen, trying to read what was going on in his mind. 'Know what I didn't like about the place, though?'

'The price of a pint, I expect.'

'There was that. But I can't be doing with chuffin' standing all bloody night. Not one chuffin' chair in the whole frigging place. I ask you.'

'You get more punters in that way.'

'Suppose you do. So what about this studio then? You buying it, or what?'

'Renting to start with, like, until the paperwork and that gets sorted.'

'It's none of my business, like, so you can tell me to piss off, but how come you can afford it? I imagine Niamh must have something to do with it.'

'Ma left me a bit, like. Just about enough. Mind you, I had to knock the woman down a bit. But soon as I saw it I knew it were right for what I wanted. Tom came along, and he were bowled over with how well the place is kitted out.'

'So the old gal had a few quid under the mattress. Good luck to you. What's the plan then? You going to record your own stuff? The band, I mean.'

'We should be able to, but hopefully I can rent it out to other bands and make a bit of money out of it. An investment, like.'

It was Phil's turn to stare out of the windscreen. 'Righto.'

'I want kids to come and use it as well. Ones who can't afford lessons, like. Or whose parents can't.' Stan had suddenly woken up.

'Uhu.'

'I'll call it *The Stan Booker Music Academy*. Chalkie reckons I might be able to get some funding for it. You know, sponsors, or even the council. It needs a bit of marketing, which is where Niamh would come in.'

'Good idea.' He almost added *Ah! I knew she'd chuffin' well be in there somehow.* He screwed the top onto his flask. 'So you going to carry on with the winderin?'

'We'll have to see how it goes. I'll carry on for now, like, but we'll just have to see how it all pans out. Anyway, you'll be able to see what it's like later on, if you're still coming.'

Phil had one foot out of the door. 'The boys' final, by the way, is a week Sunday, deffo.' He named the semi-professional club ground where it would be played. 'You up for it? The county provide all of the officials, like for the semi.'

'Wouldn't miss it,' replied Stan. 'They've done really well.' He joined Phil on the pavement, looking up as the sun burst through a gap in the clouds. 'Who'd have thought it, aye? Heady times, Phil, me old. Heady times.'

Stan had been given a key to the studio. He'd fallen in love with it at first sight. He did inspect a couple of others, but they were barely larger than a shoe box, so the choice was simple. The price was the difficulty, but the owner was keen to see a quick sale. Needing an immediate source of income, she agreed a relatively knock-down price and that in the meantime Stan could use it on a rental basis, as soon as the solicitors could draw up the agreement.

That evening, he sat in the control room, on one of the two plush leather chairs which rolled on castors. On the work surface in front of the glass panel overlooking the performing area was a range of equipment, including computer screens and keyboards, sound mixers, other black boxes with winking lights and whose function he could only wonder about, plus headphones and mics. On the wall behind him were two TV screens and a bank of smaller screens which were part of the security monitoring system. He would know whether anyone was standing at the door, entering the hallway, coming upstairs or in the upstairs corridor. Phil would be along in few minutes to give the place the once-over. All he saw for the moment was the occasional shadow of someone walking past the entrance. He collected a can of fizzy drink from the fridge adjacent to the door into the other room, and walked through. Standing in the centre of the room, which measured approximately six metres by five, he was impressed by the total lack of sound. The building was on the first floor of a converted house on a street off the busy London Road, not far from the railway station. On the ground floor was a shop which was open from six in the morning until ten at night, selling everything you could expect to buy in a supermarket and more. It was the more which had intrigued Stan, particularly the sex aids in the 'adults only' box room. There was a constant flow of customers going in and out, but neither this nor the road or rail traffic could be heard in the sound-proofed studio. On one wall was a bank of keyboards, against another were stands with a choice of guitars, and in one corner was a percussion set. All was available to any musicians that didn't have or want to bring their own equipment, and Stan had agreed to pay an additional five thousand for the equipment. .

He walked over to another leather castor-wheeled chair by a wall, and sat on it. He found that by giving a firm push with his feet, and lifting them off the floor, it could travel from one side to the other, stopping just short of the opposite wall. He turned it round, this time shouting as it rolled across the floor, arms raised high: 'It's all mine. It's all mine. Well bleeding well soon will be.' On checking the monitoring screen, he could see Phil waiting to be admitted. After giving him a quick Cook's tour, they amused themselves for several minutes by racing backwards and forwards across the room on the chairs, egging each other on and singing lines from some of the band's songs, safe in the knowledge that nobody could see or hear them.

Tuesday, May the second, 2016, would be a noteworthy day in the life of Stan 'The Man' Booker. And of many of his friends, and their friends and friends of friends in Leicester and beyond. Stan was able to make first use of the studio, and to mark the occasion invited as many of his and Chalkie's band, plus Phil, to join him for a jam session. Tom, Angie and Daniel could not, due to work and other prior commitments. Fortunately, all bar Chalkie's rhythm guitarist were able to get along, so for two hours 'they had a right good go at it, and loads of laughs', as Stan said afterwards. At eight fifteen, they packed away instruments and made their way by arrangement to Mandy's home for drinks and nibbles, in time to watch the second half of the match between Chelsea and Tottenham Hotspur on TV. Theoretically, Leicester City could become champions that evening, provided that Spurs lost or drew the match, but two minutes after the television had been switched on and seats found, Spurs scored the goal which gave them a two-nil lead just before half time.

There were groans all around the room, and even suggestions that they go back to the studio rather than watch Spurs fans gloat over a victory against their London rivals. A mass brawl involving most of the players on the pitch sparked some interest in the room, but once the half-time whistle was blown, the volume on the TV was turned down and the game was largely ignored, except by Phil, as the beer and wine flowed, anecdotes, jokes and memories were shared. Until, that is, Phil became animated.

'Aye up, everyone, this is beginning to get interesting.' Chelsea are having a real chuffin' go, and Spurs don't look happy at all.' They turned to watch the game for two or three minutes, but most preferred to return to their drink and previous conversation.

'Yessss,' shouted Phil, gleefully, and clenching his fist. 'Now it gets fucking interesting.' Chelsea had reduced the deficit to two-one. TV watching positions were resumed, and they looked on in disbelief and anticipation as the Spurs' play became increasingly ragged and players resorted to persistent fouling to prevent Chelsea from scoring the all-important second goal.

'They're falling apart,' said Chalkie, after the fifth Spurs player was booked by the referee for foul play. 'Never thought I'd find myself cheering on bleeding Chelsea. Go on,' he shouted.

A few minutes from the end of the match, most in the room were on the edge of their seats as one of Chelsea's players bore down on the Spurs goal.

'Go on my son,' shouted Stan, poised like a coiled spring to jump to his feet. Which they all did as the ball hit the back of the net. Pandemonium broke loose in the room. There were shouts and hugs, slapping of backs, men dancing jigs, standing on chairs and jumping off them. Beer bottles were opened, then fizzed and overflowed.

'Mind the glasses,' Mandy shouted, unheeded. Stan put his hands on her hips and pulled her towards him.

'Give us a twirl, duck. Don't worry. If owt gets broken I'll cover it.'

There was a gradual calming down, as they tried to listen to the commentary. The referee blew his whistle to signal the end of the game, and there were shots of members of Leicester City's squad, many of whom had gathered in the home of one of the players, celebrating the result and their status as champions.

'Championi, championi, we are the champions,' they could be heard singing. This was probably the extent of their Italian. The club's manager, Claudio Ranieri, was then seen beaming from his apparent location in Italy.

Spontaneous gatherings were being shown, including one outside the home of the player in which the squad members were partying. Very soon, shouts of celebration could be heard in the street outside Mandy's house. People had taken up the 'championi' chant. Stan led the way to watch as the party atmosphere grew.

'We could play something to get them singing,' said Chalkie, having to raise his voice. 'What do you think? Suggestions?'

'*We are the Champions*, an obvious one,' said Stan.

'*We've Got the Best Team in the Land.*'

'*Johnny Be Good.*'

'They'll dance to whatever,' suggested Mandy. 'They just want to party.'

Instruments, mics, amps, speakers and extension leads were collected from vans and cars, and after a quick sound test, off they went.

'Hallo Leicester. Champions,' was all Chalkie had to say to generate a load cheer from the street. Something like a hundred people, from toddlers in parents' arms to elderly in wheel chairs had turned out already, and more were joining all the time.

'No one believed we could do it, but here we are.' More loud cheering. The impromptu band played for over an hour, and could have continued for much longer but for the onset of fatigue and thirst for more beer. Thanks to mobile phones and social media, news travelled fast. Passengers ran from parked cars driven from across the city, eager to join in the celebrations. Some brought fireworks, trumpets were blown, and no one on this and many other streets in Leicester would be sleeping peacefully for a while yet. Both the local radio and TV station sent crews to relay the scene to listeners and viewers.

'Un-chuffin'-believable,' said Stan, his arm around Mandy's shoulder, as they looked on from her doorstep. 'And what makes it especially unbelievable is the fact that the old gal had placed a bet on City winning the title. Back in August.'

She gave him a puzzled look. 'Who? Your Mum?' He nodded. 'So how much did she bet then?'

'Just a tenner, like. She wouldn't want to throw her money away.' He turned to her, trying unsuccessfully to prevent the smile. 'They gave her five thousand to chuffin' one.'

'Oh my God!'

## Phil

It's hard to describe the chuffin' feeling. It's like.... What? You're so proud, so happy. It's as good as it gets, kind of thing. Everyone is smiling, and you know why they're smiling. They feel the same. It's not like being a Man U fan. Oh, we've won the premiership. Again. Yeah, yeah, yeah. It's normal. Teams like City just don't win the Premiership. Or didn't used to.

In the centre of town, by the old Clock Tower there's a statue of three famous Leicester sportsmen, which was put there to celebrate three trophies which they won in about 97' I would say. You'd have to remind me who they're supposed to be. But we won the friggin' County Championship at cricket, some rugby cup, and the chuffin' Coca Cola Cup, which is Mickey Mouse compared to the Premiership or even the FA Cup. So it kind of sent the message that we're good at sport in Leicester. So I don't know what they'll chuffin' well do about winning the Premiership. You've got to have a statue of Claudio. The very least they can do, like. Maybe give all the fans a free ticket for the next match, or the first one of next season. Not frigging likely though is it? What Claudio might do though is give us all some pizza. I wouldn't put it past him. He's all right, Claudio.

## Stan

All I can say is that to celebrate, Mandy and me had the best sex ever.

# Thirty-Nine

## Closer to You

Phil and Stan eventually made it to the start of their round for the following day. It took several knocks on Mandy's door and presses on the bell by Phil before Stan eventually roused himself. 'Better show willing,' Phil had said. Their working day started in the van, sharing the coffee and cake collected from Ursula's en route to Beaumont Leys. They had managed to find a quiet side street, but even here every driver that passed by beeped the horn and had the inevitable blue and white scarf trailing from the car or van window.

Stan had bought a copy of the Mirror, and they both had a copy of the early edition of the local newspaper. They were sharing anecdotal reports of fans who had placed bets at various odds on City to win the Premier League title.

'Here's a cracker,' said Stan. 'This nurse at the General, right, was bought a bet by the doctors she works with in her department. Apparently the medics are all Tigers fans and took pity on her for being a chuffin' City fan. They clubbed together, like, to buy her a ten pound bet back in August, and pinned the old bookmaker's slip onto the notice board in their meeting room. It was still there went she turned up for work this morning. What odds do you reckon they would've frigging well got?'

'Dunno. Thousand to one?'

'Only five chuffin' thousand to one.'

'Gordon Bennett? You're joking. So what's that, fifty thousand. Holy shit. Fair play to her mates though, not touching the slip. Must've been tempting, like. Did you hear the one on the old radio this morning, about the bloke who didn't have a bet? No? Well this bloke, right, been a City fan like for ever, always has a friggin' bet on them winning something. I mean every year, like. So when they won League One, what, three, four years ago, then promotion from the Championship, yeah? Well he was quids in, weren't he. So last year he moved to New York, and in all his chuffin' excitement he forgot to put his usual twenty quid bet on.'

'So probably cost him a hundred thou then. Or he lost out on a hundred thou, more like.'

'Your old gal would have had a flutter as well, wouldn't she? She'd have been so chuffed, your mum. Shame she didn't live to see it.'

Stan looked wistfully out of the side window. He had resolved to not share news of his winnings, courtesy of his mother, with anyone other than Mandy and Niamh, pledging them both to secrecy. He had been at pains to stress to Phil that his inheritance would not affect their relationship, as far as he was concerned, but he could sense that Phil was struggling to come to terms with it, and at times appeared to be slightly distant. Most of Stan's friends and acquaintances were what he regarded as staunch working class, and Stan felt they might not be too impressed by the knowledge that he had come into some money. That he was an additional fifty thousand pounds richer on top of his inheritance would almost certainly not sit comfortably with Phil, nor many others for that matter. On the other hand, suggested Mandy, they would probably find out sooner or later, and may well all be very pleased for him and wish him the best of luck. In her opinion, the best policy was to be open and up front with everybody. Stan wasn't sure whether he was prepared to take the risk.

Via social media, news was spreading about the band's performance at The Brown Cow the previous week, and of the impromptu playing at the street party to celebrate Leicester City's success. Neil and Angie had got wind of this and warned Stan that there could be a bigger crowd for the second gig, but none of them was prepared for the hundred yard long queue, four or five people deep, outside the pub an hour before they were due to open the show, as the supporting act. The average age of those in the queue was noticeably younger than it had been for the first gig.

It seemed that the whole of Leicester, if not of Leicestershire, was basking in the reflected glory of their team's success. Virtually everyone inside and outside the pub wore a Leicester City shirt, and to while away the time those outside would burst into celebratory songs or chants. The pub closed the door when just over half of those waiting had been admitted. The owner, who had been somewhat aloof at their first meeting the previous week, welcomed Stan as if they were close friends of long-standing, and showered the band members with compliments.

'Just don't get cocky, right,' was all Stan said to them before they took to the stage. They could probably have got away with a shoddy performance, given the mood their audience was in, but they played and sang confidently and well. When it became clear they were expected back on stage for a second encore, they were stuck for what to play, until Neil suggested 'How about *We Are the Champions?*'

The following day, Stan met Niamh for lunch in Ursula's café. He had invited Phil along. As they waited for the soup to arrive, the boys stood either side of Niamh, laughing and smiling as they huddled together over the photograph on the inside pages of the early edition of the local paper, which Niamh had brought along. There was also a short piece about the band's performance the previous evening. Stan proudly read the article out loud for a second time, then pointed to each band member in the photo, saying how it had caught them all in a typical pose, except for Malcolm.

'Looks like he needs the toilet, poor lad. Shows the chuffin' effort he's putting in.'

'It's a great shot of you all though,' said Niamh, 'and a good bit of publicity.' Ursula brought the soups to the table.

'Ah, I saw that too. What a fantastic photograph. I must ask the newspaper for a copy so that I can hang it up on the wall. I know just the spot.'

'Let me guess,' said Phil. 'In the gents, next to the condom machine.' They all laughed.

'Well I did think about that, but then I thought the ladies would be better. Actually, just to the right of the bar, where it would catch the light.' She turned to Niamh. 'Are you sure I can't tempt you with the Leberknödel? It comes all the way from my home town. Stan loves it, don't you Stan.'

'Aye alright then. I'll join Stan and give it a go. But just the cabbage, mind, no potatoes. I have to watch the figure.'

Niamh reflected on the previous evening's gig, and thought that they were all much more relaxed than the previous week and had benefited from the experience. Consequently they gave a much improved performance. The pressure would be on for the following week, because expectations would be higher, but the key was to try and stay relaxed. She also advised Stan that as a general rule the band should add something new to each gig to freshen things up, for the band as much as the audience. Stan and Phil high-fived when she confirmed that the band would be in the line-up for the festival in Derbyshire in June. Stan let out a whistle after she had listed some of the other bands and singers who would be preforming. Niamh then went on to talk about the studio.

'I'm really excited by the whole idea, Stan. And if you'll let me, there are three, maybe four things I would like to do to help move things along. Would you like to hear them? Tell me if you think I'm interfering.'

'OK, go on then. I'll chuffin' well tell you if I need to.'

'Right. First is to find some sponsors to put some money behind it, and that goes hand-in-hand with publicity. Have either of you heard of crowdfunding? No?' She explained how it works, and gave some examples.

'How does that sound, Stan?'

'Well, uh. I dunno really. I suppose if other people are willing to back us, a few quid here and there, then why not. But you're saying it's a few quid from lots of people.'

'It could be lots. Some schemes are more successful than others. There's no guarantee, but I think yours is a real goer. So next, can you be free on Monday afternoon? There's someone I'd like you to meet.' Stan looked at Phil, who shrugged his shoulders, as if to say 'Don't look at me. I haven't a clue.'

'Well if it helped, like, I could be, umm, available on Monday. Are you going to tell us owt about this bloke, or do I have to guess?'

'Who said it was a bloke? OK, I can tell you that this person represents a group of people who provide grants to non-profit organisations, which, like yours will, have a scheme which benefits the community. And they are very interested in hearing what you have to say.' Stan looked hard at her, squeezing nose between finger and thumb.

'My Ma used to say that if something sounds too chuffin' good to be true, like, it almost certainly is. Presumably these people, who I guess might be friends of yours, have some money behind them. So what I'm asking myself is where does it come from, and what's in it for them, like?'

'Those are questions you'll have to ask them yourself, Stan. They'll be honest and up front. I'm confident they'll come up with an offer. But this is only a suggestion. Feel free to say no. OK?'

'Maybe.'

The final part of Niamh's plan was for her publicity team to contact every school in Leicester, primary and secondary, once there was some funding in place, to outline the scheme and to invite them to nominate boys and girls who they think would benefit from the tuition on offer. Stan would need to establish some selection criteria, and she could help him with this. Coupled with this would be some media publicity, including on TV, when the first students turn up at the studio.

'Now I like that idea. And you,' he said to Phil, 'could get to meet your heartthrob again, me old.' Phil looked blank at first.

'Oh yeah, if she's lucky.'

The food arrived.

'And what is that about a heartthrob?' asked Ursula, looking at Stan. Realising that she was starting to blush when he returned her look, she turned away, saying she would fetch some water. It all happened quickly, but it didn't escape Niamh's notice. Stan kept his head down and tucked into his food. Phil gave Niamh a wink.

Mandy estimated that there were about a thousand people altogether in the two small stands on either side of the ground, and she joined in the loud cheer as the two teams ran onto the pitch side by side. She and Stan were surrounded by a significant contingent of the support for Phil's team, including Jane, Esther and all of the band members. Putting two and two together, Jane realised who Esther must be, but resisted the urge to ask Stan to confirm this. Feeling and looking decidedly awkward about the situation, she moved towards the safer territory of the group from the working men's club.

The opposition team was from Wigston, a suburb on the south side of the city. Everything about them struck Stan as being a notch or two up from the Fosse Boys, from the noticeable difference in height and trendy smart haircuts to the banners and flags being waved by their supporters on the other side of the pitch. While the Fosse Boys either stood around in groups of three or four passing a ball around, or having shooting practice at the goalkeeper, the Wigston lads went through well-rehearsed 'give-and-go' drills. They wore track suits which on removal after the warm-up revealed shirts with their individual surnames on the back. At least the Fosse Boys' shirts were clean this week, he reflected.

Effort, Dedication, Devotion, Glory. Stan imagined this would be the gist of Phil's last minute team talk as they huddled in a circle, arms on each other's shoulders. In his attempts to inspire the boys, Phil had recently started to use these words, after learning that they were displayed in the Portuguese football academy in which the famous player Ronaldo learned his trade. Stan smiled to himself and thought that they might need a bit of divine intervention as well. Phil waved and gave thumbs up as he jogged towards his dugout just in front of the stand housing most of his team's supporters.

The referee blew his whistle and Phil's team kicked off, to a roar and shouts of encouragement from the crowd. That was about as much as the team saw of the ball for the next five minutes, as the opposition intercepted a pass and then played keep-ball, with some short crisp passes. The Fosse Boys ran back and forth chasing the ball, until a longer pass found a Wigston striker who took the ball in his stride and shot first time, beating the goalkeeper. Silence descended on the Fosse supporters, while on the other side of the pitch there were gleeful celebrations.

'Shit,' said Stan to no one in particular. 'It could be a long chuffin' afternoon.'

The following ten minutes followed a similar pattern to the first five, but this time it was a midfield player who burst through the Fosse Boys defence to collect a pass before calmly rounding the goalkeeper to score. Phil emerged from the dugout to shake his fist and shout encouragement, in true managerial fashion, before retreating to sip from his water bottle. The cheering from across the pitch was on the verge of gloating. There was some unsubtle advice from the Fosse fans, both to their team and to the opposition supporters.

'Stop pissing about and get stuck into these wazzocks,' from one of the mothers was one of the less crude calls.

'Why can't our boys get the ball?' asked Mandy, as they continued to chase shadows.

'Well, duck,' replied Stan. 'There are two or three seriously good players in the other team, and our lads can't get anywhere near them. They're running the bleeding game at the moment.' There was a brief moment of encouragement as a long pass from a Fosse player caused confusion in the opposition defence, until the goalkeeper rushed out to collect the ball.

Heeding the advice to get stuck in, some of the Fosse boys were flying into tackles and giving away free kicks. This appeared to unsettle their opponents, who for the rest of the first half seemed to be content with avoiding the tackles and keeping their two goal lead. Although they had hardly touched the ball, Phil's team managed to not concede another goal before half-time. Seeing that the Wigston team had three adults with them for the break, Stan made his way to the dugout, collected the water bottle carrier and made his way over to join Phil and his team.

'Right lads, we're still in this game. We get a goal back and they'll start panicking. We just need a bit of self-belief.'

'But we can't get the ball off them, Phil,' said Moz.

'Yeah, I was just coming to that, thanks Moz. So what we need to do is go back to chuffin' basics. It's no good trying to pass our way up the field against these. Cos we're not good enough in that department just yet. But from where I'm sat their defence looks a bit dodgy, a bit suspect under the high ball, wouldn't you say, Stan?'

'That's exactly what I were going to say. And those two lads in midfield, they're too cocky by half, so let's rough them up a bit. Give them a bit of verbals, and wind them up. You know, tell them they're a pair of tossers, like. Or you've heard they've got a small dick.' The boys laughed. 'That kind of stuff. But not where the ref could hear you, mind.'

'And maybe a bit of man-to-man marking on them as well. Who fancies a bit of that?' asked Phil. Two hands went up, and Phil told them who to mark. 'Good stuff. Let's play two up, and four across the middle, crowd the midfield a bit more. Put those long balls down the middle and let's get into them. Route one. Can we do it?'

'Yes we can,' came the reply in unison. Stan joined Phil in the dugout. They looked on in dismay as the Wigston boys scored within thirty seconds of kicking off.

'Well that were a waste of fucking time,' said Phil. It was Stan's turn to be managerial. He shouted at the boys to look at him, which they did. He glared and shook his fist.

A long pass into the opposition defence was headed half-heartedly by one of the centre backs, who was knocked over by the Fosse striker challenging him. The referee gave a free kick for the late challenge, but the defender then reacted to something that had been said to him by the striker and gave him a push, unseen by the referee.

This acted as a signal for the half-time pep talk to take effect. The combination of strong challenges and verbal teasing broke the concentration of the Wigston players, and after a few minutes one of the star midfield players, clearly frustrated by the hounding from his new marker and unable to find the space to make his passes, turned and swung a punch which knocked his opponent to the ground. Phil and Stan, along with the fans in the stand were on their feet, baying for blood. Stan ran on to the pitch with the water bucket and sponge to tend to the lad still on the ground, while the referee dealt with the melee around him. He theatrically produced the red card, and signalled to the midfielder to leave the pitch, before advising Stan that his player would have to be taken off the pitch and be substituted, on the basis that he had received a head injury. The player was escorted to their ambulance for an assessment by two members of the St John's Ambulance Brigade.

The resulting free kick was floated into the opposition penalty area. It landed between the Wigston defenders who were too slow to react, and Moz pounced to score. Five minutes later it was the Wigston's supporters turn to be silenced, while the celebration of the second goal went on behind Phil and Stan.

The game became a scrappy end to end affair. With ten minutes of normal time left, a long kick from the Fosse Boys' goalkeeper bounced over the head of the defenders, leaving Deano with a clear run at goal.

'Go on my son,' shouted Phil, on his feet.

He made no mistake. Three all. Phil and Stan stood arms aloft, their friends behind them ecstatic. Over the next few minutes the Fosse Boys were so busy teasing and tackling their opponents that they seemed to forget that they needed to have the ball if they were to stand any chance of winning the game. Extra time was looking distinctly possible, when disaster struck. A speculative shot from one of the Wigston players, which was clearly going to miss the goal, struck a Fosse Boys defender on the arm before he could avoid the ball. The referee awarded a penalty. Stan and Phil looked at each other, incredulous. There were boos from the stand behind them.

'No way a penno,' said Phil. 'I'm not having that. It was ball to arm.' He ran towards the referee. Stan called after him. 'Shit.' He chased after Phil, just managing to intercept him before he did something he might regret. He stood in front of Phil to block his path.

'Leave it mate. It's not worth getting into trouble over.' They jostled as Phil tried to get past him, and Stan had to shout at him to stop. 'Look Phil, mate, having a go at the chuffin' ref ain't going to do anybody any good. It's down to our goalie. I'm going to bet he saves it. Look at me. Look at me.' He had Phil's attention, and spoke quietly. 'Good. Right. We both know it shouldn't be a penno. But you having a go at the friggin' ref is only going to get you fined and the club in the shit. You'll be letting the lads down. Yeah? So come on, leave them to it.'

While this had been going on the ball had been placed on the penalty spot, and all the players were waiting as the referee held up proceedings until Stan and Phil were back on the touchline near the dugout. They watched as the goalkeeper did his Kasper Schmeichel impersonation on the touchline, waving his arms above his head and dancing sideways back and forth on the goal line. The few seconds of silence as the crowd waited for the kick to be taken seemed to stretch into minutes. The goalkeeper dived to his right. The shot was well struck but he managed to get his finger tips to the ball and deflect its path onto the post. It bounced away from the goal. Players from both teams ran towards the goal to either clear the ball away or follow up and score. All of the spectators were on their feet, not knowing whether to cheer or groan, as it wasn't clear what had happened to the ball. Then as the goalkeeper stood up his dejection told the story. It had evidently bounced off the post then off his back and into the goal. There was just time for the re-start before the referee blew his whistle to indicate the end of the match.

'Right, come on,' said Stan. 'You can chuffin' well sulk later. These boys need you over there. Bloody well tell them you're proud of them, cos you should be. They gave it a right old go. And don't say a friggin' word to the ref. Got it?' Phil nodded. Bottom lip quivering, he muttered that the boys didn't deserve to lose, at least not by a dodgy penno. As they walked over together, Stan also told Phil he should be proud of himself for getting the team to the final. It would be a day they wouldn't forget in a hurry. 'So, head up mate.' The players from both teams were shaking hands, several of Phil's boys wiping away the tears as they did so. To Phil's surprise, many of the parents came and shook his hand, saying thank you and well done for getting them to fight back in the second half, what a great job he was doing. Phil in turn shook the hand of each of his players, even managing a hug for the most distraught.

As the boys collected their runners-up medals at the presentation, Phil wondered how they would feel about it the next morning. Or perhaps more to the point, how they would feel about it the following weekend, after receiving their medals as league title winners. He slipped away quietly, before anyone suggested going for a drink.

## *Phil*

I was given a certificate once. It were for *Most Promising Young Boxer of the Year 1969*. Still got it somewhere. It never really came to owt. I didn't stick at it long enough, like I should've. We used to have prize days at school. Kids would go up for sports trophies, books and stuff for doing well in class and that. The 'boffs', as we called them, were given a bit of a tough time, mainly by those kids who were never going to be good at owt much. I was one. Funny sort of attitude really. We should be saying well done to them. Stan were one of the few who could get away with being bright, cos he managed to stay one of the lads, sort of thing. Some of those kids in my team, like, well I doubt whether they'll be much good at studying and that, but winning the league and runners-up in the cup should mean they feel good about themselves, at least for a bit. Makes it all worthwhile.

## Stan

Phil were right. It shouldn't have been a penno. But it happens don't it. Was it life changing? Did anybody die? You have to keep things in perspective, like. Life does sometimes change in them small moments, though, and we don't even know it. For example, one or two of Phil's lads have been a bit naughty at times, and taken a dive on the area to con the ref into giving a penalty. If they hadn't have done you could argue that the team wouldn't have won their league. I don't believe in destiny or fate, or the meaning of life for that matter. It's all a load of bollocks. Some things you have control of, but lots you don't, and most things you can't predict. It's all total random stuff. Like Niamh leaving me. Phil cocking things up with the taxi. Meeting Angie in the music shop. Niamh turning up again. And you look at how things went for her.

It still weren't a penno though.

## Forty

# Steppin' Right Along

iamh was looking up at the camera, two men standing in the shadows behind her. Stan pressed the button to let them in, then walked over to the table in the centre of the main room of the studio. He wanted to appear relaxed and master of the situation, and not subservient to anyone just because they had shed loads of money. So after practising a number of positions he had decided to be seen sitting on the corner of the table as the group walked through the door, and he would then stride over to meet them. He remembered some advice he had once been given about preparing for important meetings. XYZ. He looked down at the zip of his jeans. It was open. Horrified, he stood up to rectify the situation only to find that the zip wouldn't budge. He was heaving on it as his visitors entered the studio. It took just a couple of seconds to pull the reluctant zip up, by which time his three visitors were looking on with quizzical smiles.

'Sorry,' he said, straightening his jeans before walking over to them. 'Thought I ought to check, like, before….You know, and the bugger wouldn't budge.'

'Don't worry, Stan,' said the taller of the two men, almost as tall as Stan. 'We've all been there at some point. My Da used to say to me don't forget XYZ.' There was the hint of an Irish accent, and he had the fresh complexion and a smattering of ginger freckles some might associate with his countrymen. He was prematurely bald, but Stan suspected he had once been red-haired. He also thought there was something familiar about the man.

He introduced himself as Paul and his colleague Nigel, a solicitor. Nigel was short and wiry. He had a pointed nose and the rest of his features seemed to have been chiselled out of his small face. His neatly cut black hair had been given a random shape with the help of some gel. He had the air of a man used to doing business in more exalted surroundings. Hands were shaken, Nigel's feeling sweaty to the touch. To Stan's relief they were not 'suited and booted', but dressed in the smart casual mode. Stan invited them all to have a seat, and offered to make tea or coffee. They were content with the water available at the table. Niamh briefly outlined the purpose of the meeting, expressing the wish that it should be informal. Paul then explained that Nigel would be making notes during the discussion, as they would be accountable to the group which they represent and for any decisions reached. He asked if Stan was happy with the arrangement.

'Of course. I understand.' He sat up straighter. 'Have we met before somewhere? I mean, you look familiar.' Paul looked at Niamh, who smiled.

'We wondered if the penny would drop, Stan. This is my little brother Paul. Well not so little now, is he.'

'Of course. Well bugger me. Paul Duffy. Just look at you.' Stan's feeling of inferiority evaporated. Here was someone who had walked and kicked balls on the streets of a Leicester council estate, who had learned to fend for himself and to charm everyone with his mischievousness, skills which Stan suspected had served the man well as he climbed the ladder. The man, who as a young lad whose family home was besieged by thugs, had run to call Phil to the rescue. The two stood and reached across the table to shake hands again, this time with real warmth. For the next quarter of an hour they caught up on the highs and lows of their respective lives, there being significantly more highs for Paul. He did well at school, and went on to gain a first class honours degree in aeronautical engineering, and discovering that the banks liked to recruit engineers he went to work for one of the big European establishments in the City. From there he went on to work for a venture capitalist company, before setting up his own.

'Married?' asked Stan.

'Happily. Two gorgeous daughters, one the spitting image of her mum, the other of Niamh.'

'Public school, I expect.'

'Absolutely not. Local schools. They have their feet well-grounded Stan. But we do have some perks, like nice holidays in our farmhouse in France.'

'Oh ah? Well I usually manage to get to Skeggy for a couple of weeks.'

'And bloody shiver.' They laughed.

Nigel tapped his pen on the edge of the table and looked at them both with a fading smile.

'Shall we umm…'

They got down to business. Paul outlined the function of the foundation he represented, which was essentially to make grants to innovative community schemes, particularly in the arts. Although Niamh had told him about Stan's idea for using the studio to support young musicians, he asked to hear it directly from Stan. Niamh watched on, smiling, as Stan talked, bursting with pride and passion about his ambitions.

'So how much are we talking about?' he asked on a finishing note.

'We'll come to that in due course if that's OK, Stan,' said Paul. 'There are a few things that Nigel will need to explain to you first, and which you need to take on board. What we can't do is just hand money over to an individual, umm. Well, I'll let Nigel explain.'

Nigel handed Stan and Niamh each two pages of A4 with bullet points which he said would summarise what he was about to go through. The summary was as free of jargon as he could make it, but there were some terms he couldn't avoid using.

'The first of these is *Limited by Guarantee Company*,' which he went on to explain. Other areas he covered included the need to set up a board of directors, keeping accounts, and producing an annual report to the venture capitalist group. Nigel paused at the end of each paragraph to give Stan the opportunity to ask questions. He was reluctant to ask any, but Niamh had a sense of when to ask Nigel to clarify something, for example *Articles of Assocation*.

'Chuffin' Nora,' said Stan, breaking the silence that followed once Nigel had finished speaking. 'I had no idea it would be so bleeding complicated. So I definitely need a Board of Directors?'

'Yep,' said Paul.

'So what's stopping me from doing all this off my own bat, like? Just getting a few kids in and teaching them to play guitars and stuff?'

'Absolutely nothing, Stan,' Paul replied, 'and good luck to you if that's what you want to do. But you'll have to cough up the money yourself.'

'Mmm. So how much might you lads be talking about then?'

'Ten k. Ten thousand a year, tax free, maybe increasing if your scheme is successful.'

'Shit. Serious dosh then.' Stan did some quick sums. 'So that would pay for about four hundred lessons. Where do I sign?'

'And it might get even better. Niamh, do you want to tell Stan about your plan?'

Niamh's plan was to raise additional money through crowd-funding, which she had previously mentioned to Stan. She explained once again how it would work, and added that Paul, or rather his group would match, pound for pound, the additional money raised. She also offered to get her publicity team to get some press coverage for Stan's project, hopefully including the TV people.

'You realise what you've just done,' he said to her. She looked blankly at him. 'You've probably gone and got Phil to meet his sweetheart from the Beeb again, and worm his way onto the bleeding screen.'

Stan's head had been in a swirl after the meeting, and he sat on his own in the studio, silently reflecting and unpicking the long discussion that had taken place. More than once he had asked himself whether he was out of his depth, and whether he really wanted to get involved with a bunch of money-grabbers, even if one of them was Paul Duffy. But gradually the logic of the situation took hold, and he felt that it was too good an opportunity to miss if he was sincere in his ambition for the studio. By a possible quirk of fate Neil, Angie and Tom were all available to meet with him that evening, although it had to be in the café at the hospital, as Tom was due on shift.

Starting with the day he learned of his inheritance, Stan told them about the studio, his plans for it and his meeting with Paul. As he spoke, their faces gradually took on looks of wonderment and disbelief. Neil asked him if he had just made this up. Sounding slightly patronising, Angie said 'What an amazing idea Stan. Well done you.' Tom looked at his watch and at a clock on the wall then sat back with his arms folded.

'And you want us to be your directors, don't you?' More a statement than a question.

Stan looked at each in turn. 'Bang on,' he said. 'What do you think?' There was a discussion about the amount of time and responsibilities involved, and it took two more rounds of teas and soft drinks before Stan was able to convince them that the role was essentially about making sure the accounts were accurate and everything was above board.

'Well I'm up for it,' said Neil eventually. 'I think it's a heck of thing to do, Stan, and I'll give you as much support as I can.' The sentiment was echoed by Tom and Angie. Tom stood up to indicate that he had to leave.

'I would like to see the small print all the same,' he said. 'Just so we know that we're not liable if it all goes tits up. Ask Niamh to bring along the paperwork when we see her would you. And just another thought. Might Malc be a bit upset to not be asked?' Stan explained that he had a more hands-on role in mind for Malcolm, in the form of giving some guitar tuition if he was willing.

Things moved quickly over the next two or three weeks. On the same day that Leicester City were officially crowned as Premier League champions, Fosse Boys received their trophy and medals as winners of their league. The boys were in the sea of blue and white that lined the streets of Leicester as the open-topped bus carrying the Leicester players paraded through the city. Graffiti images of the manager Claudio Ranieri appeared on walls and posters. The third and final gig at The Brown Cow was another success, the place packed out again. As the weekend of the Derbyshire festival drew nearer, the band's practices took on a renewed sense of creativity, driven by a collective nervous energy. Neil, Angie and Tom signed on the dotted line as board members for Stan's project, after Niamh had talked through the role of director with Tom. On the basis of the written offer of the grant from Paul, Stan decided to use some of his own money to start the ball rolling, and the publicity went into schools and the local press, with a tight deadline of one week for applications to reach Stan and Niamh. Agreeing that Neil and Angie's experience as teenagers of music tuition and playing in orchestra's would be helpful, Niamh and Stan had sat down with the two of them to draw up a set of selection criteria to help prospective students put together their applications. Niamh was encouraged by, and Stan disappointed by the number of applicants, which was around the twenty mark.

'What's the problem with these kids,' said Stan. 'I thought there'd be hundreds, well dozens, of them wanting to be musicians.

'This is only the beginning Stan, early days,' Niamh had replied. 'Word will spread, and there'll be more second time round.'

'And some of these duffers can barely string three words together. Look at this one.' Niamh glanced across at Stan's iPad screen.

'You said yourself you weren't looking for, what did you say? Smart arses? You want kids who are prepared to graft.' Stan grunted in response.

'And look at this one. Biggest musical influence. My Grandpa, he says. Not John Lennon, or Gary Moore, or owt like that, but his bleeding grandpa.'

'Have you seen his surname?' Stan looked at the email.

'Dorsey. So?'

'Could be related to Gerry?' Stan looked blank. 'Gerry Dorsey?' It took a few seconds before Stan got there.

'Ahhh. Got you. Engelbert. Yeah, could be I suppose. In which case why doesn't he ask his old grandpa to pay for tuition? He'll have shed-loads.'

'Would you prefer a kid who relies on handouts or one who makes his own way?' Another grunt from Stan.

'It's chuffin' hard this, ain't it?' he commented after they had agreed on the six they would invite along to an audition and a short interview, which would be held ten days before the gig at the Derbyshire festival. 'I mean. This could be life changing for them kids.'

'And you're the one giving them the chance, Stan.' There was just the hint of a suggestion of pride in Stan's smile.

On the morning of the day which might just improve the life chances of these teenagers, Stan and Phil had their morning break on the patio of a client, at her suggestion. After several days of working in warm sunshine, their arms and faces were nicely tanned. There was a fierceness about the sun on this particular morning, and they sought the shade of the sun umbrella. Swifts screamed as they flashed through the garden in spitfire battle formation, then dispersing and circling overhead, before diving once more. A robin sang happily from its perch on a shrub, before dropping down to pick up a caterpillar it had spotted.

'Beats sitting in the chuffin' van, my old,' said Phil. 'What do you suppose them birds are? They look to be enjoying themselves.'

'Swallows or summat. Don't know really. I do know a robin when I see one, but that's about it. I've always preferred birds of the unfeathered variety.' They laughed together then sipped thoughtfully on their coffee. 'Things alright with you and Jane, after them shenanigans?'

'Yes ta, mate. I think we've sorted things out. You? Have you kept any feelings for Niamh under lock and key?' Stan watched the swifts fly by once more.

'Well and truly, me old. In fact, there was never any danger really. Me and Mandy are dead strong, like, and apart from the odd reminder, you know, a smile, or that sideways look she gives you sometimes, I haven't felt attracted. Know what I mean? She has got a good business head on them chuffin' shoulders, I'll give her that.'

'Still taking them tablets?' asked Phil.

'Yep. But I've been getting the heebie-geebies lately. Not sleeping and stuff, and it's all about the chuffin' band and this friggin' festival coming up.'

'What, you're worried you're going to cock things up?'

'Yeah, that, and thinking what's an old git like me doing playing with these kids, who are all loads better than me. That kind of stuff.'

'I thought that's why you take the chuffin' tablets, to cut out all this negative shit.'

'Yeah but it doesn't mean I can't fret from time to time, me old. It's only in the night, that's the thing. I get up to go for a bleeding pee, and that's it. I'm wide awake, churning it all over. Last night I was up for over an hour supping a cuppa and reading a Dick to take my mind of it.'

'Sounds normal to me, mate. That goes on in our house sometimes. Listen me old. For what it's worth, me and Jane think what you're doing is frigging amazing, and you deserve all the good stuff that's going to come your way. Neil and them are good musicians, very good in fact. But you're up there with them, Stan, and your playing has got better cos of it, believe me. Well you must know that yourself. And the way things are frigging well going you'll be able to give up this shitload of a job and go professional. And this thing with the studio, the kids and that. You're old Ma would be dead chuffed. In fact I bet she is, up there looking down on it all.'

'Thanks mate. I appreciate all that. But this frigging job you know, it's alright. I mean. We're working in the fresh air, doing something that's worthwhile and people chuffin' appreciate. And we're our own bosses. No one's here telling us to pull our bleeding finger out, are they? No. Here's to all window cleaners, heroes all.' Stan raised his mug and chinked it against Phil's. 'No I wouldn't want to give it up. Not yet a while. Maybe go part-time if I need to put more into the band, like. Who knows?'

Phil was on his feet, indicating it was time to get back to work. 'Stone me,' he said. He spread his arms out wide. 'Winderers of the world unite,' he called out. 'And get back to chuffin' work.'

## Stan

When we was in hospital just before Christmas, Harry said to me that people are happiest when they're in their element. What he meant was when they're doing something they enjoy and are good at. Some of us, not many though, are lucky enough, like, to earning a living by doing something we're good at and enjoy. What I've learned by playing with Tom and the others is that I'm in my element when I'm on that frigging stage, playing my guitar. We might make it as a band, we might not. And I don't know whether you're any good as a writer, my old, and whether anyone will read this story, but one thing I will be trying to do in my studio is help them kids find their element. And tell all them parents out there that life is too frigging short to spend it doing stuff you don't enjoy, and to help their kids find what it is they're good at. I drifted for thirty years and nearly missed my chance.

## Phil

Stan's right. There are far worse jobs than being a chuffin' window cleaner.

## Forty-One

## Let's Get the Show on the Road

'How much time do you think you should give to practising?' This was the question which was turning out to be the tie-breaker. Answers ranged from '*Dunno really. Depends on me boyfriend,*' to '*All day if I could. I just love it. Know what I mean?*' Neil, Angie and Stan chose three of the candidates to be the first to benefit from Stan's project, twin black brothers who both showed promise on guitar and keyboard, and a girl who had been playing the saxophone for a few months, and whose Polish parents both worked in the NHS. She and one of the brothers were able to join Stan and Niamh in the studio the following evening for the TV interview which Niamh had managed to negotiate.

Phil inevitably tagged along and hovered in the background, hoping to catch more than a glimpse of his favourite BBC East Midlands presenter. He was wearing a brand new blue and white striped shirt, and for the first time ever had slapped on some gel onto his thinning hair, to try and produce a random effect that he had noticed on some younger men. He was frequently checking his hair in a mirror and straightening his shirt, forgetting that he had gel on his hands. Intending to project the image of a smart businessman, Stan had bought himself a new suit, but instead opted for new black denims and a *Leicester Rocks* tee-shirt. As always, Niamh managed to look glamorous and on-trend with the minimum of effort, in sandals, three-quarter length pastel-red jeans and light blue blouse. They were disappointed to discover from the film crew that the interview with the presenter would be conducted from the TV studio. Disappointment turned to near-devastation on Phil's part when they learned that the female presenter was on holiday and the interview would be with a male colleague.

'Don't know why I chuffin' bothered,' said Phil. 'Waste of chuffin' effort. I'll be in the pub across the road.' He checked his hair again on the way out.

'Phil,' called Niamh. He turned. 'It wasn't a waste of effort. You look lovely.' She blew him a kiss. He smiled back at her, blushing slightly.

'Oh Phil,' called Stan. Phil turned again, hand on the door handle. Stan mouthed a kiss, for which he received a one-fingered salute.

Niamh gave a few minutes of coaching to the teenagers, suggesting what questions they might expect and what response they could give. In front of the camera they were both confident and looked very much at ease, laughing and joking with each other, and at the end even suggested that one day they could be playing in a band together. Stan was given the opportunity to talk about his hopes and plans for the studio, but Niamh could see that he was slightly peeved that the teenagers had stolen the show. 'You were great,' she said quietly to him.

There was further coverage in the local newspaper, and there was a lot of interest in the studio's new social media account. The combined effect of all the publicity was the promise of considerable funding from businesses and individuals, and the support through the crowd funding was growing. For several days Stan walked around with a permanent grin on his face.

While everyone else around the table in Ursula's Café chatted and smiled, Daniel looked glum. Squeezed between Neil and Phil, there as an honorary guest in a pre-festival gig lunch for the band, he was staring at the screen of his iPad, earphones plugged in. Phil tapped him on the shoulder and removed one of the earphones.

'Come on, me old. Why not put that thing away for now and talk to us. What's up anyway? You look like you've lost a fiver and picked up granny's old knickers, as my Dad used to say.'

Daniel had been watching a YouTube posting of the band playing *Midnight at the Oasis* at The Brown Cow, and had noticed that he had made two mistakes. Neil joked that he himself had made several mistakes, but the audience wouldn't have noticed. And he certainly hadn't picked up that Daniel had made any.

'Yes, you did make mistakes,' said Daniel, 'and so did everyone else, except Angie.' By now they were all listening.

'Well we all know that Angie was made in heaven,' said Tom, 'so she has an unfair advantage. And if you only spotted two mistakes, and they must have been teeny-weeny ones

Danny, then that's near-perfect. So give yourself a break, and enjoy the food and company.'

'Well that's another problem.' They looked at him.

'What is? The company?'

'No, I like the company. Well mostly. But not the food. I can't even say the names of the things on the menu.' Neil looked across at Daniel's menu. He turned it over.

'Try these, mate. Look, everything with chips, even chip butties.' Daniel chose scampi and chips, and orders were given to Ursula.

Angie then picked up on Daniel's comment that he likes the company, well mostly. She asked what it was that he didn't like, but having second thoughts, suggested instead that a much more positive thing to do would be for each of them to share what it is about the band they liked the most. There were moans and groans.

'I hate that sort of thing,' said Malcolm.

'Angie, you never stop trying to micromanage us,' said Tom. 'Why don't we relax and just enjoy the moment.'

'That is so unfair, Tom. I was only trying to get something positive going.'

'I'll tell you what I like,' said Phil, in the hope of nipping in the bud anything which might spoil the occasion. 'About the band. The lot of you, like.' They all turned to look at him expectantly.

'I do like to see a pert bum, and of all the bands I've seen over the years, which including all those on Top of the Pops is a very lot, this band is the one with the best chuffin' collection of bums I've seen.' There was laughter around the table and Stan spluttered into his beer.

'Not the music then, Phil, but our arses,' said Malcolm.

'Oh the music is great, but it's umm, well it's your bums that set you apart. Know what I mean? Like I couldn't say that of, well let's see, of Fleetwood Mac, for instance, of whom I am a big fan. Or Chalkie's lot.'

'Careful,' said Stan.

'Mandy's apart, of course. There are definitely one or two squidgy bums and one or two, shall we say have seen better days.'

'Well I'm with you,' said Malcolm. 'I'm an arse man myself.'

'I'm beginning to see you in a new light, Phil,' said Neil, mischievously.

'No, no, no. It's not like that,' replied Phil, to hoots of laughter. 'I'm not swinging both ways or owt. Shit. I'm beginning to regret opening my bleeding mouth.'

'So on a scale of one to ten, how would you score us all then, Phil?' Neil asked. 'Just out of interest, like.'

'Now I'm not sure I want to go down that road. It's all a matter of taste. Know what I mean? I don't want to go upsetting any of you, nor build anyone up, so to speak.'

'And I guess on the matter of taste,' said Tom, 'you wouldn't want to be seen to be doing any arse-licking'. For the next minute or so none of them could stop laughing. It took the arrival of the food to calm them down.

Over the course of the meal they discussed travel, accommodation and meeting up arrangements for the Derbyshire festival. Tom, in charge of sorting out accommodation, had booked them onto a campsite adjacent to and owned by a pub on the outskirts of a village two miles from the venue. He pointed out that there was a second pub in the centre of the village. Angie would be driving up in her parents' campervan, and offered beds to Mandy, Ursula and Esther, who were all going along. Stan suggested that Niamh would have booked into a posh hotel somewhere. There was a sudden realisation that only Neil possessed a tent and sleeping bags. He and Tom were unable to get away until Saturday, and would travel up during the morning. Malcolm had been given the responsibility of renting a minibus large enough to carry everyone else and all of the equipment, and was asked to requisition tents and sleeping bags for those that needed them.

'All systems go then,' said Stan. The group gradually split up to go their separate ways. The last thing Stan wanted to do was go home and be on his own. He helped Ursula to clear the table and then asked her to join him for a cup of coffee. For the next hour or so they talked about a range of topics. Friendship, families, growing up, growing old, life in general. At one point she asked if Stan would prefer the privacy of her office, but he politely declined. She looked away briefly then smiled at him.

There was just the matter of the practice the following evening. Everyone arrived full of enthusiasm and also early, which gave them fifteen minutes additional practice time. The band played and sang well. People drifted in and out between the bars and the room, and towards the end of the evening there was an appreciative audience of about thirty.

'Just what we needed,' commented Stan. 'I only hope we haven't peaked too chuffin' soon.'

Stan had not slept in a tent since he was a teenager. Sitting outside The Green Man pub, his body ached after an uncomfortable night spent in a sleeping bag on top of a foam mat which had been laid out on the sloping grass, and his head was still ringing because of the loudness of the music booming out from the speakers at the festival. His mood didn't exactly improve with the news from Neil that Tom had been called in to the hospital to help with an emergency, and it would be a few hours before they could set off. Malcolm, Phil and Daniel had been complaining about the situation almost as much as Stan, but the women told them to stop whinging. At least the sun was shining, they had a glass of decent beer in front of them, and they had discovered that the village shop sold sandwiches and pasties, which made up for the disappointment of finding that the pub did not serve food at lunchtimes.

Just as he was beginning to feel human again, Stan heard the sound of music which he recognised but at first couldn't place. Then a group of Morris dancers, led by their musicians, appeared from around the corner fifty yards away and processed up towards the pub. Angie and Mandy joined in the applause from the fellow customers, some of whom had appeared from the bar, clutching their glasses.

'For fuck's sake,' said Malcolm. 'I do not want to see a bunch of tossers Morris dancing. I vote we go somewhere else.' Angie explained that her father was a Morris dancer, and she enjoyed watching it. So they stayed put. There were in fact two teams, and when the local team had performed one dance their leader introduced their guest team from Leicestershire. As they lined up Stan said that he knew this lot.

'Harry's team. The bloke that died in hospital. These came to dance for him in the chuffin' hospital.'

An hour later, Angie was dragging an ever-so-slightly reluctant and sheepish looking Malcolm onto the tarmac to Morris dance. Stan had introduced himself to the Leicestershire team, and before he realised what was going on, he found himself manoeuvred into position amongst the dancers.

'This next one is our joining-in dance, Stan,' said the lead musician. 'I'm sure Harry is up there watching on in approval, so why not get your friends up and have a go.' And they all did.

There was joking and teasing as they made their way up the hill to the campsite to collect their things and prepare for the drive over to the festival. Angie challenged Malcolm to deny he had enjoyed the dancing. It had been a gas, he replied. He might even take it up. 'Not,' he added. Stan believed that Morris dancing must be good for the soul, as he was feeling 'tonnes better' than he was earlier.

As the van was being unloaded behind the stage where the band would be playing, Tom and Neil were on the A50 heading out of Leicester to join them, Neil driving, so that Tom could try and relax. He had been called in at seven in the morning to help out in life-saving heart surgery which took the best part of five hours. They had decided to take the M1 as far as junction 24 and then drive cross country through Derby, rather than go further north and cross country through Matlock.

'Shit. I've forgotten my phone charger,' said Neil. 'Mine's dead. Where's yours Tom?'

'Ah! Well, I was hoping you'd have yours, as mine's on the table at home. I forgot it the panic this morning. And my phone's pretty flat as well. So I guess we won't be listening to any music on the way up.'

'How about the cricket? Have you been following the test match?'

They had a shared love of the game and talked animatedly about their favourite players and matches they had been to. They had both been hoping to get along to one of the test matches later in the summer, and Neil offered to try and buy tickets. As they drove past Trowell services and the traffic slowed to a crawl, Neil realised he had missed the turn off for Derby. Tom looked at his watch.

'We've got a couple of hours leeway,' he said. 'So we're OK for time as long as this lot keeps moving.

Stan stood on the stage arms akimbo, taking in the scene from this, one of the smaller stages. Daniel, Angie, and Malcolm were alongside him. Apart from the small village close to the site, it was surrounded by open countryside. To the north the Kinder Scout plateau was just visible. In stark contrast were the eight other stages, hemmed in by the many dozens of blue Portaloos which lined much of the perimeter. To their left as they looked out were various food outlets, rows and rows of igloo shaped tents and festival-goers in their hundreds moving between them, accompanied by a cacophony of music which drifted across to the stage. A hundred or more were gathering in the space in front of the stage, ready for the first act, although it was still a couple of hours before they were due to be on stage. *Leicester Rocks* were the second of four bands performing on this stage, before the big names appeared. To their right were the massed car parks, stewards directing new arrivals to the few places left. In the lane leading up to one of the entrances were cars, vans, motorbikes and pedal bikes, and a stream of pedestrians on both side of the queue. Beyond the lane, raised on a high embankment was the line of the old Cromford to High Peak railway, now part of the High Peak cycle trail.

'Take it all in Daniel, me old. This will be a day to remember. First Morris dancing, and then the big moment on stage. This lot are going to love watching you.' Daniel managed a smile as he looked down at his feet.

'It must have taken an army weeks to put this lot up,' said Angie. 'And in a week's time they'll have taken it down again, and the sheep and cows will be back.'

'What? You mean this lot will be standing in sheep shit while they watch us?' asked Malcolm.

'Who knows, duck?' replied Stan. 'Some people will friggin' well do anything to get a glimpse of you on the guitar.'

After a few minutes they turned to exit through the small band of people setting up and checking instruments, amplifiers and speakers. Amongst them was Phil.

'Happy as a pig in shit,' commented Stan.

Once they were past the Nottingham exit the traffic thinned and Neil was able to put his foot down. As if in celebration, the radio commentary team announced the arrival of cake into the studio and the England captain completed his century of runs.

'Things are looking up, Neil.' But as he spoke they could both see the erratic driving of a Ford Focus a couple of hundred yards ahead, as it wandered across from the inside in to the outside lanes and then back again. Cars bunched together quickly as drivers braked, some sounding their horns, before they picked up speed again as the situation seemed to right itself.

'I should just hang back for a minute, mate,' said Tom, whose instincts told him all was not well inside the car which had crossed lanes, and which was still a hundred or so yards ahead. He could make out the driver slumped over the steering wheel and the woman passenger struggling to lift him away from it. Again the car moved from the inside lane without indication, causing the driver of the car alongside it to swerve. The knock on effect was instantaneous, as cars travelling at high speed in the outside two lanes braked hard, more horns sounding. There was the hard thud of metal on metal as cars in those lanes drove into the back of those on front. Meanwhile, the car causing the problems drifted back towards the hard shoulder, catching the front wing of another car which pirouetted and came to a halt on the hard shoulder. There was more screeching of brakes, and the sound of cars shunting behind Tom's car. Tom had quickly switched on the hazard warning lights and somehow his car had managed to escape unscathed.

Vehicles in all four lanes were now at a standstill, and the tailback was quickly building up. Tom reached behind him for a bag.

'That was pretty cool driving Neil, mate. Phone nine nine nine would you, and tell them what's happened. We're between junctions 26 and 27. I'll go and see what's going on in that Focus.'

'Just one problem mate. No charge on the phone.'

'Shit. OK, I'll ask one of the other drivers, although someone will probably have done it already. Keep an eye on me, will you, and if I give you a wave come over and give me a hand. We could be here for some time.' The thought had already occurred to Neil. Tom was running towards the Focus.

Stan was prowling in the space outside the stage area. He had exchanged a few words with the young members of the band due to be on first, as they had passed him. There were cheers and whistles as they walked onto the stage. With half an hour to go, the audience area was well over half full, and fans were still streaming in. From what he could hear as the guitarists checked the tuning of their instruments, he thought they would be playing rhythm and blues. He caught sight of Niamh walking towards him. She waved, and he stopped and waited for her. She asked if they were all set to go. Stan explained that Neil and Tom hadn't arrived yet and he was slightly worried. He'd tried a few times but couldn't get hold of either of them on the phone, and thought it strange that neither of them had called. Give me five minutes, she said, and I'll see if my team can check out the traffic situation. She hurried away in the direction from which she had come.

She returned shortly, slightly out of breath. 'We might have a bit of a problem, Stan. Seems there's been an accident on the M1 coming north, and it's been closed for a couple of hours. Long tailbacks. Things are expected to be moving again in an hour or two, but you can't tell with these things. No reports of any fatalities as far as we know.'

'Shit. Why the fuck haven't the duffers phoned?' They looked at each other, both having the same thoughts.

'I'm sure they're fine and will get here. They're possibly in a pocket where there's no signal.'

'But what do we frigging well do? How long can we give them before we have to chuffin' well call it off?'

'No one's talking about calling it off, Stan. We might have to bring the third act forward to give Neil and Tom time to get ready, depending on how late they are. So I'll go and find them to give them the heads up. And if needs be we'll bring the last one forward as well. They won't be happy, but that's tough.'

Stan found the others in the porta cabin reserved for their use, playing a version of partner whist which Angie had taught them. Phil was with them, and he and Daniel had evidently just won a hand. Everyone seemed to be in good spirits. Stan caught Phil's eye.

'Any news?' asked Angie.

'Niamh's on the case, duck. There's been a bit of a hold up on the motorway, but they'll be here soon. Phil, can you give me a hand for a mo, me old. It's a step needs fixing.'

As they walked away Stan put Phil fully in the picture. 'How do we handle this with Danny Boy? I didn't want to tell him in front of everyone, in case he freaked. Know what I mean?'

'Let me take him to one side like, while you talk to the others, and I'll tell him that the boys are going to be a bit late and you might have to play a bit later than planned. I'll keep it low key. He should be alright, especially as he's enjoying the card game. He remembers all the frigging cards that have been played, so he keeps winning.'

Later, the five of them found a spot from where they could watch the young band playing. Their brand of rhythm and blues had a very contemporary feel to it, and for a while it provided a distraction. But as time passed beyond the point when they would stand any chance of being next up, even if Neil and Tom were helicoptered in, a cloud of despondency enveloped them, despite Angie's attempts to lift the mood. Out of the corner of his eye Stan caught the flashing blue lights of a police car travelling at speed up the lane which ran alongside the festival site.

'Bleeding coppers,' he said to himself. 'Last chuffin' thing we need is them crawling all over the shop.'

Five minutes later five phones pinged simultaneously as the Whatsapp message came through. 'They're here.'

'Well bugger me backwards with a banjo,' said Stan. 'Into action.'

Tom and Neil had been given a police escort at high speed, from the scene of the pile up on the M1 to the backstage entrance, where they were standing talking to Niamh and two policemen.

'Evening all,' said Stan as he approached the group. It had been all he could do to stop himself running. 'What's going on here then? What were you lads up to, chasing a police car?

Don't tell me. You got lost and asked a policeman the chuffin' way.'

'We're pleased to see you too, Stan,' replied Neil. 'We're lucky to be here at all.'

'Yeah, sorry mate. You're a sight for sore eyes, I tell you. We was worried about you, like. Specially as we heard nowt from you.' Tom told them about the mobile phone situation, adding that his new best friends, nodding in the direction of the policemen, had called and spoken to someone here to explain what had happened and that they were on their way.

'Really!' exclaimed Niamh. 'I'll just go and check on that.' She hurried off.

'The escort was the least we could do,' said one of the policemen. 'Your mates here are heroes, and you should be proud of the two of them. Saved at least three lives. Doc here gave CPR to one poor bloke who'd had a cardiac arrest, and your mate stopped a couple of people from bleeding to death. They kept all three alive long enough for the paramedics to take over.'

It was the driver of the car which had brought the M1 to a standstill who had suffered the cardiac arrest. Seeing Tom run over to help, Neil wasn't able to sit and wait. Stepping out of the car, he looked around the chaotic scene. Cars, vans and lorries had come to a halt at various angles, and there had been several collisions. For a moment or two the only sound of which he was aware was of the traffic in the other carriageway, but gradually people began to emerge from vehicles, most looking dazed but some clearly distressed, a few calling for help. He soon found Tom, and together they managed to get the driver out of the car and onto the ground. Tom quickly assessed the need to give him CPR.

'Take my first aid kit,' he said pointing to his bag. 'Any heavy bleeders Neil, there are sterile compression pads in there. Press on the wound, as hard as it feels OK to do, and try and get them in a position so that the bleeding part is higher than their heart. Lift arms and legs. Anyone in shock, recovery position. Do you know what that is?' Neil nodded, then got up and left Tom to tend to his patient.

He went from vehicle to vehicle, checking whether there were any injuries. Several people had suffered minor bumps and cuts, but three needed urgent attention. One passenger with a broken arm had gone into shock, and in adjacent vehicles two more were badly injured, bleeding heavily. He called out for anyone with first-aid experience to come and give him some help. A woman was able to tend to the person with the broken arm. A few other people came to him, all saying they had no first-aid training, but were willing to help if he could tell them what to do. Neil was thinking on his feet, and took two of the helpers to a car in which a passenger was hurt. He passed on Tom's advice on how to staunch the bleeding from the man's leg. The man was conscious, and they should try and keep him awake. Neil went to help the second person, who had managed to get out of his car before collapsing. His head and face were covered in blood. With help Neil was able to get the man into recovery positon, cushions under his head to raise it. By the time the ambulance arrived and the paramedics took over, some fifteen minutes later, the man was awake and talking, and his head wounds had almost stopped bleeding.

Given the number of vehicles involved there were relatively few injuries. As the police went meticulously and efficiently through their procedures, which included taking statements from drivers and passengers at the front of the long tailback, and supervising the removal of damaged vehicles to the hard shoulder for recovery, all Tom and Neil could do was sit in Tom's car and wait. That was apart from when they gave statements themselves, which gave them the opportunity to explain their situation. They were told that it could take up to three hours before the traffic would start moving, but the officer they spoke to offered to find the number for the festival site management, and give them an estimated time of Tom and Neil's arrival. They passed the time discussing and singing together some of the songs from the band's set for the evening, and came up with ideas for improving the arrangements of one or two for future purposes.

Frustratingly, for half an hour they sat looking at an empty road ahead of them, after those vehicles ahead of them had been removed to the hard shoulder.

Neil looked at his watch.

'Looks like it ain't going to happen, Tom. At this rate it could be getting towards midnight when we eventually pitch up.' Tom agreed. A tap on the passenger side window made them both jump.

'Right sir,' said the policeman to Tom. 'If you'd care to drive carefully over to the hard shoulder in front of the other vehicles, a colleague of mine will be with you shortly.' Two minutes later they were under police escort, and forty-five minutes later they were greeted by a concerned-looking Niamh.

'So are you up for this then?' asked Niamh. She had returned, furious that the message from the police had not been passed on. 'I mean it sounds like you've been through a tough few hours.'

'Are you kidding?' asked Tom. 'I haven't driven like a bat out of hell just to use the bloody toilet. But I am desperate. It's surprising how long you can hold it when you have to.'

Eleven of them were standing roughly in a circle; the band members, Niamh, Phil, and the two policemen looking slightly incongruous. There was an air of sudden expectation.

'This lot are about done,' said Stan, referring to the band on stage. 'Then we need to pull our fingers out to set up and sound check.' He turned to the policemen. 'Officers, you're welcome to join us.' They thought they might manage to stay for the first few minutes.

Niamh herself stood at the microphone to welcome the band onto the stage, apologising for and explaining the delay. There was enthusiastic applause as they walked on. Feeling almost euphoric as well as nervous, Stan looked out at the sea of happy, smiling, yet expectant faces, played a couple of chords to calm his nerves, then thanked everybody for coming. He turned to face the band. They too were smiling and looking expectant. Mandy, Esther, Ursula and Niamh were waving and shouting from their places in the front row of the audience. This was just as Stan had imagined it would be. One finishing touch was needed. He looked directly at Mandy, and for a moment everyone else was invisible. He pointed to her and held up his mobile phone. There were just four words in the message. She made a pretence of giving it deep consideration, frown on her face, hand to her chin, then smiled back at him. Stan read her reply, simply *YES*.

'Chuffin' brilliant,' he said into the microphone. As they were setting up, Stan had announced that he wanted to open with *Walking By Myself*. He gave Daniel the nod, then counted himself in. The timing was perfect.

# Acknowledgements

*M*y sincere thanks go to the following people for their support, either with the development of the storyline, proof reading or editing.

Simon Beckett, Pam Hatfield, Joyce Janes, Christine Tarpey, Chris Thompson.

Paul Merrison (for his work on the cover design)

# Chapter headings/ song titles

Walking By Myself – written and performed originally by Jimmy Rogers, covered by Gary Moore on the album Still Got the Blues

Come on in My Kitchen – Robert Johnson.

Come Rain or Come Shine – Ray Charles, inspiration taken from Eric Clapton/B.B. King arr.

It's a Jungle Out There – Buddy Guy

Ursula's Café – Leicester Rocks

Not Alone – Harry Gardner (song about suffering from dementia)

Crossroads – Cream

Danse Carribe – Andrew Bird

Black Magic Woman – Fleetwood Mac, covered by Santana

Autumn Leaves – many covers, including Nat King Cole and Eva Cassidy

There May Be Trouble Ahead – Nat King Cole

Further on Down the Road – Bobby Blue Band, various covers including by Gary Moore and Eric Clapton

Blue – Joni Mitchell

Some Kind of Wonderful – Buddy Guy

Tupelo Honey – Van Morrison

All Along the Watchtower – Jimi Hendrix

Another Brick in the Wall – Pink Floyd

First Impressions – Leicester Rocks

Listen to Your Heart – Roxette

We're All in This Together – Leicester Rocks

Now Is the Cool of The Day – Coope, Boyes and Simpson

You Might Need Somebody – Ronny Jordan, featuring Crystal Gaze.

To Live Is to Fly – Cowboy Junkies.

In the Bleak Midwinter – traditional Christmas carol.

Journey's End – Tommy and Liam Clancy, cover by The Teacups

Kind Hearted Woman Blue – Robert Johnson, covered by Eric Clapton
     and others

Fields of Gold – Sting, cover by Eva Cassidy

We're Going Wrong – Cream

The Payback – James Brown

Moving On – Gary Moore

Say You Love Me – Fleetwood Mac

Still Got the Blues – Gary Moore

Ticket to Heaven – Dire Straits

Dream on Dreamer – Brand New Heavies

Be Careful What You Like – Leicester Rocks

Fightin' Hard – Alvin Youngblood Hart

Somewhere Over the Rainbow – Judy Garland, and many covers

We Are the Champions – Queen

Closer to You – Ronny Jordan

Steppin' Right Along – Bill Withers

Let's Get the Show on the Road – Leicester Rocks

# Some useful Lestah slang and dialect

Ark at it – Listen to that noise

Ain't yorn – Sorry, but that doesn't belong to you

Ay up, me duck – Hello

Ayumashed? – Have you made a pot of tea?

Bap – Cob

Chip 'ole – local fish and chip shop

Chisit – Nickname for Leicestrians

Citeh – Leicester City (not to be confused with 'tahn' – city centre)

Chewie – Chewing gum

Cob on – Upset

Co-ville – Coalville

Council pop – Tap water

Cozzeh – Swimming costume

Croaker – Doctor

Dobber – Condom

Duck – What most people are called.

E's gorra chin on – He's being very grumpy

E's gorra cobbon – He seems to be upset

Fount it in the cupbut – It was in the cupboard

Footeh – Football

Frit – Scared

Gawping – staring

Gerronwirrit – Please continue

Gerrout o' me road – Allow me to pass

Gerroutuv it – I don't believe you

Gis a bit – Could I have a piece.

Gisit'ere – Could you pass that over?

Gorra bag on – In a mood.

Gorrago – I have to leave

Guwin down the offeh – I'm going out to the off-licence

Guwin dentist – I'm going to the dentist

Guwin kahzi – I'm going to the toilet

Guwin up tahn – Travelling into the city centre

I'll do that straight the way – It'll do it immediately

I'll have no truck wi' him – I'll have no dealings with that man

I'll lamp ya – I'll give you a good thumping

It's black over Bill's mother – It's going to rain soon

Jawonowt – Would you like anything?

Laggy bands – Elastic bands

Like – To be inserted at regular intervals within a sentence (e.g. It was like it just like came from nowhere like)

Lekeh – An electrician

Larreh – Cheeky/mouthy

Liccle – Small

Mardeh – Upset

Me tabs ar fruz – My ears are frozen

Old cock – Friend

On ya todd? – Are you alone?

Or'ight me ode – Hello my friend

Ooh yar beauteh – Exclamation of surprise

Ow much chissit – How much is it?

Ospiccle – Leicester Royal Infirmary

Pack puggin! – Stop picking your nose

Parky – Cold

Plaggy bag – Plastic carrier bag

Propah – Proper (e.g. Propah mardeh)

Puthering down wi' rain – Bucketing it down

Roaring – Crying

Sen – Self

Seyor – Goodbye

Sh'urrup ya wazzock – Be quiet you fool

Skank – Leave someone

Skanks – Pants, underwear.

Snap – Lunch

Soz – Sorry

Summut – Something

Tahn – City centre

Throw a wobbler – Lose one's temper

Treat ya sen – Treat yourself

That fellah – Him, over there

There owt else on? – is there anything else on (TV)?

Wannacroggeh – fancy a lift on my bike?

Wanna twos – Fancy sharing

Warrayaupto – What are you doing?

Well I'll go to the foot of our stairs! – What a surprise!

What's going off? – What's going on?

Wossermarrerwiyu – What is the matter with you?

Yakit – Throw it

Youluvitdonchaar – You really like that, don't you?

# Walking Through Lincolnshire's Seasons

## with Hugh Marrows

# Acknowledgements

For this third volume of walks, taken from those published in Lincolnshire Newspapers, I must yet again thank the many other writers who have gone before me, though not necessarily as country walkers, in writing about Lincolnshire's landscape, its history and its architectural heritage and from whose work I have learned so much.

Those newspaper editors who have been kind enough over the years to publish my work must be thanked first and foremost, for without their indulgence, my ramblings – in both senses of the word – would probably not have seen the light of day.

Again my wife must receive her dues for acting as part-time secretary, accompanying me on some of the walks and for allowing me time to complete the remainder. She has also, in addition to offering constructive criticism, suffered me spending many hours in research and at the computer keyboard typing everything out.

Thanks too to David Cross, a walking companion over many years; and the staff of the county archaeological service who have dealt with many requests for information.

And finally, to the landlords and landladies of inns around the county who have allowed the use of their carparks as starting points.

Cover image: St Peter's church, Ropsley.

First published in 2008 by
At Heart Ltd
32 Stamford Street
Altrincham
Cheshire
WA14 1EY

in conjunction with
Lincolnshire Newspapers Ltd
5-6 Church Lane
Boston
Lincolnshire
PE21 6ND

Text and images © 2008 Hugh Marrows

ISBN: 978-1-84547-211-5

Printed and bound by Ashford Colour Press, Gosport.

I am very pleased (not to say flattered) to have been asked to put together a third book of my Lincolnshire country walks, again all taken from my articles published in various editions of Lincolnshire Newspapers over the past decade. Some of these have, where necessary, been slightly revised in order to update them and to provide a standard format.

And a good way to begin this particular volume, it seems to me, is with a quotation from our very own Lincolnshire poet, Alfred Lord Tennyson (1809–1892), who aptly captures the theme to this book, and the rapidity with which the years seem to roll by, with his words from 'Will Waterproof's Lyrical Monologue':

*As on this whirligig of Time*
*We circle with the seasons.*

The chosen theme for this volume, you will have gathered by now, is 'The Seasons' and the selected walks each have some characteristic that makes them particularly attractive at a certain time of year. However, they all have other features of interest too and, I hasten to add, they are all good at any time. For example, woodlands can be equally enjoyable in spring or autumn; a beach or coastal walk is refreshing either in the summer sun or on a bracing winter's day.

There are of course a few practicalities that need discussing. These walks are fairly short and easily accomplished in half a day, so expensive hiking gear is not essential. Clothing is a matter of personal preference, provided you bear in mind the prevailing weather and any likely changes.

Having said that, I always think that boots and waterproofs do need to be of as good a quality as you can afford, for obvious reasons!

The detail in the route guides and the accompanying maps should get you round these walks without problems, but I would counsel having an Ordnance Survey map with you. If possible, make this the relevant Explorer sheet, for these contain greater detail and can be useful in helping you to understand your surroundings and to locate the start points more easily. I have used grid references quite frequently and the technique for working these out is easily and quickly learnt, as each map has an explanation and example of this map reading skill. From a safety point of view it is always useful to know just where you are – particularly in case of an unforeseen emergency. Most walks have an inn or café close by but carrying a small supply of food and (especially) drink is always prudent. Remember too that where permissive paths are used they will not appear on OS maps!

One of the great things about living in Britain is our wonderfully varied seasons. With our busy, modern lives it is surprising how rapidly they go by, and a good antidote to the pace of 21st century living is to relax amongst what seems to be (although it is not always so) our quiet and unchanging countryside; something that Lincolnshire has in abundance.

Each season gives the countryside its own special attractions. Spring for flowers such as the primrose; summer for the fresh green colours and wayside and hedgerow flowers; autumn for the vivid russets and golds on the trees; winter for crisp frosts on a cold, sunny day. And perhaps that most imperceptible change of seasons is when winter fades away and spring arrives – which takes us back to the beginning of the year, and of the book, again.

One final thought: on reflection, it has dawned on me that readers could quite reasonably ignore my recommendations and simply go out and do these walks whenever they felt like it, and they would be right to do so. In reality they are all good at any time of year; indeed, each would amply repay four seasonal visits. So by my reckoning, that's eighty walks for the price of twenty!

I must end by reminding readers to obey the Countryside Code, and by so doing show respect for the countryside, its wildlife, other ramblers following in your footsteps and the farmers and landowners on whose goodwill all walkers rely. Once again, Happy Rambling to you all!

**Hugh Marrows**

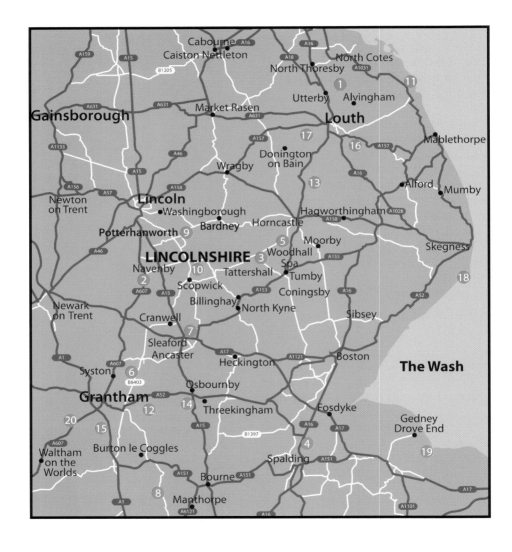

# *Spring*

# *Autumn*

# *Summer*

# *Winter*

# *Spring*

*I dreamed that, as I wandered by the way, Bare winter suddenly was changed to spring.*

'The Question' – Percy Bysshe Shelley (1792–1822)

To most people, spring is a season that offers a sense of renewal after the short and sometimes dreary days of winter. As the daylight hours increase and the temperature rises, this is a season with promise in the air that uplifts the spirits.

As the countryside bursts into life again, what better time is there to get the walking boots out and enjoy it? The blustery 'Lion days' of March magically clear the atmosphere so that we can enjoy the views, something for which Walk 2 is particularly recommended. The new growth all around should also tempt us out to enjoy the fresh crop of woodland and hedgerow flowers, abundant in Walks 3 and 5.

# Covenham St Bartholomew
# & the Reservoir

This grand spring walk is found to the north of Louth and explores
Covenham along with its nearby reservoir. And it's short enough
to be feasible either before or after a pub lunch.

Both the Covenhams (St Mary's and St Bartholomew's) have a church and the two villages blend together almost imperceptibly. The boundary is close by St Bartholomew's church, where a sign shows the name of both villages; one on either side. The names come from the Old English *Cofa's Ham* (homestead) and both were distinct, separate villages by the mid-1400s, being known then as Covenham Sancti Bartholomei and Covenham Sancti Marie. However, we only see St Bartholomew's on this walk.

St Bartholomew's church is an appealing patchwork of chalk and greenstone repaired with red brick, with an unusual slate-hung bell turret instead of a tower. Some 13th century stonework survives a substantial restoration in 1854. The church has been redundant since 1981 and you will probably find it locked, though it is possible to peer inside through the windows. Look too for the impressive (but weatherbeaten) carved head over the porch door. The churchyard is now a nature reserve known affectionately as 'God's Acre'.

In contrast, Covenham Reservoir is obviously a modern landscape feature and is managed by Anglian Water with the dual role of satisfying 21st century demands for both water and leisure facilities. Its construction began in 1967 and took two years. Once built, it took another year to fill with water drawn from the Great Eau and the Louth Navigation. It is a considerable size, with the surface area of the water measuring 218 acres, a depth of 15 metres and a circumference of almost two miles. One corner is designated as a nature reserve, and because of this there is public access to a perimeter path that allows observation of the many water birds that use it, especially during the winter. Its leisure uses include a flourishing sailing club, with wind surfing and water skiing facilities also available.

In the large meadow crossed near Manor Farm on the return to Covenham St Bartholomew's, the noticeable earthworks are remains of the original village site that clustered around the manor. Prehistoric flints indicating an even earlier history of occupation have been found in the fields between Grange Lane and Birketts Lane. These fields have also revealed traces of overlying mediaeval settlements through finds of pottery going back to Saxon times.

When you return to the inn, look for the huge terracotta plaque on the end wall bearing the date 1898.

NOTES. Readers may begin from the Plough Inn at Covenham St Bartholomew's by kind permission of the landlady (please use the back of the carpark). Alternatively, park at the reservoir (GR340964), putting the inn half way round the walk. You can picnic by the reservoir too, but NOT within the embankment wall!

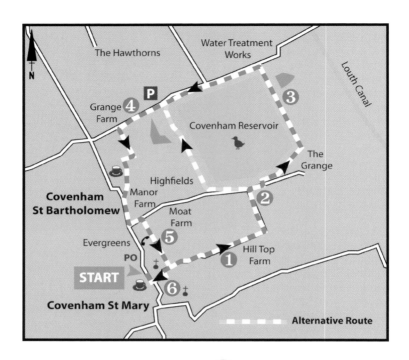

START: New Plough Inn
(GR338945)

MAPS: OS Landranger 113
(Grimsby) or Explorer 282

DISTANCE: 4¾ miles :
7.5 kilometres

REFRESHMENTS: New
Plough Inn

① Leave the inn carpark and turn right
for a few yards to St Bartholomew's
church, and then bear left down Birkett's
Lane. After about three-quarters of a
mile, the road ends. Now keep forward
along a grassy track that soon bears left
to meet another road.

② Turn right for 25 yards, then go over
a stile on the left and climb the steps
onto the reservoir embankment to join
the perimeter footpath. (The public may
use this, but it is not a right of way.)

You can walk round in either direction. If you go left (which saves half a mile), pass in front of the Boat Club building to reach steps just around the next corner and descend to the road. However, I recommend turning right to walk round three sides of the reservoir, where the high vantage point provides wonderful views over the marsh and inland towards the Wolds. At the corner before the Boat Club, descend steps on the right to the road.

Turn left for 500 yards (taking care with children or pets) towards a footpath sign and footbridge on your left. From here, cross an arable field aiming just left of a bungalow on the far side. Once across, keep forward to the left of a line of trees and when these end, turn right to join a lane. After about 50 yards, a footpath sign points left into a house's drive. Where the shrubs on the right end, veer right over the garden to a waymark at a footbridge. Now bear half right, cutting a field corner (or use the field edge), to a ladder stile and from it turn half left over a large meadow, taking a diagonal line to the far corner; aim between Manor Farm and a house. There you'll find a second ladder stile; join the road and turn left.

At the Grange Lane junction you can merely keep ahead back to the inn but my choice is to turn left for 100 yards and then take the signed footpath from a stile on the right. Walk between a

fence and hedge to a second stile, climb over and then turn left to continue in a meadow, now with the hedge on your left. In the corner is a footbridge; cross this into a third field. Aim slightly left to a hedge gap on the opposite side containing another stile. In the final field, head towards the right hand one of two large trees, to a final stile and a lane.

This is Birkett's Lane again. Turn right back to the village and inn.

# Navenby & Wellingore

This walk heads from Navenby onto the Lincoln Heath to tread in the Roman legionaries' footsteps down Ermine Street and then along part of the Viking Way and the dramatic Lincoln Cliff.

At first sight, the line of cliff-edge villages stretching south from Lincoln seem poorly sited on high ground. In reality, though, there are spring water supplies, meaning the area has been continuously settled since at least the Iron Age. The Navenby Archaeological Group has identified one of these prehistoric sites just outside Navenby, which proved to be of unexpected interest because it had subsequently been covered by a later Romano-British settlement. This is hardly surprising, however, for it lies alongside Ermine Street. The area has now been landscaped and opened to the public with colourful information boards detailing the discoveries made.

In East Street, Navenby, stands Mrs Smith's Cottage; this too is open to the public from time to time. It dates from the mid-1800s but remained virtually unmodernised until its last occupant (Mrs Hilda Smith) died at the age of 102 in 1994. Since then, with an eye to saving Navenby's heritage, the villagers have managed to secure its preservation as part of their local history.

Arriving at Wellingore we pass the Hall. Parts of the building date from the 1750s, but it is mostly of the 1870s. The Hall was once home to the Nevile family who left Auborn to live here, but have since returned to their original home. Offices now occupy the building, but you

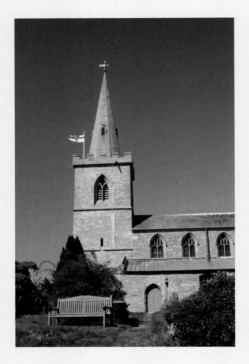

southern part of the churchyard (with seats for a rest) offers fantastic views.

For the mile and a half back to Navenby from Wellingore we use the Viking Way. This too offers remarkable views, both northwards along the cliff towards Lincoln and westwards over the Witham and Trent valleys. Once back at Navenby, get a peep into St Peter's church if you can, for its chancel contains an outstanding Easter sepulchre. This remarkable carving is widely regarded as one of the finest in Lincolnshire (if not in England!) and gets a mention in virtually every book written on church architectural history. The churchyard itself is managed as a nature reserve and a seat offers the chance of a rest before the final few yards back to High Street and its beckoning attractions. If you look for the Lion and Royal you will be impressed by the large emblem over the front door topped by the Prince of Wales's feathers. It was presented after the Prince (later King Edward VII) stayed there in 1870, though only very briefly.

And finally, watch out in both villages for their distinctive silver-coloured, lion-headed water hydrants. These date from the 1930s when the first mains water supply was installed.

NOTES. Navenby has plenty of parking space along the High Street plus several choices for refreshments. There are also inns at Wellingore.

can still peer through the gateway; the house's splendour remains, even down to the prominent private chapel adjoining the eastern end.

A few yards further on stands Wellingore's All Saints church, which contains two marvellous tombs in the north aisle, of Richard de Buslingthorpe and his wife Isabella, and the altar reredos based on Leonardo da Vinci's 'Last Supper'. It's worthwhile walking around the tower too where the

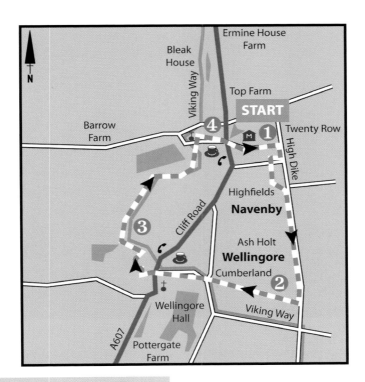

## ABOUT THE WALK

START: High Street, Navenby

MAPS: OS Landranger 122 (Lincoln) or Explorer 272

DISTANCE: 3¾ miles : 6 kilometres

REFRESHMENTS: Inns, tearoom and chip shop in Navenby, and The Marquis of Granby and the Red Lion in Wellingore

① From High Street, Navenby, locate and turn into East Street. Pass Mrs Smith's Cottage and keep going until you reach Ermine Street. Turn right. At the next junction (with Chapel Lane) turn right again and after only a few paces go left into the large open area. Here you will find marked paths and the archaeology information boards; you can walk across to join Ermine Street again at the far left hand corner.

2 Turn right and in half a mile you will see a signed footpath on the right heading towards Wellingore. The way is clearly marked over two arable fields, beyond which it meets a road. Cross carefully and keep ahead into the village, passing the Hall to reach the church and the A607. (The inns are off route to the right before the Hall.)

3 Cross into Vicarage Lane. At The Green turn right and then go left and right again before making a final left turn to reach the Memorial Hall. You will see a play area to your left; walk past it and beyond that a clear path crosses some rough ground. At the far side turn right, following the Viking Way along the hilltop. The path is distinct and easy to follow until it arrives at Clint Lane in Navenby. Just past a pond, take the first left turn, the narrow path signed as 'The Smoots', bearing left at the bottom. Turn right when you get to a metal kissing gate and on reaching a second gate, look for a stile nearby just across to your right. Climb it and cross a meadow to another stile below the church. Across the road, a few paces uphill, there are steps near a wall, which lead up into the churchyard.

4 Turn right and from the churchyard gate keep straight ahead back into Navenby High Street.

# Woodhall Spa & Kirkstead Abbey

This Woodhall Spa to Kirkstead route is ideal for a spring walk, all on well-established paths and lanes through woodland and open countryside.

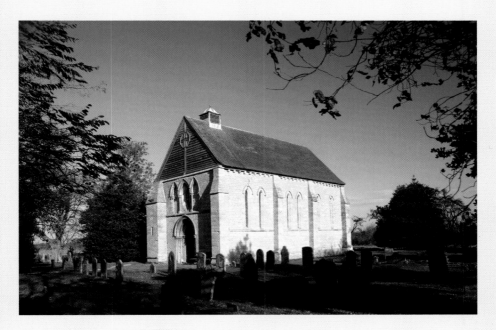

The stories surrounding John Parkinson's fruitless search for coal at Woodhall in the early 1800s, the subsequent (and almost inadvertent) discovery of the spa waters and the establishment of a thriving spa resort are well known. Despite having now lost the spa the town remains a bustling place, but we quickly escape all this, for immediately behind the main street shops are the Pinewoods, eight hectares of mature woodland owned by the Woodland Trust. They were formerly known as Scrub Wood until planted with pines in 1811 by Parkinson to provide the pit props for his ill-fated coal mining enterprise. A little further on is the spa site and Coalpit Wood where the mineshafts were sunk.

The spa was set up in the 1840s following the discovery of bromide and iodine rich waters in the abandoned, and by then flooded, mine shafts, the locals having noticed the water's beneficial effects on both ailing cattle and people. Woodhall's popularity increased markedly once the railway arrived in 1855 and continued throughout the Edwardian era. Although becoming less popular as the 20th century progressed, the spa struggled on until abruptly forced to close when the shafts collapsed in 1983. Nevertheless, road signs remain pointing to vanished institutions like the Rheumatism Clinic. (There's one in Coronation Road.)

stone after the Dissolution, and nearby in the fields to the left are the distinct earthworks of the abbey fishponds. We then come to the abbey site itself.

Kirkstead Abbey was founded as a Cistercian monastery in 1139 and dissolved in 1537. The present remaining stonework is over 50 feet high and the moat, which retains some water during wet weather, encloses some 13 acres. It is worth taking time to explore and it's good mental exercise to try to deduce the abbey ground plan. Here's a clue; the tower remnant is the southeast corner of the south transept. A good time for doing this is when everything is picked out by low sunshine.

St Leonard's church, dating from around 1230, stands nearby, just outside the point where the abbey gates once stood. It has been described as 'a very precious little church' (Rev H. Thorold). Measuring a mere 20 by 44 feet, it is still considered to be one of the finest examples of 13th century architecture in the county. The striking west doorway is particularly impressive, along with its elegant, narrow windows. (I'm sure there was once a notice saying where the key could be obtained but this now seems to have disappeared!)

We return to Woodhall alongside a stream called 'The Sewer' on OS maps. Don't be put off; this is simply an archaic name for drain or ditch.

Another Woodhall institution, of course, was the Teahouse in the Woods (now McCauley's restaurant), an evocative name to many generations of Sunday afternoon motorists and their families. Woodhall also lies on the Viking Way, the long distance footpath linking the Humber to Oakham in Rutland. We use a short section of this as we head for Kirkstead Abbey. Although within a housing estate, the path occupies an unexpectedly secluded, grassy avenue of trees, though I (and doubtless many others) remember it as open fields when the Viking Way was first created. On approaching the abbey site we pass the Old Hall, built from looted abbey

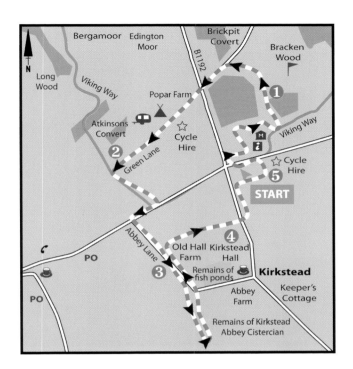

START: Royal Square,
Woodhall Spa
MAPS: OS Landranger 122
(Skegness) or Explorer 273
DISTANCE: 5¼ miles :
8.5 kilometres
REFRESHMENTS: Various in
Woodhall Spa

From Royal Square, cross Station
Road and locate the footpath on the
right immediately behind Bell's Estate
Agents; this leads into the Pinewoods.
Keep forward for 100 yards then turn left
through the trees to reach Coronation
Road. Now turn right to pass the Kinema
and the old spa buildings, going left
at the footpath sign by McCauley's
restaurant. Follow the clear path through
woods, behind the spa and beside the
golf course to a road.

23

2 Turn left and at the crossroads keep forward along Green Lane for three-quarters of a mile to where the Viking Way crosses. Now turn left again on the footpath between fences and trees to reach the Kirkstead road.

3 Bear right for 300 yards and then cross into Abbey Lane. Continue past a footpath on the left (our return route), the Old Hall and earthworks of the abbey fishponds. At a bend, enter the abbey site ahead. Walk as far as St Leonard's church, then return to the lane.

4 Go back to take the footpath (now on your right just after the farm) that leads via field edges beside a stream ('The Sewer' on OS maps) to a stile into a paddock. At the far end after a second stile, the path goes to the left of a hedge, emerging onto a drive to reach the road. Turn left.

5 In 300 yards, look for a footpath sign pointing to the right. You may now either keep ahead back into Woodhall, or cross into Long Avenue (another footpath) following it to Stanhope Avenue. There turn left for Broadway and left again back to the start.

# Surfleet, Seas End & the Reservoir

This delightful riverside walk makes a fine spring ramble. Easy underfoot, it follows grassy riverbanks, quiet country lanes and (an added bonus!) links three inns.

Most ramblers' bookshelves contain a little volume bearing a title that reads something like 'Great Pub Walks'; indeed there are some such books just for Lincolnshire. This walk, however, reigns supreme in this respect for it allows the possibility of visiting not one, but three inns! One at each end and one at the halfway mark too!

Settlement in the Surfleet area only really began following the Roman occupation, for it was then that the earliest attempts at drainage began. At first, these were sporadic and largely

ineffective until, in the 1650s, various drainage schemes were devised by Dutch engineers. Before that time, river silting was a serious hindrance to vessels and for a time in the early 17th century, boats were actually carried overland between Surfleet and Fosdyke some six miles away on the River Welland. However, solving the drainage problems unexpectedly led to the surrounding land drying out and shrinking, so that pumping became necessary to avoid flooding. Again, attempts to deal with this new problem were somewhat ineffectual, with real success only coming in the 1820s when reliable, steam driven pumps could be built. The first sluice at Surfleet Reservoir was built in 1759 with the present one dating from 1879. As we stand on it today, many miles from the sea, it is surprising to reflect that Surfleet, still a further two miles inland, was once a coastal village. At Surfleet Reservoir you can rest whilst indulging in that timelessly enjoyable occupation of watching people 'messing around in boats'.

Back in Surfleet, St Laurence's church merits a visit. The most striking feature, of course, is the leaning tower. This began to tilt very soon after being built (probably between 1270 and 1350) and the tip of the spire is now over six feet from the true perpendicular; Lincolnshire's very own Tower of Pisa! A church guide leaflet explains many other interesting features, both inside and out. Across the road stands the welcoming Mermaid Inn, with its grand, columned doorway, and which once had its own malting and brewery.

The River Glen provides the principal interest throughout the walk and there is plenty to see in the way of boats and wildlife, especially waterfowl, with grebes diving for fish being a common sight. The riverside sections of the walk are part of the Macmillan Way (the long distance path from Boston to the south coast) and of the Brown and Black Fen Trails criss-crossing the fens. They also

feature in a local Millennium Walk, one of a series devised by the South Holland District Council and shown on a display board at Surfleet village hall. Leaflets for these are available from the SHDC or tourist offices.

NOTES. In Surfleet there is room for considerate parking in the lane behind the church and running parallel with the river (opposite the Mermaid Inn). See the final paragraph of the route instructions for suggested alternatives.

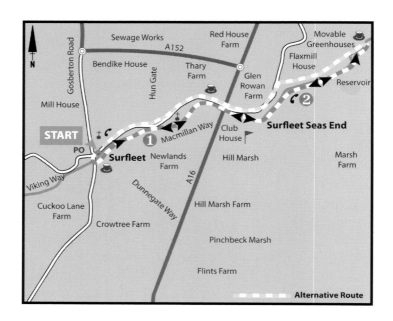

## ABOUT THE WALK

START: Surfleet village

MAPS: OS Landranger 131 (Boston & Spalding) or Explorer 249

DISTANCE: 4¾ miles : 7.5 kilometres

REFRESHMENTS: Mermaid Inn, Surfleet, Riverside Inn (by the A16), The Ship Inn, Surfleet Reservoir and Fish & chip shop, Surfleet

1 At the main road, carefully cross over (to the Mermaid) and turn left to use the pavement over the bridge above the river. Then re-cross the road and join a signed footpath (the Brown Fen Trail). Walk between a house and the riverbank and then along the edge of a large garden, with trees between you and the riverbank, to emerge into an arable field. A grass path along the riverbank soon widens into a track and continues to the A16 road. Unless doing a short walk and returning to Surfleet, from here use the underpass and turn right up the

steps at the far side before bearing left onto the golf course, paying due heed to the (unintentionally?) humorous notice board.

2 Keep to the left hand edge of the golf course for 100 yards or so then rejoin the riverbank just after a bungalow. After about a mile, pass to the right of a large shed and cross a bridge over Blue Gowt Drain. Now turn left along a concrete road. After 60 yards, bear left again down onto a grass path between the chalets and the water's edge. On reaching the sluice, climb steps up to the road and turn left above the water, before turning right at a footpath sign pointing along the opposite bank. In

a few yards you will find steps on the left leading down to the Ship Inn.

3 Return by the same route.

Study of the OS maps will reveal alternatives to the walk described above. You could return using the lanes on the opposite bank to that walked on the outward section. Doing so creates a circular walk. Indeed, roads could be partly used to reach Surfleet Reservoir in the first place, thus making a figure-of-eight walk. Also, turning back on reaching the Riverside Inn converts the walk into two separate, shorter ones (see map).

WELCOME TO

MARTIN PICNIC SITE

LINCOLNSHIRE COUNTY COUNCIL

## Spa Trail & Martin

This walk uses part of the Spa Trail between Woodhall and Horncastle. It is an especially good springtime outing because of the glorious profusion of spring flowers in the local woodlands.

I must warn readers that this route unavoidably involves a quarter of a mile or so on the B1191, so take care here, especially with children! There are fairly good verges, however, so use them whenever possible. Remember too the vagaries of the English climate, for the woodland tracks particularly will get muddy after rain, though the wettest bits now have boardwalks. Don't let these considerations put you off though, for on a sunny spring day this is an extremely pleasant walk! But do it in the springtime (although it's still lovely at other times) or you'll miss the flowers!

The Spa Trail forms part of the Viking Way, the only National Trail within Lincolnshire, as it wends its 148 miles from Barton on Humber to Rutland, and the section used here is entirely along the old Horncastle Branch Railway, which was operative between 1855 and 1971.

Tucked away at Martin stands St Michael's church, described by Henry Thorold in his books on Lincolnshire churches (and accurately too!) as 'lost among farm buildings – a precious forgotten little building'. There is a magnificent Norman doorway with very well preserved carvings, and amongst the greenstone masonry are colourful, contrasting patchworks of brick repairs. There was some restoration here in 1877.

White Hall Wood is also an ancient landscape feature which, together with the adjacent Highall Wood and Thornton Wood, may well precede Domesday in age and thus be the actual woodlands mentioned in the Domesday Book. Within White Hall Wood – to the left on our walk, though unfortunately not visible from the right of way – is a moated grange site and causeway. This may possibly be the grange known to have been leased by Ralph Cromwell (builder of Tattershall Castle) from the monks of Kirkstead Abbey.

However, the primary reason for doing this walk, especially in the springtime (roughly from late April onwards), is to see the spectacular display of spring flowers beside the railway and in the woodlands. The blooms include literally thousands of primroses, celandines and wood anemones; a sight that will lift the most jaded of spirits!

Martin is also a deserted mediaeval village (a DMV to archaeologists) and its entry in the Domesday Book indicates that there were probably more residents there then than there are nowadays. There was also particular mention – and remember that this was in 1086 – of the extensive woodland and woodland pasture that is still a feature of the area today, as we shall see during the walk. As we leave Martin, heading towards the woods, the grass mounds in the meadow give very clear traces of the old village house plots and streets.

NOTES. Alternatively, start from the small carpark at Sandy Lane, Roughton (GR218647). This adds half a mile. If you begin there, simply follow the old railway to Martin Bridge, joining the route described above as you go, and on reaching the railway again after White Hall Wood, turn right instead of left to return to your car (see map).

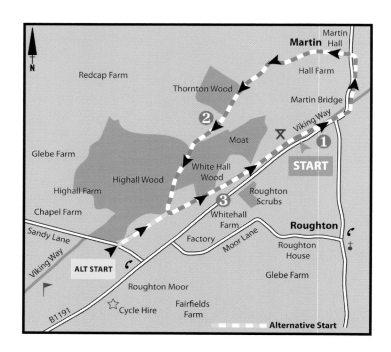

## ABOUT THE WALK

START: Martin picnic site (Spa Trail GR235658) (see notes)

MAPS: OS Landranger 122 (Skegness) or Explorer 273

DISTANCE: 4 miles : 6.5 kilometres

REFRESHMENTS: None en route but Woodhall Spa and Horncastle are both nearby

① In the picnic site, face the road and then turn left, walking along the old railway as far as the Martin road bridge. Immediately before this, look for a pathway that has been worn away on the right and which leads up to the road. Turn left across the bridge and walk a quarter of a mile to a turning on the left for Martin. This is signed for Hall Farm.

**2** From the footpath sign near the farm and the church, keep ahead past a large barn and go through a bridle gate. As you continue through more bridle gates a delightful, wide grass track develops. There are even views to Lincoln cathedral from this section! Once through a 'double bend' the track keeps ahead to enter Thornton and White Hall woods where an obvious way continues through the trees to eventually rejoin the old railway and the Spa Trail.

**3** Now turn left back to the start, with many more flowers to be seen beside the old trackbed.

# Summer

*Sumer is icumen in
Llude sing cuccu!*

Anon (13th century)

All the elements of an ideal day in
the country are incorporated in this
selection of summer walks. The
warmer days at this time of year are
more conducive to short walks, and
those that wander beside cooling water
are especially welcome. So too are
those that offer the chance to while
away an hour with a picnic beneath
shady trees or enjoy a relaxing drink at
a village inn after your exertions.

The first of these requirements is
satisfied by Walks 7 and 9, which are
both partially beside waterways. A
chance to dine in the fresh air comes
in Walks 6, 8 and 10, each of which
offers contrasting and unusual places
to eat out of doors. The hilltop at
Bellmount near the end of Walk 6 is a
particularly good scenic vantage point
at which to a take a picnic break.

# Londonthorpe & Bellmount

This walk is admirably suitable for a family woodland walk and picnic. It is partially on National Trust land near Grantham and starts from their Bellmount carpark.

Belton's deer park towards Grantham with St Wulfram's church spire prominent and the hills of the Vale of Belvoir in the distance, while the views from Londonthorpe on its hilltop are equally grand.

Londonthorpe is mentioned in the Domesday Book under the name 'Lundetorp', but St John the Baptist church is now the only surviving mediaeval building. Its tower is 13th century and has a saddleback roof, of a style that is unusual in Lincolnshire and which was added in Victorian times. Indeed this estate village is almost entirely mid-Victorian in date, so that the architectural style of the cottages gains its attractiveness through its consistency and is yet typical of the period. Look out for the ornate bus shelter converted from an old conduit (water supply) house.

Some of the paths used here are permissive, being within the National Trust estate and adjacent Woodland Trust woods, so they do not all appear on maps as rights of way. Before you return to your car, the grassy slopes below the Bellmount tower make a wonderfully elevated picnic spot with a view.

Though short in distance, it is these views that make this walk memorable, for they are quite disproportionate to the effort required to get to them. Those from the Bellmount Tower are quite outstanding, looking out over

Nikolaus Pevsner, quite rightly, in his *Buildings of England: Lincolnshire* points out that the Bellmount Tower is not a tower at all, regardless of being so named on OS maps, but an arch. In 1719, Sir John Brownlow was created Viscount Tyrconnel and it was to his memory that the 'tower' was built between 1750 and 1751. The windows are Venetian in style and there is an upper room (not accessible to the public), originally used for picnics; though I guess they would be grander than the ones today's visitors will be carrying! Restored by the National Trust

1993 and 1995, comprises 155 acres. It is the Trust's local showpiece and a popular local attraction with its own carpark, information boards and maps provided.

Belton is of course one of England's great country houses. The Brownlow family purchased the estate around 1617 and the house we know today was built in the 1680s. In 1936, the then current Lord Brownlow was Lord in Waiting to Edward VIII and was, as a close friend, heavily involved in the abdication scandal involving Mrs Wallis Simpson. Belton House was also the setting for the popular children's fantasy novel *Moondial* by Helen Cresswell, and there's a great outdoor adventure playground too! So a good day out is guaranteed!

in 1989, it commands perhaps the best view of the whole walk. Locally it has the rather odd nickname of 'Lord Brownlow's Trousers'.

The Woodland Trust is a national organisation that has its headquarters in nearby Grantham. It was founded in 1972 and since then has acquired well over 1,000 woods throughout the country totalling more than 47,000 acres. Londonthorpe Wood, planted between

NOTES. The start is reached either from Belton village or from Ermine Street with an approach via Londonthorpe. Although the walk is short, it is intended that it be combined with a visit to Belton House nearby, though being a National Trust property there is an admittance charge for non-members.

# Walk 6

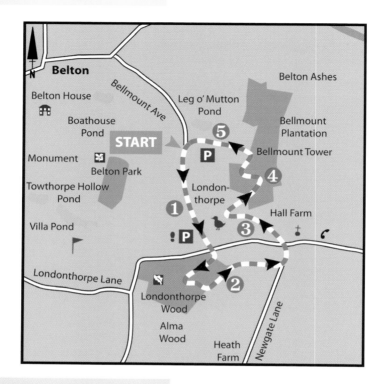

## ABOUT THE WALK

START: Bellmount carpark (GR944389)

MAPS: OS Landranger 130 (Grantham) or Explorer 247

DISTANCE: 3 miles : 5 kilometres

REFRESHMENTS: Stag Inn, Barkston (off route) and Café at Belton House (NT)

**1** From the Bellmount carpark entrance, turn left along the road until you reach a junction. Cross into the unsurfaced lane opposite and after a few yards, as it begins to steepen, go through the gate on the right into Londonthorpe Wood. Follow the grass path ahead to a path junction then bear left to wind uphill until you eventually join a clear path within the trees of adjoining Alma Wood, which stretches along the hilltop.

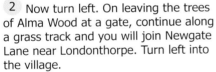

2  Now turn left. On leaving the trees of Alma Wood at a gate, continue along a grass track and you will join Newgate Lane near Londonthorpe. Turn left into the village.

3  At the road junction, look for the footpath sign and kissing gate that are just across to your left and in front of a house. (But before continuing the walk, first explore Londonthorpe by turning right then left down Church Lane – and return.) From the kissing gate, walk diagonally down a meadow to a stile in a hedge and keep forward in the next field to the second stile and gate, accessing another section of Londonthorpe Wood again. Keep forward for a few yards and then take the first path on the right.

4  Climb a stile into a grass field and turn sharp right beside a hedge for a few yards to another stile. Now head diagonally through the large meadow up to a stile in its top left hand corner. A gentle climb through the Bellmount Plantation now begins. When the path splits, bear left making another left turn at the top of the hill, before swinging right to reach a final stile with Bellmount Tower seen ahead.

5  From the 'tower' turn left downhill back to the start; though there are other paths within the woods to explore first if you wish.

# Sleaford to Evedon

Partly beside the Sleaford Navigation, this easy route starts from Sleaford's old canal wharves to explore the nearby countryside and visit the quaint 'leaning' church at Evedon.

Opened in 1794, the Sleaford Navigation linked the town to Chapel Hill on the River Witham 13 miles away. The term 'Navigation' (rather than 'Canal') is used to describe it since it was engineered by straightening and deepening the New River Slea, a pre-existing river. That name is itself something of an understatement, for the 'New' river dates from the Middle Ages when the 'Old' river was originally diverted to power watermills.

We begin outside Money's Mill, built in 1796, within a loop of the navigation that allowed vessels to turn round for their voyage back to the Witham. Remnants of this loop remain near The Hub Arts Centre and alongside East Banks. Look out, too, for the original Navigation

Wharf gateway preserved in Carre Street, and Navigation House (1838), the former company office near The Hub, which is now restored as a museum. Over its door, though rather weathered, is the Navigation Company motto: *Leve Fit Quod Bene Furtor Onis*. Suggested by Sir Joseph Banks (the Lincolnshire naturalist who sailed to Australia with Captain Cook), it is a quotation from Ovid and translates as 'A Heavy Burden Correctly Carried Becomes Light'. The navigation closed in 1881.

Just beyond the Leisure Centre, the Old River Slea departs to the right over a sluice but we meet it again near Evedon. At Cogglesford Mill, the large open area on the right was the site of Old Sleaford, the 'capital' of the prehistoric Coritani

tribe. It remained strategically significant throughout the Roman occupation as their road between Bourne and Lincoln, today's Mareham Lane, crossed the Slea here at a cobbled ford. The site was an Anglo Saxon settlement too, and has been the source of many archaeological finds. Cogglesford has probably had a watermill since Anglo Saxon times though the present one is mainly early 18th century. It is in working order and often open to the public.

At Evedon, St Mary's church leans noticeably down the hillside because the underlying clay has subsided. The churchyard contains rare 16th century lidded gravestones. Nearby, the 16th century Manor House and a huge water tower from 1915, now an unusual private home, can be seen.

At Holdingham Lock, the garden on the far bank still contains an original 1790s octagonal toll booth, a unique bit of the navigation's heritage. Again, there has been a mill here for centuries, the latest being 18th century.

Back in Sleaford, the Lollycocks Field area was formerly occupied by osier (willow) beds, grown for the local basket making industry. The North Kesteven District Council currently maintain this wetland habitat as a nature reserve.

To round off this interesting walk, pop into The Hub, a former seed warehouse now transformed into an ultra modern arts and crafts gallery. There is a café inside, and the splendid aerial views over Sleaford from a roof terrace should not be missed.

NOTES. Money's Yard carpark is short stay, allowing sufficient time for the walk only; to gain extra time use the Eastgate carpark. Both are Pay and Display. From the Eastgate carpark get to Money's Yard by cutting through (or round) The Hub to the old wharf area and Carre Street. Admission to Cogglesford Mill, Navigation House and The Hub is free.

# Walk 7

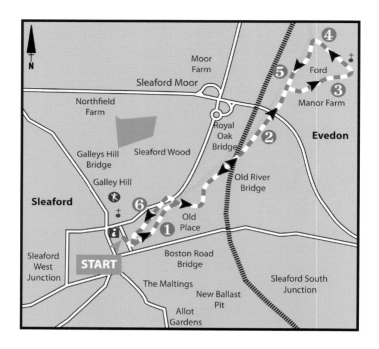

## ABOUT THE WALK

START: Money's Yard carpark (off Carre Street), Sleaford

MAPS: OS Landranger 130 (Grantham) or Explorer 272

DISTANCE: 4½ miles : 7 kilometres

REFRESHMENTS: The Hub in Sleaford

1 Leave Money's Yard into Carre Street and turn right to use the zebra crossing to gain East Banks beside the navigation. Continue past the Leisure centre to Cogglesford Mill.

2 Keep ahead, still by the navigation, for another 200 yards before turning right by a hedge. In a few yards at a gap, turn left over grassland close to the Old River Slea until you reach the railway. Bear left and go under the railway at the first bridge (we return under another bridge seen a few yards

away) before going left again and rejoining the navigation. Now turn right. At Bonemill Lock, go under the dual carriageway bypass, up steps and continue beside the navigation again for a further 350 yards. Now look carefully for a waymark on a post on your right. Go down to a narrow footbridge to follow a field edge to another footbridge and stile.

3 Climb over and turn half left over a meadow, aiming towards Manor Farm (you may find mown paths through lots of wild flowers!) to another stile in the far corner. There, join a track that passes through the farmyard and leads to Evedon church, with the Manor House and water tower visible ahead. Near the churchyard wall, a seat offers extensive views.

4 Continue the walk down the stony lane, seen on the left as you approach the church. Cross the Old River Slea at a ford (and footbridge!) rejoining the navigation at Holdingham Lock. (Turning right provides a short 'there and back' stroll to Papermill Lock, whose name is self-explanatory.)

5 Otherwise turn left. On meeting the outward route, return under the bypass to the railway, this time using the bridge with the white kissing gate and walk back to Cogglesford Mill.

6 Now cross the lock to follow the footpath on the opposite bank by Lollycocks Field. At the next bridge re-cross the navigation to return to Money's Yard. On the way, another footbridge gives access to the Eastgate carpark.

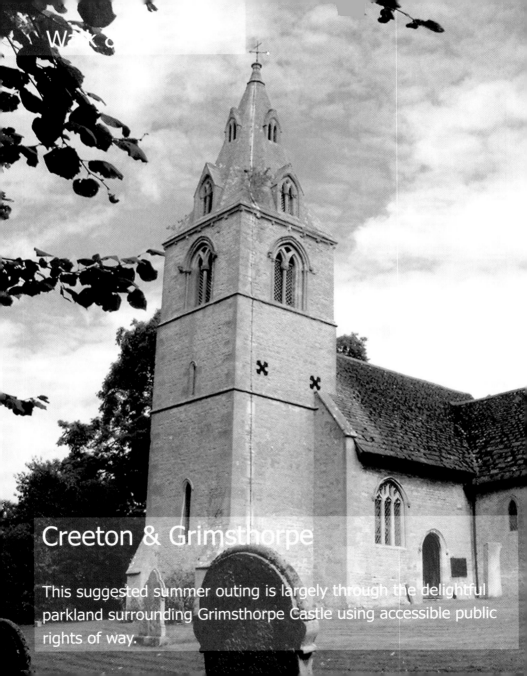

# Creeton & Grimsthorpe

This suggested summer outing is largely through the delightful parkland surrounding Grimsthorpe Castle using accessible public rights of way.

To the west of the market town of Bourne lies Grimsthorpe Castle and its 3,000-acre estate. In contrast to many such estates, Grimsthorpe does have several public footpaths through its magnificent park and this walk is designed to take advantage of these at a time when the woods and wildflowers are at their summer best.

Grimsthorpe Castle was built in the 13th century, being altered and added to until 1722 when the famous architect Sir John Vanbrugh completed a new north front. It has been the home of the Duke of Ancaster since 1516 in the reign of Henry VIII. We only see the castle distantly from our route (though it is often open to the public) but we do explore much of the park, including some of its wilder wooded areas.

There is a real mediaeval atmosphere here, especially as we head back towards Creeton through avenues of ancient trees. Amongst the wildlife you may be lucky enough to see fallow deer, or even red deer. During the Second World War, the park was used for military training and many deer escaped into the surrounding countryside, so they are common hereabouts. Watch out too for buzzards, particularly whilst crossing the park for the first time where the ground is more open. In the valley to the south of the castle is the site of a 12th century Cistercian abbey, the Vallis Dei, still shown on maps as 'The Vaudey'. As you enter the park near Little Bytham, also at the Pebble Gate and finally as you exit towards Creeton, make a point of looking at the gates, all of which have a most peculiar hinge design (especially the lower one), which I have never seen elsewhere.

Creeton has fine views over the valley of the West Glen River. Some of the best are from St Peter's churchyard, noted for the carved Saxon crosses still standing there, and there are also a few remnants built into the walls. Search out too the poignant and poetic gravestone by the chancel south wall to Clement Nidd, who died aged 74, and which is shared with his wife who died aged 18. The nearby coffin shaped graves are believed to be those of monks from Vaudey Abbey. If you have the good fortune to find the church open, go inside to see a copy of a 'Judas' bible of 1611, in which the printer has mistakenly put 'Judas' instead of 'Jesus' in Matthew 26:36 and the error has been amended by hand.

Although this is included as a summer walk it is one that is particularly suited to any time of year to enjoy the park's

varied seasonal glories. This is one walk that should definitely be done more than once!

NOTES. The lay-by where we begin is just south of Creeton, near the road junction at GR011197. The nearest inn is The Windmill at Swinstead. Take care on the first section where the roadside footpath is narrow. For a picnic try a large log seat in Grimsthorpe Park at approximately GR027204.

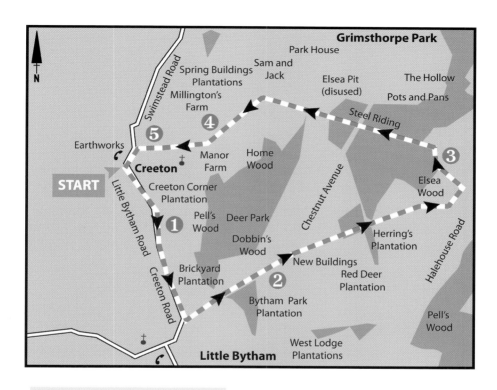

## ABOUT THE WALK

START: Lay-by on the B1176 near Creeton

MAPS: OS Landranger 130 (Grantham) or Explorer 248

DISTANCE: 5 miles : 8 kilometres

REFRESHMENTS: None on route

**1** From the lay-by cross the road and turn right along the footpath. In 300 yards re-cross (where the footpath continues) and finally re-cross again after Bytham school. Approaching Little Bytham village, take the signed bridleway on the left, going down to the West Glen River, then uphill to enter Grimsthorpe Park at a bridlegate.

# Walk 8

2 Follow a wide grassy avenue until you meet a park road with a house to your left. Walk ahead a few yards, then bear right onto a track with a footpath sign a few yards along it. From this, go left onto a grass track towards and past some woods. In about a third of a mile join a firm track. Keep ahead, ignoring a turning to the left, and when the main track bears sharp right keep, ahead on a rough grass path until you eventually join another track, this time with a stony surface. Turn left.

3 In 200 yards at a footpath sign turn left again towards woods, soon bearing right alongside them, then go left and re-enter Grimsthorpe Park at the Pebble Gate. Keep forward now, continuing to a road where you can glimpse Grimsthorpe

Castle beyond the site of Vaudey Abbey. Cross to a stile and keep ahead over a second stile to reach the tree trunk bench, then maintain your direction to another gate. Leave the park and bear left.

4 Now with hedges on your left, a headland path leads through three fields. After the gate into the fourth field keep to the left hand edge by a wire fence. When the path begins to steepen downhill, and passes an overgrown area, look for a stile on the left and climb over into the lane beyond.

5 Turn left to visit Creeton church, then return and follow the lane down to the main road. Make a final left turn over the river to get back to the start.

# Potterhanworth & the Car Dyke

A lovely short walk for a summer's day, this route follows meadow paths, woodlands and a section of the Roman Car Dyke.

Potterhanworth is situated to the southeast of Lincoln, just where the Lincoln Heath slopes gently towards the Witham fens, here bordered by the Roman Car Dyke. And with the Ermine Street passing a few miles to the west, there may well have been a Roman settlement nearby.

The 'Hanworth' part of the village name derives from the Old English, meaning 'Hana's homestead' whilst the 'Potter' prefix refers to local mediaeval potteries. However, these two elements of the village name, though both ancient, only became one word in the 1940s. Close by is the hamlet of Potterhanworth Booths, a 'booth' being a temporary settlement near summer pastures, typical of this low-lying area. Another unusual local dialect word is 'barff', a hill beside low ground, which again is an apt topographical description.

Architecturally, the church is usually the dominant feature of most villages but at Potterhanworth it is an unusually massive water tower that first catches the eye. Built in 1903, it draws water from local boreholes and is an early example of a public water supply. Across the road stands St Andrew's, looking somewhat diminutive by comparison. Although a church has existed here since before Norman times, the oldest part of the present building is the 14th century tower, while the rest dates mainly from an 1856 rebuilding. On the nearby green

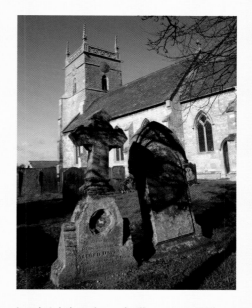

is a brightly coloured village sign, with the war memorial across the road on Stocks Hill. Opposite that is a bus stop built to commemorate the 1951 Festival of Britain.

Opinion is divided over the purpose of the Car Dyke, a Roman construction, which from Cambridgeshire covers 76 miles before joining the Witham and providing a route via the Fosse Dyke to the Trent, the Ouse and so to York. Was it built to transport supplies (an explanation strongly championed by William Stukeley, the 18th century antiquarian from Holbeach)? Or was it simply a drainage system? It closely

# Walk 9

follows the five-metre contour and so could well have been designed to divert streams from the heath away from the low-lying fens. Then again, bearing in mind Roman engineering ingenuity, perhaps it was both! In the vicinity of the Car Dyke (seen on the walk) there are extensive views towards Bardney, Woodhall Spa and the Wolds.

The Domesday Book recorded large areas of woodland around Potterhanworth and some of this remains today although in fact these local 'Limewoods' – named for their pre-dominant species, now quite rare – probably originated in pre-history following the retreat of the last ice age

some 10,000 years ago. Potterhanworth Wood is managed in a number of traditional ways, for example by coppicing. Together with surrounding fields and hedgerows, the woods provide many diverse wildlife habitats, so there is always something interesting to see. Our walk passes through Potterhanworth Wood.

NOTES. Parking space in Potterhanworth is limited so be considerate; try Barff Road or Middle Street. Paths through Potterhanworth Wood may be muddy after rain. The Plough inn at Potterhanworth Booths is a few minutes' drive away – or a walking detour to it is described below.

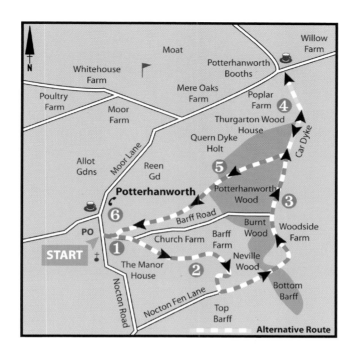

## ABOUT THE WALK

START: Potterhanworth village

MAPS: OS Landranger 121 (Lincoln) or Explorer 272

DISTANCE: 3½ miles : 5.5 kilometres

REFRESHMENTS: The Chequers, Potterhanworth; The Plough, Potterhanworth Booths (off route)

1 Go down Barff Road, noting the chapel on the left; the footpath beside it is our return route. Continue to the edge of the village.

2 Now take the footpath on the right across pasture to a fence corner, keeping forward with the fence to your left towards the narrow, far end of the field. Cross a stile, a footbridge and a small arable field to meet a farm track. Turn left, staying on the track through a double bend until a signed footpath bears right along a grass track. At a waymark turn right again, beside woodland (Neville Wood) and, keeping

outside the trees, bear first right, then left to reach a road. Turn left.

3  When the road bends right, keep forward on another track that soon crosses the Car Dyke. In a further 150 yards take the bridleway going left, rejoin the Car Dyke and continue to a road. Keep forward along this until it bends right then continue ahead beside the Car Dyke until a footbridge crosses it on your left.

4  [To walk to the Plough Inn at Potterhanworth Booths, keep forward here for half a mile to the B1190 road, joining it opposite the inn. Return the same way to the footbridge.]

5  Cross the Car Dyke into Potterhanworth Wood and always

keeping directly ahead, partly on paths and partly on a track, walk to the far side and exit via a kissing gate and footbridge. Now turn right, but only for a few paces, then go left beside a ditch, shortly to turn left over a small footbridge. Cut a field corner to a hedge gap and walk along the right hand edge of the next field until it begins to slope away, then zigzag first right, then left down to another footbridge by a lake. From it, walk up to a fence and kissing gate seen on the skyline, cross a track and keep ahead to another gate in a hedge corner. Press on through more meadows, and kissing gates, until you can veer left to rejoin Barff Road at the chapel.

6  Turn right back into Potterhanworth.

# Blankney & Metheringham

This gentle stroll visits two delightful villages where the edge of
the Lincoln Heath meets the Witham Fens.

In the Domesday Book of 1086, Blankney's entry appeared as *Blachene*, meaning 'Blanca's island'. By the early 1400s, a large estate had developed which 300 years later, in 1719, came into the ownership of the Chaplin family. Charles Chaplin (1786–1859) had the most recent Blankney Hall built in the 1820s. He was also responsible for the appearance of the present village with its ornate stone cottages, built during the 1830s and 1840s. His son Henry became an MP, a confidant of the Prince of Wales (later Edward VII and a regular visitor to Blankney) and a celebrated racehorse owner. His horse, Hermit, won the 1867 Derby and is buried on the estate. Unfortunately, the hall burnt down in 1945 and was never rebuilt, although farm buildings and stables survive. Blankney's church, St Oswald's, stands near the hall site and has a lytchgate dedicated to Henry's wife, Lady Florence, who died in 1883. Some mediaeval stonework remains within, but all that we see from the outside was rebuilt in the 1880s.

On the approach to Metheringham, the village mill (1867) is clearly visible on the skyline. It originally had six sails but as these inevitably broke over the years they were not replaced, and by the time it finally closed about 1930 only three were left.

Much of Metheringham village was destroyed by a disastrous fire in 1601 and of St Wilfred's church only the Norman tower survived intact. Rebuilding was undertaken quickly, however, and inside it is still possible to see some charred roof beams that were reused. The porch door, also rebuilt, dates from 1602, and it retains its original wooden lock in working order bearing the monogram of Queen Elizabeth I. Also inside is an impressively carved monument to Lucy Skipworth who died in 1763. The parishioners manage the churchyard as a wildlife sanctuary.

The village centre has two stone crosses. The first stands near the library and is the shaft of an ancient village cross, possibly 13th century. The other, isolated in the middle of the road, commemorates the coronation of George V. Nearby is a lion-headed water hydrant, a relic from the days when mains water was first piped to the village.

The railway that we cross twice on the outskirts of Metheringham was opened in 1882 by the Great Northern and Great Eastern Joint Railway and at one time formed part of the route for the Liverpool to Harwich boat trains. The Chaplins built their own private roadway from Blankney Hall to Metheringham station, allowing them to travel there without being on public view, and near the start of the walk we glimpse a short section of it.

NOTE. The Stepping Out carpark is signposted from the B1188 road.

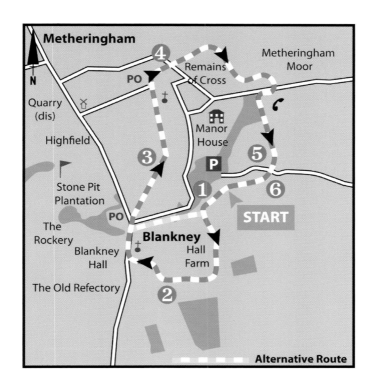

## ABOUT THE WALK

START: Stepping Out carpark, Blankney (GR075606)

MAPS: OS Landranger 121 (Lincoln) or Explorer 272

DISTANCE: 4 or 4½ miles : 6.5 or 7 kilometres

REFRESHMENTS: White Hart, Star & Garter, shops in Metheringham

**1** Look for a waymark on your right as you enter the carpark. Follow its direction and, at a metal fence, glance right into the trees to see the bridge over the Chaplins' private carriageway from Blankney to Metheringham station. Go left beside the fence to reach a stile on your left. (The short route bears right here through trees to a road, then turns left through the village to the T-junction with the B1188. Join the main route there by turning right; then go straight to step 3 on page 67.)

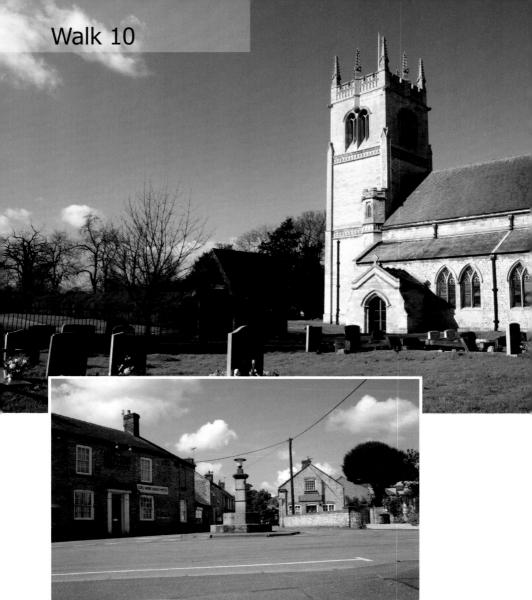

**2**  The longer walk crosses the stile. Go along the field edge to a concrete bridge in the corner, cross it and proceed with a hedge to your left over a second footbridge. Keep ahead to another waymark and there turn right along a grass track leading to a farm. At a surfaced track, keep forward and turn right in order to pass round the high wall of the old hall garden. The track soon swings left and then, once beyond the old stables, bear right over the green that fronts the church and join the main road (B1188). Go right, using the pavement, to reach a T-junction. (The short route joins from the right here.)

**3**  Keep ahead and pass through the kissing gate just after the last cottage on the right. Walk diagonally over Blankney's cricket field, aiming for a small gate by a large conifer tree. The path now runs beside a fence to another gate with views to Metheringham mill. Pass Metheringham cemetery to join a walled path by St Wilfred's church; this is Church Walk. At the end turn left into the village centre.

**4**  Bear right past the library and right again on reaching Fen Road (by the Methodist chapel). Cross the main road into Fen Lane, go over the railway bridge and almost at once descend steps on the right into the paddock. Follow the left hand hedge to a kissing gate, go through it and immediately turn right along a field edged by trees. As this path swings gradually left, watch carefully for a waymark and steps on the right leading into a small business park; walk through this to the main road.

**5**  Turn right along the pavement and, once over the railway again, cross the road onto a footpath through the woods opposite. On leaving the trees continue ahead, soon joining a short track to a surfaced lane.

**6**  The footpath opposite soon crosses a track to a stile from which a final meadow path leads back to the Stepping Out carpark. Alternatively simply turn right along the lane itself.

# *Autumn*

## *Seasons of mists and mellow fruitfulness*

'Ode To Autumn' – John Keats (1795-1821)

The transition from summer to autumn often seems the quickest seasonal change of the year; a time when morning temperatures plummet suddenly and out of the blue comes a hint of frost in the air. But there is usually a spell of 'Indian Summer' weather that, combined with the dramatic autumn colours, should encourage us out while the sunshine lasts.

Keats' words about autumn undeniably carry an air of melancholy. But life's best pleasures are the simple ones, and one of these is the childhood enjoyment of shuffling through drifts of fallen leaves! We have two woodland outings here – see Walks 12 and 15 – where this innocent activity can be indulged. And since corn stubble is almost as good as leaves, we scrunch through some of that on Walk 14. At this time of year the seaside can be enjoyably bracing too, so Walk 11 visits the coast at Saltfleet.

# Saltfleet

Autumn provides a good excuse to visit the seaside for a bracing stroll. And we start from Paradise too – not something you do every day!

New Inn is dated 1673 but was certainly built earlier, for in October 1643 Oliver Cromwell is said to have slept under its roof before (although some say after) the Battle of Winceby.

The diminutive Wesleyan Methodist chapel nearby was built in 1815. The Primitive and Free Methodists also established themselves here but their chapel has closed, so this one holds the longest record of continuous worship. It has a delightful garden, always open for visitors, and makes a peaceful spot in which to rest or to picnic. It is also sometimes open for refreshments, including excellent homemade cakes (recommended!). Just beyond the New Inn, on a former old sea bank, is the mill. This probably dates from the 1770s and was rebuilt and made taller in the 1890s. It remained working until around 1951, and has now been converted into a private house.

Until 1791, Saltfleet was a market town, having originally been a royal port required to provide ships and men to the King in times of national emergency. Although much has been lost to the sea over the centuries, including St Katherine's church in 1679, Saltfleet revived as a popular bathing place during the late 18th century. The New Inn dates from that time and Saltfleet is still a small but well-liked resort to this day. However, despite the depredations of the North Sea, much of historic interest remains. The Manor House opposite the

As our walk enters Saltfleet it passes the Freshney Memorial Pump. This commemorates Frederick Alan Freshney, a trooper of the Imperial Light Horse. He was an adventurous local lad who studied engineering in Lincoln before going to work in the gold mines of South Africa and volunteering for service during the Boer War. He was wounded at Colenso on 5 December 1899 when a bullet went through his left eye, then his shoulder, before finally lodging in his lower back. Paralysed, he was brought back to Saltfleet where he died on 20 May 1906, aged just 32.

At Saltfleetby, St Clement's church was re-erected on its present site in 1885 using the stones of the former church, located 400 yards away, which had been in a bad state of repair since at least 1841. The new St Clement's has been redundant since 1973 and is now private property, but a footpath goes through the churchyard to pass just yards from where the former church stood. Forlorn gravestones still peep from the undergrowth of the old churchyard. The Rimac National Nature Reserve is a Site of Special Scientific Interest and stretches for five miles along the coast

to the south of Saltfleet. It consists of dunes that began forming around the 13th century and is presently managed by English Nature. Near the entrance are information boards and route maps for 10, 20 or 30 minute nature trails. It is worth a visit at any time of year and is well known for its orchids, but is especially famous as a stronghold of the natterjack toad.

NOTES. The Paradise carpark is on the right as you enter Saltfleet from the south. Anyone tempted to explore the foreshore should heed the warning notices and be well informed about tide times. Take care on the two short road sections.

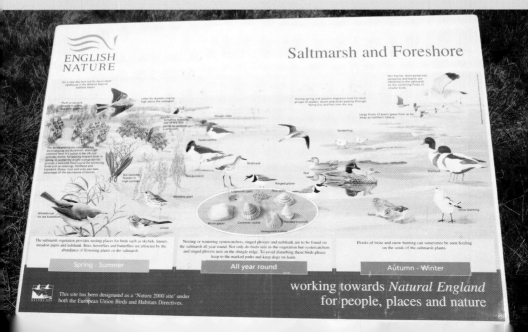

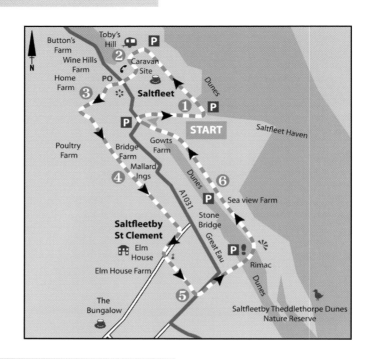

## ABOUT THE WALK

START: Paradise carpark, Saltfleet (GR457934)

MAPS: OS Landranger 113 or Explorer 283

DISTANCE: 6 miles : 9.5 kilometres

REFRESHMENTS: Crown Inn or New Inn, Saltfleet (Occasionally available at the Methodist chapel)

**1** Turn right on leaving the carpark and, in a few yards, turn right again along Haven Lane. At the carpark and picnic area, cross the dunes to your left and follow the foreshore, keeping forward where at one point low dunes bear off towards the sea. In half a mile go left inland up a concrete ramp near a flagpole; this leads into Sea Lane.

**2** After about 200 yards, look for a footpath going left into a caravan park and follow the driveway to a waymark where the path goes between a hedge and a fence. This soon turns right,

dyke and, after crossing a brick bridge, keep forward with the Mar Dyke to your left, eventually reaching a footbridge and a road.

⑤ Turn right for 400 yards to reach St Clement's church, and take the footpath going left through the lytchgate (with seats) and the churchyard. It then leads ahead by meadows and two stiles to the A1031 road. Turn left and, using the verges when possible, walk for 400 yards to a bend. Now leave the road, keeping ahead along a lane to Rimac Nature Reserve carpark. Explore at will!

⑥ Ignore the footpath on the left just near the Rimac entrance gate and head directly forward to an information point and observation platform overlooking the foreshore. Bear left in front of this, along a foreshore path, for about a mile. After crossing the Great Eau, a track leads directly back to Paradise.

passing over The Hill into Saltfleet village and emerging by the Memorial Pump opposite the Crown Inn. (Explore the village now or later; the chapel, Manor House, mill and New Inn are all a short distance away to your left.)

③ Cross the road into Pump Lane and, at the end where this bends left, take the footpath over the footbridge on the right. Walk ahead over an arable field, then follow a grass path to a road and turn left.

④ At the first bend take the footpath departing to the right. This soon joins a

# Walk 12

# Ropsley & Little Humby

This walk is between two pretty villages built from the local Lincolnshire limestone. Neighbouring woodlands make it a particularly attractive outing for autumn.

Ropsley, originating from the Old English *Hroppa's Lei* (or wood), was recorded as Ropeslai in the Domesday Book. St Peter's church, elevated above the surrounding cottages, is a glorious amalgam of architectural styles from the Saxon and Norman periods onwards, and has an impressive broach spire, a more common feature in south Lincolnshire than elsewhere. Restorations took place in 1894, 1903 and 1928. Several of the gravestones in the churchyard are of ornately carved slate, an alien stone to Lincolnshire (though perhaps a cheaper alternative despite probably being 'imported' from Leicestershire!). The village has won awards as a best-kept village from the Council for the

Preservation of Rural England on six occasions between 1975 and 2000.

Little Humby is a quiet and secluded spot, attractively built mostly of local stone and sharing its name with Great Humby just over half a mile away, which is actually the smaller of the two. Old houses surround a long green that slopes up from the ford, where pride of place goes to the Manor House with a datestone proclaiming 1631. There is no church – Great Humby has that – and the Roman road King Street, linking Bourne to the Ermine Street at Ancaster, passes to the east. Incidentally, Great Humby was the former seat of the Brownlow family before they purchased the Belton estate near Grantham and departed in the early 1600s to build their magnificent new home there. So perhaps they just perpetuated a grander name – preferring to live somewhere 'Great' rather then 'Little'!

Just before we re-enter Ropsley near the end of the walk, we pass the site of a ring dam, just discernable amongst some trees, and shown on the OS maps. This name implies (in archaeological terms at least), that it was once a fishpond area. Although it is first firmly identified in the local Enclosure Award of 1796, and appears on maps of that date, a land deed of 1335 mentions something similar, a fishery called the 'Mickledam', that may also in fact be referring to it. This is, therefore, almost certainly a mediaeval landscape feature and is recorded in the county records as such.

Finally, a few words about Bishop Richard Fox. He was born at Ropsley around 1448 and is believed to have been educated in Boston, before going on to Oxford and Paris and then travelling around Europe. On his return to England he may have been headmaster at Stratford-upon-Avon Grammar School, before becoming chancellor of Cambridge University. However, his real fame rests on his rise in royal court circles, where he became the Secretary of State to both King Henry VII and King Henry VIII. He was subsequently Bishop of Exeter, Wells

Durham and Winchester, where he was buried after his death in October 1528. He did not forget his native Lincolnshire, however, for he was the founder of Grantham Grammar School, where some 200 years later Isaac Newton was a scholar. His birthplace at Ropsley is commemorated by a plaque on the wall of a farmhouse (formerly an inn) just a few yards to the south of the Green Man.

NOTES. Within the woods and at the remoter parts of this walk you may (if quiet and lucky) see some of the local deer. The woodland paths can be muddy. Roadside parking is possible in Ropsley; please do so considerately.

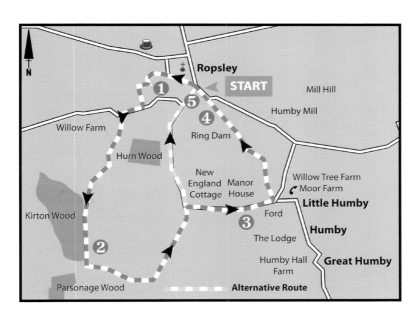

## ABOUT THE WALK

START: Ropsley village; near the Green Man inn

MAPS: OS Landranger 130 (Grantham) or Explorers 247 & 248

DISTANCE: 4½ miles : 7 kilometres

REFRESHMENTS: Green Man, Ropsley

**1** Set off from Ropsley up Church Lane – almost opposite the inn. At the end, continue into a lane signed as a 'No Through Road' and onto a footpath; follow this leftwards and round field edges to reach a footbridge. Turn left over this and walk straight over a small golf course to a road; now turn right.

**2** After about 200 yards, take the first signed footpath and stile on the left and after a footbridge, swing right then left behind a hedge. Keep forward from another footbridge to Kirton Wood and a further footbridge. Continue along the path in front of you just within the trees, and at the end of the woods turn sharp

left along a green lane. In just over half a mile, at a track junction, turn left again and continue to a road.

Keeping ahead here is a short cut back to Ropsley – all on road – but it misses out Little Humby entirely!

**3** The main walk follows the road to the right into Little Humby. Just beyond the ford take the signed track on the left – but explore the village first! About 100 yards along the track look for a stile in the hedge on your right. Walk along the left hand lower edge of two meadows, and then go left from a footbridge to reach another in a field corner. In the

next field, aim towards a stile near the middle one of three tallish trees, and maintain your line over the next field to a stile approximately one third of the way along the far hedge.

**4** Cross a narrow meadow and go through another hedge, keeping to the right of some trees ahead, to a further stile and footbridge. Pass through some trees (the ring dam is amongst them) to proceed left of a hedge by a house gate. After more stiles the path leads between hedges to a gate.

**5** Join the nearby road and bear left back into Ropsley village.

# Belchford & Fulletby

Here we visit the Wolds to explore Belchford and Fulletby. Partly along the Viking Way, this is a popular local walk through some fine scenery.

there and none of its 'sons' becoming famous. Taking into account the fact that it lies beside the River Waring, the village name seems a bit odd, for one would expect 'Waringford' or some similar reference to the river. Nevertheless, there is a ford along Ings Lane to the north of the village, close to the course of the Lincoln to Wainfleet Roman road. The village name probably derives from a local man with the Old English name of 'Belt'.

Belchford's little St Peter and St Paul's church stands just round the corner from the Blue Bell Inn. It has been a religious site since before Domesday, though the present building dates largely from 1783 with alterations in 1859 and 1885. Finally, in 1900, the tower was removed. There is a colourful village history information board near the adjacent village hall.

Although Fulletby is one of Lincolnshire's highest villages and stands at an elevation some 200 feet higher than Belchford, the climb there is mostly quite gradual. Both the ascent to Fulletby and the return to Belchford down in the valley offer wonderful views.

By all accounts (or rather lack of them!) Belchford seems to have slumbered peacefully through the centuries with no great historical events taking place

Fulletby has always been a small, quiet place too, but has achieved fame of a sort. Here, on 23 January 1816, one Henry Winn was born, and the village was to remain his lifelong home for 98 years. Henry grew into quite an extraordinary character whose achievements eventually gained him an entry in the *Guinness Book of Records.* His boyhood schooling was in Belchford, but when he was ten his father died and he was forced to take on the responsibility of supporting his mother and the younger members of the family. Undaunted by this setback, he continued to educate himself at home. When he was 24 he married and opened a general store (which remained a business until 1980) in his home opposite the church, but he also mastered the trades of decorator and auctioneer's clerk, as well as becoming the village constable, Sunday School teacher, and local tax collector. He inaugurated a village sick club too, and in his spare time (and there can't have been much of that!) wrote poetry and newspaper articles. In 1850 he and his wife also founded Fulletby's first school and a free library, mostly stocked with his own books. And, unbelievably, they found the time (and energy!) to have 21 children, though tragically only four daughters survived to adulthood. Henry died in 1914.

Another important role of his in village life was that of parish clerk and it is this that is commemorated in the *Guinness Book of Records.* Henry first assumed this duty in 1830 at the age of 14 for the simple reason that the elected clerk could neither read nor write. However, in 1845 Henry became the full-time clerk and stayed in the post until 1910, a total of 80 years, qualifying him as England's longest acting public servant. His

gravestone is in St Andrew's churchyard. It stands close to a large memorial to his 15-year-old nephew, Matthew, carved by Henry's brother Richard, a skilled sculptor, who also lived in Fulletby.

Fulletby's village name, with its familiar '-by' ending, denotes a settlement established after the Danish invasion. All traces of an early church have disappeared and the present St Andrew's dates from 1705, being much restored in 1857 by James Fowler from Louth.

NOTE. Park considerably in Belchford near the Blue Bell Inn or the church.

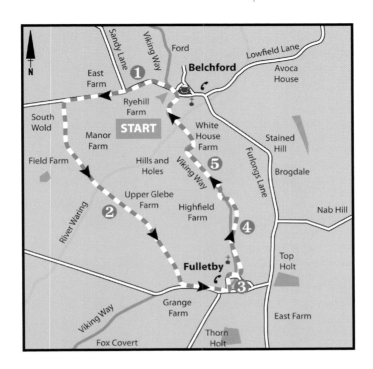

START: Belchford village

MAPS: OS Landranger 122 (Skegness) or Explorer 273

DISTANCE: 4½ miles : 7 kilometres

REFRESHMENTS: Blue Bell Inn, Belchford

① Follow Main Road westwards and uphill (the steepest part of the walk) out of Belchford, towards the A153, for just over half a mile. Turn left onto a signed footpath.

② After crossing the hillside, the path veers left slightly and descends to the River Waring, though it's more like a stream here! Cross the footbridge to begin another uphill section, rising steadily until the path bears right on a track past Westfield House and continues

to the public road near Fulletby. We join the Viking Way here and it is a fine viewpoint too!

3 Turn left and walk into Fulletby, turning left again immediately after passing the garage. The first right turn will then lead you to the church. Pause here to visit the churchyard and Henry Winn's grave and look back towards his old shop opposite, now a private house.

4 On leaving the churchyard turn left, making a second left turn down Paradise Lane, which becomes School Lane where Henry's school once stood. After 200 yards, climb a stile on the right and walk down the middle of a large meadow where grassy mounds indicate the site of mediaeval Fulletby. Head for another stile by a gate and over another meadow to a third stile. Now follow a grass path briefly uphill beside a hedge, and at the top bear left a little to a stile situated on your right.

5 Descend by hedges towards Belchford, keeping forward for a few yards when you join a track. Then turn sharp right, although only briefly, until the path angles left again to continue downhill once more. After re-crossing the River Waring, the path climbs a short way to join Dams Lane. There, turn right back into Belchford for the Blue Bell Inn.

# Folkingham, Pickworth & Walcot

Those interested in architecture will enjoy these three attractive churches, all of interest but Pickworth particularly so! There we find an exceptional series of mediaeval wall paintings.

All the indications are that the field paths used on the three 'sides' of this roughly triangular walk are quite ancient. They still lead, even with occasional modern diversions along field edges, on fairly direct lines from village to village taking the shortest line.

Folkingham sits on a hilltop and its wide, picturesque marketplace slopes up to the Greyhound Inn, a former coaching inn probably dating from the early 17th century, with St Andrew's church nearby down a short lane. Down the sides are lovely old houses, many Georgian, whilst at the lower end is the fine mid-17th century stone Manor House. An extension to the east

end of the Greyhound in 1788, where there is a large Venetian-style window, incorporated the local magistrates court.

Below the village is the site of a Norman castle built by the de Beaumonts after the conquest. This was reportedly ruinous by 1535, but in 1825 a House of Correction was built on the site. This closed in 1878 but the imposing gatehouse survives as an unusual holiday cottage. The motte and bailey, however, remain well defined; there is a footpath round part of it.

We arrive at Walcot close to a pretty ford to follow a quiet lane into the village. Here, St Nicholas' church is in the early

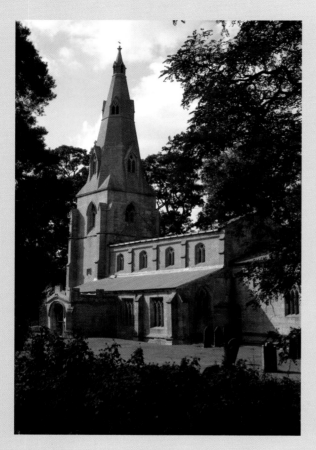

However, Pickworth church (another St Andrew's) remains the prime objective of this walk with its famous treasure trove of mediaeval wall paintings. These were revealed after the vibrations from German bombing nearby shook flakes of whitewash off them; fortunately the coats of whitewash hadn't adhered to the paint too well! The largest painting, over the chancel arch, depicts 'The Doom' with various demons, flames and cauldrons, but also Christ in majesty. Along the nave north wall are the Ascension, and 'the Three Quick and the Three Dead'. All the paintings are believed to be late 14th century. There is a detailed church guide and an interpretive leaflet for the paintings.

Keyholder details are on display in the porch – do make an effort to obtain the keys should the church be locked!

14th century 'Decorated' style outside, but there is older work within. The richly crocketed spire is unusual in that it bulges slightly (what architects call 'entasis'). The church and mellow old farm buildings overlook the village green.

NOTES. The walk crosses several arable fields. Paths are generally marked in any crops but dry conditions underfoot are preferable.

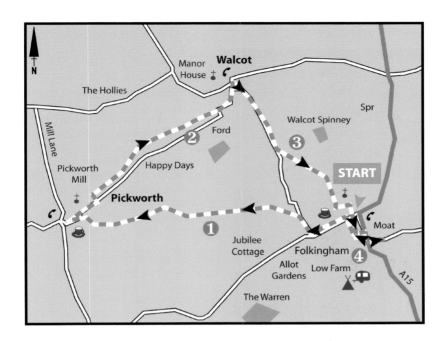

## ABOUT THE WALK

START: Folkingham Market
Place (GR073337)

MAPS: OS Landranger 130
(Grantham) or Explorer 248

DISTANCE: 5½ miles :
9 kilometres

REFRESHMENTS: New Inn,
Folkingham, and two tea
rooms in the Market Place

① Leave Folkingham Market Place via
West Street. At the edge of the village,
take the first right (Walcot Lane) and in
150 yards go left into the playing fields.
Cross these diagonally to a gate in a high
wire fence on the far side, bear right to
the field corner and then left by a hedge.
At the next corner, cross a footbridge
then keep ahead over an arable field,
aiming slightly right of the left hand
one of two twin electricity poles. From
another footbridge in the hedge at the
far side, Pickworth comes into view.
Bear half right to a footbridge and walk
to a waymark by a hedge, then turn left
beside it on a grass headland to another
footbridge, again in a field corner. Keep
ahead now to a hedge corner seen

across the next field with a stile and fingerpost. From this, veer only slightly away from the hedge running along the top of the next meadow, until a hedge corner is seen jutting from the far side; this is near a new house. Head for it and follow a path between two hedges down to a road. Turn left for Pickworth church.

2️⃣ Return the way you came, but this time continue along the lane and go left at a footpath sign along a short track, before turning right at a hedge corner. At the field end, cross a stile and then keep ahead with a stream (and marshy

area) on your right to reach a footbridge. Cross this and go left to a second footbridge a few yards away, near a ford. Cross this too and bear right, roughly in the direction of Walcot church, keeping parallel to the hedge in the field bottom, towards a stile in a hedge. Keep forward again to cross a footbridge over a stream in a shallow valley, then, as you near houses at Walcot, veer down to the right to climb two stiles and emerge near Walcot ford. Follow the lane up to the village green.

3️⃣ Leave Walcot along the lane signposted for Folkingham and in just over half a mile look for a footpath sign to your left. Cross an arable field in the direction indicated, aiming for a gap in trees just left of a line towards Folkingham church. At these, go over a footbridge and veer left, passing close to twin electricity poles, towards a waymark in the field corner. In the final two fields, aim for the left hand end of a row of new houses and at a lane keep ahead, turning left at a gate into the graveyard. Go through a gap in the churchyard wall and exit back into the Market Place.

4️⃣ To explore more of Folkingham, go along West Street again and turn left down Chapel Lane. At the bottom, turn left along Spring Lane. Before turning back up the Market Place, make a right and then a left turn (into Billingborough Road) to see the old castle and House of Correction.

# Stoke Rochford

Despite its proximity to the A1, Stoke Rochford remains a haven of peace and quiet, with the parkland surrounding the hall being especially colourful in the autumn.

Stoke Rochford nestles in a hollow with trees all around and with St Mary and St Andrew's church serving both Stoke, northwest of the A1, and Easton, to the southeast of it. For generations, the economic and social life of these villages was dominated by the Turnor family (Stoke) and the Cholmondeley family (Easton). Indeed, the Cholmondeleys still own the park at Easton Hall (the house is now gone) and have recently made great progress in restoring the formal and terraced gardens.

Inside, the church reflects its dual role in an unusual way by having two chapels, one either side of the chancel – north (for the Turnors) and south (for the Cholmondeleys) – specifically dedicated to their respective families and containing their splendid family memorials. Also worth seeing are a double effigy carved from a single stone block, an ancient parish chest, a beautiful painted font cover and a memorial to the 2nd Battalion Parachute Regiment, billeted locally and famous

for its exploits at the Arnhem Bridge during the Second World War. In the churchyard, watch out for some very unusual metal gravestones which look like gearwheels from some ancient machinery. Nearby you can admire the impressive village pump.

Stoke Rochford Hall, passed twice during the walk, stands in rolling parkland, some of which is now a golf course, offering views across its numerous lakes. Remains of Roman villas have been found locally, for the Roman Ermine Street is only just over a mile away to

the east. This early history of occupation was followed with a succession of halls, documented as far back as the 14th century, as the Neville, the Rochford and the Coney families all went on to live there. When the Turnor family arrived in around 1665, they set about building their own new hall. By the time Christopher Turnor inherited the estate in 1829 he was, with in excess of 20,000 acres scattered around the county, the third largest landowner in Lincolnshire. He was thus wealthy enough to be able to reorganise the estate, move the village to its present location (out of sight of the hall!) and even have part of the Great North Road diverted. The present hall, begun in 1841, is now an educational college and teachers' union (the NUT) conference and training centre, whilst a substantial part of the park has been made into a golf course.

By the carpark overlooking the hall stands an enormous obelisk, aligned with the centre of the house and dedicated to Sir Isaac Newton who was born in the neighbouring village of Woolsthorpe but who received some of his early education in Stoke. Erected in 1847, the obelisk bears a commemorative inscription in praise of the great man, although it all seems rather wordy nowadays. On either side of the road near the park entrance are two grand gateways from the stables of a previous hall built in 1676, moved and re-erected as follies to impress visitors.

NOTES. There is limited space for careful parking by the roadside as you approach the village just after leaving the A1. Watch out for the Post Office and shop, for that is where the walk begins. This walk varies from that previously published, as permission to use the private Cringle Road within the estate is no longer possible.

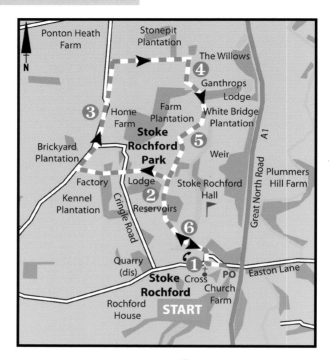

## ABOUT THE WALK

START: Stoke Rochford Post Office (GR923273)

MAPS: OS Landranger 130 (Grantham) or Explorer 274

DISTANCE: 4½ miles : 7 kilometres

REFRESHMENTS: None on route

**1** First of all, locate the footpath sign and kissing gate near the Post Office. From here, walk downhill to the footbridge over the Cringle Brook and then up through the churchyard to rejoin the road. (Keep ahead for a few yards if you wish to see the village pump.)

**2** Otherwise, bear right and follow the road a short way until you can turn left into the grounds of Stoke Rochford Hall. Enter the gate and follow the drive up to the carpark at the Newton obelisk where there is a good view of the hall. Just ahead, a bridlegate leads into the park.

Go through that, and in a few yards a track bears left along an avenue of trees; follow this until it reaches a lodge and a lane.

③ Cross the lane and the field opposite to a bridlegate into some woods. A winding path leads to the far side, exits and continues down the left hand edge of a field to reach a road. Turn right to pass some cottages and at a T-junction (just after a lake) keep ahead along the road. Near a double bend there is a footpath inside the hedge to your right, but using the lane or its wide verge is easier! Continue until you reach a stile by a gate at a signed track to the right.

④ Follow this until it reaches another signpost at a track junction and there turn right. On nearing some woods the bridleway swings left, but almost at once, at a footpath sign, there is access to Stoke Rochford Park on your right.

⑤ Look for a yellow waymark post, walk towards it and maintain your line through a group of trees. From them, keep forward past more trees and a seat to join a metalled track below the 13th tee. Turn right and follow this back to the gate into the carpark near the obelisk.

⑥ Return to the start via the outward route.

# *Winter*

*The summer hath his joys
And winter his delights.*

'Winter Nights' – Thomas Campion (1567–1620)

To many, this is the season to hang up one's walking boots, stow the rucksack away and hibernate. Being out in a blizzard is, of course, wisely avoided but there are bright, crisp days when it is a shame to be cocooned indoors.

The winter countryside has much to offer. There is still greenery in the fields as the winter wheat breaks through, and don't forget the comforting anticipation of thoughts of tea and scones by the fire at the end of a frosty afternoon's walk!

At this time of year, arable land perhaps is best avoided (unless hardened by a good frost!), and this is something I have done as far as possible here. The coast still has its attractions at this time of year, especially around the Wash where vast flocks of geese and wading birds may be seen; hence my inclusion of Walks 18 and 19. There are plenty of birds, too, on inland waters such as Denton Reservoir on Walk 20 – an ideal winter afternoon outing.

# Little Cawthorpe & Muckton

Our first suggested winter walk is an easy one from Little Cawthorpe to Muckton and back. It is largely on country lanes plus some grass tracks.

Little Cawthorpe is arguably the prettiest village along this eastern fringe of the Wolds and its inn, the Royal Oak, (together with countless others) commemorates the occasion in 1651 when King Charles II hid for a day and a night in an oak tree to escape his enemies after the Battle of Worcester. A particularly picturesque part of the village is the ford, which provides the inn's alternative name of 'The Splash'. Both feature on its splendid sign – and if you phone up, the landlord and staff even answer 'The Splash'!

At the other end of Little Cawthorpe is the Seven Springs Pond, the source of the Long Eau, which flows over the 'splash' near the inn and onwards to the sea at Saltfleet. The area has been landscaped over the years but even from the roadway some of the springs can still be seen bubbling away.

Above the pond is the little church of St Helen's. It is quite modern as churches go, having been built in 1860, and is strikingly designed in red and black brick, though some people may feel that it looks a bit town-like and lacks sympathy with its village surroundings. Directly across the road is the Manor House. Dated from 1673, it is a private property but can be glimpsed from the road and is a fine example of Dutch gabled Tudor brickwork.

Two miles away, Muckton has lost its church altogether. An earlier Holy Trinity church had been rebuilt in 1878, though it still contained some original Norman archways; sadly however all was demolished in 1983. Now only the poignant, abandoned churchyard remains, with gravestones still in situ, and is approached through a splendid, albeit lonely looking lytchgate. Across the road on a gate pillar is a rare Victorian letterbox.

For three-quarters of a mile our route runs close to (and twice crosses) the course of the old East Lincolnshire main line between Grimsby and Peterborough that was the first to be built by the Great Northern Railway. It was completed in stages and this section opened on 3 September 1848. In addition to passenger services it became an extremely busy freight line conveying fish from Grimsby and local produce to the capital. Closures of stations, passenger and freight services began as early as 1939; final closure for this line was on 5 October 1970.

About half way along the walk is a quiet lane, which mostly sticks close to the 50-metre contour and is therefore raised above the marsh, but still below the hilltops. This modest elevation nevertheless gives impressive views towards Saltfleet and the sea.

On the way back to Cawthorpe, the walk also passes Legbourne Wood. This 86-acre wood has been owned by Lincolnshire Wildlife Trust since 2004, having been partially purchased by public appeal. It is the largest of the Trust's woods and is a special example of authentic, ancient woodland, probably undisturbed since the time of the Norman Conquest. For this reason it is notable for its range of woodland flowers; though you'll have to come back in spring and summer to see those! You may detour to explore if you wish, but do stay on the marked paths.

As you return to Little Cawthorpe, notice the Greywacke Stone by the ford, a glacial boulder transported from Scotland as many as 20,000 years ago. It was retrieved from the Seven Springs pond at the far end of the village where for generations it had provided a footrest as villagers collected their water.

NOTE. Readers may park and start the walk from the Royal Oak by kind permission of the landlord. Please use the rear carpark.

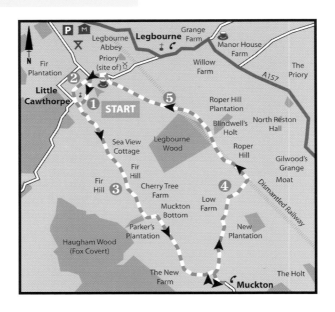

## ABOUT THE WALK

START: Royal Oak, Little Cawthorpe

MAPS: OS Landranger 122 (Skegness) or Explorer 283

DISTANCE: 4¾ miles : 7.5 kilometres

REFRESHMENTS: Royal Oak, Little Cawthorpe

From the Royal Oak there are two options for the first part of the walk. The first is to turn left from the inn and walk through the village to a T-junction by the church, and then go left again. (You will then have joined option two.)

The second option crosses the road below the inn into the narrow lane of Coggles Way. After crossing a stream, turn right on a path that leads through woods to a road. Turn left to reach the church and this time keep ahead at the T-junction.

The combined route now heads straight out of the village into the countryside. Follow this quiet road for two miles along the edge of the Wolds,

enjoying the fine views over the marsh. In Muckton you will find the abandoned churchyard with its lytchgate.

④ To return you will then need to head back towards Little Cawthorpe for 200 yards before bearing right into an unnamed 'No Through Road', continuing ahead when this becomes a grass track. At a track junction bear left, close to the old railway line, until in half a mile, at Legbourne Wood, the path crosses the abandoned trackbed. (Go left here to explore Legbourne Wood; you can emerge at the far end to join the main walk.)

⑤ Otherwise, follow the public right of way over the railway and leftwards as it loops round amongst the trees on the far side, continuing roughly

parallel to it until the path veers left to re-cross it. Now follow the lane ahead until you reach the water splash. Cross a footbridge onto the raised waterside path; this leads directly back to the ford and footbridge below the inn.

# Walk 17

# Hubbard's Hills, Hallington & Raithby

This walk begins from Hubbard's Hills, one of Lincolnshire's most popular beauty spots, to explore two local hamlets, one with a fascinating church.

St Peter's at Raithby was designed and built in 1839 by W.A. Nicholson at the behest of the Reverend Henry Chaplin. The architectural style is the neo-Gothic that was then in fashion, although the appearance of masonry was achieved by cementing over brickwork. However, there is some real late 13th century masonry in the north arcade as well as pillars, and contemporary furnishings include a west gallery. The windows were repaired in 1963 but still contain oval medallions of early German/Flemish glass. One curiosity there is a barrel organ, dating from 1839, that is the only one in Lincolnshire still in working order. The three barrels each hold ten tunes.

To reach Raithby we cross a former mediaeval village site. The village name comes from the Old Norse name of 'Hreithi', plus the suffix '-by' meaning farmstead. Raithby was for centuries combined administratively with the neighbouring hamlet of Maltby, situated a quarter of a mile to the south (shown on the Explorer map at GR310842) but which has now vanished. The population records of 1563 show 21 households at Raithby-cum-Maltby, so there were probably more people living there then than now! As we approach Raithby over a large meadow, the house platforms and streets of the former village are exceptionally clear and well defined. Notice, too, the ancient village pump beside the road, opposite the church.

The former railway, crossed twice during the walk, was the Great Northern Railway Company's branch line linking Louth with Bardney. Its construction involved steep gradients and tunnelling through the Wolds in places, raising the cost to a level that almost scuppered the whole project. The western end

from Bardney opened first, in November 1874, but it was not opened throughout for passengers until December 1876. Passenger services ended in 1951 with goods trains continuing until early 1960.

Hubbard's Hills has an interesting history too, the gorge itself having been carved out at the end of the last ice age by meltwater torrents. In 1875 Auguste Pahud, a language teacher, came from Switzerland to work at Louth's King Edward VI Grammar School. Through marriage he subsequently became a wealthy farmer and it was discovered after his suicide in 1902 that he had left a large sum of money for the purpose of benefiting the townspeople of Louth.

With it, his trustees purchased the valley and landscaped it into the beauty spot we know today; it was formally opened to the public in 1907. The story is told on a tablet within a small Grecian-style 'temple' standing beside the River Lud.

NOTE. During the winter, the café in Hubbard's Hills only opens on Saturdays and Sunday afternoons. Longer opening hours will prevail from Easter onwards.

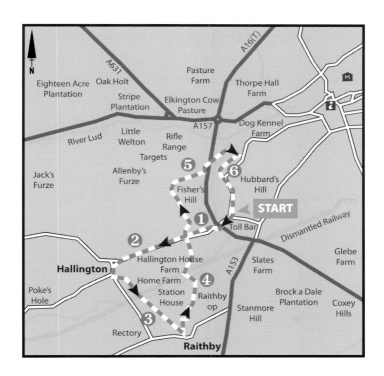

START: Hubbard's Hills, west carpark (GR315861)

MAPS: Landranger 122 (Skegness) or Explorer 282

DISTANCE: 4 miles : 6.5 kilometres

REFRESHMENTS: Hubbard's Hills Café (or in Louth)

1. Leave along the road away from Hubbard's Hills. Just after the bypass, climb some steps on your right to a stile leading into a meadow. Keep parallel to the lower edge of the field until you see a bridle gate on your left and then rejoin the road.

2. Turn right along it and at the first junction go left, and downhill into Hallington. Just beyond the entrance to Home Farm, take the permissive footpath on the left through an orchard and from the far corner walk to another fence corner. Next, proceed diagonally

107

over a large paddock, again to its far left hand corner where a stile leads onto the old railway.

③ From a footpath sign, bear very slightly left across an arable field. Take your line from the sign if the path is not marked on the ground (if the field is very muddy, you could turn right and walk round to Raithby by road). Otherwise

footbridge on the right, and from that walk up to a bridle gate just to the left of a house. Now turn left along a grass field-edge path. On reaching a three-way footpath sign, go left over a causeway and footbridge between two lakes and re-cross the old railway. Next, veer right over an arable field to a footbridge before going left to pass a house and walk up its drive to a road where you rejoin the outward route. (You could now simply turn right back to the start or use the meadow path opposite again!)

5 For the full walk, go back into the field opposite and head uphill to a bridle gate to the right of a large tree. Continue through a shallow valley until reaching a footpath sign pointing up to the right. Go up the slope and follow the field edge, eventually turning left through a copse of trees to reach the bypass. Cross with care to another stile opposite, climb over and keep left by a hedge. In the second field, veer right towards Hubbard's Hills café.

6 Get back to the start by turning right through Hubbard's Hills valley.

aim towards Raithby church tower; once this comes into view, and from a stile in a hedge, continue across the meadow containing the mediaeval village site towards a large house. Pass round this to the road, arriving opposite the church.

4 After visiting St Peter's, return over the same meadow but now veer right past a small brick building to a

## Gibraltar Point

This is only a short walk, but makes an ideal part of a winter day out visiting Gibraltar Point, one of Lincolnshire's leading nature reserves.

There is so much to see here that you could well find that, even though the walk is short, your explorations occupy a good deal of your day! If you have not been to Gibraltar Point for some time you will find that visiting again is particularly worthwhile, for the Lincolnshire Wildlife Trust has now opened its redesigned visitor centre. Extensive alterations have created room for fresh displays, a new observation lounge and – very importantly – new tearooms! I give my preferred route below, but on this occasion readers may freely ignore my instructions and follow their own inclinations, as many other footpaths offer both shorter and longer options.

The Gibraltar Point area has an interesting history. The Lincolnshire coastline here has developed over many centuries and the inner (west) dunes alongside the road from Skegness were mapped as far back as 1779, but could be a century older. From mediaeval times, the nearby River Steeping gave access to the then busy port of Wainfleet, which eventually fell into decline because of river silting. Gibraltar Point took over Wainfleet's role for as long as larger boats could reach it, and a small village with an inn developed, with a coastguard station eventually being added in 1859. The sea's retreat continued, however, as yet more dunes built up to the east and by the 1920s

viewing hides constructed and most recently, a further area of ponds with three more hides has opened on Jackson's Marsh to the west of the approach road from Skegness.

The Wash area, of which this reserve is part, forms a major staging post for

shipping ceased to use the Steeping Haven. The coastguards finally left in 1925, and the place became deserted.

The County Council took on ownership in 1937 and the Lincolnshire Wildlife Trust, founded in 1948, took over the management of the 1,000-acre nature reserve in 1952. By the 1960s there was a small visitor centre. When larger premises were needed the coastguard station was converted for this purpose, with David Attenborough performing the official opening in October 1974. The Wash Viewpoint followed in 1986, opened by another wildlife broadcaster Julian Pettifer, by which time Gibraltar Point was sufficiently important to be designated a National Nature Reserve. In subsequent years, new meres and lagoons have been developed,

migrating and over-wintering birds, and during the walk a Heligoland trap will be seen. This is basically a netting tunnel used to catch birds for ringing and so aid population and migration studies. The reserve is also important for its range of diverse habitats for plants, insects and seashore wildlife.

There will be plenty of birds on the foreshore too, and fine views across the Wash to Norfolk, so bring binoculars. Having said all that, don't feel bound by my route; you will find lots of other options to explore!

NOTES. There is a small car parking fee. Visitor centre opening time information is available on the reserve website. The paths used do not appear on OS maps.

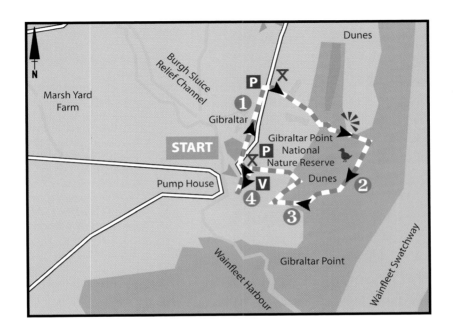

## ABOUT THE WALK

START: Gibraltar Point, main carpark

MAPS: OS Landranger 122 (Skegness) or Explorer 274

DISTANCE: (as described) 3 miles : 4.5 kilometres

REFRESHMENTS: Café at Gibraltar Point visitor centre

**1** Set off from the carpark along the approach road by which you arrived. Beyond the flood bank, leave the road to the left and walk through the trees onto Jackson's Marsh. Turn left out to the first hide. Return and bear left again on a footpath running alongside the road and you will find more hides overlooking another lagoon. Near these, cross the road and go through the north carpark to reach the hide at the Mere, which was excavated in 1972. From here, a good track now heads towards the foreshore. A path off this track to the right leads to the Fenland Lagoon East hide.

Norfolk. Descend the far side and (although there are other paths) walk out over lines of new dunes onto the open foreshore and turn right. After some 350 yards, bear right at the first significant break in the dunes to return inland. Before long you should bear left parallel to the shore and reach a boardwalk over the inner dunes. (This is a short cut back to the visitor centre.)

③ However, I recommend keeping ahead and turning right on reaching the warden's summer hut instead. A path now heads inland again and cuts over the dunes near the Heligoland trap to join a track. Back at the boardwalk, turn left to return to the start.

④ Complete your exploration by continuing past the visitor centre alongside the Steeping Creek to the Wash

② After visiting this, continue along the main track to the sleeper steps, climbing the dunes of Mill Hill. This is the highest point on the reserve, offering an amazing 360-degree panorama stretching inland to the Wolds and in the other direction to

viewpoint. The views here extend over miles of marsh to the Wainfleet bombing range; Boston Stump is even visible on a clear day!

# Sutton Bridge

A bracing winter walk along old and new sea banks returns with extensive views across the Wash and the River Nene.

There is nothing strenuous about this short walk, and at a reasonable pace it should occupy a little over two hours. It will provide a breath of bracing, fresh sea air on any bright winter's day with skeins of geese flying overhead and the plaintive call of the curlew in your ears. Bring binoculars if you have them; there may be shipping to watch if it is high tide and there are usually plenty of birds to see. However, readers are warned to remember that going out onto the marshes can be extremely dangerous.

To reach the start, leave Sutton Bridge along New Road. At the edge of town, on the right, is the local golf course occupying an 11-acre site where Sutton

Bridge docks were constructed in 1875. Only some half a dozen boats had used them for a few days when all the earthworks collapsed; all this even before the official opening ceremony had taken place. Repairs proved impossible, and the scheme was abandoned virtually before it had begun.

Halfway out to Guy's Head you will also pass King John's Farm, where King John reputedly stayed after losing his way, his treasure and nearly his life whilst crossing the Wash fens in 1216.

Following the last ice age, rising sea levels meant that it penetrated some 30 miles inland and Holbeach (now so far

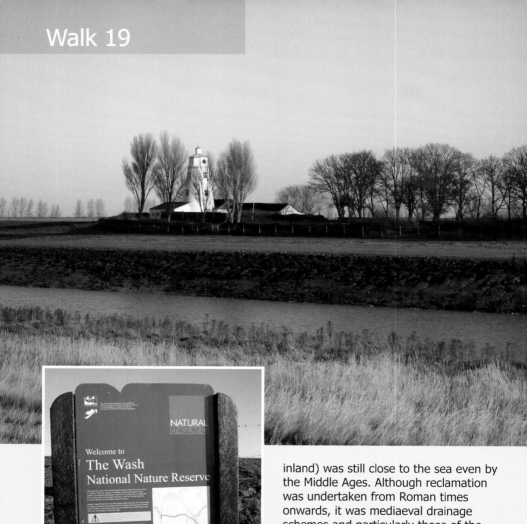

inland) was still close to the sea even by the Middle Ages. Although reclamation was undertaken from Roman times onwards, it was mediaeval drainage schemes and particularly those of the Dutch engineers in the 1700s that achieved the most progress in creating thousands of acres of new land. The OS maps chart later work by dating many of the successive sea banks.

And when is a lighthouse not a lighthouse? The two at Guy's Head were intended to operate as such when the Nene outfall was constructed in 1831, but were never actually used. The work of building the Nene outfall was undertaken by two of the best-known names in English civil engineering: Rennie and Telford. Until that time, Lincolnshire had no well-defined boundary with Norfolk, for the river here was simply one huge estuary and Cambridge technically still extended out into the Wash between them. The East Lighthouse is famous as the home for six years in the 1930s of Peter Scott, the naturalist and painter, and marks the start of a ten-mile long walk to King's Lynn dedicated to his conservation work.

Some 24,500 acres around the Wash – including all the marsh seen from the walk – are now designated as a National Nature Reserve, the largest in the country. It is home to many seabirds and is a particularly important winter base and feeding ground for huge numbers of ducks and geese. Out on the horizon, 2½ miles away, is a large circular island constructed in 1975 during a study into establishing freshwater reservoirs. This too is now an official seabird sanctuary.

To complete your day out, readers might wish to return to Sutton Bridge and explore. Worth a visit is the Victorian St Matthew's church, which dates from 1843 and is built of knapped flint. Nearby is the famous swing bridge. The first bridge here was built in 1831 (as part of the new Nene outfall); a replacement was built by Stephenson in 1852 and the present one dates from 1897. A road along the east bank of the river leads to a viewing area and information boards opposite the docks and then on to Peter Scott's lighthouse where there is a carpark and picnic area.

Finally, those with energy to spare could try some of the walk from Peter Scott's lighthouse.

NOTES. For refreshments there is an inn at Gedney Drove End (GR462293), a short drive northwest of the start. Otherwise return to Sutton Bridge for the Bridge Hotel, New Inn, or shops.

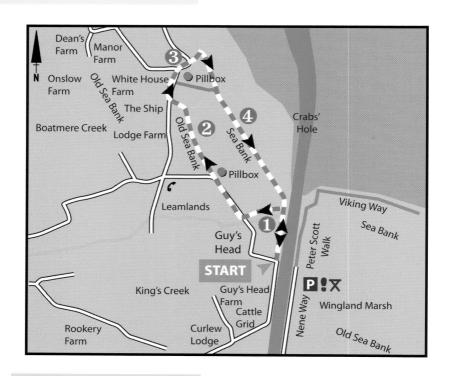

START: The Lighthouse, Guy's Head (GR491257)

MAPS: OS Landranger 131 (Boston & Spalding) or Explorer 249

DISTANCE: 4½ miles : 7 kilometres

REFRESHMENTS: None on route (see Notes)

**1** Start off from the carpark at Guy's Head along the footpath between the lighthouse and the river. After a stile, cross the Lutton Leam drain and turn left to reach a road.

**2** A footpath goes right here along an old grassy sea bank, but this is rough and tussocky so some may prefer to use the road itself. Either way, where the

road bends left, near a World War Two pillbox, the continuing sea bank should be followed. In half a mile, the path descends to a farm track and bears left to join the road again.

③ Turn right now. (In a few yards a path to the right may be used to shorten the walk slightly.) The main walk continues for about 300 yards to a road junction and turns right there. At a left hand bend by an Ordnance Survey trig point and another pillbox, leave the road, keeping forward along a track out onto the modern sea bank.

④ Turning right will, in about 1½ miles, return you to the start with a short overlap of the outward route.

# Harlaxton & Denton Reservoir

This route includes a new permissive footpath linking the
Grantham Canal and Denton Reservoir.

Recently, whilst meandering along the Grantham Canal, the chance discovery of a new permissive footpath led me to choose this walk as ideal for a winter's day. It also opens up several new variations to other walks on local footpaths.

We start from the Gregory Arms, by kind permission of the landlady, and walk first down the the 'Drift', an old drove road which probably linked up with Sewstern Lane to the south of Harlaxton, known to be another important droving route from prehistoric times. The Drift leads to the Grantham Canal.

A first reference to this canal comes in the Grantham Corporation minutes of 1770 but it was 23 years before an Act of Parliament approved a scheme and construction of the 33-mile waterway began. Although engineered to closely follow the contours of the Vale of Belvoir, 18 locks and 68 bridges were still required; the latter costing £120 each, including materials. The canal opened in 1797 and was initially reasonably prosperous; until the coming of the railways, that is! The Ambergate, Nottingham, Boston and Eastern Junction Railway (ANBEJR) took over the management of the canal in 1854, but was soon taken over in turn by the Great Northern Railway, which saw the canal as business competition and allowed its slow decline to begin.

Even so, it coped better than many canals. It survived until after the First World War, and only ceased operation in 1929, to be formally abandoned in 1936. Fortunately for us, legal obligations to provide water supplies for agricultural purposes meant that it stayed relatively intact until it became recognised as a heritage and leisure asset and restoration began.

Like other villages near the canal, Harlaxton and Denton each had a wharf. At Harlaxton, this was close to Harlaxton Bridge and where the Harlaxton Cut began. The low hill to the east could not be avoided and a mile-long cut, with over 20 feet of hillside removed in places, was necessary to reach Grantham. This can be viewed from Harlaxton Bridge.

Look, too, for what is known as a 'winding hole' (where boats could be

turned round) dug into the far bank about halfway between Harlaxton Bridge and Denton Bridge. Denton Bridge is an original from the 1790s and is now a listed building. The Grantham Canal Restoration Society has renovated the wharf area here and added a slipway, a project that won it an award in 1991.

The purpose of the Denton Reservoir was to supply the canal with water and its construction was itself a major engineering feat. Its 27-acre surface area comes as a quite a surprise when seen for the first time, being well hidden and only approachable on foot. It holds up to 61 million gallons of water and is nowadays a popular fishing venue. (It's a good picnic spot too!)

Back in Harlaxton the village church, St Mary and St Peter's, is mostly built of local ironstone and has some 15th century work, but was drastically restored by the Victorians. The village

itself is very appealing, with many old stone houses. From near the inn there is a grand view of Harlaxton Manor, described by the late Henry Thorold as 'one of the greatest 19th century houses in England'. Built between 1831 and 1837 for George de Ligne Gregory, it is now the UK campus of Evansville University, USA. The inn commemorates the family name.

NOTES. We begin from the Gregory Arms carpark by permission of the landlady. The inn stands beside the A607 to the west of Grantham.

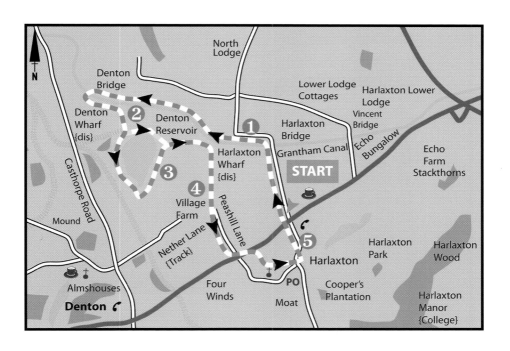

START: The Gregory Arms, Harlaxton

MAPS: OS Landranger 131 (Grantham) or Explorer 247

DISTANCE: 4 miles : 6.5 kilometres

REFRESHMENTS: The Gregory Arms, Harlaxton

① From the inn carpark, turn right and right again down the Drift. Immediately after crossing the canal, turn right down onto the towpath and then double back under the bridge (No. 66). This was once the site of Harlaxton Wharf. Follow the towpath for 1¼ miles to reach Denton Wharf and Bridge (No. 65). Turn left over the bridge and at the bottom of the approach ramp, look for the permissive footpath sign and access map on the left.

Go over the stile and briefly bear left towards the canal, then turn right on grass to a hedge gap to the left of a wood. Head diagonally over the next meadow and from its far corner bear half right alongside more woods to a stile at a track. Turn left, then right at a corner, to ascend the reservoir embankment. (You could now save half a mile by going left; if you do this look for a footpath and steps on the left after about 250 yards.)

The main walk, however, turns right to circumnavigate the reservoir in an anti-clockwise direction. At the far end, cross a footbridge over the feeder stream and keep left to reach the footpath, steps and footbridge on your right. Walk along the right hand edge of two fields to a second bridge, then continue along the edge of another field to a stile by a gate.

Immediately over this, bear right up a track (grassy at first) following it to the A607 road. Turn left along the pavement for 200 yards then cross carefully to a stile and footpath sign pointing towards Harlaxton church.

Walk down two meadows and go left through the churchyard. At the far end, an enclosed path leads down into the village and emerges opposite the war memorial. Turn left back up to the A607 and the Gregory Arms.

# Other walking guides from Hugh Marrows

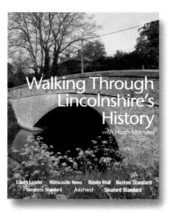

## Walking Through Lincolnshire's History with Hugh Marrows
### £8.95

- Full colour
- 1½-7 mile walks

Follow in the steps of a Roman legionary down Ermine Street, or visit the county's abandoned World War II RAF airfield.

These 20 step-by-step routes around the county's historical landmarks explore some of Lincolnshire's varied past and most beautiful scenery.

## Walking in the Wolds with Hugh Marrows
### £8.95

- Full colour
- 3-6 mile walks

With clear maps and easy to follow routes, Hugh Marrows' selection of 20 walks is packed with interesting historical information and helpful hints.

For lovers of the Wolds or walkers heading in this direction, this book is an essential companion.

For more information or to buy any of these titles visit **www.atheart.co.uk**

**At Heart Ltd:** 32 Stamford Street, Altrincham, Cheshire, WA14 1EY
**Tel:** 0161 924 0159  **Fax:** 0161 924 0160